Resurgence of Dawn

Quest of Fire

BRETT ARMSTRONG

Published by Expanse Books,
an imprint of Scrivenings Press LLC
15 Lucky Lane
Morrilton, Arkansas 72110
https://ExpanseBooks.pub

Printed in the United States of America

Paperback ISBN 978-1-64917-347-8

eBook ISBN 978-1-64917-348-5

Editors: Erin R. Howard and Linda Fulkerson

Cover by Linda Fulkerson, bookmarketinggraphics.com

This is a work of fiction. Unless otherwise indicated, all names, characters, businesses, events, and incidents are either the product of the author's imagination or used in a fictitious manner. Any resemblance to actual persons, living or dead, or actual events is purely coincidental.

Scripture quotations have been taken from the Christian Standard Bible®, Copyright © 2017 by Holman Bible Publishers. Used by permission. Christian Standard Bible® and CSB® are federally registered trademarks of Holman Bible Publishers.

This book is dedicated to the glory of God without Whom there are no words worthy of writing and to my son who tells fantastic stories of his own and whom I hope to inspire to dream boldly and follow God passionately.

ACKNOWLEDGMENTS

I often thank them among the last on my list, but there is no amount of gratitude sufficient to cover what my family does for me to make being an author possible. Late nights, time away from them, and having to pick up the pieces when hard times come (as they inevitably do in publishing). Plus, the unending airing of ideas, posts, sketches, and all manner of other elements of storytelling ... My wife and son and parents keep reminding me that their love is precious and inspiring and invariably finds its way into the words and worlds of the stories I write.

My extended family, church family, and friends have also been a huge source of encouragement over the years. As are my growing group of writer friends whose focus on the craft and devotion to our Lord are dear to my heart and much-needed guideposts along the way.

A huge thank you is owed to my publisher, Linda Fulkerson, for being patient with me as I both struggled with meeting deadlines and continue to share the pieces to this complex story. Thank you to Erin Howard, too, for being such a fantastic editor and encouragement.

Thank you to my bosses Andrew Neely and Daniel Mead for allowing me to take time off when needed to make the big writing pushes and attend events that keep my author career moving forward.

There are so many others to whom I owe thanks. Whether

for little or big things, you never know how acts of kindness can impact their recipients. Or how much a little encouragement will help an author to persevere.

Last, just as first, I must thank the LORD for inspiring me, leading me to the people I needed to meet for this book to be published, keeping me and others safe while driving after late nights working on it, and Who is the Source and the only deserving recipient of the honor for every endeavor. Without His love in Christ and Light to guide me, there is no doubt in me that this book and every other I've written would never have been. Benevolent, merciful, and painstaking in tending to me. To God be all the glory.

Western Lowlands
(Middle Era)

Ice Shelf
Gulf of Fenres
Udknor
Magknor
Lake Presia
Grand Knorstok
Knorland
Ivorsbad
Castork
Bechast
Versik
Mazsk River
Icereel River
Ermsford River
Vigthex River
Hildecrest
Narrowville
Lake Earlbald
Ostenis River
Hook River
Hearcrest
Caldeness
Anon-carson
Ordemair
Pepin's Fjord/ Pepin's Folly
Sagby (Aagen)
Vogteremark
Glassombury (Estona)
Glastus
Glastonvale
Glowerrythes
Seabridge
Eigh
Albaron
Bay of Bris
Erinoir River
Bracken River
Creston
Falconcleft
Carmine Glades
Mostra River
Little Mostra
Bestance River
Stormridge
Ecthelowall
Canewith
Culla Cover
Port Valence
Mertoo
Fairwinds (Bonus Mare)
New Caledonia
Castle Letolix
Abaross
Ironhold
West Haven
Rareabruck
Maple Point
Tenchyford
Durble Down
Isle of Geasts
Kinsbane
Tislatna
TISLATNEAN SEA
NUTSDENE SEA
Libertias
Youngland
Kirke
Knebb River
Black River
Lake Pax
Peter's March
Bright Pond
Elenwis
Port Jareeth
Fell Inlet
Endas River
Gradlingbok
Highland Foothills
Varangerex
Tyreenes
Carvenna
Onfer
Nalice
Karakhum
Horse River
Cross River
Ansedeaux
Buroquist
I'ves River
Rehaley
Port De'Ston
Lacfortes
Lake Poire
Lake Albolixeus
Firess Marsh
Carvenna River
Poireville
Vrs River
Beggar Pond
Quarentz
Calaguerra
Orduedo
Cennamar
Dovet River
Corcos River
Lyrscony
Lyscea
Neinth
Parthes
Byzel River
Yulidistan
Rioca River
Menga River
Anstara
I'jon
Edes Oasis
Ziljafu Desert
Andgulch
Gado Mines
Santesso
Verdeja
Lago Amargo
Valencia River
Riodelta
Ash Dunes
Gerisk Ruins
Surcalido
Paravencia
Kasson
Isla Volcán
Portlanders
Shield Islands
Straits of Calide
Garcenilles
Yesmar
Nostoreo River
Luzano River
Bosquermeral
NOTIOSANEMOS SEA

WESTERN LOWLANDS
MODERN ERA
(JASON'S ERA)

Gulf of Fenres

ECTHELOWALL COMMONWEALTH

KNORLAND

VOGTEREMARK

Caldoness
Glastonae
Glaston River
Ecthalon
Grimndale
Brackenburgh
Middleborne Islands
Siochail Plains
New Ecthalony
Bonus Mare
Abaross
Falconcleft
Carmine Glades
Geisle
Havenor
Stormridge
Port Jarreth
Black River
Falkirke

REHALCYON

Carvenna
Lacfortes

Lyrscony
ANSTARA - CLIENT KINGDOM
OF REHALCYON EMPIRE.

I'jon

Cennamar
Arridgulch
SURCALIDO

ZILNEN

GARCENILLES - ECTHELOWALL PROTECTORATE

N'jafu

Ruins of Gerisk

Central Lowlands (Middle Era)
ICE SHELF
BAY OF CROZMAL
Huntsend
Bózlyk
Kepke
Zarsam
Arnukhan
Vodanaya
Ivberria
Psilmos
Clerva Flats
Mem
MENSAR FOREST
Deepwood
Doreslek
GLACIA LAKE
Muzdy
ORMAN THICKET
Knorland
FROZEN PLAINS OF ARNUK
FISNUL RIVER
RECCAGOR RIVER
Lesnaygora
NURNOK RIVER
Opuska
THE HIGHLAND
City of Light
LOWER HIGHLANDS
LOWER HIGHLANDS
BEULAH PLATEAU
CIYACEM RIVER
LAKE OBTESEK
KEVNDAR FOREST
PILPHRATES RIVER
LAKE EBERAS
Tsnkachvok
Geghetsik
Qirthen
Trtloh
TelBron
Shanfara
Avanchaluk
Yusbilsi
Ikesias
CHARIS RIVER
Ermonh
ELBNON FOREST
Hündürqala
Uhrico
Uldim
ZILJAFU DESERT
SYKONOS MOUNTAINS
Centras
ENDOCHORA SEA
Uldiquim
Zunri
Siginacaq Yerl
Hepthel
STROFES RIVER
Fort Varos
Mononi
COKACHIK RIVER
Quimethra
KIZOS OASIS
Variiliman
GULF OF HULAPI
Rybe
Uthtar
Kizosa

CENTRAL LOWLANDS
(MODERN ERA)

ICE SHELF

Itzknor
Pezund
Memsar
Vodanaya
Ivberria
Reccaknor
Bözlyk
Estepe Pass
Dareslekya
Kepkevina
Leknuk
ARNUK
Psilmos
Clervu Flats
Mui
Nimucs
KNORLAND
Lesnaygora
Opusk
Krak O'ysailles
Urkhastvania
LOWER HIGHLANDS
HIGHLAND
Togaman
NDARVU
Ciyacem City
LOWER HIGHLANDS
LOWER HIGHLANDS
Pekadesh
REHALCYON
Montégris
Lesjou
Chomigny
Prasteha
LOWER HIGHLANDS
MBISAI
Vuhoso
Tsnkachvok
Geghetsík
Qirthen
Ipthfur
Phosphan
Tel Bronthus
SHANFARA
Ermonhalo
Uhrico
Avonchauk
YUSBILSI
Hündlúrqala
Ikesiapolis
Centros
Sol Uldim
Siğmacaq Yeri
ULDIQUIM
Zunri
ZILNEN
Fort Varos
Hopthora
Endochora
Mmoni
Quimethra
Rybe
Kizosa
Varliliman
Uthar

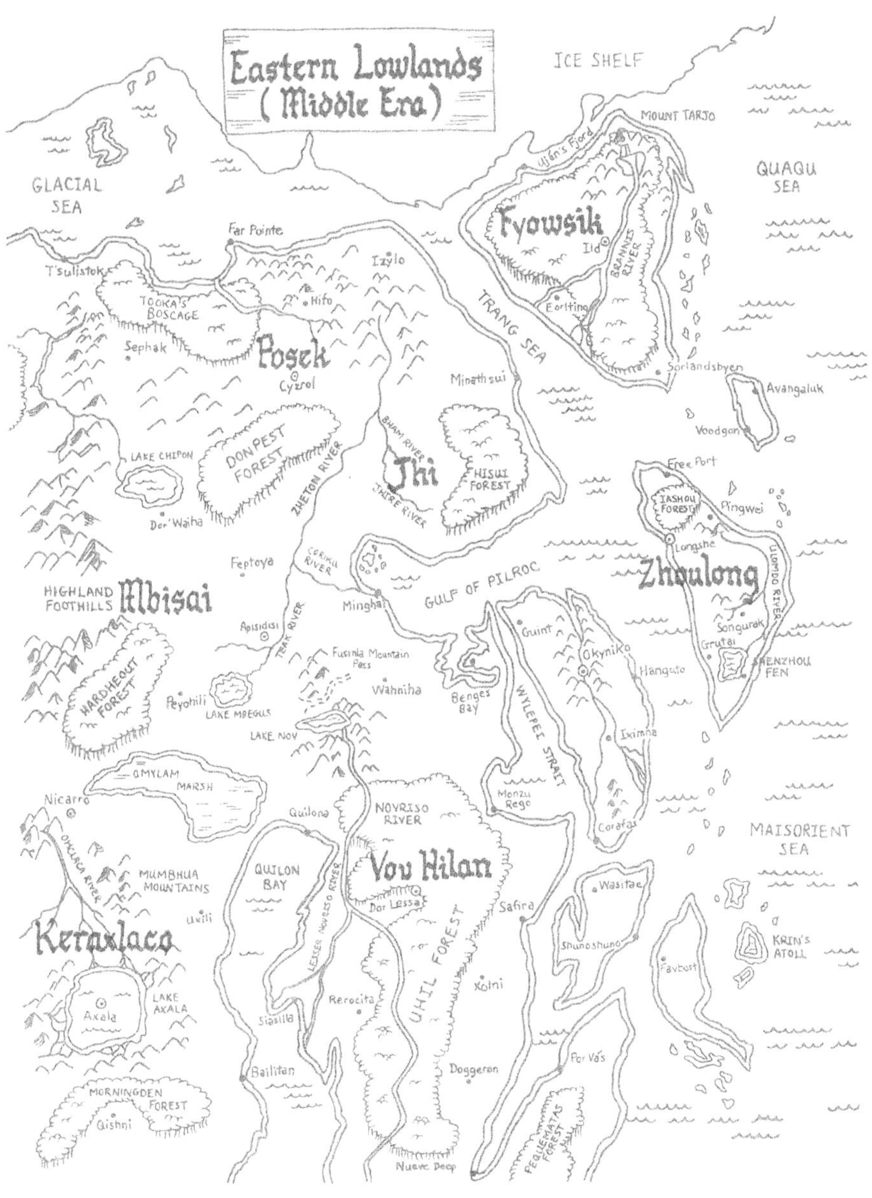

Eastern Lowlands
(Middle Era)
ICE SHELF
GLACIAL SEA
QUAQU SEA
Far Pointe
MOUNT TARJO
Uián's Fjord
Fyowsik
Ild
BRANNIS RIVER
Eorltino
Sorlandsbyen
TRANG SEA
Izylo
T'sulistok
TOOKA'S BOSCAGE
Hifo
Sephak
Posek
Cyzrol
Minathsui
Avangaluk
Voodgon
LAKE CHIPON
DONPEST FOREST
BHAM RIVER
Jhi
HISUI FOREST
Free Port
IASHOU FOREST
Pingwei
ZHETON RIVER
SHIRE RIVER
Longshe
Dor'Waiha
CORIKU RIVER
Zhaulong
Feptoya
LUOMBO RIVER
HIGHLAND FOOTHILLS
Mbisai
GULF OF PILROC
Minghai
TEAK RIVER
Apisidisi
Guint
Okyniko
Songurak
Grutai
RENZHOU FEN
Fusinla Mountain Pass
Hanguto
Peyohili
LAKE MBEGUS
Wahniha
Benges Bay
WYLEPEE STRAIT
HARDHEOUT FOREST
LAKE NOV
Iximne
OMYLAM MARSH
Nicarro
Monzu Rego
Corafas
MAISORIENT SEA
Guilona
NOYRISO RIVER
QUILON BAY
Vou Hilan
Wasitae
Uxili
Keraxlaco
LESSER NOYRISO RIVER
Dor Lessa
Safira
Shunoshuno
KRIN'S ATOLL
OMARA RIVER
MUMBHUA MOUNTAINS
UHIL FOREST
Kolni
Favbost
LAKE AXALA
Axala
Rerocita
Siasilla
MORNINGDEN FOREST
Gishni
Bailitan
Doggeron
Por Vás
PEQUEMATAS FOREST
Nueve Deep

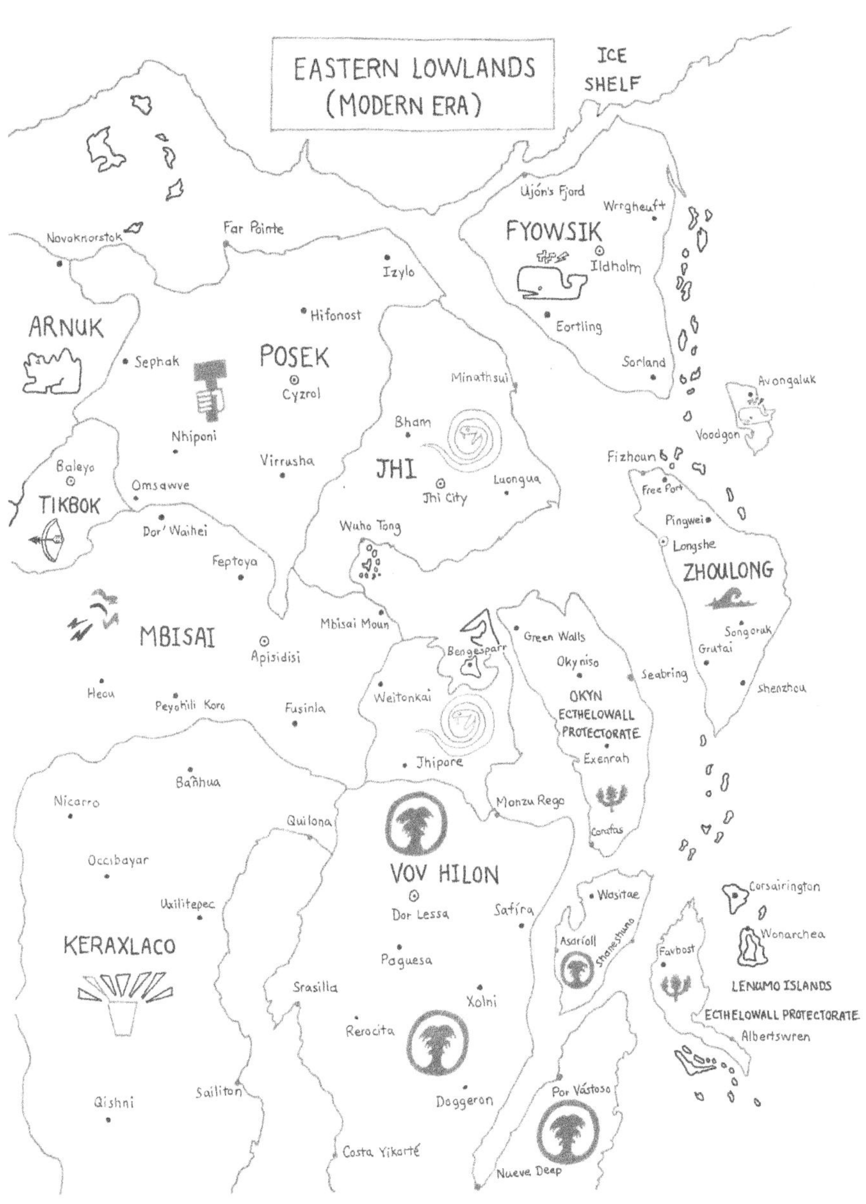

EASTERN LOWLANDS
(MODERN ERA)
ICE SHELF
Novaknorstok
Far Pointe
Izylo
Ujón's Fjord
Wrrgheuft
FYOWSIK
Ildholm
Hifonost
Eortling
ARNUK
Sephak
POSEK
Sorland
Avongaluk
Cyzrol
Minathsui
Voodgon
Nhiponi
Bham
JHI
Fizhoun
Virrusha
Luongua
Free Port
Baleyo
Omsawve
Jhi City
Pingwei
TIKBOK
Longshe
Dor' Waihei
Wuho Tong
ZHOULONG
Feptoya
Songoruk
Mbisai Moun
Grutai
MBISAI
Bengesparr
Green Walls
Shenzhou
Apisidisi
Okyniso
Seabring
Heou
Weitonkai
OKYN
Peyokili Koro
Fusinla
ECTHELOWALL
PROTECTORATE
Jhipore
Exenrah
Bañhua
Monzu Rego
Corsairington
Nicarro
Corafas
Quilona
Wasitae
VOV HILON
Shanethuno
Wonarchea
Occibayar
Safíra
Asaríoll
Favbost
Uxilitepec
Dor Lessa
KERAXLACO
Paguesa
LENUMO ISLANDS
Xolni
ECTHELOWALL PROTECTORATE
Srasilla
Albertswren
Rerocita
Por Vástoso
Qishni
Sailiton
Daggeron
Costa Yikarté
Nueve Deep

QUEST OF FIRE—THE STORY SO FAR

...

Jason returns to Brackenburgh after living on the run. He stops at an inn to escape the rain and there is captivated by the innkeeper's daughter, Aria, and the innkeeper's story of another teen from centuries past, Anargen.

Anargen lives in Black River a small village of Libertias, and has just joined the ancient order Palatini Lucis Aeternae, or Knights of Light, who serve the divine High King of All Realms. Few in the Lowlands outside the Order still obey the High King's laws or submit to his rule. Soon after joining the Order, Anargen's friend, Caeserus, tells him he had a vision of four Knights defending a Tower of Light from an attack that would topple the tower and leave everything in darkness and ruin. He believes he and Anargen are part of the four and enlisted their mentor Sir Cinaed's help in determining how to fulfill their part in the quest. This is heartbreaking for Anargen, who has just started a courtship with the girl he loves, Seren. Following his oaths, Anargen, Caeserus, Sir Cinaed, and two other teens from the village—Bertinand and Terrillian— all leave for a location Sir Cinaed vaguely hints at being of importance.

As they travel, the group is assaulted by a centuries-old monster, the Grey Scourge, and Sir Cinaed reveals they are traveling far north to Ordumair, the homeland of the Ords, a group of dwarfs who are coming to a historic peace treaty with the men of the powerful Commonwealth of Ecthelowall. Cinaed has been summoned to witness the historic moment and believes it to be key to the tower quest.

However, on arriving, Anargen and the others find the Ords hate Knights almost as much as the Ecthels, and when the peace talks falter are caught between the two sides as a battle breaks out. Very quickly, it becomes clear that the Grey Scourge was orchestrating the false accord and uses his dark powers to transform parts of the Ecthel army into werebeasts like himself. With the combination of evil sorcery and the latest siege weapons, the Ords are overwhelmed, and all seems lost. Rallying the battered Ords, Cinaed reveals he is actually Meredoch MacCowell, Defender of the Northern Realm, and has rescued the true leader of Ecthelowall, Viceroy Ecthelion, who the Grey Scourge tried to execute. The Scourge wants something in Ordumair, a lost treasure that had at one time been shared jointly by the Ecthels and Ords.

As the defenses start crumbling, the Grey Scourge breaks in and is confronted by the Knights, who defeat the Scourge and discover an oracle from a past ruler of Ordumair that is remarkably similar to Caeserus's vision.

Outside the fortress walls, the battle for Ordumair takes a turn as the dark powers of the Scourge have been broken, and aid arrives in the form of Knights from Albaron and the Vogteremark, sent for at Sir Cinaed's request.

Back in Jason's time, the Storyteller is interrupted by a city councilman who places him under arrest along with Jason, who is charged with conspiring with the old man. Outside the inn, however, the councilman reveals himself to be a doppelgänger, a changling, who posed as the councilman to get the Storyteller alone and murder him. The Storyteller, also named Cinaed, reveals himself as a Knight of Light and defeats the councilman. He then invites Jason to come with him as he goes back to the inn to get Aria and promises to explain more once there.

Upon arriving back in the inn, the pair splits up to find Aria. Jason succeeds but is forced to run with Aria from the inn as her grandfather defends them against an attack by werebeasts serving the same mysterious master as the doppelgänger.

Aria, also a Knight of Light, is soon after forced to defend them both from a Sombra, mystic assassins who can merge in and out of shadows at will. The Sombra, once defeated, reveals he was actually after Jason.

The pair flees Brackenburgh and hides out at an inn in the nearby town, Windward, to wait for Cinaed the Storyteller to rejoin them. While there, Aria begins to reveal more of Anargen's story.

With Ordumair delivered, it is decided that Anargen, his friends, Viceroy Echtelion, and a group of Ords will travel to the ruins of the Ord city Glastonae to search the archive there for more about the Tower of Light. There they find an oracle from the Ord ruler that is almost identical to Caeserus's vision. The group however must defer completing the quest as it becomes clear Ecthelion's son orchestrated the Grey Scourge's coup and has taken control of Ecthelowall. The group pledges to help retake Ecthelowall but must sneak back into the country to rally restoration forces for the Viceroy. To do so Cinaed recalls the kindness he and Anargen's father showed to a secretive man who arrived in Black River some time ago,

Arnauld Nerebold, who is actually a famed Ecthel privateer fallen on hard times. Trusting Captain Nerebold can guide them secretly back into Ecthelowall the group heads for Black River and stops at Falconcleft where the Count of Stormridge, Eidolon, takes interest in them. Shortly after that meeting, they are attacked by a group of Sombra, intent on assassinating the Viceroy. Barely escaping, to better mask their plans the group splits with Anargen, Caeserus, and Bertinand heading to Black River to send Anargen's father, Glewdyn, with Captain Nerebold, to meet the Viceroy, Sir Cinaed, and Terrillian at West Haven.

Anargen reunites with Seren, who reveals she pledged loyalty to the High King and has become a Knight of Light as well. Their blissful reunion is interrupted when mercenaries raid Black River. Anargen and his friends lay down their arms rather than risk harm coming to the villagers.

Taken captive to a secret location to labor on an enormous construction project, Anargen and Caeserus have a chance to escape, but when Anargen realizes he would have to leave Seren behind and the potential danger she would be in he again surrenders.

Months pass with Anargen and his friends released to live in Stormridge under watch to ensure they don't speak of what has happened. Anargen forgets his oaths to the High King during the time and lives a normal life until one night he sees something that stirs his memories—the Grey Scourge has been watching him and that very night, Anargen discovers a package that contains his spiritsword. Holding the divinely blessed blade reignites his zeal for the High King.

Soon after he is brought to a Knight Hall in Stormridge where Glewdyn and Sir Cinaed have already rescued Caeserus. They travel to get Seren back while Caeserus and Anargen go to retrieve Bertinand. They find him beset by a direnoir. A monstrous parasitic creature that feeds on the fears of its host. After defeating it, the Grey Scourge attacks, intending to keep them from returning to the Quest of Fire. They defeat the Scourge and bring him prisoner back to the Knight Hall. He reveals that he has been working for Count Eidolon and that the Count's plans for conquering the Western Lowlands are almost complete. Confronting Eidolon, the evil ruler does not hide his dabbling in dark sorceries from the cursed land of Tislatna, long ago destroyed by the High King for its wickedness.

Escaping the encounter with their lives, the Knights try to rally the few members of their Order in Stormridge they can trust, only to find they're too late. Eidolon has used the sorceries of Tislatna and an enchanted fruit that grows in the region to take control of the entire city's population. Mindless servants of his will, called carrion, they overwhelm the Knights with only a handful escaping. Sir Cinaed, Glewdyn, Anargen, Seren, Caeserus, and Bertinand along with a Sir Kyreneas, Lady Lyncia, and five other Knights make it atop the enormous reservoir that holds a secret escape tunnel from the city. There they find Eidolon waiting for them. He intends to sacrifice them in a ritual that will allow him to summon a wyvern long dormant in the mountains of the region and fuse it with a goblin to create a dragon, the first of an army of such creatures he wants to use to conquer the Lowlands and the very forbidden sorcery for which Tislatna was destroyed.

A battle ensues as a storm threatens to overflow the reservoir. The Knights attempt to escape, but Sir Cinaed, Glewdyn, and Anargen are still on the artificial lake's retaining wall finishing off Eidolon when the wyvern he summoned arrives. The creature rejects the weakened Eidolon, destroying him, and then sets out to do the same to the Knights and everything in its path. Sir Cinaed sacrifices himself, leaping onto the wyvern and slaying it as the reservoir gives and the water and stones plummet with the Defender Knight and the wyvern to the valley below. Anargen and the others escape, heartbroken.

In the Modern Era, Jason and Aria receive a message that her grandfather has had to slip out of Rehalycon to the Ecthel island, Geisle, and wants Aria to meet him there. Before Aria and Jason part ways, however, Jason is attacked by a group of mobster thugs who work for his family. The Wernstrums are the preeminent crime family of the Lowlands. They almost beat Jason to death when Aria steps in and rescues him. Jason confesses to Aria he had been running from being a part of his loathsome family till he received a letter giving him an ultimatum to either rejoin the family or his younger brother, Dorian, would be forced to take his place in the gang. Aria convinces him to come with her and they will figure out what to do next.

They arrive on Geisle and meet up with Cinaed the Storyteller. He leads them to the mansion of Professor Goulder, an old friend and fellow Knight of Light. Along the way, Jason and Aria acknowledge the romance between them and decide to formally begin dating, such as they can. Arriving at the eccentric professor's home, he shares his secret communications and seconds a plan Cinaed proposed to have all the Lowlands' Defenders of the Realms assemble to address the disturbing signs and growing darkness they've observed and endured. While discussing their next steps, the mansion is attacked by werebeasts and again Jason and Aria flee while Cinaed defends them.

The couple almost escapes when Sombra ambush and overwhelm them, taking Jason captive. Jason is brought to the Gerisk Ruins in the Southwestern desert nation Zilnen. There the Sombra hold him in wait of word from their client on whether to bring him in or finish him off.

Jason escapes with some aid from the High King and after encountering the horrifying powers of Tislatna buried in the ruins, makes his way to a small desert ksar where he's caught by the Sombra but liberated by Cinaed and Aria. The Sombra vow revenge.

From there, the group travels north to I'jon where Sadiq Kharoum, Defender of the Southwestern Realm resides. Zilnen is hostile to Knights of Light, so they meet in a secret library. There Jason is introduced to Aria's close friend, Tirzah, and encounters some books that cast doubt on whether what he had experienced was truly marvelous or rather the whole Quest of Fire was a sham. While gripped in doubt and uncertainty, Sadiq flies into a rage, having learned Jason is a Wernstrum. The Wernstrums had been helping the Rehalcyon Empire with a secret project on the southern shores of the Notioanemos Sea and Sadiq as a loyal Zilnian noble accuses Jason of treachery and espionage.

Cinaed, Jason, and Aria leave in a rush, and on the train ride, Cinaed confirms he is not the Sir Cinaed from the stories Jason has been told. Torn by not having helped his brother and convinced he'd been conned into believing a fairy tale, Jason jumps off the train and abandons Aria and Cinaed. He heads home to Brackenburgh and turns himself over to his family. It was a ruse and a trap all along. Dorian isn't in danger at all, he is now the head of the family and behind the attacks on Jason. He reveals that he has embraced the dark powers used by Count Eidolon and others and chains Jason up to endure a slow and painful death.

While chained, Jason cries out to the High King, broken and penitent, realizing once and for all the Quest of Fire is real.

In a blaze of glorious fire and light, the High King frees Jason from his bonds.

Meanwhile, Aria and Cinaed visit Dr. Gregorio Antoni to further their work in uniting the Defenders of the Realms. Aria is wistful and misses Jason. But they can't lament long as Sombra attack forcing them to move on. Cinaed instructs Dr. Antoni to help Jason find them, because he is certain they haven't seen the last of the teen.

During the events in Stormridge of the Middle Era, Thomas Fenwrest is a squire serving his uncle Baron Fenwrest under the captain of his guard, Sir Hurstwell. Thomas and Hurstwell are tasked with delivering the Baron's young son, Gregor, to Yerst Castle along with his betrothed, Lady Delia Sornfold and her sister Mia. The war to restore the Viceroy has been underway for months and things seem hopeful when the group stumbles upon the ravaged field of a battle that dealt a decisive blow to the Restoration Army. Having lost his own family, Thomas comforts Mia who believes her father, Baron Sornfold, died in the battle. The group also finds a survivor, the foreign Knight and friend of Anargen, Terrillian.

Sir Hurstwell advises that they all retreat to Port Valence, a fortified position on the coast. They arrive along with a steady stream of refugees from the collapsing Restoration front lines just as the Monarchists launch a surprise attack on Port Valence. Fleeing inside the city, they only just catch their breath before it becomes clear Valence too will fall and they make a narrow escape from its docks onboard a ship bound for the island of New Ecthelowall, known to its residents as Emeral.

On Emeral, Mia discovers her father is alive, and as Baron of Emeral welcomes the group, and Viceroy Ecthelion who also arrives at the same time, promising safety. Things are quiet long enough for Thomas to think on the lessons Terrillian has been giving him about Knights of Light and for Thomas to begin to see he and Mia have feelings for one another. A celebratory ball is thrown by Baron Sornfold and Thomas is invited to attend as Lady Mia's guest. However, Gregor has fallen ill since their escape from Valence and must be tended to. Shortly before the ball begins, Thomas has a vision of the Tower of Light under siege. He doesn't know it at the time, but it is eerily similar to Caeserus's vision almost a year earlier. He pledges himself to the High King and is at once aware that there is something unnatural about Gregor's illness. A dark force seems to be binding him.

Thomas delivers Gregor from the enchanted illness and is warned by Gregor that he had been poisoned by Lady Delia. The pair dash to the site of the celebration and reach it just in time to see Delia murder her father and proclaim her loyalty to Monarch Ilyron. Thomas, Terrillian, Sir Hurstwell, Mia, Gregor, Viceroy Ecthelion, and the Viceroy's guards fight their way out and make a desperate escape into the Emeral countryside. Their plan is to reach the other side of the island before word that they weren't captured reaches there and sail to Libertias to plead for aid from the Viscount of Libertias.

The attempt fails and they are forced to turn back where they are intercepted by Captain Nerebold. The captain takes the Viceroy and Terrillian to Libertias to petition the Viscount as planned, but Gregor and Mia are deemed too valuable to risk keeping with the Viceroy, as they each now represent the most powerful noble houses in Ecthelowall's Restoration forces. They travel with Thomas and Sir Hurstwell to the Isle of Geists (later called Geisle) to hide until a safer passage north can be arranged. While hiding deep in the foreboding interior of the island, they discover a darkling creature that reveals an evil far greater than Monarch Ilyron is orchestrating the events unfolding.

The monster mortally wounds Sir Hurstwell, before he and Thomas are able to defeat it. In a frantic bid to save Sir Hurstwell and get needed supplies for Mia and Gregor, Thomas seeks help from the residents of the island only to find they've been slain by Monarchist forces after they failed to find Gregor and Mia. The trio remains on the island until Captain Nerebold returns, and they sail with him, determined now to seize the hope that their most desperate hour was past and to warn the Viceroy about what they've learned.

DRAMATIS PERSONAE

MIDDLE ERA

- Anargen: Eighteen-year-old Knight of Light from the small town of Black River and part of the Quest to defend the mysterious Tower of Light.
- Seren: Anargen's fiancée and Knight of Light originally from Stormridge and swept into the Quest during an attack on Black River.
- Glewdyn: Anargen's father and elder Knight of Light. He and Sir Cinaed helped rescue Anargen and the others in Stormridge.
- Sir Cinaed: Anargen's mentor, also known as Meredith MacCowell, Defender of the Northern Realm. He sacrificed himself in Stormridge to save everyone.
- Caeserus: Anargen's best friend who had the initial vision of the Tower of Light that pulled them all into the Quest of Fire.

- Bertinand: Anargen and Seren's friend and another Knight of Light on the Quest who has been through all the triumphs and trials thus far.
- Sir Kyreneas: An elder Knight from Stormridge. One of its few survivors.
- Lady Lyncia: An insightful elder Knight from Stormridge who foresaw Sir Cinaed's heroic death.
- Sombra: League of assassins who use dark Tislatnean sorcery to merge in and out of shadows at will.
- Count Eidolon: The ruler of Stormridge and wielder of dark powers who was defeated and destroyed with Stormridge.
- Maldes Ilyron: Usurping Monarch of Ecthelowall and son of Ecthelion.
- Viceroy Ecthelion: Deposed rightful ruler of Ecthelowall and leader of the Loyalists in the War of Restoration.
- Ords: Race of northern dwarfs who were delivered from destruction in large part thanks to Sir Cinaed, Anargen, Caeserus, Bertinand, and Terrillian's efforts.
- Dag Votere: Citizens of the Vogteremark, a northern nation that sent Knights to aid Anargen and the others in liberating the Ords.
- Viscount Geralian: Ruler of Libertias, Anargen's home nation.
- Thomas Fenwrest: Ecthel teen who joined the Knights of Light while rescuing Mia and Gregor from the collapse of Loyalist defenses in Ecthelowall.
- Mia Sornfold: Daughter of the murdered Baron Sornfold, and heir to his lands. Sister to the bride of

Monarch Ilyron.

- Gregor Fenwrest: Thomas's cousin and the last remaining legitimate rival claimant to the Monarch's throne.

MODERN ERA

- Jason Landsby (Wernstrum): Eighteen-year-old who stumbled upon the Quest of Fire while trying to rescue his brother from their sordid family.
- Dorian Wernstrum: Jason's younger brother who embraced the dark powers offered to him and tried to imprison and execute Jason.
- Jerome and Glinda Chesterton: Kindly innkeepers in the small Rehalcyon town of Windward. Old friends and allies of Cinaed Black.
- Werebeasts: Savage werewolf-like monsters who retain the reasoning of a man and are servants of Dorian and those wielding the dark powers of Tislatna.
- Aria Black: Jason's estranged girlfriend and Knight of Light whom he abandoned after being deceived into believing the Quest was a lie.
- Cinaed "The Storyteller" Black: Aria's grandfather and current Defender of the Northern Realm. His stories about Anargen's adventures drew Jason into the Quest of Fire initially. Plans to unite all the Defenders of the Realms to stop the coming darkness.
- Melania Tsyket: Jason's childhood sweetheart and heir to a rival gang. Believed to have died years ago.

- Verdun Tsyket: Melania's uncle and head of the family's gang. One of the foremost criminals of the Lowlands.
- Direnoir: Hideous parasitic monsters that feed off their victim's fears until they've destroyed their host. They serve Dorian and those like him.
- Doppelgängers: Creatures capable of changing their appearance to that of another person in order to replace that person. They serve Dorian and others wielding the dark powers.
- Dr. Gregorio Antoni: A Knight of Light from the Lyscea province of the Rehalcyon Empire who secretly supports Cinaed Black's efforts.
- Sadiq Kharoum: Current Defender of the Southwestern Realm and ardent patron of Zilnen. Hates and blames Jason for Zilnen's troubles.
- Tirzah Kharoum: Sadiq's middle daughter and Knight of Light. Shares a sisterly bond with Aria.
- Kaveed Amine: Tirzah's beloved and expected successor to Sadiq and the throne of Zilnen. Pledged by force to Sadiq's older daughter to appease Mesnara.
- Mesnara: Ex-wife of Sadiq and noblewoman of Zilnen who wields considerable influence in the patriarchal Zilnian society.
- Farzhad: Cousin of Kaveed and middling ranked officer in Zilnen's army.
- Carrion: Ordinary individuals controlled by Tislatnean sorcery such that they cannot feel pain and single-mindedly follow the bidding of whoever cast the spell.
- Kazim Cuzibaum: Current Defender of the West Central Realm.

TWENTY-THIRD INTERLOGUE: ON THE RUN

The frantic thrum of Jason's heartbeat drowned out everything. His heart raced as if it could batter its way past his breastbone. They were coming for him.

A flash of lightning lit the darkened stone streets outside his alley. Standing across the way in the pounding rain were two of his family's enforcers. They beamed their torchlights into a flivver parked beside the road.

Jason slunk back deeper into the alley as one yelled an obscenity and smashed in the windshield glass of the automobile. The second gripped the other by the arm roughly and uttered hushed words to him. Jason couldn't hear them from here, but he knew what was being said. It was a reminder that if they failed to find Jason and kill him, then Jason's younger brother Dorian would kill them.

A shudder ran through Jason that had nothing to do with the chilly winter rain. He all too vividly remembered the dark creature that looked and sounded like his brother as he mocked him and left him to die in the dungeon beneath his family's mob headquarters. Jason had been there to rescue his brother from his family's wicked heritage. He never saw the betrayal coming.

Both bruisers took off down the street, heading to the city's northern districts. Jason settled back within his alley haven and leaned against the wet bricks. Taking in a shaky breath, he forced himself to breathe normally. He shouldn't be so scared. This wasn't the closest he had been to death tonight. And it wasn't by his skill he had escaped it.

A warmth enwrapped him as he remembered the flames burning through his chains. The brilliance of the light emanating from the throne, the splendor of the High King's visage as he looked down on him through fire that consumed Jason without destroying him. The music and majesty of the Sovereign of All Realm's voice alone would be with Jason to the end of his days. Never mind the unbelievable sequence of events that transported him from that dismal dungeon to this street.

A whisper of the magnificent voice came to Jason again. He winced at the instructions he received.

"It looks like I'm going to be walking an awfully long way unarmed on foot. I could easily fashion a makeshift crankshaft to take one of the flivvers down the street."

The heat around him intensified, and the voice of instruction took on a tone of rebuke.

"I'm sorry, my King. You're right. My allegiance, my life is pledged to you. You know best."

Steeling himself, Jason dashed out from the alley and wound through the lamplight-dotted streets of Brackenburgh. With every step, marveling at how readily he'd just said those words. As recently as the previous morning, he had been certain the legendary High King of All Realms and his *Palatini Lucis Aeternae*—Knights of Light—were fables. Myths he had rejected as powerless to help him. If only Aria could see him now.

A pang of regret and longing gripped his chest, and he rounded the next street corner and stopped. He breathed in and out, the ache building as he recalled their last minutes together.

Everything seemed to point to him being misled by her grandfather's stories about the Knights. At the time, Cinaed's fiery quest to hold back the darkness seemed like a foolish distraction from Jason's goal of rescuing Dorian from his grandmother. He had been so callous in that moment when Aria asked him to stay. Even now he could see the pleading in her emerald eyes as he flung himself off the train and dashed away. With that, he had broken both their hearts. Jason was only eighteen, but he was pretty sure he had razed his haven of true love.

Hot tears mingled with the frigid drops of rain pelting his face as he took off again, heading for the western road out of the city. He wiped them away.

What is wrong with me? My brother is a vessel for dark sorcery, and I'm crying over a girl? Did becoming a Knight suddenly make me fragile as glass?

Though he couldn't strictly say how, he knew that wasn't it. When he left her, the only thing that made it bearable had been his conviction that the whole Knight Order was a false myth and that he could save his brother by his sacrifice. But he had been wrong on both counts. Added atop his stack of guilt and regret, his foolishness left him with the immense weight of knowing he'd hurt her. Not to mention the question of how many more of the mystical assassins who merge with shadows, the Sombra, had attacked her after he left? She was in greater danger because of him.

Honk!

The goofy tinny sound of a flivver honking its horn gave him just enough time to realize he was running in front of the clunky car. Diving away from it, he landed on the slick hard cobblestones with a groan and watched as the flivver puttered out of sight.

That was close.

Getting to his feet, he nursed his sore arm, unsure whether it was a new contusion that hurt or an old one. Probably both. Standing under a street lamp, he could see he had a little red stain at the epicenter of a damp splotch on his sleeve.

As he looked up from his injury, he froze. The two goons pursuing him were down the street by two blocks. There wasn't anything between him and them.

Maybe they won't notice me.

A second later, he saw one of them cock his head and then point and exclaim, "It's him!"

Jason took off running across the street, not even trying to sort out a route. He needed more distance and a place to hide out, especially through the night.

Rounding the corner, his heart sank. He was in a section of town filled with stores shuttered for the night. Where could he go?

Jason looked up and down the street. He blinked, eyes wide with surprise. Was that light shyly shining out of a shop window about halfway down the row?

"Stop there you little blighter!" the closer of the thugs bellowed.

Jason didn't hesitate. Sprinting as fast as he could down the street, he made for the lit shop. Sliding the last five feet along the rain-slicked sidewalk stones, he used the iron railing on its stairs to swing up and land on the shop's stoop. The lettering on the large glass window beside the door was faded but looked like it said, "Lowland Antique Treasures."

Hope they don't mind me passing through.

Jason pulled on the handle and found it was stuck. He tugged again and again, each time more franticly. Sparing a glance over his shoulder, he saw the mobsters were rounding the corner onto this street.

Help me, my King!

Jason yanked, and the door gave. He leaped through the opening and tumbled down. As he crashed onto the floor, the expansive room went dark.

1

BROKEN

*"We stumbled down from the slopes of Stormridge's mountains
in a stupor, the bleakest of nightmares. I don't know how long
we all wandered without speaking, without stopping. The horror
of all we had endured, all we had lost cut deeper than our hearts
could bear."*

—*Anargen's King's Day Journal*
18 Fómhar 1606 Middle Era

Through the window, Anargen could see the trunk of an enormous tree felled by a recent storm. Its sorrow was his own. He sank down heavily onto the bed, continuing to look out. Removing his helmet, he rubbed his face and ran his fingers through the mess of his sweat-soaked hair, getting the dark strands out of his face. After days on the run with no rest and no chance to sit and reflect and grieve the unmendable wound he had suffered at Stormridge, he had come to the small town of Cattingsford. North along the Knight's River from

Youngsland, it was the quiet chance for solitude he and his companions needed.

Like the tree outside, however, Anargen understood now that the initial wound that shattered the tree and the swift plummet were not the worst things it faced. Worst was laying there on the dampened grass, unable to right itself. Unable to mend itself. Laying there dying, decaying, never more to rise. Anargen was terrified that now might be that moment of catching his breath and facing his fall in full. He closed his eyes, willing himself to not think about it all, to just focus on his breathing.

A few moments later, he felt a hand wrap gently over his own. Without realizing it, he had been digging his fingers into the bed's sheet, handfuls of straw bunched in them, poking through to prick his bare hands. He had been imagining the damp mossy bark of the trunk, growing softer as toadstools, insects, and time ravaged it.

Anargen didn't need to look to know his comforter was Seren, but he did, and he wished he hadn't. In her sorrel eyes were the bottomless fathoms of compassion he had always been drawn to, and he knew in her love she ached for him. But he couldn't bear it now.

"You didn't come to dinner again tonight," she pointed out in the gentle nursemaid's tone she had taken when speaking to him since their escape from Stormridge. It was almost as painful to hear in her voice as if she had scolded and chided him for his malfeasance. She had tried that once as well. Reminding him that he was her fiancé and it was her duty to tend to him. In either approach, the underlying meaning was the same—his despondence was only serving to hurt her further. Strangely, this paralyzed him instead of galvanizing him to action. Other nights, he had simply sat there stoic, his eyes fixed on the distance until she left him. More than once, tears were in her eyes.

"I still can't face them," Anargen croaked, his voice tight. He'd barely drunk anything since their escape, either. It hurt to speak, but he couldn't bear it if she cried over him again tonight.

"The Knight Hall of this town has taken care of us," she pointed out. "You can't eschew their kindness anymore. They don't deserve it."

He looked at the floor, unable to hold her gaze. Her pale complexion seemed more so in the dim candlelight of the room, and he could see the tightness in her cheeks, the pursing of her lips. It wasn't just the benevolence of the Cattingsford Knights he couldn't keep turning aside.

"I know," he managed to say, his eyes drifting back to the window and downed tree.

After several seconds of silence, she prompted, "Well?"

Turning his gaze to her again, he drew in a breath. It was then that he took stock of her more fully. Her long straight hair had been done into an intricate braid tied with a black ribbon. It matched the dark dress she'd been given. "You look beautiful," he commented, speaking the first thought that came to him. "Your braid is lovely."

She huffed out a sigh and blinked. "Thank you. You could have seen it better in the main hall, by the fire. It was lonely seated by myself."

He nodded. "It was lonely on my walk. The townspeople don't seem quite so happy to see us as the Knights here."

"Some people are superstitious. Watching someone slowly killing themself with sorrow isn't often taken as a good omen."

That got his attention. Was that really what he was doing?

All it took to confirm it was to look into Seren's eyes and see there that she was already mourning him. Mourning a husband she would have loved for a lifetime but never married. A life together that would have been like two vines winding about each other, supporting one another, bound together, more one than two. He had already buried that happiness in his own heart, but he hadn't realized she was doing the same.

Anargen coughed, trying to work moisture into his mouth and failing. Voice raspy, he replied, "Then you won't be alone tomorrow. No more mourning."

Her brows raised. "Truly?"

"You have my word," he vowed and raised her hand to his lips. He was sure it must have felt more like shagreen than a lover's kiss.

The transformation was instantaneous all the same. Seren seemed to be filled where a moment ago she was empty. She stood quickly. "Well then, why wait?"

She gave a knock on the still-open door to the room. Apparently, it had been an agreed-upon signal because in came his father Glewdyn and Lady Lyncia, bearing with them plates of cured meat, hard rolls, blueberries, and early harvest winter greens. Two flagons of a warm beverage, perhaps a cider, were included. The meals were sat on the small table bearing Anargen's lone candle.

Before heading back to the hall, Glewdyn bent down and gave him a tight hug and a kiss on the top of his head. If Anargen could have cried, seeing his father's expression through the whole thing would have brought tears.

"You can stay if you like," Seren called to Glewdyn and Lyncia. "Even here, it is proper to have chaperones."

Turning to Anargen, she added, "You aren't wrong about the townspeople disliking us. Something is going on, and there is no need to add to their gossip by flouting social mores."

Propriety aside, Anargen would never take advantage of Seren. But it was a moot point. Drinking the steaming apple cider with slow, purposeful sips, Anargen nodded. Try as he might not to, the cider was quickly downed, and with it, all the food. Seren was much more dignified in her eating, so he spent the next several minutes watching her, not speaking, just taking time to appreciate her presence. Occasionally, he would spare glances up at Glewdyn, who had one of his equally quiet grins that spoke louder than any wine-spirited revel. Even Lady Lyncia's sharp old eyes and tight-lipped reservation seemed softened for this moment.

After several minutes, Seren finished, and they shared a low conversation. Light. Distant from everything that had happened and from the future. Mostly about the growing of winter greens, grinding grain at a mill, and the kind women of the Hall who had helped Seren with her hair and clothes. Occasionally, Glewdyn or Lyncia would offer an anecdote or comment. Until an hour later, Anargen felt the stirring of something akin to happiness threatening to crack through the ardent defenses of his despair. He did not resist and treasured giving Seren a goodnight kiss. When he lay down after all had left, he knew he would sleep tonight without the terrors that had woken him every night prior. And if they did threaten his dreams, he could bear them.

But he stirred awake, and it seemed to him he had not been asleep for more than a few minutes. Though he knew that wasn't true. The candle was out, and the room was full dark, with the only light being stars shining through a haze of clouds. That and the burning blade of his father, as he stood over him in full armor, shaking him awake.

"Get up, son," Glewdyn instructed, no room for disagreement in his tone. "We have to go."

"What's happening?" Anargen asked, groggy as he struggled to strap on his armor with drowsiness-hampered hands.

"The townspeople," was all Glewdyn replied by way of explanation. "Bertinand is bringing Seren and Lady Lyncia. Caeserus and Sir Kyreneas are gathering the others."

As soon as Anargen strapped on his spiritsword and picked up his shield, Glewdyn stepped around him to the wall with the window. Plunging the fiery sword into the wall, he cut the opening much wider, section by section, taking the smoldering pieces and setting them aside quietly. The others appeared at the doorway to the room, with Seren rushing over to clasp Anargen in a quick embrace.

"It's going to be okay," Anargen soothed, even though he hadn't the faintest notion if he could guarantee such to be true.

"Now, son," Glewdyn insisted. "Go."

TWENTY-FOURTH INTERLOGUE: A KNIGHT'S ARMS

The sudden press of the dark startled Jason. After he had made such a mess of opening the door, he lost the ability to see the lights going out as a coincidence.

"Hello?" he whispered.

No answer. Jason took a few tentative steps forward, old boards creaking under his feet. His eyes slowly adjusted to the deeper dark. Long shoulder-high shelves ran the length of the long room's center. Around the room's walls were mounted shelves and floor cases with glass lids to view an assortment of items. He spotted everything from globes to antique children's toys. There were things with exotic designs from foreign lands, the purpose for which he could only guess.

A sudden flash of light from across the room caught his eye. It was faint and ever so brief, but he was sure he saw it.

Licking his lips, he dithered over what to do. Something strange was happening, and after the night he'd had, his imagination happily supplied any number of horrible things that could be awaiting in the darker areas of the shop.

After a few moments, he heard one of the fiends chasing him call out from next door, "He's not in here."

I have to get away from the shop window.

Risking the deeper dark, he crept among the shelves at a crouch. Toward the back, he spotted something out of place. Amidst pots and other odds and ends was a weapon—a sword.

For several seconds, he just stood there, staring at it. It looked to be a dusty old saber, something from almost a hundred years past. It had an ornate hilt with some kind of etchings along the blade and handguard. Peculiarly, Jason felt the compulsion to grab it. His hand reached for it before he even realized he was doing so. He hesitated, hand hovering over the hilt as the intense pull to lay hold of it raced up his arm. The sensation was so potent it startled Jason. Was it just his imagination, or had the air around the sword grown warmer?

It wasn't his imagination. The longer his hand lingered, hovering over the hilt, the hotter the air became until it felt like he was warming his hands beside a fire on a winter's day. The pull to take hold of the sword intensified in equal measure until he couldn't help but brush the tips of his fingers across its aged leather grip.

He gasped. The moment his hand touched it, little streaks of light dashed along the length of the blade. It would have terrified him if he had never witnessed something like this before. But he knew exactly what he'd found, and he tightened his grip on the hilt, lifting it from the shelf and holding it up as flames raced with a rush of heat and brilliance to cover the entire blade.

"A spiritsword," he murmured. Tilting it back and forth to examine the glowing inscriptions, he realized he had never held a spiritsword before. If he had, he hadn't known it. In school, he had been required to learn a bit of fencing, and with his family being what it was, he had held more than one blade in his life. None had felt like this.

The heat traced up his arms, burning through his sinews and enwrapping his bones. The sensation should have been torture, but the closest thing Jason could come to it in description was delicious. This was the cold drink of water on the hottest Zilnen midday. This was the shelter of Falkirke's sturdy walls in the blustery gale of a summer storm. It calmed and exhilarated him in one.

"Magnificent," he murmured aloud and let out a contented sigh.

"It is indeed," a deep, clear voice agreed.

Jason spun to find a tall man watching him. Clothed in a heavy overcoat that reached to his knees, the speaker was well-tanned and had dark hair. His clean-shaven face seemed taut with a gravity of person Jason had always imagined the Emperor of Rehalcyon possessed. But it was absurd to think the Emperor, or anyone of near echelons, was in this modest antique shop. More likely, it was the owner of the shop, and this was how he expressed being piqued.

Trying to clear his throat to offer an apologetic reply, Jason found himself cut off.

"I see you have found the spiritsword. It burns brightly for you."

Jason hesitated to reply, unsure whether he could admit to such a thing without being identified as a Knight of Light, new to it though he was, and possibly tossed into the street without. Once more, the other man spoke. "I know you are one of the *Palatini Lucis Aeternae*. I see clearly how the blade burns in your grasp."

Jason took a step back and straightened as he did. Only two groups of people, such as he understood it, could see the fire of a spiritsword. Those who pledged themselves to the High King and those who utterly rejected him and instead sided with the Dark Prince.

Which is he?

As soon as the thought formed, however, Jason regretted it. For some reason, it felt painfully foolish to imagine this man as a servant to the dark. "I'm a Knight of Light, yes," Jason agreed. "I came in for safety from two terrible men. I apologize for the intrusion."

"The two men are just outside and waiting to rend you to bits. I suggest you claim the armor as well."

Jason's attention snapped to the window. He could see two dismal shadows lurking just beyond, their forms blurred by the dark. It seemed to him the night had grown deeper and colder.

Turning his attention back, he found the other man looking past him. His gaze was so fixed he may well have been looking beyond the city itself. The sensation of that thought was unnerving. "I, uh," Jason faltered. "It isn't my armor. That is, I can't pay you for it."

"It is not mine to require payment," the man replied once more, looking directly at Jason. "But if you fret over it, check your right pocket."

Confused but feeling compelled to comply, Jason reached into his pocket as he watched the man with anxious fixation. His hand found a cloth with something hard wrapped up. Producing it, he unbound it and gasped. There were two gold solidi from the days of Rehalcy, before the Empire's rise. Such currency was prized, and one was worth enough to purchase the shop, let alone the old arms and armor.

Brow furrowed, Jason looked up at the mysterious man. "How? Where?"

"Don't you know?" the other prompted.

"Cinaed," Jason murmured, suddenly recalling him passing the handkerchief to Jason to wipe his brow after being rescued from the Sombra in the burning Ziljafu desert ksar, Sayeh. "It's a miracle my brother's thugs didn't take this from me."

There was a contentment about the man's face, but he said nothing. Suddenly, his expression darkened. "You must ready yourself. They are coming."

From across the shop, the sound of the door opening drew Jason's attention. Peering around the shelves, he saw the two brutes clomp heavily in.

Turning back, he found the other man was gone. Looking around the back edges of the shelves nearest him, Jason gaped. The man was just completely and utterly gone.

"Come out, little Wernstrum. We can smell your stench. You had to know you can't hide from us."

At the end, the words became mixed with a gruffness akin to a bestial growl.

Taking in a shaky breath, Jason slipped the armor off the shelves beside him and put it on piece by piece as quickly and quietly as he could. He had just grabbed a modest buckler shield to complete the suit when he heard a low whistle at his back. One of the two enforcers stood at the head of the aisle. "Look here, Sven. This one fancies himself a knight."

All Jason's muscles tensed. What stood before him was a weirdly stretched version of the enforcer, his eyes remote and dark, his voice gravelly.

"Isn't that sweet? Playing pretend at his age," another equally gruff-toned response came from behind Jason. "Where's your horsey, little knight? Did it run off with the rest of your armor? That's a right shame."

Jason scrambled away from the looming and equally grotesque version of Sven. This earned a throaty chuckle from both attackers.

Undertones of something sinister rumbled from deep

within them. Their cruelty galled Jason, stirring up a new sort of indignation in him and, with it, courage.

Rising to his feet, he pointed the spiritsword toward each in a slow arc, back and forth. Flames crackled and swelled from the blade, flooding Jason with warmth and strength.

The two men leaped back and snarled in near unison. Jason could see the dark pall marring each man in the light of the sword's fire. He imagined these two were much like Mr. Keeper from Cinaed's stories. At this point, the facade was the human form and the reality, the monster underneath.

After years of living on the streets and traveling to survive on his own, Jason had heard a pretty broad range of curses. Many leveled at him. The ones spewing from the fiends on either side of him were by far the vilest he'd ever heard.

As they spat them, they each began shuddering, their profanities blurring into inhuman growls.

It's just like Cinaed's story from Bracken. These two are werebeasts!

Not giving a moment longer in wait, Jason vaulted the shelf beside him and dashed out the front door. To his surprise, he moved so fast that it only took seconds to be outside, turned, and standing with his spiritsword held at the ready.

By the time his pursuers sauntered out of the building, Jason had caught his breath. The two fiends wreaked with swagger. They had abandoned normal human mannerisms and were now half crouched, moving opposite each other to try to flank him.

With each step taken, Jason could see them twist and warp from human toward their beast form. Tales he'd heard about Anargen and the others having faced such creatures conjured horrible images of their ferocity and prowess for wanton carnage. Jason stepped backward to keep himself from being totally flanked, but he was running out of space. The row of buildings behind him had no alleyways nearby, and this was the start of an unusually long block.

His guard faltered, and he started to lower the spiritsword. With wobbling steps, he shuffled toward the way he came down the street, hoping he could get there if he ran. There were canine-like chuckles from the two thugs, and their eyes showed ochre now.

They can tear me to shreds. What am I doing?

In his hand, the spiritsword dimmed. The change drew his eye, and he caught upon a few familiar words. "Perfect love casts out fear."

Anargen said that so many times. In moments like these, when he felt overwhelmed, he trusted in the High King to deliver him ... and the High King did. The stories tell that the werebeasts are terrifying, but they also tell that the fiery blade of a Knight of Light can slay them.

Jason's grip tightened on the spiritsword, and once more, the heat of it danced up his arm, coursing through his veins. He stopped edging away and stood stock still.

"You should rethink your allegiances," Jason called out to them. "Me 'playing' Knight is more worthwhile than a thousand centuries spent bound by the dark sorceries you've given yourselves over to."

One of the creatures snarled at Jason, and he realized they'd stopped transitioning. They were covered in a fur coating, and their faces were twisted with sharp teeth sticking out at odd angles from lupine snouts, but they were hardly the beasts he'd been told of. It was like they were unfinished.

Suddenly, Jason's eyes leaped to the sky, where he realized the moon was only in its waxing quarter.

"New moon's bane, full moon's gain ..."

Should what he remembered from the stories be true, then these werebeasts were created on the recent new moon. They had never yet achieved their full monstrous state and so were far from that strength and prowess. "You're just pups, aren't you?" he blurted out. "Werebeast pups. Or cubs. Or whatever you're called."

"We're called death," one of them warbled out throatily, his voice keening with petulance. It sounded as though human speech was becoming difficult to maintain in his current state.

Before Jason could call out a retort, the other beast charged. Pivoting, Jason threw up his buckler to deflect sharp claws swiping at him. They raked across the buckler's burning surface, and the creature squealed in pain. It leaped back a good five feet and shook its singed hand.

A whisper told Jason to jump forward, but he hesitated, feeling confident he could similarly handle the next such charge. That's when he noticed the other creature had wheeled around and was attacking from the side to scratch him. It had broken a chunk of a support to a building's portico off and lobbed it.

The chunk of heavy wood hit Jason square in the chest and sent him tumbling to the stones of the street on his back. Shaking his head, he struggled to get up, but the first beast was on him. Leaping over to take swipe after swipe at him, battering his desperately thrown-up defense.

Help me, my King!

Furious blows rained on him as the thing sought a weak point in his wavering guard. Jason realized the whisper had been help, if he'd only listened.

I'm sorry. From now on, you lead. I follow!

A whispered instruction to roll came, and Jason wouldn't have hesitated, but he was pinned between the clawed feet of the monster.

At that moment, the creature jumped up, and Jason rolled along the stones and scrambled back up to his feet. Across from him, the fiend landed with a terrific crash onto the street.

Another whisper told him to duck and then roll to the right. As he did, he saw the wild swipe from the other monster cut through nothing but the air of where he'd been. As he came out of the roll, Jason surged back up into a slice that caught the werebeast across the chest, sending small smoke tendrils spiraling off the creature.

It whimpered and retreated several steps, nursing its smoldering breast and abdomen. The other must have seen because it let out something between a roar and a howl and charged.

Jason stood still and dove right at the last second, just as the whisper had guided him. He caught the werebeast across the back, leaving a glowing line from shoulder to hip.

Both creatures fumbled about on the ground, whining and whimpering. As Jason advanced on the one freshly cut, it let out a shriek, got to its feet, and ran back down the street away from Jason.

Seeing his comrade flee, the other let out a pitiful semi-bark and bolted after.

Standing there, almost too stunned to breathe, Jason watched them until they were out of sight around a corner building. He drew in a jagged breath and let it out slowly.

Thank you, my King.

Sheathing the spiritsword, Jason rubbed his face. Was his first fight with genuine creatures of darkness really over so soon?

"Well done," called someone from across the street. Jason's benefactor from the shop was standing there. In his hand was a gleaming sword.

2

BETRAYAL

"Amid our greatest fears since passing beyond the enclosure of Stormridge's mountains is that the farther we move from them, the more exposed we feel. There are certain to be enemies who have felt the blow delivered to their forces. Where we are grievously wounded, they may only be so much so as to be angered and hungry for vengeance."

—*Anargen's King's Day Journal*
18 Fómhar 1606 Middle Era

With great care to be as silent as stone, Anargen dropped to the ground from the hole in the wall of the Knight Hall's room. Checking to the right and left, he motioned for Seren to come and helped her down. He did the same with Glewdyn, who landed with a grunt and more violent noise. Together, they each got Lady Lyncia down.

Bertinand hopped down last and of his own, voicing a hushed *"Oof!"* as he hit the ground. "Let's try not to make a habit of doing this."

"*Shh*," Lyncia chided.

He held his hands up placatively and shot Anargen a look like he thought the old woman was a grouch. When Lady Lyncia eyed him scathingly, he managed to beam a hasty smile.

Anargen couldn't understand how Bertinand could be so glib right now. This was perhaps their most ignoble hour, and if they didn't hurry, it could certainly be their last in the Lowlands.

"We are to meet the others at the stables on the west side of town," Glewdyn informed him. "The Knight Errant here, Sir Nathan, is securing supplies with some others from the Hall. They will meet us at the stables as well."

Giving a nod, Anargen dashed along the length of the big wooden Hall, set wider and shorter than most structures he'd seen. He was careful to keep low under the windows and kept a wary eye on each alleyway.

A small stand of trees stood between the Knight Hall's back wall and the river, which wound around the town to the south and west. The stables on the west end of town would be a good place to ride out from to ford a low spot in the river, but where from there? If they continued south toward Youngsland as planned, they would have to cross the river again. They didn't have funds for a ferry, and the waterway would be too deep to cross. If they turned north, they could go to Raresbruck and West Haven. Or, a bit farther south, they could return to Black River. At least whatever ruins remained after Count Eidolon's mercenaries destroyed it.

Anargen pushed that from his mind. He carried enough pain over more recent events than his heart could stand. Lading onto them the memory of his childhood home being destroyed so he and the others could be taken captive to Stormridge and pressed into forced labor would break him.

Passing into the less frequented streets of the town,

Anargen noticed small parties of townsmen going from building to building, knocking on doors and entering some against any protests raised. What could have so thoroughly turned the townsmen against them? Surely not a depressed young man struggling with his grief.

Their one advantage was that the town's layout merged its buildings with the tree line in a number of places, allowing them to slip among the vibrant foliage and back around buildings without much risk of exposing themselves fully. Cattingsford wasn't a very large town either. It had a few stone buildings and was half-over the size of Anargen's home village of Black River.

They were in view of the stables when Bertinand came and shook his shoulder. "Bad news. It looks like Caeserus and the others were intercepted."

Anargen doubled back a couple of streets with Bertinand and confirmed his suspicions. Caeserus and Sir Kyreneas's tall forms in their glowing armor were being directed back away from the direction they needed to go by a dozen townspeople with torches and spears. They were being led toward the city's center. The civic focal point had a large bell and a well on a stone plaza. More importantly, stocks and gallows were erected there.

Gnawing on his lip, Jason glanced back to where Seren and Lady Lyncia stood, poised to race to the stable. They could all make for the stables now and escape for sure. But that would condemn Caeserus and Sir Kyreneas to whatever fate awaited them. It also left the question of what had happened to the other Knights from Stormridge who had escaped that city's destruction with them. Only five remained, but where could they have gone? Were they also captured and being led away?

"We're going to help them, right?" Bertinand asked, sounding almost rhetorical.

"Right," Anargen confirmed, looking to his father for the affirmative. The older man nodded.

Sparing a glance toward Seren and Lyncia, he saw they were dashing back up to them. "What are you doing?" Glewdyn whispered once they were close enough. "You should keep to the plan. Grab the horses and go. We'll join you once we're able."

"Please?" Anargen requested, directing it to Seren.

"We're Knights as well," Lady Lyncia reminded them. "We all stand, and we all fall, united."

It was no use arguing. Anargen could see the same fixedness in Seren's expression. Her qualities of stability and strength were sometimes as frustrating as they were endearing.

"Fine, then what's the new plan? Anyone got one?" Bertinand prompted, looking from person to person.

"The plan is for you to die, phosphila," a raspy voice hissed behind them.

From the shadowy depths of night formed the shape of a man, then two, and finally a third. They wore black robes with hoods and cowls under heavy grey armor.

Sombra!

Supernatural assassins capable of merging in and out of shadows and using them to ruthlessly murder their marks. As the trio reached out, hauberks formed from the dark and shot forward, thrusting at the Knights and forcing them into the open street.

The thought crossed Anargen's mind to draw his sword to fight back, but he caught a stern look from his father. He raised his hands and watched as Seren, Bertinand, and the others did the same.

"*Ha!* I expected more from this lot. They hardly seem to be the troublesome group from the fiasco at Falconcleft," one of the three Sombra chuckled.

"Their numbers were greater then," another protested.

"Hush, you louts," the first Sombra chided them. "All of you, to the town square. *Now!*"

Crunching along the street, Anargen noticed several lanterns hung around the square and in the hands of the townspeople, who had formed a loose semicircle around the town center. Caeserus and Kyreneas stood on stone platforms. Before the pair of Knights was an array of three more Sombra, each bearing a different shadowy implement that glinted wickedly in the light from the villagers' low-burning lanterns. As Anargen got closer, he could make out the mixture of miens worn by the townspeople. Some scowled furiously as if hating the very sight of the Knights—one man jeered at them, a cruel sneer turning up his lip. Most simply looked ill at ease. One by one, Anargen and the others were goaded into the center with Caeserus and Kyreneas.

One Sombra of the central three, with a cruel-looking flail, wore more impressive armor than the others. From the way they were angled around him, it seemed he was their leader. Anargen remembered Cinaed had called Sombra of this kind "ancients." Centuries old and regarded by their caste as semi-divine. A bittersweet irony because it was Sir Cinaed's humbling of Karanlik, another of their ancients, that no doubt landed them in this current predicament.

Oh, Cinaed! We need you now more than ever.

Thinking about the loss of his mentor was sure to cripple him, and Anargen couldn't afford that now. He tried to focus on what was happening around him to keep from slipping back into the endless mire of grief.

The clouded eyes of the Sombra ancient slowly looked over them. "There were five others?"

"Three have fallen. Two escaped into the forest. It was the

sound of their flight that alerted these to their danger," one of the Sombra informed their captain.

"On whom does the blame for this failure rest?"

One of their number stepped forward. "Mine, excellent one."

There was only the slightest tilt of the ancient's head in the direction of his charge. His ghoulish countenance seemed to darken considerably, though. "Wev, go now and finish them both. Fail again, and you shall be our next quarry."

Wev bowed low and twisted his body, becoming a cyclone of dark mist. Just as swiftly, the mist spread into darkness and was, by all appearances, gone.

That business concluded, the ancient turned back to the assemblage before him. Reaching into the folds of his cloak, he made a sweeping gesture. Shadows pooled around him and swirled upward, forming an elaborate ebony seat with a feathered dragon looking down from above. Its forelegs formed armrests, and its hindlegs held up a seat cushion. The tail coiled to become a slight dais, and the wings curled around to partially enwrap the throne.

With a wheezy grunt that sounded as if it had passed through a desiccated corpse's lips, the enchanted assassin seated himself. "Now we shall render judgment on those who have defied the Sombra."

He addressed the townspeople, "First, you have all done well. Your cooperation has spared your town destruction. For now. Know that if you ever speak of our kind or what you see here this night to anyone, you shall all suffer far worse remunerations than these before you."

Anargen caught the gaze of a man among them who fussed with a cap he'd removed. His hands were trembling. None of these people looked familiar, so Anargen guessed the Knights of the Hall weren't among the betrayers. Having heard what happened to the five Stormridge Knights not with them now, he could guess what had become of them.

None of Cattingsford's citizens uttered a word of dissent. Once one has made a deal with the darkness, the danger of turning back and the cost of it must seem very steep. Too high for any of them. Anargen knew from experience that redemption was worth the pain and risk.

"You're all cowards!" Caeserus lashed out, startling Anargen out of his introspection. "Every one of you deserves whatever these fiends have devised for us and more, tenfold!"

One of the Sombra beside the ancient leaned forward and, with a swipe of his hand, made a whip materialize and struck Caeserus across the cheek.

Caeserus grunted, seeming to fight the impulse to cry out in pain. A furious red welt rose up, and a trickle of blood dripped down from it.

"Speak again, and those words shall be your life's last."

"Perhaps wise ancient, it would be easier for us to face our fate if you named our crimes against your people?" Kyreneas offered with an ingratiating tone.

The lash struck out and hit him across the shoulder.

"You presume much phosphila," the ancient chided. "You believe we must have causes to act as you do. A compulsion for your sort of 'justice.' Perhaps you think because you are of light and we of shadow that we are crude, dark reflections of the things you reveal. We are not. We are heirs to ancient sorceries and powers of the Lost Realm. Your impertinence is cause enough to kill you without a second's repose.

"But we are in the employ of greater forces still than Tislatna ever bore. And we are bound by our contract with them to do as instructed. Thus, we shall proceed with this night's ceremony."

He gave a wave of his hand to the Sombra with the

halberds. The point of their spear tips lifted in front of Anargen's face, and he understood he was being forced forward again. Once more, he shot a glance at his father. This time, Glewdyn looked conflicted but seemed in the earnestness of his expression to be pleading to hold just a little longer.

"Do your employers realize you're wasting so much time on such an elaborate scheme for vengeance? Surely such important forces would not be worried with the likes of us," Glewdyn commented with a twinge of derision in his tone.

The lead Sombra glowered at him. "You were not at the Falconcleft attack," he noted. "But you did aid in Count Eidolon's fall, and your impertinent tongue has earned you the privilege of being the first to die." He gave a nod to have Glewdyn brought forward.

"Just as I thought," Glewdyn mocked. "The only reason you would hold such a spectacle in front of a town full of witnesses is to restore your sullied image. Try to dupe everyone in the Lowlands into believing the Sombra are still a force worth fearing."

Their leader rose off his throne. "You speak so boldly for one being led to his execution. A pity you will not live to see us strike the blow that sets your Libertian capital on its knees." Settling once more back onto his place of honor, he waved to his men. "Let us begin."

A soft voice spoke up with urgency, and Anargen perceived its simple instruction: "*Now!*"

Dropping to a crouch and shoulder rolling to the side, Anargen managed to draw his spiritsword as he did so, such that when he was back onto his feet again. A hastily raised block caught the Sombra guard's halberd. Pushing it off, he was able to block and then parry a quick pair of jabs from the halberd wielder.

Yelping with surprise, the Sombra made a violent thrust

with the spear-tipped head of the weapon. But Anargen was ready and dodged just in time. Grabbing the weapon shaft with his off hand, Anargen brought his spiritsword around, cleaving it in half. While the Sombra was dazed from the strike and swiping at the smoke roiling off his weapon, Anargen went on the offensive, and with a deft sortie, he pushed forward and scored a deep hit into the Sombra guard's abdomen.

Immediately, fire caught on the wound, and the Sombra slid back, dropping to the ground, writhing and cursing. That was one down, at least.

The next instant, Anargen was grabbed from behind and slung down. Standing over him, Glewdyn had drawn his spiritsword as well and brought it up to deflect a strike from another halberd.

By now, the elder Sombra was on his feet and shouting, "Which fool of you did not first take their weapons?"

Looks like your underlings' hubris will cost you this night.

Rolling out of his father's way, Anargen got to his feet and found another of the Sombra bearing down on him with an axe and dagger. The suddenness of it forced Anargen to back up, but the Sombra was already morphing into a haze and slipping behind him to press his attack.

A whisper told Anargen to swing his sword around at level as he turned. Doing so would require committing totally to the strike and leave no room for recovering or defending himself if it did not land.

At your command, my Great King.

Anargen spun and put all his might behind the spinning strike. As he turned, he spotted Seren surging forward, her spiritsword drawn. She was almost on their foe, and as the attacker reformed, he noticed her as well, raising his axe to hack her down before she could get to him.

It was a devastating miscalculation on the Sombra's part.

Anargen's blow landed, slicing deep and undefended across the Sombra's torso, cutting through the dark mist of his body even as it sought to return to solid form.

The assassin gasped and then shrieked as the flames flared to a fierce bloom around him as if someone tossed an entire cruse of oil onto a fire.

By now, the reversal of fortunes was almost complete, with Lady Lyncia, Bertinand, and Glewdyn finishing off the other two of the common Sombra present. Only the Sombra ancient remained. Strangely, he stood stoic as he watched his underlings fail and fall. As the last of them dissipated into cinders, he seemed to stir from his stupor. Striding forward, he produced the flail Anargen had noticed earlier, a cylinder covered in spikes. In his other hand another flail materialized, this one terminating in the wicked curve of a scythe.

"You phosphila do your Order service while my pathetic servants have failed the Sombra miserably. A shame that you must die. Were you to abandon your foolhardy allegiance to your king, you would all make excellent warriors for the shadows. As it stands, I must now destroy you all."

Bringing his right arm over his head, the Sombra leader snapped his black scythe flail at Glewdyn, extending its chain farther on command.

Glewdyn dropped to the ground, narrowly avoiding it. Unconcerned with it, the ancient Sombra twisted around and swept low with his other flail, forcing Lady Lyncia to retreat.

Anargen tried to advance but had to leap out of the way as the scythe was snapped back and stabbed deep into the street stone where he had just stood. Little shards of block were shorn from the path and showered over him as the Sombra recalled his weapon.

The ancient arced and twirled, rising into the air above them all. Churning in a spiral, he launched one attack after another, scattering all five of the armed Knights and sending the onlooking villagers of Cattingsford fleeing in a panic.

Blow after blow missed its mark and slipped in and out of the narrower confines of the battle area. Each failure elicited curses in some foreign tongue.

Out of the corner of his eye, Anargen caught sight of Caeserus and Sir Kyreneas recovering their weapons. They were keeping back and hadn't drawn them, but even so, Anargen wasn't the only one to notice this development. The Sombra ancient muttered something, and the cylindrical flail in his one hand drifted into black smokiness and dissipated. In its place, the ancient drew out a series of throwing knives and tensed to sling them at Caeserus and the others.

Springing forward, Anargen leaped up and brought his sword down just in time to catch the Sombra's arm at its full extension. His blade connected and cleaved off the shadowy appendage, but the throwing knives arced out as obsidian missiles.

It was impossible to see who, if anyone, was injured because the ancient roiled in pain and slung his scythe to catch Anargen, who had left himself exposed with his attack. He tensed for the stabbing pain of the blow.

In place of the pain, there was a metallic clang as Glewdyn intercepted the strike. Bertinand followed him with a stroke that severed the chain from the scythe blade, and on his heels, Seren charged forward and, with a desperate dive, plunged her blade into the nebulous vortex at the base of the ancient's abdomen.

Fire caught onto the Sombra's haze, and a bright swirling cyclone of fire twisted upward. Collapsing from his height, the ancient crashed on top of the throne. Groaning, he tried to reform his legs and lower torso but cried out as the flames collapsed inward with the coalescing mists they were caught upon. It appeared he was trapped between states.

"Do you yield?" Glewdyn asked breathily from the exertion of the quick and decisive battle. "You need not cling to the darkness—"

"Save your pity and propaganda, phosphila," the ancient snarled. "Your victory is a hollow one. My order will complete our next contract in Kirke. Then that exiled fool Ecthelion will get what he deserves, and you will all find the Lowlands far darker than you've ever known them. In the deep shadows, your ruin will be swift and excruciating!"

The last words the Sombra gritted out as through clenched teeth. Wretched creature that he was, it was still difficult to watch.

He gripped his throne, which dissolved into gloomy tendrils that arced out around him. Like a fish leaping out of the water, the ancient Sombra heaved himself up into them, and when he came down, he disappeared into a pool of shadow. The dark stain on the ground streaked away from the town, with lines of fire tracing after.

Stunned, Anargen started to pursue him, but Glewdyn caught his shoulder and shook his head. He whispered, "Tend to Seren and the others."

As he turned to face her, he saw Seren's hands were trembling as she sheathed her spiritsword. They had all come so very close to death this night. Had the Sombra been less arrogant, not split their forces, or the High King not favored them, the outcome would've been far different. Their eyes locked, and they dashed toward one another.

TWENTY-FIFTH INTERLOGUE: GUIDANCE

Jason peered across the street at the mysterious man from the store. Looking now, he seemed less like a shopkeeper and more like a warrior pulled from the legends of Tislatna. Armed with a sickle sword that had a bent handle, the shopkeeper held the blade at his side in a neutral stance as Jason had once seen fencers do. His helmet was shield-like and went around to his back, and his armor plates overlapped almost like waves of the sea. More impactful than the peculiar arms and armor was the change in effect around the man's face. It had deepened in tone until he looked like liquid copper in the forge, ready to lash out with such heat that anything and anyone in his path would melt away in an instant.

"Thank ... you ..." Jason muttered, awestruck. He felt as though he had to keep his eyes on him but desperately wanted to look away.

"You are afraid?" the man asked, sounding neither amused nor annoyed.

A nod was the best Jason could manage. Moments ago, he thought the werebeasts were terrifying, but this was far more so. The beasts were cruel and monstrous and sought to induce fear, whereas this being was noble and magnificent, commanding fear by his nature rather than demanding it.

"Do you know the High King of All Realms?"

"*Huh?*" The question threw Jason. It seemed silly, given the man already knew Jason was newly joined to the Knight Order.

"Do you know the High King of All Realms?" the being repeated.

"I do know him," Jason replied. Finding the answer too brief, he scoured for something else to add and came upon something intensely personal. "He's the breaker of my chains."

The being smiled at this. "That he is Jason Landsby, once Wernstrum. Again, you have acquitted yourself well."

"Thank you again," Jason replied and immediately felt like a child, parroting things with no thought.

Nodding, the other picked up the conversation, rescuing it from Jason's slack-jawed awe. "There is no need to feel inadequate. You have not seen any of my race before. Few in this era of the Lowlands have seen we elves. I assure you, we are, as you, servants of the Most High King."

"An elf?" Jason tried to cobble together anything and everything he'd heard about such beings. All his attempts produced bizarre and insufficient odds and ends that didn't add up to what he saw now. A few things were salvageable, though. Elves were the first servants of the High King. Some rebelled, as men did, and followed the Dark Prince. Others continued to serve the High King. They could change form and had some kind of relationship with fire. Though from the collection of children's stories Jason had to draw from, it was hard to assemble a coherent picture of what the nature of that relationship could be. Looking at a real-life elf, he thought being formed from fire might be accurate.

Given that the elf said nothing further, Jason sensed he should say something. Or rather a compulsion to fill the charged silence. "What's your name?"

"My name is more wonderful than your tongue can handle. But if you must call me something, Vif will suffice in simplicity and purpose."

"Vif," Jason repeated as if testing it. Taking a steadying breath, Jason tried to calm his ragged heartbeat and gradually forced himself to relax from his tension to run. A question came to him the moment he was able, the thing most fixedly on his mind naturally. "You know what happened to my brother?"

The elf's brows knitted as if in contemplation, but at length, he replied, "Yes. I also know you blame yourself. You should not."

"You don't understand. I left him. I left him with monsters, and now he's become one." Jason sank down into a crouch and put one hand on the stone pavement. He suddenly felt dizzy from the flood of wistfulness and regret. He was mourning Dorian. "All of that darkness inside him. I should have been here to prevent it."

The elf gave a curt shake of his head. "No. You would have been destroyed. Your brother is not new to darkness. Perhaps it is because your kind cannot see into the heart and must only look at the slow-growing fruit of each man's spirit. This path would have found him, and he would have taken it, even if you had not left your family."

Shrugging, Jason countered, "Well, then I have to save him now. Get him away from it all before it's too late."

The elf bent down in front of Jason, looking at him squarely in the eyes. "You are not ready for such a thing. Try now, and you will die."

Jason fell backward from his crouch and hit the stone beneath him heavily. It was one thing to feel he could do nothing. Being told it by a creature of legend made it something wholly else—despair—the deepest ravine from which there was no scaling, no possible ascent. "I've lost him then. I lost ..." His voice gave out.

"There may come an hour when you may help him," the elf allowed, his posture and demeanor not faltering a millimeter. "For now, you must find Sir Cinaed and Lady Aria."

Hearing their names drew Jason up from the depths he'd fallen enough to speak. "How will that help?"

"They can help you determine what your family's involvement has been with the Rehalcyon Empire. That will be a key to facing the darkness gathering in the Lowlands."

"Don't you know?" Jason asked, genuinely thrown rather than combative.

"I do not. The High King knows, of course, but he has not chosen to share this with me."

"If he knows what is happening, why would he keep that from us? Why not just tell us?"

"He leads his servants to roads of plenty and roads of hardship. The plenty out of benevolence and the hardship to shape you. If he has you search for these answers, the journey will help to prepare you as much as the knowledge at the quest's end."

"If you had said that to me a couple days ago, I'd have called you crazy. But somehow, I know you're right. I even have ... peace with it."

"Good." The elf straightened, walked across the street, and gestured to the door to the shop. "Retrieve the rest of your armor, then. Keep to the familiar roads. That much I am permitted to know and share with you."

Jason scrambled to his feet. "Wait, you're leaving me? What happens if those things come back?"

Once more, the elf looked vexed, his face severe from

contrasting light and dark. "You have the *Machira tou Pneuma*, spiritsword, sharpest of dual-edge blades. With this burning blade, nothing will be beyond you to overcome. You have also the *Thyreos Pistis*, a shield forged of faith in the High King. No flaming arrow or wicked missile of the Enemy will be able to strike you with it in hand.

"Within the shop are further implements. Each bit of armor you have learned well of already from the tales you've heard. Did you think it mere chance you are so knowledgeable of that which is discounted as myth by others?"

"I suppose not. It would just have been nice to have someone with me for what's ahead."

A flash of light and wave of heat smashed into Jason, its intensity forcing him to raise an arm defensively. "You have the High King watching over you always. Never will he be far from you."

With that, another surge of flames swirled around and, in an instant, collapsed onto the elf—a brilliant light, enough to outstrip what this block saw during the daytime. By the time Jason's eyes adjusted, Vif, the elf, was gone.

As if in a dream, Jason staggered into the store and found everything Vif had instructed him to take and nothing more. Once dressed, he emerged from the shop, low flames crackling and rolling off his divinely provided armor and arms.

Taking in a deep breath and letting it out slowly, he said, "Great King, I'm with you. Lead the way."

3

PARTING WAYS

*"I had never known what it was like to lose a sibling. The pain
of losing a brother then was something I was wholly unprepared
for and hurts beyond my ability to justly describe."*

—*Anargen's King's Day Journal*
18 Fómhar 1606 Middle Era

Anargen wrapped his arms around Seren. They'd done it. Or rather, the High King's favor had done it through them. They were alive and had bested the trap laid for them.

When Anargen pulled back from the embrace, he was surprised to see Seren's expression nowhere near the euphoria he was experiencing. He turned to find Caeserus glaring at them, his wounded cheek still bleeding. He also favored one arm, holding his other palm tight to his forearm. He didn't have his armor on as Anargen had thought. Only Sir Kyreneas did. Caeserus's sleeve was stained red, where his hand clenched. One of the knives the ancient had thrown must have hit him.

Before Anargen could separate from Seren and walk to

38

him, Caeserus called out, "What in the Lowlands were you thinking, gambling with our lives like that?"

"Gambling with our lives?" Anargen repeated, not comprehending where his friend was coming from.

"Your swords hadn't been confiscated, and you waited till we were all about to be beheaded to act!" Caeserus was yelling.

Anargen looked to the others with them and found a mixture of sentiments playing on their faces, mostly apprehension over the conflict. Using a soothing voice, he replied, "I was surprised as well. We were favored by the High King that they didn't take them. I suppose that was the wisdom driving us to surrender without an initial fight."

Caeserus's eyes went wide, and he looked away, biting his lip. Then he shook his head and coughed out a harsh laugh. "Surrendering again, *hmm*? That's becoming your signature tactic, isn't it? Who will end up dying in the long run from it this time, I wonder."

Anargen felt as if his friend had just driven a dagger through his belly. How could he use what happened to Cinaed against him? He tried to respond and couldn't form any words.

At his side, Seren bristled. "You might try having a moment of thought before speaking. Anargen led the way in saving your life and the Quest."

"Quest?" Sir Kyreneas spoke up. "What Quest? All I see is a ragged group of survivors who escaped a calamity only to find themselves prey to enemies and allies alike."

"You know good and well the Quest we're on," Glewdyn countered. "The Tower of Light's defense is what we all seek to safeguard." He looked at Caeserus as though he wanted to remind him it was his vision of that Tower and its fall that had drawn all of them into the Quest in the first place. But he didn't say it. Anargen's father was too noble for cheap point gathering. "Besides that," he continued, "If you need someone to blame, it should be me. I signaled to Anargen to wait."

"No, it wasn't just you," Anargen interjected. "I was guided by the High King to act when I did."

"Right. The king really guides you that way. You, the traitor to his oaths," Caeserus scoffed. "It rings so false that it makes me wonder if we haven't all been deluding ourselves."

Anargen squeezed Seren's hand to preempt a scathing counterattack on his behalf. "What do you mean? We know what this is, what we've been doing since Ordumair."

"From where I stand, you all seem insane," Sir Kyreneas snapped. "Defender MacCowell told us about Ordumair. Given how he perished, I, too, wonder if he wasn't a charlatan and false Knight. Reaping a liar's dues."

Anargen gaped at the older man. How could anyone say something so terrible, let alone of Cinaed, who died saving them all?

It was Caeserus who found his voice first. "Maybe it wasn't him who was a fraud but all of us. All of this. The Quest. The king. Maybe it's all a bunch of rot."

"Surely you don't mean that, Caeserus," Glewdyn said, his voice taking on his most fatherly tone of concern.

The teen shrugged. "Is there any evidence to the contrary from how we've suffered or others have?"

"Sometimes we are called to make a stand, even if it ends in sorrow," Anargen reminded him. "Sometimes it is the stand which is the most powerful implement for the High King to cast off darkness. If we turn back now, if we forsake our oaths, then truly we fail. It would be better to die clinging to the High King's banner than to forsake it and remain in the Lowlands a hundred lifetimes."

"How dare you say something like that to me?" Caeserus shouted, giving Anargen a shove. "You gave up on the quest in

Stormridge, remember? And now, you want to lecture me about being steadfast? About what's worth living and dying for?

"No. You don't get to say a single word about this. Not you. Not Seren. Not Bertinand. None of you kept your oaths like I did through those dark months. And let me tell you, they were nothing compared to now. Nothing!"

To the rest of the group, Caeserus jabbed his finger accusatorially, "We all had a chance to do something magnificent. To change the fate of the Lowlands, or so it seemed. But you know what? I can't tell a bit of difference between how these monsters end up and how supposed knights of light do. Both fall. Brutally. Bloody. Unsung. What exactly are we even fighting for at this point? If we can't even save our own lives, what better day is there?"

"Caeserus, no!" Anargen grabbed his friend by the shoulder, which the other shook off. "Caeserus, please, don't say those things. You know we're all waiting for the King's Day."

Throwing his arms up to gesture all around again. "Are we? And what exactly does that mean? Is today anything like 'the King's Day'? Dark and us nearly swallowed by death?"

Anargen shook his head. His heart felt just as fractured and contused as when he saw Sir Cinaed falling. Except now, it was happening slower, each strident chord of pain plucked with added malice and purpose. "The light and goodness we stand for, the High King we serve ... they're worth dying for. The reward comes at the end of all things in the Highlands. We only need to hold on as best we can in the Lowlands. Honor our oaths, protect those who can't protect themselves, bear the light into the dark ..."

Looking around at the group, Anargen couldn't believe what he was seeing and hearing. Caeserus was backing away, shaking his head. Bertinand sat on a fence rail, staring intently at the ground but looking profoundly annoyed. Sir Kyreneas had removed his scabbard and held it up.

"I have carried this sword for almost my entire life. Never once in those days did I think I would lay it down by choice. But this is a pain I had never foreseen. We are totally abandoned by the King," Kyreneas said, sounding as if he felt ill and would throw up any moment.

"It's almost as if we've been fooling ourselves all along about the king," Caeserus commented darkly. "Dreaming fanciful dreams into our waking hours, and now we've woken up and see the Lowlands are more despicable and drearier than any nightmare."

"That's enough of that," Glewdyn spoke up. "I cannot speak for what any of you have seen in your lives save the horrors of the latest hours. I've heard stories about what you, Bertinand, and Anargen endured at Ordumair. It is all painful, hard, and filled with cruelties no one should endure.

"But you look at the brokenness and darkness and say there is no light. How can you forget so quickly those hours when the light and the High King have been so clear and evident? You see defeats mounting, but with them have been victories. Ordumair was devastated but not destroyed. Stormridge, too, is swept away, but the evil that was slowly twisting it has been extinguished in those very same waters.

"If you only open your eyes to the night, you'll never see the day. I've seen it in so many little things as I cared for things growing, and in their cycles, there is life and death. But in death, many future lives are secured. Anargen is right. If we don't keep faithful to our oaths, then all that is left is death, but if we hold steady, then a harvest of life comes. When the High King's Day arrives, then the dark, death, all this brokenness none of us can bear of our own— it will all be swept away just as Count Eidolon and the wyvern and their influence were.

And yes, till then, there will be night and sorrow, but dawn is not so far as you imagine. Only hold fast, and we shall all see it."

Sir Kyreneas hooked his scabbard back to his belt. "Perhaps you are right, Sir Glewdyn of Black River. But my point about the state of the Quest you were on still stands. I cannot in good conscience lead any other of my charges into danger, certain to claim their lives. Lady Lyncia is an elder as well and must make her own decisions, but for myself and those who look to me for guidance, we will make for Lake Pax and join the Knights there. One day, we may find a genuine Quest favored by the High King, but it is not this one."

Without entertaining a further point in counter to his own, Kyreneas waved to the other remaining Knights from Stormridge and called, "Come to me, dear ones." He began walking off before any of the others moved to join him, but after a few moments of reluctance, they followed. None of them met the eyes of Anargen and the rest left standing behind.

Anargen's gaze turned to Lyncia, who never once contradicted Kyreneas in his tirade. But she looked distant, distracted. Struggling with her own opinions on the matter, no doubt.

"I can't believe they're leaving," Anargen mumbled once they were out of sight.

"Seriously? You can't believe they left after all we've been through, all that we've just discussed?" Caeserus snorted. "You know what, Kyreneas is the only one of you with any sense left. Whatever we were doing, it's clearly a failure, and I've had enough taste of pain and death and sorrow for fancies of my childhood. It's time to wake up from dreams."

With that, Caeserus stormed off through the midst of the group, heading in a separate direction from Sir Kyreneas's group. Where he was headed was impossible to say from his bearing.

Stunned beyond words, Anargen watched his friend stalk away. In all their disagreements and setbacks, never once could he have imagined this moment. Not the bitter taste of bile rising in his throat, not the dizzying panic and devastating pain concentrated in his heart. He might have fallen, but he and Seren were still in one another's arms, supporting each other.

With Caeserus's departure, only Seren, Glewdyn, Bertinand, and Lyncia were left to stand firm.

All of a sudden, Bertinand dashed out from the middle of the group and jogged in the direction Caeserus had headed. "Bertinand?" Anargen called out, feeling like all the Lowlands were sliding into the abyss.

Bertinand, who had been silent through the arguments, stopped and gave a heavy sigh. "Someone has to go after him. And, well, I could use some time away from ... this." He gestured to Anargen and Seren, who separated from their consoling embrace.

"Bertinand, please," Seren called after. "We need you. The Quest needs you."

He looked down and huffed. "Maybe, maybe not. Either way, I have to do this. I ... Goodbye, Seren."

And then he, too, was gone, dashing off into the gloom, leaving only the four of them there to bear the banner of the High King.

Anargen did not know if they would survive the heartache of the loss.

TWENTY-SIXTH INTERLOGUE: FAMILIAR FACES

Dawn had not yet reached out its arms in its daily embrace with the landscape when Jason arrived at the village of Windward. No one was in the streets this early, so it took little time to navigate the central walk lined with flowers and squat log cabins. His intended destination was the inn he and Aria had stayed in when they first fled Brackenburgh months ago. It was already shaping up to be a crisp but beautiful winter day, though clouds far on the horizon suggested it could become stormy by nightfall. Given he'd been traveling on foot the whole time, perhaps staying at the inn until the next day would be wise.

Jason paused in front of the modest pine doors and prepared himself. He desperately needed the innkeeper to remember him from the last time. The waifish older man had seemed kind during his last visit and certainly had been recommended to him for aid. But that didn't mean he was accustomed to being sent anyone by mythical warriors from the High King nor trusting the word of penitent gangster family heirs. Not to mention, how would Jason not come across as a villain if he had to explain abandoning Aria and Cinaed?

Yeah, definitely easier if he remembers me.

Giving three solid knocks, Jason stood back a few steps, expecting he would probably be waking the innkeep. There was no answer, but through the thick glass of one window, Jason could see a light shining. Whether that was a candle or electric lighting, someone was awake and stirring within.

While he watched the window, the front door swung open. A bony hand reached out, grabbed Jason by the shoulder, and yanked him inside.

Jason stumbled in and spun loose of his assailant's grip. It put him off balance, and he fell back into the desk where the innkeeper would greet travelers. Scrambling back to his feet, he saw the person who grabbed him was actually Jerome, the keeper of the inn.

Before Jason could offer an apology, the man put a bony finger to his lips and nodded past Jason to his wife, Glinda. A plump little woman in a puffy antique dress, she was going about closing the window shutters all along the commons area of the inn.

Jerome gripped Jason's shoulder and gestured for him to follow. The innkeeper led down a hall off the main one, bearing to the right. It wasn't the same room Jason and Aria stayed in before.

The strange behavior twanged on Jason's already tightly strung nerves, but he followed. A few seconds later, he was treated to seeing the innkeeper tap his foot against a section of wall a chair had been in front of. The place where Jerome's foot touched sank in. There was a mechanical grinding sound as a secret latch released, and Jerome was able to push in the section of wall to enter a secret room.

What could an inn in a speck of a town like Windward need

with a secret room? Better yet, what does Jerome have to say to me that necessitates it?

With a wary eye to the hall beyond them, Jerome put the secret door back in place. His stern blue eyes peered out at Jason from under the thick grey tufts of his brow. He gave his short bristly beard a scratch and said, "You know, you're not the most discreet person, are you?"

"*Uh*, pardon?"

The older man shuffled over to the far side of the room about five strides away and opened a small chest there, covered in an impressive amount of dust. Most of the room was in a similar state of apparent disuse. A hidden room no one ever used, along with Jerome's odd behavior, made Jason wonder if he was dreaming.

"Here." Jerome tossed a brown long coat, somewhat like Sir Cinaed the Storyteller's.

Looking it over as the scents of must and leather bombarded his nose, Jason replied, "Thank you?"

Jerome glanced over his shoulder as he rummaged through the chest further. "The elf Vif told us you had joined the Order. He didn't warn me you'd be so painfully obvious about it. The coat's to help you not attract the notice of everyone between here and Vov Hilan."

"Oh." Jason looked down at the fire-traced inscriptions on the armor he wore. Grimacing, Jason realized how walking around in centuries-old armor would startle anyone encountering him. He looked up and intended to give a real thank you to Jerome, but the feisty innkeeper was already back to focusing on his chest. Inside, it mostly looked like there were clothes.

At length, though, the man extracted a satchel, and with a grunt as if it were heavy, he proclaimed, "*Aha*, found it."

"What is it?" Jason asked, looking it over as Jerome sat it on a small table along the left wall.

"What Vif said you'd need for your journey." Reaching in, the innkeeper produced several weathered papers, a bound tome, and a stack of letters.

Holding each letter out, one by one, for inspection, Jerome stopped at one with swooping lettering. It had an imperial postage mark, so it had come from somewhere in the Rehalcyon Empire's lands.

Not bothering to extract the letter's contents, Jerome handed it over to Jason. "There you are. You'll need this to prove your trustworthiness to Antoni."

Taking the letter, Jason looked it over. It had the same faintly musty smell as the coat, along with a hint of cedar. The letter's sender had not left a return address. Jason peered at Jerome, not bothering to mask his befuddlement. "I'm sorry, but why are you giving me this?"

"Didn't Vif tell ya?"

"No. All he told me was, 'Keep to familiar roads.' I remembered your hospitality to Aria and me, so I came here hoping to get a room for the night before heading south."

"To where?"

"I hadn't planned that far. I just know Aria and Sir Cinaed are south. I was trusting the High King would guide me to them."

Rubbing his bristly chin, Jerome agreed, "Aye, he will. Seems the first step he led you to without you even knowing it. That's good. But, this time, you'll need to listen. Everything is happening fast, so I'm sorry to say I can't put you up for the night. You took longer than expected to get 'ere, so I'm guessing you walked?"

Jason nodded, feeling like he was being evaluated by a

teacher at the academy he had attended before he ran away years ago.

"*Mm*, well, I can get you a horse to help make better time. You'll probably need to cut across the Siochail Plains instead of sticking to the coast. Maybe take a ferry down the Glaston River. If you can get to Falkirke, then you take the train to Lyrscony."

"Lyrscony—that's in the Lyscea province," Jason replied. "Is that where Aria and Cinaed are?"

Shaking his head, the older man sighed. "No, it's where they were, but where you'll need to go. I only know what I've been told, so there's not much more that I can give you than that. We all have as much truth as we need to follow the High King's leading. Right now, it looks like neither of us needs much to show ourselves faithful. *Eh?*"

"I'll do my best, sir. To be honest, I've never been one to just go by faith. Coming from my family, living without a plan always seemed like a good way to end up in a ditch somewhere feeding worms, if you catch my drift."

At last, Jerome smiled. "I do, and I've never been much good at minding my own business. So maybe there's something to be learned in this for each of us. Building us into better Knights, as it were."

Patting Jason on the back, he added, "Come on, Sir Landsby, I'll get you all set up to go with some food for the road and that horse. Just be careful not to make much noise around here and to stay off the main roads. Elves aren't the only ones watching you."

Jason grimaced. He wasn't sure who Jerome meant, but whether the shadow assassin Sombra or the werebeasts his brother had unleashed on him, there was no shortage of terrors hungry for his demise.

Turning to follow Jerome back out of the room, he caught sight of the bound tome again and hesitated. It felt weird, as though he had been pulled back, halted by the book. It was unremarkable. Dark leather and worn faded parchment. Its battered exterior gave no hint of its contents, but Jason couldn't take his eyes off it.

"*Um*, not to pry," he said, "but what is that book there?"

Jerome leaned back into the room. "*Eh?* Oh, that is something Sir Black left me some years back. A journal from a long time ago. It was pretty special to him. Said to return it to him once I finished it. Of course, my fogged old brain didn't remember to ..."

The old man laughed. "Of course. You take it. Return it to him for me."

"Are you sure?" Jason asked, taking it as it was pressed in his hands.

"*Mm-hmm*. And the bag too. That was his. It's a whiz-bang of a story. You should give it a read while you're traveling. Help pass the time."

"Thanks." Jason put the letter and journal into the bag. After sliding on the coat and fastening it closed in the front, he slid the satchel over his shoulder. Wrapped in the scents and tokens of the past, he felt oddly comforted, as if their age and weathering made his future seem a little less doubtful.

4

PETITION

*"Every day since leaving Cattingsford, it has rained. The days
are gloomy, and as we traveled northward, the sense that the very
Lowlands itself wept for the sorrow of our hearts has only
intensified."*

—Anargen's King's Day Journal
4 Premgelee 1607 Middle Era

Looking out the rain-streaked pane of glass onto the square, Anargen sighed. Estonbury was a place of intense memory and importance to him. It was here they had met Sir Orwald before finishing their fateful journey to Ordumair. But it was also here he had been greatly encouraged. Even in the dismal gloom of this stormy evening, he could make out the details of the statue of Thane Ornand. Standing stalwart, defiant, insistently pointing to the Highland in the distance. At a pivotal moment in the Quest, that very statue had reminded him of the reward awaiting them in the

Highland, in the City of Light. It had been enough to help him press on despite the dangers.

This evening, Anargen needed a new lesson from the statue. If they were going to succeed in this journey, he must be carved from the same stony resilience and persistence as Ornand. Seren and his father were all that was left of the Quest. Even Lady Lyncia had taken her leave of them, albeit her claim was to stay behind and help re-establish the Knight Hall and Order's presence among the citizens of Cattingsford.

Noble as that was, here, leagues away, her absence felt immense. Never mind the way the wound of Caeserus's departure and Bertinand's afterward continually galled him. There wasn't a day when Anargen didn't ache within and wrestle with the angst born of their absence.

How did it come to this?

There was a knock on the room's door. "Come in," he called, though he needn't do so. This was the Knight Hall's library, not his personal quarters. Most of those in the Hall had given him a wide berth as though they could sense his wounds. They treated him like an animal sporting an injury and being the more dangerous and unpredictable for it.

The entrant did not announce themself. And Anargen did not turn to ascertain the other's identity. Perhaps the wide berth was only so expansive because he doubled that distance with his own behavior.

Even so, he was only somewhat surprised when Seren's arms took hold of his, and she rested her head there. Such tender affections were welcome warmth in a frigid season.

"I knew I would find you in the library," Seren commented, her voice gentle, soothing. "Though I expected to find you book in hand."

"I tried to read but couldn't focus."

"They're waiting for us," she reminded him.

"I know," he admitted. He left out the part where he couldn't bring himself to go in yet. How he dreaded it.

"It's painful," she noted. He arched a brow, and she gave a little nod. "Speaking about what happened. To Sir Cinaed, but also to us. I've never heard of Knights of Light being betrayed by the citizens of a town they serve."

"Not in the Northwestern Lowlands, at least," he amended. "But nothing like what happened in Stormridge has taken place since the Ancient Era."

"Nobody blames you for what happened."

He turned toward her. Seren's cocoa eyes were bright and filled with the concern and caring that captivated his affections and would never let them go. "Your insights shouldn't surprise me by now. You know me better than myself."

She shrugged. "Maybe not that well, but what I'm passionate about, I learn and keep in my mind."

He kissed her hand. "I don't deserve your love."

"It's good then that you have it no matter how you feel about your worthiness." She leaned up and brushed his lips with a kiss. Seren tugged on his hand. "But we can speak more about that later."

"Absolutely," he agreed with a playful grin.

Giving him a little nudge as her cheeks reddened, he moved over to the library door and motioned for her in deferral. "Mi'lady."

She gave him a formal curtsy with the deep green dress she had been given by the women Knights of the Hall. Passing through the door, she led him by hand to the meeting chambers, which were broad and open, lit by more than a hundred candles. It was impressive with soaring glass windows, long oak tables filled with magnificently armed and attired Knights of the Hall, and smooth, polished stone floors. It seemed out of place, knowing that Sir Cinaed had been the preeminent Knight of the Realm and worked from this Hall for years. At least when compared to the humble circumstances Anargen lived in at Black River. Someday, he wanted to find out the reason why Cinaed had stepped back from his identity as Merodoch MacCowell, Defender of the Northern Realm, to be a simple Knight Errant in the tiny village so many leagues from here. It's something perhaps Glewdyn knew, but Anargen couldn't bring himself to ask yet. Not with the loss still fresh. Maybe he would never be able to speak it aloud.

At the front of the room, an elderly man, tall and waifish, Sir Matthias, spoke, "Hale evening, Sir Anargen and Lady Seren. Thank you for coming before us." His voice sounded off, heavy with something that he strained to bear up under.

"Hale evening," he answered on their behalf. "It is our honor."

Glewdyn stood and motioned for them to join him at the room's front alongside Matthias.

As they approached, Glewdyn explained, "I told them what befell us at Stormridge. What became of Sir Cinaed and his heroism on our behalf."

Anargen's throat tightened, but he managed to whisper a thank you to his father. Knowing the group before them might judge him guilty for what had transpired was hard, but having had to bear the tragic news would have been crushing for him.

Matthias gestured to Glewdyn. "I believe now, good sir, you were about to counsel with us on the full matter of your arrival."

Glewdyn nodded. "I appreciate your directness," he said. "Would that I could say we were coming to you with words that would soothe the loss of Defender MacCowell. But, in the spirit of your directness, I will also be forward. We need your aid. After the tragedies of Stormridge, we became privy to a plot against an important official whom we believe to be Viceroy Ecthelion—"

At this, there was a sudden surge in side conversations and murmuring around the room. Glewdyn waited for these to fade away before continuing, "And we need letters from you commending us to the Viscount of Libertias to allow us entry to his court at Kirke so we may deliver this message of peril. The Viscount can then reach out to the Viceroy and warn him of the impending threat to his life."

Contrary to moments earlier, there was a dreadful quiet as if all words had been stolen from the room. It was hard to say how much time passed before Sir Matthias at last shattered the silence. "Friends, this seems like an important matter, but surely not so much so as the Quest? You have not yet identified the location of the Tower of Light nor the explicit nature of the threat against it. With Defender MacCowell gone and so many of those devoted to the Quest deserted from it, should you not be focused on it instead?"

Rubbing his chin, which sported a thickening patch of a greying beard, Glewdyn countered, "You are right that the Quest is in danger of faltering and that it's of incredible importance. But we agreed mutually between us that this is what the High King has led us to, and we have received no convictions otherwise. It may seem like only one life hangs in the balance, but I feel certain there is far more to this than we perceive now."

Scowling, Matthias nodded and shot a glance at the other elders. Their faces were unreadable to Anargen, but the Knight Errant of Estonbury seemed to explicate the sentiments embedded in their stony facades. "Since you are determined to pursue this course, then I must be frank. I'm afraid there are a number of issues which make it impossible for us to provide the letters you seek. Not the least of which being that Viceroy

Ecthelion is living in exile. His restoration army has almost been obliterated and is certain to lose the war. As such, the Vogteremark's leaders have been keen to forge a peaceful relationship with Monarch Ilyron."

"But he was the one who almost destroyed Ordumair, who summoned all those beasts that would have murdered every last Ord out of sheer cruelty!" Anargen blurted out. He surprised himself as much as the others in the room with the outburst.

"It is actually because of our aid to you and the dwarfs of Ordumair regarding that attack that we were rebuked by the Vogteremark's leaders. If we render you aid in defiance of them now, we almost certainly will lose our privileged status or worse."

Had Anargen heard that rightly? He looked at his father, whose face was largely impassive except around the eyes, where he could see a slight tightening. Gentle as ever, Glewdyn replied, "You are, of course, free to give letters to whom you choose. However, I would be lying if I said I understand the reason for your refusal. How can we stand by and not act when the life of another is certainly at stake?"

Matthias grunted heavily as if he feared this would be the reaction to their decision. "Yet you do not know for sure who is in danger. Can you say with all certainty that you really know anyone will perish?"

"We would not have come to you otherwise," Glewdyn insisted.

For a brief moment, Sir Matthias looked like he wanted to say one thing but caught the eyes of a number of the other elders and worked his jaw for a bit before settling the matter. "Our decision is made. You ask us to risk the well-being of the many to possibly aid one. That we cannot do.

"You may go, however, with our respect and gratitude for all that has passed between us."

"This is absurd!" Anargen blurted out. "Do you hear yourselves? If Sir Cinaed were here, he would not let this stand. Knights of Light cannot simply dismiss each other's urgent needs to keep life simple and easy. It is not our way, our Great King's way."

Several of the sterner members among the Estonbury Hall's ranks began squabbling loudly, and for the space of a breath, Anargen thought they were reconsidering. Then he read the harsher truth written in the sullen expression Sir Matthias wore, and he realized that wouldn't be the case. Minutes later, he, Seren, and Glewdyn were brought not only outside into the rain storm but all the way to the edge of Estonbury.

As they sought cover from the rain under a nearby stand of trees, Anargen looked back at the gates to Estonbury. Gates, he had been told, would no longer welcome any of them again. It was as though when Sir Cinaed fell, the Order fell with him. Painful as it was to admit it, perhaps Caeserus had been right in one regard. The Quest very much looked as though it was at an end and had utterly failed.

TWENTY-SEVENTH INTERLOGUE: THE LIGHTS OF FALKIRKE

The sun had long since set by the time Jason guided his weary steed, Apellate, into the city limits of Falkirke. Cold winds whipped around, threatening to carry with them flakes to the higher elevations. He had actually been in what he considered urban spaces for some time now, but here, the change was punctuated. In the near distance soared buildings like grey stony fingers of giants, reaching to stroke the sky and snatch clouds from it. Brackenburgh was impressive but laid out broadly, with the intent to see the entire city from the top of the Ministry of Justice building. Falkirke, the capital of the Rehalcyon Empire, was not so constrained and boasted great things commensurate with the nation it governed.

The electric lights and telephone and telegraph lines new to Brackenburgh were run like veins and arteries in Falkirke. And already Jason could feel the city's pulse thrumming from its heart as it awoke with the second life that comes with night's arrival.

It was strange. Jason had traveled all over the Empire and never once visited its capital. Partly because he always imagined it to be a stuffy, stodgy place, crammed full of sycophants angling for some kind of gain. Nothing unusual, just another place to drift past rather than through. Now that he was walking into it as a Knight of Light and knew firsthand the darkness moving the Empire's highest circles, he felt like he was entering a bear's den with the intent to prod the beast.

Centuries ago, when Falkirke was known as Kirke, it supposedly had a moat around it with four bridges, one for each cardinal direction, to signify all were welcome to partake of the freedom of the new nation of Libertias. This was a bold offer and one that ultimately could not last. As Jason's horse trotted across one of the famed bridges, now considered part of the city center with its outskirts far past, he wondered if the story was true. Whether Anargen and the others saw Kirke, saw that freedom before it ended. Jason's history was a bit fuzzy, but Anargen and the others must have lived close to the final years of the Middle Era, which culminated with the Second Battle of Kirke and the city's fall. Did Anargen sense it? Could he perceive he was living in precipitous times? Would he say the same about the world now? Having seen the darkness hidden in it made plain and the light of the High King who ultimately rules over it still clearer, Jason certainly felt like the Lowlands had come to a moment on which its entire history would turn, which was a terrible, wonderful feeling.

The horse ride, deeper, deeper into the man-made oasis of concrete, glass, and steel, quickly revealed new civic wonders. Jason initially followed the widest, most crowded thoroughfares through wealthy mercantile districts. There, even the frames around the doors and windows were gilded with gold, and the luxurious homes were carved from marble, some perhaps even the rare and forbidden stones from the Lost Realm of Tislatna.

He was growing tired but could not bring himself to rest in the epicurean districts, even if he could have afforded it.

Instead, he made his way through districts reserved primarily for foreigners, immigrants, and servile labor. These set clustered on the periphery of factories where smoke roiled thick and black enough from broad chimneys to blot out the sky and made the air taste of sulfur and ash. Through dingy windows into the poor's tight, squalid towers, Jason saw the impoverished families clinging together. No doubt grateful for even the meager meals they put by as they hovered around stoves, forced to double garb against the night chill in their threadbare shirts, dresses, and slacks. From street corners, he eyed the unsavory onlookers back, knowing their type too well. The pickpockets and worse—ever at the ready to swoop in and take whatever they could by any means necessary. Jason had seen wealth and poverty in abundance because of his escape from his family. But the contrast had not seemed so stark, so obvious, and so tightly bound together as here in Falkirke. Perhaps the difference really lay in him, and the dichotomy had always been so pronounced. Whatever the case, he couldn't escape the sensation that the torturous disparities were indeed in sharper relief here.

It was all so wearying. But for some reason, he couldn't bring himself to pull off the streets at an inn or hotel and get the rest he sorely needed. Not until he had come upon the Chencepar Hotel. It wasn't in the worst parts of the city, but it certainly wasn't the glamorous broad streets and capitoline towers of the wealthy parts.

Inside, the scent of tobacco and various spirits was strong. Just a glance was needed to confirm the structure included a bar as a haze drifted out from a corridor beyond the entry desk, carrying with it the sound of soothing music mingled with dozens of idle conversations. The hotel manager waved Jason over. He was a squat little man with a round, smooth-shaven face and well-oiled hair, newly popular across the Empire.

"Greetings, gent, welcome to the Chencepar Hotel. How may I assist you?"

"I could use a room for the night and directions to the train station providing passage to the old provinces of the Empire."

"Ah, of course. The lines to Rehalcy, Tyreenes, and Lyscea are serviced from Prominence Station's South Platform. May I inquire as to your business in the 'old provinces'?"

Jason tensed. Perhaps he had misspoken. Rehalcy, Tyreenes, and Lyscea had joined to form the Rehalcyon Empire just before the Modern Era and so were referred to as the old provinces by many. Though much of what had been Libertias was now so long part of the Empire, it would be hard to call them new lands. Falkirke itself among them. Sometimes, those from Falkirke took umbrage over being seen as separate from the Empire's origins. Usually because those making the distinction were from the old provinces and had potent elitest attitudes regarding their historical pedigree. The old provincials, in turn, could be riled by emphasizing the Empire's capital was now in the "new lands." The question was, which side of that divide did this man fall on? Jason could already tell picking the wrong side would be a good way to cause a stir.

In the past, Jason had gotten by without having to give two figs about who he annoyed at hotel desks, but he was supposed to be skirting notice. Any little trail he left could be devastating for more than just him.

"Of course," he answered as breezily as he could manage. Some of his experience hustling might serve him well now. His grandfather had told him more than once, "A good lie is the best tool you have available. The truth may get you somewhere, but the right lie will get you anywhere you want." Jason started to open his mouth and let himself slip into the familiar smooth mode where truths could be bent as easily as softened clay.

"Gent?" the man behind the desk prompted when Jason

failed to say anything. The manager's large eyes found their way to a nearby city policeman with his back against the wall. As if summoned to alertness by the glance, the officer shifted forward from his otherwise exemplary statue imitation.

This was spiraling sideways faster than Jason would have expected. He reached for his familiar excuses and once more could not force any out. They tasted vile in his mouth, and it did not take long to realize that the High King's fire must have purged that proclivity to falsehood from him. Trying again, this time with a limited dose of the truth, Jason managed to admit, "I have colleagues in the South who summoned me to discuss our latest research into some historical documents in my care."

He patted his satchel with the journal and gave the manager a wry smile that looked every bit as put on as it was. To a true Falkirke native, the clear annoyance with his circumstances should be winning, and if the manager were from the old provinces, he would be amused by the notion of Jason being "summoned" and the chagrin it seemed to induce in him.

The manager chuckled. "Oh yes, those pompous old blowhards in the old provinces are always yanking on their decrepit, nepotist puppeteer rigging, aren't they?"

Wow. Definitely from Falkirke.

"Clarence Smythe III, at your service," the manager announced, proffering his hand.

Giving it a single curt shake in the custom of the Empire, he replied, "Jason Landsby."

"Here." Smythe handed him a key. "I'll give you a quiet room in our solidly 'newlander' wing. If any old province snobs trouble you, send them to trusty Smythe." He slid the key over.

"Thank you, gent," Jason said, sticking to the manager's jargon of choice.

"Of course. I'll need thirty Imperial chevrons."

Jason reached into his satchel and counted out the bills needed to cover the cost. Jerome and Glinda had helped him to exchange the remaining rare solidus for the common currency he'd need for his journey.

As he took the bills, the manager noted, "By the way, you might want to work on masking your accent. The old provincials are most condescending to you northerners."

Jason nodded. "I'll keep that in mind."

A flicker of something flashed across the manager's round face. "Ah, as it happens, two other travelers from Brackenburgh arrived here earlier. An older man and a young lady. Perhaps you'd enjoy their company?"

It was good Jason controlled his initial impulse to roll his eyes at the insinuation he'd know and enjoy the company of everyone from the north. He was in a better position to stymie the surprise and hopefulness he felt swell within him at the description of the other pair's origins. "You don't say," he replied.

"I do say. I literally just did," the hotel manager said, looking puzzled.

"Sorry, a quaint northern custom. Thank you again for the room and all your helpful information. I don't suppose the Brackenburghers mentioned where their business was taking them?"

"They did not, but they're in the bar presently if you would like to inquire yourself. I can have a hop bring your things up to your room if you would like to go meet them."

"Ah, no. Thank you, Mr. Smythe. I travel light. But I will take your suggestion and go meet them at once." Hesitating a moment, Jason added, "Is it common to have an officer stationed in this establishment?"

"No," Smythe said with some annoyance in his voice. "Normally, the Chencepar is the epitome of tranquil. However, there have been some … odd stirrings in this district of late. The hotel's owner felt it best to have a, *um*, presence to deter riff-raff."

Odd that a middling hotel at best would hold itself to such epicurean standards. But that might have simply been Mr. Smythe's perceptions coloring things. "I appreciate the consideration of your guests' well-being. Hale evening."

Jason hurried off before the manager could delay or redirect the conversation. Something about that officer unsettled him, and he wasn't sure if it was because of echoes of his old life or his new life spoke warnings to him. Whichever was the case, he couldn't pass up this chance, and as he slipped into the bar past another pair of officers, he scanned the crowds in hopes of spotting Aria and Sir Cinaed.

TWENTY-EIGHTH INTERLOGUE: EMPTY HANDED

Jason dropped down heavily at a table in the bar. One hand was balled into a fist, gripping absently at the burgundy cloth spread over the small circular blackwood table. He'd been all around the room twice, including passing by the officers in the room a couple times apiece. Each time he did so, they seemed to take a deeper interest in him. The memory of his last brush with the "police" in Brackenburgh still haunted him. Even though he had not done anything to deserve it, he felt an anxious weight bearing down on him under their gaze.

Worst, he hadn't spotted the purported pair at all. If it had been Aria and Cinaed, and he realized now how improbable that really was, they wouldn't linger out in a crowded open bar like this. He let a long sigh. Maybe it was for the best. It gave him plenty of time to sharpen his apology speech for Aria.

Aria.

His heart ached just thinking about her. When would he get over hating himself for how he handled things?

The smokey room and somber tune played by the band didn't help. A song of love lost in time of war wound its way around him, into his ears and gripped tight his heart—precisely the sort of thing he did not need to be distracted by right now.

"Care for some company?" A light voice inquired from behind him. Jason turned, surprised by the familiarity of the tone, and almost fell out of his seat backward. There was a good reason for him to recognize the speaker, but it was impossible because the woman it belonged to should be dead. The first girl he had feelings for.

"Melania?" he asked somewhere between a whisper and a croak.

A smirk turned up one corner of her thin lips as it did when they were younger. But that was where the similarities grew much fainter. Her once strawberry blonde hair had faded to something more akin to ash and was done up in curls, tucked under a wide jade cartwheel hat. When they were younger, she had already begun dabbling in makeup, but now she was a mistress of its arts, with smokey eye shadow and blush that accentuated her high cheekbones. Her dress matched the color of her hat and was layered with a silk sash around her waist that he presumed was purely meant to draw attention to her figure. It had been four years since he'd seen her last, and apparently, she'd become the epitomized image of the Modern Era woman.

"You're staring," she pointed out, an amused lilt to her voice. To the tall, broad, but most of all grave, man beside her, whom Jason recognized as her uncle Verdun, she commented, "He either likes what he sees, or he wants to know how I survived that gunfight on Strayler Street years ago. You know, the one that broke up our family's business in the North?"

Jason swallowed uncomfortably and glanced up at Verdun. He had been the head of Melania's family, the rival gang that Jason's own family, the Wernstrums, had bested to claim sole shadowy rule of Brackenburgh. Verdun hadn't said anything yet. From under thick grey tufted brows, he glowered. His cold blue eyes told Jason this wouldn't be anything akin to a pleasurable run-in.

"Oh, now he's wondering if you're going to kill him for what his family did to ours," Melania said again as if a delighted spectator. Her smile grew still more sly, and she leaned down so her mouth was beside Jason's ear and whispered, "It hurt when you ran away from us. We were going places, me and my little heartbreaker. Now? *Hmm.* What to do?"

A chill rippled down Jason's back. Not from fear or the velvet tone Melania had thickly garbed her words in. Something was off. Never mind her surviving the Strayler Street shootout or her finding him now after all these years. There was something wrong with her. Something that made his hand drift toward the spiritsword strapped under his cloak.

"Take him outside," Verdun concluded, his voice the husky gravel that still unnerved Jason. "Some cool air will help us decide what to do from there."

Melania supplied an elbow draped with the silky hanging fabric of her sleeves. It exposed the several gold bracelets on her forearm, along with a tattoo they were obscuring.

"If it's not too much trouble, I think I'll stay in here. Thanks for the offer, all the same," Jason replied.

Melania put a hand lightly on his shoulder and sashayed around behind him. "In that case, maybe we should just join you here. Reminisce about old times. Catch up on what's new."

Taking a cue from her, Verdun sat down opposite Jason and beside her. His bulky form dominated the table. "Plenty to discuss," he agreed.

"What do you want?" Jason asked under his breath.

Lips pursed, Melania chuckled airily. "So much more than you can imagine. But presently, to keep your brother Dorian happy. And nothing would make him more so than if you were to share the whereabouts of whomever it is you're bent on finding. Whoever they are, they must be important to rush you all the way to Falkirke as winter sets in."

"Can't a guy go south to get away from the cold?"

"*Mm-hmm.* You know I see through you. I always could." She caressed his wrist with her thumb and let her hand rest there. "You haven't found someone to replace me, have you?"

Her mock concern grated at his nerves. She knew about Aria and probably Cinaed. "Replace a sixteen-year-old girl who stabbed me in the back and then apparently faked her death afterward? Nope, I haven't been in the market for that kind of crazy in a long time."

"And yet, here you sit, disrespecting my niece in front of me," Verdun countered. "Conspiring with the enemies of the Empire. Working against the Wernstrum Family and its chosen leader. Seems crazy to me."

Out of the corner of his eye, Jason caught one of the officers looking at him. A few seconds later, he motioned to another officer and whispered something, pointing in Jason's direction.

Great. Just what I needed.

Either the officer overheard the comment about him being a traitor to the Empire or the Wernstrums. It would be a development to have his family's influence stretch this far south. But then again, that wouldn't be the craziest thing he had discovered lately. Especially if Melania and her family were concerned with keeping his brother happy.

Why did they wait until now to confront me? It would've been easier to snag me on the way here. Less crowds to disappear in, and no chance for a clean policeman intervening.

"So, what? I tattle on my friends, and you let me go?" Jason pushed back, ignoring Verdun completely.

Melania gave a throaty chuckle. "*Ha!* Silly boy. Don't you know your brother has been looking for you? Last I heard, he even hired 'shadow assassins' to bring you in. We aren't the only ones looking for a reunion with you. He'll be very pleased to have you back."

It took all of Jason's years of practice at keeping a straight face not to react. They didn't know he had turned himself in before. Word must not have reached them that he had escaped his brother. The question was how to play that off to his advantage.

"You're scheming something, aren't you?" Melania observed.

Jason started to answer but noticed on the periphery of his vision that the officers were clustering. They were prepping to make a move. As much as he might hope that they were actually going to target Melania and Verdun, he had strong suspicions that it was, in fact, him they were after.

Jason put on a big grin and stood, putting his hand on top of Melania's. The gesture startled her because he felt her tense under his touch. Verdun leaned forward as well. Otherwise, they were both disciplined enough not to ruin the scene he had attempted to set. "You know it's a lovely night. Let's continue this discussion outside, shall we? Maybe drinks after?"

Without waiting for an answer, he added, "Wonderful!" Clapping his hands together, he finished, "I'll see you out there." He pushed in his chair and headed for the door out of the bar.

The officers moved that direction but were too far away to get to the door through the crowds before him. He didn't stop once he was in the lobby and plowed through the hotel doors back out into the street. Unfortunately, there would be no rest for him tonight. A shame too. Already, the temperature had dropped at least fifteen degrees, and the streetlamps glowed, glinting off the flivvers and roadsters as they drove down the streets. Jason needed to snag Apellate and head for Prominence Station. He had seen a sign directing traffic toward the enormous train station when he was navigating through the city earlier. Having some solid directions would've been great, but he was out of options. Melania and Verdun returning from the dead—insane as that was to process on its own—and being in service of his brother meant Falkirke wasn't safe for him. No doubt Aria and Cinaed were smart enough to not pass through Falkirke anyway. Smart enough or more in tune with the High King's guidance. They both always seemed to know just what moves to make.

The satchel at his side jostled as he made his way down the street, clutching tight his coat against the cold. He supposed Anargen wasn't perfect either. But he had faced a lot worse than an ex-girlfriend and some cops on the take with billy clubs. Still, Jason did feel a little buoyed that there was space for errors to be mended along the way.

Jason rounded the block to come around to where Appellate was stabled and had to stop. By the stable, four policemen stood in a group discussing something.

Bother.

Sparing a glance back to the hotel, he saw Melania and Verdun coming out. Any second, they would spot him, and whatever he suggested inside, he had no interest in speaking with them. Particularly in any place away from the deterrent of ample witnesses.

Bother. Bother.

"Hey, you there!" One of the officers called to Jason, turning his attention back to them. Sure enough, the imposing man was walking toward him.

How do situations like this keep happening to me?

Even when he was basically living on the streets hustling, his luck was never this bad. It was as though all the Lowlands were conspiring against him.

The Lowlands are conspiring against you. You took a stand

with the Ruler they're in rebellion against. You picked a side. Don't be surprised when the other side comes against you.

Jason's own thoughts surprised him. Though he supposed they were basically what he'd read Glewdyn told Anargen. It did make sense. He was on the High King's side now. He had irrevocably chosen, and now he would fall or stand on that decision.

Okay. So, what now?

There was no immediate answer. Jason knew he only had a couple seconds before one or both parties after him caught up and no doubt would do their worst.

Looking around, he ran a hand through his hair.

Calm. Trust the High King …

His eyes lighted on a dark alleyway ahead. He thought he could make out a fire escape he could climb to get to the rooftops.

Stick to familiar paths, right? Back alleys at a sprint sounds about right.

Without a moment longer in hesitation, he dashed out into the street, narrowly slipping between two flivvers passing by going opposite directions. Both cars skidded to a halt and honked their wonky horns at him. His heart thudded in his chest, but he was in one piece and on the other side of the street.

Not wasting a moment, he took off down the alley. It was narrow with uneven pavement and still slick from a recent rain. None of it slowed Jason as he ran just past the fire escape he'd noted before and jumped up and kicked off of one wall. He didn't get enough height, but the alley was tight enough that he could brace himself on either side and shimmy upward. Getting a couple feet higher than the landing on the escape, which effectively served both buildings, he jumped and landed on it with a roll. He was back on his feet in seconds.

Climbing up, he made it to the flat rooftop. From here, he could see that this building was middling height for the area. There was a shorter building to the back with a wide gap and then a taller building to the left. His best bet was to run to the sister building on the right and try to make the leap to the building behind it, which had a terrace he could land on that looked like it wrapped around the building. From there, he had the pick of hiding inside, keeping on the move and working his way to the street, or keep lighting across the rooftops at that level.

With those options, he had already unconsciously started running for the neighboring rooftop before he'd even fully settled on his plan. Getting closer to the gap, though, he realized it would be a stretch for him. He hadn't made a leap that far before, mainly because he was cautious and sane enough not to risk it.

He gnawed on his lip and looked back. None of the other choices were viable, and if any of the groups after him had come to the alley, they'd know he was trapped if he doubled back now. He either got down behind a brick stairwell outlet on this roof or went for the jump.

That jump looks pretty far. And falling from this height means, at best, I'm not running anywhere for a couple months.

There was one other thing to consider. Backing up, he tensed himself to get ready to run. Anargen had done something similar, hadn't he? While in Glastonae's Library, he had made leaps beyond his normal ability because the High King helped him. Jason could imagine the King of Light didn't want his subjects testing him on his benevolent aid and rescue but in an urgent situation like this one. Might he not intervene on Jason's behalf?

I have no other hope but your favor, my King. Please, help me now.

Just before he took off, he felt a heaviness overtake him. A pressure that, while invisible, was no less effective at completely halting him. It was as if he were being held back. It lasted only a moment, but even in its absence, he couldn't bring himself to ready for the jump again yet.

What am I waiting for? Am I not supposed to jump? Is the Great King telling me not to?

Jason turned around, hands knitted behind his head. What was he going to do?

That's when he spotted the other roof—Verdun flanked by two policemen. The brawny old mob boss spotted Jason and pointed at him.

Uh-oh.

His pursuers made their way toward Jason's building. If he didn't do something, they would be on him in a minute or less.

Again, he felt the pressure to wait. This time, there was no mistaking the origin of the directive. It didn't keep the anxiety from welling up and threatening to choke off his air. He couldn't let them grab him. Even if they only wanted to hand him over to Dorian to be tortured, he couldn't risk giving up anything.

Facing the terrace, he drew a deep breath. The pressure suddenly abated. Was he supposed to jump, or had he been guided to stay and was being trusted to do so now?

Go. We have to go.

He pleaded silently and took off running. Right away, he knew he didn't get as good a start as he needed. But he didn't stop even once on the lip of the building, looking down onto the street so far below. He had underestimated it. There was a low point, a kind of loading ramp into a storage space in the building. A fall here was almost guaranteed to be fatal.

Jason leaped, feeling the air rushing past him.

An instant later, he was standing comfortably on the terrace, easily having made the distance.

He wanted to laugh and cry and whoop for joy at the same time. But he felt he couldn't stop. Running around the building corner, he ducked behind a tall potted plant—a miniature fir tree. He took in the scene as the police and Verdun reached the edge of the building he'd jumped from. They looked around, mostly at the ground, before he heard one of them call out, "Are you certain he came up here?"

"Of course," Verdun challenged, his voice hot with annoyance. "Why else would I drag us all up here?"

"Watch your tone, Brackenburgher. You're useful to us now but not that useful."

"You mugs keep pushing with your threats. I've seen some things I didn't believe were real since Melania got us involved with you. But even freaks like you have to respect the bottom line.

"We've been keeping the shipments moving into Zilnen as asked. Do you know many officials had to be bribed and palms greased between here and Lago Amurgo? How much work to get your mystery fruit through Garcenilles customs to down there?

"You need us. We need your business, but not that bad. So, let's drop the whole whips and barbs routine anytime something doesn't happen the way you want."

Most people who were on the receiving end of a verbal scouring from Verdun were usually quick to apologize or at least had the good sense to keep quiet. Apparently, whoever was posing as or had infiltrated Falkirke's police were bolder than most. Much bolder. One of them gave Verdun's shoulder a shove.

"You forget your place, gangster," the false officer asserted, his voice taking on an icy quality and register it hadn't had before.

"Yeah, well, you can tell your boss that if he wants any more shipments going south, he's going pay triple for it now or find someone else."

Verdun bent slightly so that his face was in the other man's. "We'll see what your place will be once you have to deliver that message, *eh?*" He gave the man a shove that sent him reeling out of sight.

Jason couldn't see him, but he must have really gotten tossed because the officer sounded much farther away. "You forget, it is your organization, not you, that is of value."

If there was a gesticulation or other nonverbal cue, Jason couldn't see it. But the other officer grabbed Verdun and twisted an arm behind his back. The big gangster fought back. Freeing himself and decking the other officer, Verdun bellowed, "You can bring it on, you circus rejects! I don't get my hands dirty often, but for you, I'll make an exception."

Jason knew he should be running, using the internal strife as an aid in getting away. But he couldn't tear himself from the spot. Deep within, he felt certain this wasn't bootlegged liquor, drugs, or other contraband they were talking about. Not with his brother orchestrating it.

Verdun stood in a boxing stance, but the officer he knocked down just backed away. He stood there staring like a statue.

"What, you lose your nerve?" Verdun taunted and went for the other officer out of sight.

There was a hiss, and then Verdun screamed. The next thing Jason saw was the huge gangster's body sailing off the side of the building and the flicker of some kind of black coil or something snapping back out of sight like a whip.

Covering his mouth and jerking back around behind the

corner, Jason couldn't believe what he had just seen. Verdun lost the turf war in Brackenburgh, but he was still a major player in the Rehalcyon crime world. Those two thugs had tossed him aside like he was nothing. The ease with which they had done so instantly reminded Jason of the Sombra and their dark arts. If there were members of that order of mystical shadow assassins here, he had to get as much distance between himself and them as fast as possible.

Sprinting for the opposite corner of the building, he saw a gutter pipe leading down to street level and slid down. He turned to make for the next block and skittered to a halt. Standing square in his path with a smirk on her dark lips was Melania. "You weren't trying to ditch out on me again, were you?"

TWENTY-NINTH INTERLOGUE: FACE-TO-FACE

Jason gaped for a few seconds before reining in himself and burying his surprise. "I didn't leave you the first time. You left me. Seems fair this go around that I leave.

"How did you find me?"

"*Ha*, please. You haven't changed. Always running and jumping onto rooftops to impress me. It was trivial catching up to you."

There was a flicker of something on her face as if something had suddenly occurred to her, and the smile she wore morphed from smug to conspiratorial.

"Perhaps we could go together?" She offered her arm for him to link his own. "We can catch up on important things in private."

There was a velvety quality to the invitation. Melania had been a flirt in the past, a very effective one, but even without Aria's claim staked to his affections, the horror of what he just saw juxtaposed against the temptation before him felt magnitudes more wrong.

"I'm afraid I'll have to decline. I'm taken ... and beyond

that, I don't know how to tell you this, but your Uncle Verdun ... he's gone."

On hearing this, her face became more stoic. Pensive even. She reached up and patted him on the cheek, her fingers' touch like lines of frost tracing along the trees. With the last pat, she scratched him.

Recoiling, Jason again was in a tailspin. He didn't care for her affection, but the sudden swing was startling. Standing a few paces back, his face smarting, he suddenly could see the malice in her eyes. The malevolence in the set of her jaw. Now that he truly scrutinized her face, she did not quite resemble Melania, even an older Melania, as he had originally thought.

"No more games," he demanded, still holding his cheek as a little trickle of blood ran down it. "Who are you, really?"

Her eyes narrowed. "Why, I'm your Melania, silly."

"*My* Melania? She never saw herself that way, even when I thought we were in love. So, I'll ask one more time. Who are you?"

"Careful, master Wernstrum, your little phosphila darling isn't here to save you, and you've taken one step too far into the dark."

A trail of vapor issued from Jason's mouth as he gasped. The chill in the air deepened in a way that had nothing to do with the season. The moniker phosphila, "lover of light," was one the Sombra had often used for Knights of Light. Common enough. But her knowledge of Aria and the fell pall gathering around them made Jason certain there was nothing common or innocent about what was transpiring. Whatever was masquerading as Melania was at least as wicked and monstrous as the Sombra.

The Melania-creature gave him a cruel grin. "You have encountered the dark before, *hmm?* Dorian will be pleased to have you back. He spread the net wide to catch you once those fool Sombra failed."

Okay, so definitely not a Sombra.

"If you're not one of them, then what are you?"

"Despair for you."

Secretly, Jason reached into his cloak and undid the clasp securing his spiritsword. His hand hovered over the hilt, ready to grab it. "Right, so a just another of my brother's psychopathic sycophants."

She sneered at him. "Your fear is poorly masked. It will delight the direnoir you just escaped. Or, rather, failed to escape."

Direnoir. Anargen had faced one and barely survived. The sprawling black creature with its cobra-like head and curling, jagged tentacles that fed on fear, slowly destroying their host, were among the most horrible things Jason could imagine. They would make sure his death was miserable and painful.

Cold seemed to work its way into his veins, seeking to freeze his blood solid. The tension drained from Jason's readied muscles, and he faltered, stumbling back. His fingers brushed the hilt of his spiritsword. At once, a flush of warmth traced up his already numbed fingers.

Courage. You're a servant of the High King now. Remember.

Jason gripped the hilt of his spiritsword, and the heat spread, swelled, coursing through him, banishing the cold, utterly destroying it.

His foe stepped forward as if to grab him. Her nails seemed more like the talons of a raptor than a woman's nails.

In one swift motion, he drew the sword out and swung it around to hold it in a guard stance. Flames danced around the blade, and its light filled the alleyway. They crackled and caught on the side of the creature's face as she reached for Jason.

The Melania-thing shrieked and leaped back, crashing into a wall as she scrambled away from the burning blade. She spat and cursed him furiously.

Jason thought she would get back up and face him down, but instead, she lay half sprawled against a crate, her hands on the side of her face the fire had touched. He could see now around her palm a horrible smoothness and abject pallidness. So similar to the doppelgänger he'd witnessed Sir Cinaed best if a still distinctly feminine version. The doppelgänger trembled as she presumably struggled to hold up her Melania facade.

"You blighted cur! You have no idea what you've done. I'll savor every second of watching you die in the most excruciating tortures. Torture your mind cannot comprehend."

"Threats and boasts don't belong together. You wouldn't need one if you could deliver on the other."

Jason held out his spiritsword, pointing toward the doppelgänger. "What does my brother have you doing here? What have you been sending to Zilnen?"

The Melania doppelgänger appraised him with wariness. Her eyes flitted more than once to the flames coursing over his spiritsword. "There's nothing you can do to stop it. Zilnen's pride has finally led to its fall. All our organization did was facilitate the transfer of the pieces to expedite it all."

For a moment, Jason wondered if this monster really was Melania. The way she claimed the organization and the memories she had of Jason and her relationship fit. From what he understood, doppelgängers could only copy and replace living subjects. What if she simply hadn't used her dark powers to replace someone else yet?

If that was true, then how could he slay her? Knowing that the person she was before being twisted was still just beneath the surface.

"You don't have to be this, you know?" he said hoarsely. Try as he might not to care, he did. Even if he was solely in love with Aria, Melania was a person and one he knew, or had, very well. "There's still time to purge the darkness, to pull you back to the light."

Melania burst into laughter, a wild, almost desperate, fit. Derision as corrosive as acid dripped from her response. "You should rethink your own side in the battle ahead. It won't end well for anyone facing the returning—" She caught herself and scowled. "You and everyone you love will die. Horrible, horrible deaths."

Jason wished the biting retort and condescension in the doppelgänger's voice hadn't been all too in line with Melania's personality because she could be harsh. Particularly, she could hold a grudge. An embittered Melania all these years later, her response might have been mild. "I know you, too, Melania. You're blustering. Don't. Your Uncle Verdun was just executed. Do you understand?"

She raised herself up, fists clenched tight. "I understand far more than you! Your little phosphila gives you a flashy sword, and suddenly you think you're something? Her whole order is doomed. Anyone and anything that stands in the way of it is going to be destroyed too."

Jason sighed, glancing at his spiritsword. It was funny. Melania used to be able to get such a rise out of him. They were like a thunderstorm sometimes. Constantly booming out threats, insults, recriminations. How had he ever mistaken that for love? "I've learned more than you think. You think you know both sides of this Quest. But I've seen a glimpse of the High King with my own eyes. Compared with that majesty, that power, there is no battle. There are those who have yielded to him and those who will. It's a settled thing.

"And you're right. There's a good chance I'll die, but I promise you what awaits the High King's enemies is far worse."

By now, Melania was on her feet again, smoothing out her dress. Little tremors ran down her arms, and the side of her face not wiped blank winced as she did. "You always were stubborn and had your head in the clouds."

She glanced down the street and smirked. "Today, it will cost you!"

A whisper warned Jason to duck. An instant later, a tentacle whipped around the building and embedded a jagged barb into the stone. The chilly air off the strike brushing across his neck told Jason he had just missed being decapitated.

Shoulder rolling away, he sprinted down the alley away from Melania and her direnoir reinforcement. The whisper told him to not look back and guided him with snap decisions down a twisted path whipping past like a blur. Jason thought he heard gunshots as he passed by the alley on the other side of the building. Honestly, it wasn't his first concern. Heeding his guide at every juncture was and squaring himself with the realization that everyone and everything of his past were on the opposite side of a great gulf—one he would never again be able to cross, which would not hurt so badly except if he couldn't get through to a pragmatist like Melania, who had to have shared at least some measure of amorous feelings for him as he did her years ago. There really would be no rescuing his brother from the darkness.

GRIEVIOUS WALL

"Having no other recourse available and the imperative to act burning within us, we made the journey back to the South. Without the letters from Estonbury, the chances of getting an audience with the Viscount were greatly diminished. But what could we do except push forward until it became obvious, we could not succeed?"

—Anargen's King's Day Journal
21 Misbyr 1607 Middle Era

"I don't know how much more riding I can handle today," Seren lamented softly to Anargen. "We've been relentless in pressing on to Kirke for days."

"We're close now. Maybe just another ten miles or so, and we'll reach it," Anargen replied, reaching out and giving her hand a reassuring squeeze. He was exhausted, too, but time was running out for them. They had no way of knowing how soon after the Sombra's boast that their vicious plan would be initiated. To keep a low profile, they had skirted most signs of civilization, and it showed. Their normal clothes were tattered and dirty. At least they could bathe in rivers or ponds along the way, but if anyone came on them wearing the rags they had, he doubted a peasant farmer would let them sleep in his field until daybreak, much less the ruler of all Libertias welcome them into his palatial abode.

They wore their armor now, which shone as ever, doing much to improve their image. Almost as much as it served to help keep out the rains that had turned frigid. The showers followed them south from Estonbury and refused to give them any kind of leave. Today, an even heavier rain fell steadily across the landscape.

"No worries, children," Glewdyn called out from just ahead of them. "It won't be long now. We can stop and rest tonight in that copse ahead. There should be some berries, roots, and herbs there we can forage for a better dinner than the past nights."

Glewdyn hadn't exaggerated a bit. Anything would be better than the past two nights' meals—there were none. Before that, they'd managed to catch some wild birds and a rabbit, but with the rain's arrival, hunting became futile. It may have been wishful thinking to say that the small forest ahead would be bursting with all the sustenance their bellies ached after. There was little harm in hoping it, all the same.

Coming up to the forest, they felt an enormous relief to escape some of the pelting rain. If the storm intensified much more, then they would get little protection from the mix of birches, sycamores, oaks, and pines growing here. The woods felt more homelike, though, and after all they'd been through, Anargen felt sure that comfort was something they could all use.

Dismounting his horse, Anargen tethered his and Seren's mounts to a tree and helped her down from her saddle. The moment her boots hit the ground, she said, "I'm going to search out the berries."

Shooting a glance back at his father, Glewdyn waved him along. "Go ahead, I'll gather what we need for a fire, maybe root around for some tubers to go with the berries. Meet me back here before nightfall."

Anargen looked up at the sky. It was masked by the buoyant boughs of the pines in the area they'd selected, but just a few steps beyond, in portions thicker with the deciduous trees, there was nothing but tangles of winter-bare branches and soaring trunks, which hardly masked the steely sky and its perpetual rain. Night would only look a gradation darker than this, though deep enough in the night, it would be full dark for sure.

"We'll try to be back shortly," he promised and caught up to Seren, who had been walking slowly, waiting for him.

"You know, I hope you don't make a habit of starving me with your lethargy once I'm your wife," she commented, giving him a look that said her comment was about turning their thoughts from their painful present to their potential future together.

Except at the moment, that future felt so remote it took all he could muster within not to sully it with his doubts. "You needn't worry of that," he promised earnestly, almost aggressively so. Taking her hand, he added, "It would take a foolish man to fail to treasure a woman of the kind of beauty every artist longs to capture. With a voice that every mockingbird longs to emulate and a heart filled with wisdom and compassion that any sage and martyr would envy deeply. I promise you, I'm not a foolish man."

Seren stopped, and for several seconds, she said nothing, just looked at him. At last, she said, "If we are favored to share a long life together, I hope to ever earn the silver-sweet sound of poetry spun by your bard's tongue that puts weavers and minstrels both to shame. And I hope our love never fades."

"Loving you without bounds or end has never been a trial for me. Would that it was the worst we face," Anargen said the latter much quieter, mostly to himself.

"It looks like we are at the end," Seren commented, disappointment slumping her shoulders.

"No," Anargen reassured her, grabbing her by both arms. "No, don't say that. We don't know what lies just ahead for us."

A little pitiful smile quirked up one corner of Seren's mouth. "Actually, I do know what lies just ahead. We're at the edge of the forest, and there are no berries yet."

"Oh," Anargen said, feeling like a raving madman. "Well, then let's just peek at what lies ahead and—"

"Wait!" Seren yelled and jerked back on his arm. A furry head burst through the space between trees Anargen was about to peer through. A snapping, growling head, seeming to belong to an enormous wolf, filled the space, and then the rest of the thing burst through the tangled bunches of branches and low ground bushes.

Drawing his spiritsword, Anargen tried to get between it and Seren, but she stepped around him, drawing her spiritsword as well. It would be a wonderful testament to their unity and Seren's skill, except Anargen knew he was exhausted and barely felt like holding his blade aloft. He imagined Seren felt the same. Which meant this werebeast that just emerged was far more dangerous to them than under any other circumstances.

He debated about turning to flee, but in their present state, they were sure to be overtaken. Digging in his feet, Anargen braced himself as sharp claws raked across the shield he had just managed to bring to bear. Even the glancing scratch nearly wrenched the shield out of his hand.

Fortunately, Seren took a swipe at the beast that moment because Anargen's sloppy guard left him open for a follow-up attack. Though Seren was too sluggish in her attempt, and the monster battered her aside with one cruel arm.

She went down hard, bouncing along the roots to come to rest at the base of one of the nearby trees. Fury seized Anargen, and he sliced and hacked at the werebeast, managing to score a grazing hit after expending most of his energy. He only just got his shield up to guard as a hit from the beast struck hard enough to knock him over.

Anargen tried to scramble to his feet, but the werebeast was already advancing on him. All he could do was hold up his shield to block one attack after another.

A loud battle cry echoed among the trees, and from their midst emerged Glewdyn. Charging like a meteor plummeting into the open embrace of the ground beneath, Glewdyn was on the werebeast and delivered a fatal blow to the creature.

It took a desperate swipe at him as smoke from the wound it endured mingled with the rain. Glewdyn narrowly dodged the attack and faltered as he lunged for another strike.

This time, the blow barely connected, and the werebeast withdrew farther before collapsing.

Anargen and Glewdyn watched, both breathing heavily, until the creature went still, and the righteous fire burned away its cursed form. As soon as it had, Anargen stumbled over to help Seren up, supporting her under one arm. She groaned with each step they took.

"Thank you, father. If you hadn't shown up when you did, I don't know what would've happened."

Glewdyn dropped to the ground with a groan of his own. "Unfortunately, I do. It would have drug you out of this forest and out across the rolling plains for maybe a mile or less to crow over its victory to the others bounding across the hills."

"Others?" Anargen asked. "There are more of them out there?"

Glewdyn nodded solemnly.

"How many?" Seren asked through gritted teeth.

"I counted at least five as I was searching for the tubers. From the way they moved out there—and it sounds like madness to me—they looked like they were a patrol making rounds."

"Making rounds?" Seren repeated, sounding confused. "Why would they be doing that?"

"Because they knew we were coming," Anargen said, dropping to his knees as he eased Seren to brace against a tree trunk. "They're keeping us from getting to Kirke to aid the Viceroy."

"Son," Glewdyn spoke up, "I don't think any of us are in the shape to fight that many creatures. And that must be only one of multiple such patrols. There could be more than a dozen out there, just waiting to swarm us."

"That sounds in line with their kind," Anargen admitted.

After a couple seconds, Glewdyn suggested, "Why don't we set up camp here for the night? I did find some tubers and wild onions, and we'll use some of these trees to help us keep our tents up."

"Once Seren feels up to walking, I can help you bring them back and get everything set up," Anargen offered.

"It's all right. You both go. I'll get a small fire started and heat the tubers."

Anargen eyed her with some concern, but he knew better than to argue the point. Not with them all exhausted and needing every ounce of energy to complete the tasks remaining for the night.

By the time they got the tent materials and returned, the rain had intensified, and Seren was futilely trying to ignite the fire using some flint and rock. Every attempt fizzled under the heavy downpour. He watched Seren shivering and his father fumbling to get a couple tents set up, the fabric buckling over and over again under the rain's incessant fall. In the space of an hour or less, the wooded sanctuary had become, for them, a prison of tortures. They couldn't reach Kirke and were all cold, tired, hungry, and miserable. Worst, Anargen knew that all of it was rooted in failures that were ultimately his fault.

THIRTIETH INTERLOGUE: SERVICE

The smell of the burning coal was heavy in the air as Jason stepped off the train. A rush of steam gusted past him as if the great steely transport sighed in relief. It had made it to Lyrscony from Falkirke in three days' time. Not bad, given they only made one substantive stop at Lacfortes to refuel and let off some passengers.

Women in wide-brimmed hats with fancy dresses and men in dapper suits bustled about. It was true that the old provinces did fare better than the rest of the Empire. Wealth and prestige were concentrated here, and every Emperor since Rehalcyon's foundation had played favorites to Rehalcy, Lyscea, and Tyreenes. Even if the capital Falkirke now made it the four pillars of the Empire instead of three. The best universities and hospitals were in the South. Jason knew because had he not run away, eventually, he would've been sent to one of them. His grandfather had wanted him to have a keen mind with common sense and conventional learning to make for a worthy successor when the time was right. Even knowing that wasn't what had happened or ever would, it still left a bad taste in his mouth. So, it was with a bit of reluctance that he found his way off the platform and hailed a cab.

He sorely missed Appellate. It would've been nice to have the horse's company and even more to have been able to return it to Jerome and Glinda. In particular, he wasn't sure how he would break it to Glinda that he'd had to leave the horse behind in his haste to escape Falkirke.

"Northerner, where should I take you?" the cab driver asked brusquely as if having repeated the question multiple times.

"Oh, sorry," Jason replied, struggling to focus again. "The University of Lyrscony, please."

There, he was to meet Doctor Antoni, the contact to whom the elf Vif had ultimately been directing Jason.

Elves and intellectuals guiding my path. I really have stepped into a fantasy story.

Even after the sheer enormity and modernity of Falkirke, Lyrscony's opulence was still a bit shocking. Perhaps because it was of an entirely other sort. Where Falkirke showed its power and influence by embracing the future and building up, Lyrscony's buildings were much older but refined.

Pristine white stone facades and terra-cotta roofs with intricate reliefs, colonnades, and statues lined tight streets. Verdant foliage, often of varieties that weren't hardy enough to survive the less temperate north, hung down like the grand tresses of Queen Liliana from the old fables. People off the platform seemed less hurried and carried themselves as if they knew they were in one of the grandest cities of the Lowlands. The skies were clearer, without the smog of industrial works, and Jason got the impression artisan crafts and academia were the chief exports of this region.

It was breathtaking in both its beauty and avarice.

Pulling up to the university's campus, he tipped his driver and asked, "Which is the medical sciences building?"

The cab driver looked Jason up and down. Disheveled with his scruffy start of a beard and the age-worn leather long coat on, Jason realized he must be a sight. Perhaps the only thing that rescued him was his age made him a candidate for being a student, and his hefty satchel suggested he may be a harmless eccentric professor from the Northern regions. Either way, the cabby responded with a bit of condescension in the curl of his lips, "The large one back behind the fountains and the greenhouses. Three stories, only a blind Brackenburgher could miss it."

"Thanks," Jason replied with a tight smile. "Hale afternoon."

"*Mm,*" the cabby muttered and rumbled off in his flivver that bounced along the cobbled streets.

In all his travels, Jason could honestly say he hadn't visited a school quite like this one. The enormous campus was dominated by a tall building with a proud, round dome that he knew contained an oculus. A whisper spoken on one side could travel the distance of the room as though the many reliefs, frescos, and sculptures adorning the Floreno Hall were not sufficiently impressive. Beneath the famed Hall stretched rolling greens with stone pathways dating back to the Ancient Era, still tightly packed, and in places enhanced by mosaics created by Middle Era artists brought from Garcenilles.

Other proud brick buildings rose up around this expansive quad. A monumental library, chemistry hall, linguistics, humanities, mathematics, and on and on, but what caught his eye and held it was the astronomy building. Another relic of the late Middle Era, enhanced with a telescope that was the most impressive in the Empire. Seeing its bronzed gleam in the bright sun immediately turned Jason's thoughts to Aria. She loved astronomy. He imagined she would have treasured a chance to see this telescope, to hear a lecture from the learned professors explicating the mysteries of the night sky.

Someday, Aria, I'm going to bring you here. If you ever forgive me.

Forcing himself to focus on his purpose for being there, Jason spotted a plaza with fountains alongside a collection of impressive glass structures that he guessed to be the greenhouses. Beyond that was the recently constructed brick building, done in sharp whites and greys with geometric patterns, done in the newly popular style in the old provinces and Falkirke called Art Deco.

Before Jason could take five more steps, a pair of tall men, broad-shouldered with ramrod straight posture and stern countenances, blocked his path. What made Jason take a step back, however, were the uniforms they wore. Black edged with green highlights and bearing the symbol of the Rehalcyon Empire's Army. Each man had a pistol at his hip, and though Jason had seen Cinaed the Storyteller handle himself well against gun-toting foes, Jason didn't quite imagine himself to be so skilled.

"You there, young man. What are you doing ..." one of the men asked, pointing emphatically at Jason as he tucked something thin and boxy under one arm. He didn't allow for any answer before picking up where he left off, "for the Empire?"

The other man with machine-like efficiency extended a pamphlet to Jason. When Jason just stared back at him, he gave a crisp nod toward the document.

"Heed the Emperor's summons! Join the Rehalcyon Army

today!" shouted the bold lettering across the top. In a nice tight font with dramatic pictures of soldiers in formation and various artillery pieces, the rest was comfortingly standard jingoist fare. No danger of creatures of darkness and malevolence. Just the dogged nationalism that Jason, like anyone else, had taken for granted with the Empire. This wasn't the first time a recruiter had handed him such a brochure.

Upping the pressure, the other man spun the thing he'd tucked under his arm around to reveal a dramatic portrait of a man in a lavish robe pointing grandly into the distance. His eyes trained there. In bright colors and bold font, it boasted, "Follow the Emperor's Armies to Glory!"

Jason had to stifle a dismissive snort. The Emperor, an old paunchy man with blotchy, flushed skin, was not what was depicted here. An artist had turned portliness into stout muscularity, and his reddened skin seemed to imply vigor rather than the reality. He looked firm and formidable in his stance. All things that no one who had ever seen a live address from Rehalcyon's ruler would ascribe to him. The dichotomy between what the Empire needed its ruler to project and what he was, in reality, reminded Jason that his brother was actively involved in replacing the old dictator with someone new. Someone whom the army did not have to puff up falsely and could rally behind as it marched all over the face of the Lowlands.

"Have you ever given consideration to joining the Empire's Army, young man?" one soldier prompted.

"Of course," Jason replied, too breezily, his relief about the nature of the encounter short-circuiting his usual defensive mask of impassivity for such encounters.

The other man scowled and grabbed Jason's arm at the shoulder. "Given it serious consideration? There are men out there on the front lines of Surcalido giving their all for their country. What are you doing for Rehalcyon?"

Trying to save it and the rest of the Lowlands from monsters you probably don't believe in.

"As much as the next citizen, I imagine," Jason replied a bit clumsily. Again, lies would be so much easier to barter in to get himself past this encounter, but if he hadn't been sure in Falkirke, he was now that the High King pressed him not to tread into the shadows of untruths and deceit. "I, *um,* I didn't realize the Empire's armies were at war with Surcalido. I thought they were building up in the contested region with the Vogteremark and Knorland."

Both soldiers looked far from impressed. Poster-bearer huffed. "Do you even read the papers, boy? The Empire signed a peace treaty with Knorland to relinquish its claims on both contested regions. In exchange, they agreed to support Rehalcyon in any future conflicts."

"Which those flamenco-loving, raisin-slavering bourgeoise in the South started when they attacked the Corridor," the other added, letting some of his discipline slip in order to score some cheap insults on Surcalido's people, whose country produced most of the Lowlands best grapes and wine.

"Right, the Corridor," Jason repeated, unsure of what they were referring to and unsettled by the news in the north. Knorland and Rehalcyon had been at odds for centuries. Their rivalry had been the one thing keeping the crumbling Vogteremark from being swept away. Since both sides wanted its lands and were in contentions over it, neither could move against the Dag Vogtere. If the Rehalcyon Empire was stepping back now, then the dam would soon break on the Vogteremark, which was a shame. Jason had spent a fair amount of his first year there after running away from his family as a kid. Not to mention all of the stories Cinaed had told him that brought the place to life for him in new ways. It felt almost like he was losing an old friend.

Poster-bearer relinquished his hold on Jason by giving him a stiff push. "You're not serious. You don't know about the Corridor?"

"No," Jason admitted. "I've been rather committed to my studies for some time now. I haven't been reading the papers much."

"And what would that be that you're studying, exactly?"

Jason smiled because the truth was far more amusing in this instance than any lie he would've crafted. "Middle Era history and lore."

"What a waste of time. Surely you listen to the radio, though?" the other recruiter pressed.

"Don't own one," Jason replied with a shrug.

Shaking his head, Poster-bearer looked at his comrade and said, "Let's go. This one wouldn't last a minute on the frontlines. Got his head stuck in the past."

"What a waste," the other agreed and proceeded down the sidewalk, approaching another pair of students several yards further back.

Yeah, what a waste of devotion.

Orienting himself back to the medical sciences building, Jason hurried along the paths and across freshly trimmed grassy spaces until he reached the plaza in front of the building. A steady stream of nurses, doctors, and presumably students aspiring to be either came in and out. Jason tried his best to discreetly slip into the ebb and flow of the foot traffic and entered the building's commons area, where he spotted a large board with names of professors and their corresponding office numbers. Dr. Antoni was on floor three, room twenty-three.

Electing to take the stairs, Jason rushed up them, and as he walked the smooth tiled halls working his way toward Antoni's office, the encounter from moments before kept playing over in his mind. Try as he might, he couldn't shake off some lingering questions.

Is it wrong for Rehalcyon to be so nationalist? Expansionist?

It wasn't something Jason had ever questioned before, but faced with such aggressive displays of fervor for it, what should he make of it? Particularly given the secret undercurrents of sinister forces that would use Rehalcyon's might for their own. The mentality of conquest and domination seemed to, at the least, be ignoring the fact that all the Lowlands belonged to the High King, with nations as stewards of the lands.

Coming out of his introspective debate, Jason realized he had walked past the door to Dr. Antoni's office. Doubling back, he came to the dark oak door bearing a golden placard with "Dr. Gregorio Antoni" embossed in dark lettering. Taking in a deep breath, he knocked and waited. A couple of minutes passed by without any response, and he wondered if he should wait there or go back outside and purchase a book to read to remain inconspicuous.

The door swung open violently. There, standing in the doorway, was a spindly man sporting dark curling hair interspersed with streaks of silver. He was shorter than Jason and looked up at him with a mixture of suspicion and annoyance. "What do you want?"

Antoni's sharp tone tripped Jason up almost as much as his sudden arrival. "I'm, *uh*, Jason Landsby," he began. "I think ... well, I was told you should be expecting me. Doctor Antoni?"

If only I could convince him ... wait, of course. I do have something!

Reaching into his bag, Jason produced the letters Jerome had given him. "I believe these should help verify I'm a friend and not a foe." He held them out for several seconds before the doctor swiped them for review.

Jason gnawed on his lip as the doctor's eyes widened at the message, and the tense man in a pricey Lyscean dress suit and vest glanced in both directions. He produced a golden pocket watch on a chain, muttered something in the long-dead Lyscean language, and then motioned to Jason to come inside his office.

THIRTY-FIRST INTERLOGUE: TRYING TIMES

Within the electric-lit confines of Dr. Antoni's office, Jason had thought he would feel more secure. Guarded from the danger of wicked forces after him. From the way Dr. Antoni kept muttering in Lyscean and glancing to the door and out of his modest office's small square window, it was hard for Jason to feel any sort of ease.

"Doctor, pardon me for asking, but are you going to be okay? You're sweating pretty heavily."

The spindly man retrieved a dark blue handkerchief from his vest pocket and dabbed it across his forehead. Restoring it to its place, he flashed a glare at Jason. "We shall see how we both are shortly, shan't we? If you had come even with the remotest promptness, then neither of us would be in this precarious position."

"*Remotest promptness?*" Jason repeated, taken aback. "Sir, I came as soon as I possibly could. I might have lost half a day in Falkirke from not getting onto the train to Lyrscony right away, but that was it."

Shaking his head, Antoni stuffed several papers into a briefcase and jabbed a finger in Jason's direction. "You are late. The Defender assured me you would be coming soon after him. That was more than a week ago. I could already be safely in asylum on Garcenilles, enjoying the artist's palette of Bosquesmeral's sunsets and enjoying the comforts of its post-Tislatnean villas.

"Instead, I've been forced to look over my shoulder everywhere I went for a week. A *week*." Once more, his words blurred into some angry-sounding Lyscean words before he picked back up. "You Northerners are always loafing about, expecting the rest of us to sit on our hands and wait for you to come out of your drunken stupors."

Jason crossed his arms over his chest and watched the man bustling about, uttering his cryptic complaints in the long-forgotten tongue of the province. Ever since Jason came into the Black River Inn and was drawn into this Quest, nothing had been normal—in both the most terrifying and wonderful ways. When he was directed by an elf to meet with this man, he had assumed he would meet someone much more admirable. Someone whose devotion to the High King emboldened them to stand firm amidst the dark tides crashing down on the Lowlands.

"Is your allegiance to the High King so feeble that you can't rely on him to guard you in your posh offices and modernized insula and then criticize me?"

This seemed to bring up the physician short. He looked like he wanted to speak but held his peace. Dabbing his forehead with his handkerchief again, he very purposefully folded it into a tight triangle and, upon replacing it in his pocket, drew in a deep breath. It seemed to steady him for just a moment. "Your words cut me to the quick. I have lived my whole life pledging silent fealty to the High King. The notion of speaking it aloud and facing not only the ridicule of my peers but genuine emissaries of the darkest things I held unconsciously to be as imaginary as pixies dolloping dew on dawn-opened flowers ... Forgive me for my abrasiveness. You're, of course, correct. I should be relying on the High King.

"It is made more difficult because of disturbing information I have recently come to possess. Something beyond anything that the Lowlands have ever seen, for horror and tragedy looms on the horizon. And no matter how much Defender of the Realm Black treasures his journals, they don't offer any answers for this."

"You mean Anargen's journals?" Jason asked, surprised at how widely Cinaed had shared them.

"It's all the same thing," Dr. Antoni replied with a dismissive wave. Stuffing another round of papers into his suitcase, he tapped his fingers on his desk and clicked the case shut.

Does he mean Cinaed Black and Anargen are the same person? That would make him hundreds of years old. And—

Jason stopped himself from continuing down that line of thinking. Letting himself get fixated on who Cinaed was had blinded him to the evidence of who the High King of All Realms is, and that was a far more important question to answer rightly.

"What is it that has you spooked?"

"*Spooked?* I'm not a child! I cannot go into all the details now. Firstly, because one never knows who is listening in. Second, because while it is wrong for me to chastise you for when you came to meet me, it is no less imperative that we leave at once."

"Do you think we have time enough for you to at least tell me where it is we're going?"

Seeming to ignore Jason, the doctor produced an old brass

key from a desk drawer and stared at it for a moment. Indecision creased his head with worry lines as the seconds of silent contemplation dragged on.

Just before Jason prepared to speak up, Dr. Antoni stalked over to a large darkly stained oak cabinet and inserted the key. Swinging it wide open, he revealed a suit of armor and a short sword. The instant his hand grazed the handle to pick it up, little lines of fire traced all the way up the length of the blade and crackled there.

To Jason's surprise, the physician grabbed a bag and stuffed the gladius-style sword inside with a layer of fabric. He then hoisted the bag over his back. Shoving past the astonished Jason, the doctor stopped at the door to his office and motioned to Jason emphatically. "Well, come on then. We have to hurry if we want to catch the next train out of Lyrscony."

It took an intense effort from Jason not to roll his eyes and fire back a snarky retort. Diligently following the doctor out of his office and down the hall toward the lift bay, he managed to keep a tight hold on his tongue. As the lift dinged to admit them, Jason finally asked, "So, where are we going?"

"Onto the lift," the doctor replied in an unavoidably snippy tone. Pushing aside the entry lattice and stepping onboard the lift, he added. "You may either proceed onward with me and accept that I will tell you what you need to know when it is needed for you to know, or you can find your own way. Either suits me."

"You're joking, right? I mean, I was sent to you by an elf. An *elf!* You know? Mythical and magnificent warriors of the High King."

"Are you joining me on my terms or not?" He replied, hand on the lattice to shut it.

Rubbing his face with both hands, Jason blinked and stared

hard at the man. Of all the things he'd encountered thus far on this journey, Dr. Antoni was the most unbelievable.

"Very well. Good day, Mr. Landsby," Antoni said and pulled the lattice to close it.

Jason stuck his arm between the lattice and the side to catch it on, pushed it aside, and squeezed onto the lift. Doing so earned him a "That's better."

Moments later, the lift was on the ground floor of the health sciences building, and they were walking out into the open air of the quad. Squinting against the sunlight, Jason followed the path in the direction he'd taken from the train station. Very quickly he realized Dr. Antoni was going in the opposite direction. "Hey, what are you ... I mean, Doctor, I believe the train station is this direction."

"Of course it is," Antoni replied and continued heading the other way.

Jason dashed over to catch up. "I thought you said we're going to the train station? And we had to hurry, or we'd be late?"

"Nothing gets past you, does it?"

Flustered, Jason bit down on his lip to keep from letting some curses slip. "Thank you."

"Oh, they do teach you manners in the north, *hmm*? Well, I suppose you're welcome."

They walked for several minutes in silence, with Jason trying his best to keep his calm. He kept mentally reviewing everything he'd been instructed and witnessed thus far. Seeking out something, the slightest hint, that he should've expected this insufferable boor. Try as he might, he came up empty.

As they approached the stadium for the school's sporting events, which put them into increasing crowds as some sort of match was being played today, Jason finally lost his cool. "You know, I think I had an easier time dealing with almost being drug off by the cops being controlled by direnoirs in Falkirke than I've had with you."

Though Dr. Antoni did not stop, he did noticeably go tense at the comment. "Dire-whats? You mean the Derestal University team? No, my boy, that's not who our opponent is today. I would wager my annual salary that we're playing the University of Carvenna in groundball. Understandable mix-up, though they both do have rather ruddy school colors."

The answer was so bizarre that Jason had to wonder whether the doctor had had a psychotic break. That, or perhaps something else was going on here. This wasn't a doppelgänger of Antoni—when he touched the spiritsword, it had begun to burn as only a Knight of Light would cause it to. If he wasn't evil or insane, then what was Antoni up to?

Jason gave the other man a wider berth but stayed in step with him without another question until Antoni led them through the crowds, past the stadium, and arrived at the nicest car Jason had ever seen. The cranberry red convertible was one of the new models fueled by a petroleum-burning combustion engine instead of crank-started or steam-powered. Its wheels had thicker tires, and the engine had double the valves of the alternatives. The seats were even posh with leather coverings. The gem of a vehicle was parked unassumingly along a street hidden from view earlier. Opening the driver's side door, he handed Jason his luggage. "I trust you know what to do with this?"

"Yes, sir," he replied and loaded them into the back seat. Part of him was actually excited by the prospect of riding in what qualified as a roadster.

Antoni leaned over his door as the car started and said,

"Excellent. Now, down the street is a cab service. Avail yourself of it and meet me at the station.

"Oh, and please, no more dawdling."

A shouted protest was only reaching Jason's lips by the time Dr. Antoni zoomed down the street and disappeared around a corner. There he stood, shouting at no one like a lunatic.

6

———

THE EDGE OF DEFEAT

"With our failure to reach Kirke seemingly sealed, I stole away from our campsite in need of solace in solitude. In the seclusion of the forests outside Kirke, however, was a depth of despair and dark sufficient to destroy me."

—Anargen's King's Day Journal
25 Misbyr 1607 Middle Era

All around, the rain continued to fall, picking up instead of relenting, even after days of persistent pounding. Anargen had always loved rainstorms. The charge in the air preceding them, the steady sound as each drop landed like thousands of fingers lightly tapping a drum, and the way all the plants shone with new life at the end when the sun returned. He even oddly enjoyed the grey pall over the sky, like all the land was a valley encircled by a ring of mountains too high to perceive the peaks. Now, it was just cold, miserable, and merciless.

Where the forest floor should be almost downy with its bed

of coniferous needles, it was a muddy slog with the needles pricking out like some kind of herbaceous hedgehog. It was dark too—so dark. Perhaps they had drifted into twilight or even nightfall. It had been so long since he'd seen the sun. Days simply came to mean the time between fitful bouts of sleep. Nightmares of the mind vied with those of the waking world to keep him from any true repose or respite.

Ever since Caeserus had abandoned them, Anargen had been struggling to slay the beast of doubt. The one which insistently cried with feral glee that Caeserus was right. That the Quest was a failure, and the downfall had been Anargen's participation. Hadn't that been his concern from the beginning? When they first embarked from Black River, he had often wondered if he was meant to be one of the four Knights rushing to the rescue of the Tower of Light in Caeserus's vision. A vision that would be of questionable value and reliability given Caeserus's rejection of the Quest had Thane Ornand not recorded a similar vision centuries before.

There was no doubting the Quest was real. The High King is real. Which only served to deepen Anargen's depressive state because there was no escaping his culpability now that it looked certain the Tower would fall. If they had greater numbers, they could break the blockade of werebeasts and get to Kirke. Save the Viceroy, and the War of Restoration would not end in defeat. Then, there would be allies and minds sufficient to decipher the riddle of the Tower of Light's nature and location—its rescue would be assured.

Then, Cinaed would still be alive.

The ally Anargen most missed and who would have been the greatest aid. Here in the gloom of this dark forest, with the rain pelting him with unwavering watery volleys, he couldn't help remembering their trek, so similar in setting, through the copse around Bracken. Ringing from the past came the saddest song his home county of Walhonde's mountains ever composed. A song about a father who hadn't returned home from war that maddeningly ends before one discovers the father's fate. Anargen could still remember dimly the rich timbre of Cinaed's voice singing the verses. He found himself slipping into sync with the mournful melody,

> *"Bitter winter winds, our backs bend,*
> *Leafless trees, minders of absence lend,*
> *We stoke hearth's fire as hope suspends,*
> *Will you be home again?*
> *Will you be home? Will our wait ever end?*
> *What friend may we seek for our hearts' rends?"*

A tear slid down Anargen's cheek as he realized he knew the answer to that song's questions. *No.* Cinaed would not be coming back. The wounds his absence left would not end and had only multiplied. An infected sore that would soon claim the life of the wound's bearer.

"Such a sad song," Seren called out to him, surprising Anargen but not enough to extract him from his fixed melancholy. A moment later, she sat beside him, not even complaining about the mud that would mar and dampen her dress, which had already been abused enough from their travels. "You know, I wrote another verse to the song during the time while you were away, and I didn't know when or if you would ever return to me. One with hope, which carried me to the day your arms at last held me again."

"I remember. I heard you singing it in the woods near your family's home. It's what drew me to find you there picking blackberries. After being away so long, your voice was one of the most beautiful sounds I'd ever heard."

His eyes drifted up to see she had blushed. She reached out

her hand, but he didn't take it. Each arm felt like stone, carved into its current shape and heavy, impossible to move an inch. He watched as her expression became surprised, and her eyes looked at him and moved from surprise to pity and concern. It would have been better if she had slapped him and stalked off. Seeing the dim worry in her eyes that normally shimmered with warmth and radiated delight when looking back at him only deepened his desire to withdraw. A wounded animal, waiting its final days out, alone.

Quiet sat squarely between them, not willing to abate any more than the rain. It stretched so long that he wondered if she, too, felt inescapably held to this spot. The thought of it, of her giving up and slowly fading away, was so tragic, so terrible, it was like a chisel had been hammered into the crevices where moss had grown over his rocky arms and cracked through those stony pinions with a terrific force.

"You and my father should go back to Cattingsford. Lady Lyncia will look after you," he said, his voice sounding strange to his own ears. Hoarse, hollow.

Seren leaned away from him, her expression changing from the shattering of her own stony bonds. "What are you talking about? I'll never go back there and certainly not to leave you here."

"Then go to Youngsland or West Haven or Castle LeTolk. They're all bigger cities. At least bigger than Black River. None compare to what Stormridge was, but you'll find a life closer to what you could've had there."

"A life I could've had?" she repeated, almost as if it made no sense to her.

"If I hadn't pulled you into the Quest. It would be a life like we'd talked about before. One that better resembles your dreams rather than the nightmare I've made of this for us all."

She scowled, her expression almost angry. "*You* are the

dreams I have for my life. At least a part that cannot be removed without destroying the fabric of the whole tapestry of them." Seren gripped his hand then, squeezing it tightly. "I would rather die than leave you."

"You will die if you don't leave me," he said, his voice quavering, the words so tremulous they almost shook apart into incoherence as he said them. Within his chest, the dull ache building for days shattered the dams built for it and threatened to flood him with a pain he couldn't bear. "Caeserus was right. I've ruined things. If you stay any longer, you'll be pulled in too deep, and there won't be any escape."

He couldn't look at her now. It was hard to tell whether his words angered, saddened, or scared her. The tone her voice took was one of frustration and desperation. "You didn't pull me into anything! I told you that the High King called me to his service too. This Quest is mine as much as yours." She shook their linked hands. "We are in this together. Life. The Quest. There isn't a you and a me. There's just us. And what happened to Cinaed wasn't your fault."

There it was. She said it aloud. Anargen was on his feet in an instant. "Of course, it's my fault!" He hadn't meant to shout or to say anything more than that, but it was like the wound he'd been nursing was suddenly torn open afresh, and all of the life's blood of hope he'd tried to contain poured out with it.

"I'm the reason he had to be in Stormridge in the first place. If I had just escaped with Caeserus that night and kept to my oaths to the High King, none of this would have happened!"

He put his hands behind his head and marched a few steps away. The more he spoke, the more the hurt filled that space of gnawing tension he felt and merged into something fresh and awful. Saying these things he'd held within only made them more real. The inevitable that everyone he cared about was going to die just like Cinaed became a thing he could almost see, almost touch.

Seren put her hand on his arm gently, and he shirked it off, putting more distance between them. His mentor's sacrifice would mean nothing. Their own lives would mean nothing. The Tower of Light they were to protect would fall. The woman he loved wouldn't just lose out on a bright future she deserved, she'd be murdered and discarded like some diseased herd animal beside the road.

Doubling over, he slipped and collapsed back into the mud, his hands shaking. Clenching them into fists, he slammed them into the viscous mire. His eyes burned as the tears trickled down his cheeks, then raced like the sheeting rain above.

Seren dropped next to him, and he wanted to get up and run. Straight into the woods, crashing through the brush, letting each scrape and smack from the branches scourge him. Surely that pain would be preferable. But he couldn't move, could hardly breathe. For a creature as loathsome as himself, any relief would be a profanity.

She wrapped her arms around him and held tight. He felt shudders running through her and realized she was trying not to sob herself. Seren was fighting her grief and her fear and her pain to be a comfort to him. To keep him from resisting the treatment that might deliver him from his wound's infection.

Through the tremors of grief wracking her body, she warbled, "Cinaed was devoted to the High King and will be rewarded for his courage and sacrifice. The Lowlands are dark and full of suffering, and we all make mistakes to worsen it. But if you give up, if you forsake your father and me and the Quest and the Great King ... that's the greatest loss. The only one certain to destroy all hope. Don't abandon me. Above all, don't abandon the High King.

"Sometimes we must make a stand, and it won't end in

victory as we imagine. But there can be an example, a tower of light for others to see by that draws them to the truth and honor and hope that the High King will renew the Lowlands in his Day. And that is worth clinging to no matter how wretched the Lowlands seem, no matter how deep our mistakes and the dark things that seek to destroy us put us in the mire and gloom. You taught me that, so please, please, please don't shatter that hope for you and for me by discarding it."

He looked at her again, and in her eyes was a furious pleading, a longing. Not for him in himself, or even for the Knight he should be, but for a glimmer of the light from the High King that should be burning brightly within him. It was evident in her steadfastly refusing to be quenched. And from its heat and vibrance, he found the assurance that the High King hadn't abandoned him. Whatever the circumstances may seem.

Like a poultice, it pulled away at the infectious decay ravaging him, not erasing the pain but lessening it. Mending began. He could feel it. Warmth entered his bones, and strength coursed back into his limbs that had been slowly leeched away ever since Cinaed's death. As though his eyes were open after being closed, he saw how foolish he'd been. Crying in the woods about misfortunes that, if he'd given wisdom a chance to speak, would've revealed the High King had been with him the entire time. How could he say all was lost and he had been the source of the Lowland's ending when the High King's light and protection had been with him through every bit of it? He was falling prey to the same misguided thinking Caeserus had, rushing off to despair when hope sounded its horn's hale call to him.

"Seren?" he said shakily, then with greater surety, "Seren."

"Yes?" she replied, her voice sounding so threadbare it hurt.

"I love you," was all he could say at first, and then he

wrapped his muddied arms and hands around her in a sudden fierce embrace.

At first, he feared she wouldn't return it, but after a few seconds of paralysis, she did. "And I you," she affirmed, the health and steadiness returning to her tone.

"You're right," he replied, not wanting to let go of her for an instant. "I've failed, but the High King hasn't forsaken us. And so long as he hasn't, it's worth fighting for and following him to the end, whatever it may be."

He had not imagined Seren's hold on him could be tighter, and yet it became more tender. She laid her head against his chest, and he thought he heard her murmuring something, though he couldn't be sure. From the angle he had to see, her lips were hidden by the veil of her midnight tresses.

"Seren?" he whispered.

The murmuring continued a moment longer, low, fervent. Then she spoke up, "I was thanking the High King. I can't bear the thought of losing you, and I know I almost did."

"You did," he admitted. "And I thank him as well, especially for putting you in my life."

When she leaned forward and kissed him, it was almost as welcome and fresh as the first they'd ever shared. He found himself returning the kiss, not wanting it to end, and Seren didn't seem to either. At least until his muddy hand brushed her soft cheek, streaking it with the mirey mess.

Jerking back, startled, she wiped it away and laughed, tossing some mud onto him. It felt so good to Anargen to hear her laugh. He hadn't realized how starved for mirth he'd become. At one time, Caeserus had questioned whether Seren was preventing Anargen from keeping his oaths to the High King. It was a tragic irony that he had forsaken the Quest before he could see this moment in which she proved invaluable to Anargen, remaining faithful to those oaths.

Anargen was about to lean in and kiss Seren again when he heard a bird keen and fall silent. There was fluttering, and he saw an entire flock of pheasants take flight in the near distance.

Sharing a look with Seren, he could tell she was equally concerned by the sudden disturbance. Helping her up, he arched his eyebrow in question and got a curt shake of her head in response, wordlessly confirming he wouldn't be investigating this alone. Holding her hand as they each crept toward the source of the sound, Anargen saw a little glade with a pond in the midst of the small wood. More surprising, however, was the presence of a makeshift cabin with smoke billowing from the chimney.

THIRTY-SECOND INTERLOGUE: AN UNDERSTANDING

Running his hand through his hair, Jason blew out a long sigh. Then he started off toward the cabby, waiting down the road. Jason kept a hand in the fold of his jacket, ready to unsheathe the spiritsword the moment things became sketchy. It seemed likely Dr. Antoni had been compromised and was trying to lead Jason into a trap. That or he was the most annoying man in the Lowlands.

The latter seemed more likely as the cabby greeted him as normal, and the ride was innocuous.

Arriving at the train station, Jason spent the next fifteen minutes trying to find Dr. Antoni and wondering whether he had absconded with whatever secret information he felt too sensitive to speak aloud. In keeping with the theme of surprising him, Jason found Antoni sitting on a bench, one leg propped on the other's knee, reading a newspaper as casually as anyone might. Coming up to the bench, Jason waited for the doctor to acknowledge his arrival. When that didn't happen, he cleared his throat, equally to no avail.

Sighing, Jason dropped down beside him on the bench and

crossed his arms over his chest, trying not to let his anger and frustration push him into saying something scathing. Which meant he was utterly silent for several minutes before the muscles in his forearms relaxed, and he had control over himself again. And a modicum of compassion for the wiry physician who apparently knew things worth killing over.

"Ah, there you are," Antoni suddenly spoke up, folding his paper with a crisp crinkling. "Right on time as well. Here's your ticket."

As Jason examined the stub, Dr. Antoni stood, tucked his paper under his arm, and picked his briefcase up as if this was a leisurely afternoon in the Lyscean countryside.

Jason started to say something and then stopped himself. He was done.

My King, I've followed your guidance this far. If you rescued me from the chains and death and dark to follow this ... fellow ... around, then lead on. I'll follow you as you direct.

Antoni paused and looked back at Jason, a peculiar look of surprise and something else. Shame. Perhaps less potent. He seemed abashed.

Jason got up and walked over, joining him as he boarded the train. He followed him back to their private compartments. There, without a word, Dr. Antoni sat down and began reading his paper once again.

Jason sat on the cushioned seat opposite him and watched out the window as the steam curled up and drifted into the darkening sky. In the distance, afternoon faded into evening twilight, and deep violet bands melted into fuchsia with a thin stripe of crimson to highlight the transition. Seeing the vibrance over the wiry olive tree groves and bushy grape vines so near the low buildings with their aged architecture, but fresh vigor, he understood how people could find beauty in the sunsets here. Another experience he longed to share with Aria.

The train blew its whistle, and a moment later, there was a jerk as it started down the tracks, headed for Yuldistan in Anstara, a client kingdom of Rehalcyon. He watched as the town disappeared, and all to be seen was that green countryside punctuated by the dusty brown of well-tilled land fit for the finest olive groves and vineyard vines.

Dr. Antoni suddenly informed him, "You aren't what I expected."

"I'm sorry?" Jason replied, regretting now that he wanted the man to speak again.

"You aren't the brutish rabble I expected a Wernstrum heir to be. For a student of medicine and science such as myself, it's most perplexing. I have a colleague, a psychologist. I would derive great pleasure in baffling him."

When Jason raised his eyebrows in expectation, Dr. Antoni chuckled. "*Ah*, introducing you and your case to him would totally confound his research."

"Sorry to him too?"

Antoni's chuckle became an airy laugh, which Jason realized was the closest the thin man could get to a belly laugh.

"What's so funny?" Jason asked, proud he was able to mask his building annoyance.

Dr. Antoni reined himself in and held up a hand placatively. "My apologies. When Defender Black told me, 'All who have chosen to follow the High King are a treasure to our Lord,' I didn't believe him. But you certainly are a credit to our Order. Your patience far outstrips mine, and I had a far less … trying … childhood. I apologize for my behavior, but I had to know if it was true that you had pledged your allegiance to the High King."

Jason sank back into his seat. "So, all of that was a test?"

"Of sorts. Those in the *Palatini Lucis Aeternae*, Knights of Light colloquially, must trust the High King's will, law, and guidance without the benefit of having him always near to look over their comings and goings. 'We walk by faith, not by sight,' as it were.

"Your patience, forbearance, perseverance, and unshakable adherence to the Quest. Well ..." Antoni scowled and dabbed his brow with his handkerchief once more. "It shames me. In your place, my courage and my compassion would long ago have failed me."

To Jason's surprise, he wasn't speechless this time. "It was by the High King's gracious favor. Through the sort of foolishness you expected of me, I was shackled in a dungeon, waiting to die a terrible death at the hands of my brother. But then, the High King came to me in that awful place. He shattered my chains and offered me a chance to serve him. After I'd rejected his rule as rudely as I could manage.

"It's not what I deserved. So, it's not me you envy, it's his work in me. Which I'm sure he can do far more with someone like you."

Dr. Antoni had a very thoughtful look on his face. "Astounding. Giancarlo would be confounded. Utterly confounded."

A silence settled between them again. This time, mutually thoughtful, Jason imagined. For all his frustration earlier, it turned out Dr. Antoni was a lot like Professor Goulder of Geisle. He had enjoyed the eccentric academic's company. Whether the similarities were good or bad was an unsettled question, but there were other far more pressing ones in desperate need of resolution.

"Earlier, you alluded to some information that is critical and so secret it couldn't be trusted to be said aloud in your office. Was that all part of the test as well, or do you really have that sort of information?"

Steepling his fingers, Dr. Antoni leaned forward. "I wish I

did not have knowledge of secret things. You are no doubt familiar with the conflict going on between the Empire and Surcalido, yes?"

Not bothering to wait for an answer from Jason, the doctor continued. "I have, through various channels, determined that this is no simple war. No doubt those recruiters prowling the campus attempted to swoop down and snatch you away for their fledglings?"

Jason nodded. "I met them. Such delightful gentleman," he noted without the faintest tempering of his sarcasm.

"*Mm*, indeed. Those gentlemen have, of course, been squawking far and wide about the Empire's treaty with Knorland, which betrays the status quo of the Vogteremark. I have heard similar simmerings that Surcalido is prepared to break its armistice with Zilnen and Ecthelowall to end its war with Rehalcyon. Do you know what that would mean?"

Jason thought for a moment and shook his head. "It seems so impossible for Surcalido to do that I don't know what would happen."

"Ecthelowall would be isolated and cut off from the supplies they need to fight a war with the Empire. If Ecthelowall falls, as it would, Rehalcyon's hegemony would cover the entirety of the Western Lowlands."

The doctor drummed his fingers on the couch. "I shudder to think what the Empire could do with that much power. Particularly given we both know sinister forces are pushing the Empire toward darker aims and the destruction of any good left in the Lowlands. I don't understand dwhy we have not yet seen the King's Day."

"The King's Day?" Jason inquired. Try as he might, he couldn't recall Sir Cinaed mentioning it in conversation or story.

Antoni leaned back, surprise evident in every line of his

slackened face. "I'm stunned the Defender did not speak to you about it. Often, he encouraged and challenged me with reminders of it. From a time when I was younger than you, in fact. Perhaps even he has given up expecting it to come."

Jason shook his head. "I don't know what 'the King's Day' is, but I do know Sir Cinaed. If it is at all good, then he hasn't lost that hope."

Antoni glanced out the window of the train car at the deepening dark. "*Hmm*, then you will have to ask him about it. It is more than you are imagining, I suspect."

"Okay," Jason replied, puzzled by the doctor's reluctance to say anything about it himself. Perhaps it was another one of his tests. In any event, Jason decided not to press the point. "So, where are we headed?"

"You didn't check your ticket stub before boarding?" Dr. Antoni asked, incredulity lining his face with greater disquiet than when he had spoken of the darkest things in the Lowlands.

"No, I checked it. It says Yuldistan in Anstara. But I meant, where will we be joining Sir Cinaed and Aria? Are they in Yuldistan?"

"Dear me, no. They are no doubt already in Zilnen. But we aren't likely to just stumble upon them. Once we're there, we can attempt to send telegraphs ahead to them."

"How will they get the telegram if we don't know where to send it?"

"Well, you see, telegrams are messages sent electrically. They have armature systems that generate current, which activates a sounder to produce a click. Each click has an agreed-upon meaning and—

"Not to be rude, but I already know how telegrams function. I got a job laying new telephone lines while I was on my own to make some money. One of the phone company's engineers showed me how both work."

"Oh. Well, in that case," he opened his paper with an emphatic crinkle. "Make yourself comfortable. We have a bit of a trip ahead."

When the other man didn't look up from the paper for the next several minutes, Jason watched the landscape slip by through his window and then got into his satchel and picked up in Anargen's journal where he had left off.

A minute later, there was a pronounced thump, and the lights of the train car flickered. Jason looked up from the journal and peered outside. The view was all ebony hills with few stars visible from overcast skies to lend their light. Far ahead on the track, Jason could see the engine's headlight shining along their path. Dr. Antoni hadn't stirred. Though he felt sure something was off, Jason sat back down and continued with his reading.

THIRTY-THIRD INTERLOGUE: UNEXPECTED OPPOSITION

"This feels a little too bold," Jason commented as he scoured each direction for signs of trouble, confirming his concerns. "We stand out and are supposed to keep a low profile."

Dr. Antoni dismissed the concerns with a wave of his hand. "We made it to Yuldistan successfully. If we were going to be accosted by Rehalcyon goons, it would have been much less complicated to do it in Lyrscony. Anstara is only a client kingdom, so the Empire can't make such drastic displays of violence here."

"Can't or doesn't?" Jason challenged.

"Does it make a difference?" Antoni retorted, taking a sip from his porcelain cup. "Ah, you should try this. Authentic Anstaran tea is not to be missed."

"No, thank you. I prefer coffee." Jason continued scanning down the street from the little café they were seated. From the outdoor rooftop table, he could see a good way in either direction, but night had fallen, and even with the cities' gas lamplights, there were plenty of shadowy areas.

"There are rare occasions when one is treated to other slices of culture from the Lowlands. One should enjoy them when able." To emphasize this, he took a bite of a chewy dessert specific to Yuldistan. "*Mm*, orange and ginger. Delightful."

"So, you've said," Jason pointed out. "Besides, I've been on the move for years. I've had my share of 'slices' from other cultures."

Antoni finished off the last bite of his dessert, licking the stickiness off his fingers, and downed the rest of his tea. Finished, he sighed contentedly and announced, "Well then, I suppose we can go to that hotel near the train station for the night."

Jason frowned as emphatically as he could. "We should've gotten tickets for the first train south."

Shaking his head, the doctor again rebuffed Jason. "There was no reason to take the early train. If we had, we would've come into Zilnen at night. Supernatural threats are not the only sort we face. The Zilnians are not so tolerant of the Order as Anstarans are. Of the two, I would prefer to be there in the broad daylight, given my choices."

Jason shrugged and followed after the doctor. He missed when Antoni had been over cautious and shown trepidation for every little sound. Handling him like this was a special class of frustration.

They were about four blocks from the selected hotel when Dr. Antoni abruptly stopped in the street and whirled to face Jason. He gripped him by the arms and said, "You know, my boy, perhaps you were right. We should go to the night market and get some of the Anstaran tea for Cinaed and the others. Quite thoughtful of you."

He was overloud as he said it, and Jason blinked several times. "What?"

"Turn around and head for the train station by way of the

market," Antoni said through his teeth, the breathy timbre of fear creeping in. "You were right. Those beasts have found us."

Peering around the doctor as discreetly as he could manage, Jason couldn't see anything ahead of particular concern. Then, so fast he almost believed it to be a trick of the gas lights, he saw a shadow bulge unduly out into the street and then snap back.

"Sombra," Jason muttered under his breath.

"Precisely. Now, we must be careful not to give away our advantage."

A horrible dark bulge rose up from the ground before them and swirled into the shape of a hooded man. "What advantage would that be, Dr. Antoni?" Its hollow voice was chilling as a sharp wind in a dark wood. "A man of your learning surely knows he cannot outrun a shadow."

The doctor grabbed Jason's shoulder when the thing appeared, and his grip tightened until painful. "Run!" he shouted, yanking Jason after him as they barreled into the road, dodging an oncoming car.

Jason looked back as the blinding press of the headlights from the passing car faded, and he could see clearer. The Sombra was gone. He looked left and right for it, saw a pulsing of the shadows pooled around the road's edges, and realized it was racing over to the other side along with them.

"Stop!" he yelled and dug his heels in, jerking them both to a halt. "We can't just rush around as it directs us, or we'll find ourselves stumbling straightway into a trap."

For a moment, Antoni's face was stricken with horror. Jason sighed. "Come on, this way," he instructed, pulling the other man back across the street. He didn't have much of a plan at this point. There was no running and leaping across rooftops with Dr. Antoni. Worse still, if the terror he betrayed was genuine, Jason was alone in fighting the Sombra.

Without much time for thought or planning, the nearest

building still lit in the area seemed their best bet. Jason spotted one with at least a few lanterns burning. "There," he directed and rushed forward, tugging the doctor along. Not bothering to stop or slow as he came to the door, he battered it open with his shoulder lowered.

As he stumbled inside, the door slammed against the interior wall from the force of impact, and a woman in a purple dress with a fur shawl screamed in surprise. A man, probably her date, with close-cut hair and stiff posture, also fumbled out of the way. Both had dropped their cigarettes, which smoldered on the ruddy carpet covered in intricate flowing geometric designs.

Jason spared them each a second glance as he took in the room and realized this was some kind of piano bar. The pair he'd spooked out of the way were both definitely not native Anstarans. Understandable, since much of the subculture the bar would cater to didn't align with Anstaran norms.

At his back, Dr. Antoni was offering a very ingratiating apology. Jason pulled him along again. There wasn't time for that sort of thing, good form or not.

Jason volleyed a question to the bartender in such haste that it mostly blurred into jibber-jabber. "Is there another exit? We have some unsavory types after us."

Apparently, the bartender, an Anstaran, was used to such things. "We don't need trouble."

"If you can route us out of here, they won't come in."

The bartender drummed his fingers on the countertop. He looked out at the other patrons. They were all watching, including the pianist. The bartender simply asked, "Are you serious?"

"Unequivocally," Antoni chimed in.

The bartender scratched his chin, eyeing the two of them warily. Grumbling in Anstaran, the barkeep pointed to a door along the right-hand wall a few yards down from his counter. "Follow that hall to a door out into the back alley."

"Thanks," Jason replied and tore through the rest of the club at a sprint, not caring what those present thought or if the barkeep called the police or had lied. They had to keep moving, and even if he had to break out a window or cut through a wall using his spiritsword, he wasn't about to slow down.

He knew Aria, Cinaed, and Anargen had all handled Sombra. Still, somehow, with the mystical axes they had to grind over the trouble he had caused them and his newness to being a Knight of Light, Jason felt sure it would be safer to assume that his going toe-to-toe with them wouldn't be wise. Even without the doctor to worry about.

True to the bartender's word, there was a door out to the back alley, and the moment he stepped outside, Jason regretted the choice. It was almost completely dark, with the only light shining from lamps that filtered between buildings. But there was nothing to be done about it now. And though he wasn't sure how Yuldistanis would take to a northerner running through their back streets with a sword drawn, he let go of Dr. Antoni's arm and unsheathed his spiritsword. Immediately, the flames crackled up the blade, dispelling much of the dark pressing down on them.

"The train station is that way?" Jason asked in a whisper, confirming with Antoni that they needed to head northwest.

"Yes," the doctor replied, his voice no longer shaken with fear but still off somehow.

"Good. Sorry to say it this way, but keep up." With that, Jason took off running. Not as fast as he could, but certainly much faster than before. A few glances back confirmed the doctor was staying close enough.

Dashing down the backstreets, he got them to the edge of the rail yard. He was about to cut through a section of fence line to get in when Dr. Antoni grabbed his arm and said, "Wait! Something is wrong. From all I know of the Sombra, that was too easy. I think they let us get here."

"Why would they do that?" Jason protested, feeling both abashed he hadn't considered it and deflated that he hadn't just been successful at guiding them to this point.

"They're trying to get us to reveal the location of the others. Killing us would give them satisfaction, no doubt, but killing both us and Defenders Black and Kharoum would bring them their biggest bounties in their long and twisted history."

"If we can't get on a train to leave, then what next? Once they realize we aren't going to fit in with their plans, they'll come for us. And if there are more than one, I don't know that I could hold them off."

Dr. Antoni rested his chin on his fist and propped it with the other arm. "A dilemma indeed.

"*Hmm*, what say you to this? We cannot get on a passenger line bound for a destination they could learn and follow us to, but what if we stowed away on a freight train bound for the same locality or another near it?"

"I suppose that has as good a chance as any to succeed. Do you know which train to get on?"

"Of course not. At least not precisely this moment. The cars are marked with the lines they service. All we have to do is sneak onto a car that will be taken south, ride it to Zilnen, and jump off once we're near enough to our destination to make it on foot."

A dry chuckle was the best Jason could muster. "Well then, by all means, let's get this master plan under way."

Antoni shot Jason a withering look and stalked past him, eyeing the nearest rail cars. The rail depot here had at least fifteen rails, and they looked at cars on four of them before Dr. Antoni called out, "*Aha*. Here we are. These cars are marked for the particular line we'd need. Judging from the coupling and the brakes here being off, I think these cars might even be getting pulled out forthwith."

"Great," Jason whispered back, making emphatic gestures to remind the older man he needed to be quieter. It just earned him a quizzical look, so Jason spotted a nicer boxcar and climbed up onto it.

"It's not the hotel, but it should do," he joked. Jason reached out a hand to help the doctor climb up into the box car when he caught a glimpse of something from the corner of his eye.

The Sombra!

Jason leaped down, knocking Dr. Antoni over as the black knife clanged off the box car's frame. Rolling back onto his feet, Jason unsheathed his spiritsword and raised it just in time to deflect a blow from an urumi. The multiple blades, each like a whip, clanged against his sword and were retracted with a snap of the wielder's wrist. It was remarkably similar to the one wielded by Tumsas, the Sombra who had pursued Jason across the Lowlands and sought his destruction. Aria and Sir Cinaed had been the ones to end that pursuit.

"Lookout!" the professor yelped as another throwing knife narrowly missed embedding itself in his shoulder.

Great, there are at least two of them.

Bringing his sword around, Jason deflected a fresh urumi attack. He stepped backward as the Sombra's lower half whirled into a dark mist, and he wheeled erratically around in a spin that put him on the opposite side of Jason. The next attack set him off balance, and he ducked and rolled away from the flurry of slashes that followed, wondering how he had managed to escape unscathed.

Immediately, Jason tensed because he expected to need to

block blows from the other Sombra, but couldn't find it now, nor could he spot Dr. Antoni.

Uh-oh, I have to get back to him.

A whisper warned Jason, and he ducked as the tendrils of steel slashed across the box car inches above his head. Springing up, he just managed to avoid it as the Sombra brought a second urumi around low in a sweep.

As soon as his feet hit the ground, Jason did a diving roll forward. The two sets of urumi slashed from opposite angles through where he'd just stood. The Sombra loosed something between a snarl and a wail.

The whisper guiding Jason had prepared him for this, and even as the creature missed, Jason landed, turned, jumped, and kicked off a train car's side, swinging his spiritsword round so that he landed a blow that gashed deeply into one of the shadow fiend's arms.

Wailing became screeching, and it dropped the urumis, which disappeared into shadows as they touched the ground. Clinging to its arm, which smoked, the Sombra turned its milky eyes on him, its hairless grey brows furrowed in feral fury. It swung its good arm out and had a halberd in that hand the next instant. It yelled something in a language Jason didn't understand, but thought might have been Jhi'ish. Stepping back, he found himself with his back pressed against the train car.

Not good. Not good. My King, I need you again. Please, be my fortress of deliverance.

A jab from the shadow halberd buried its black steely blade deep into the car just beside him. It was jerked back with a metallic squeal. Another jab followed and then another, forcing Jason to dodge left, right, down, up in such a quick succession he knew he couldn't be doing it solely in his own reflexes or strength.

A whisper confirmed it, and avoiding the last sortie from the Sombra, Jason rolled forward and brought his burning sword up, shearing the halberd pole in two. With another deft slash, he just caught the Sombra across the chest.

His opponent staggered backward as the smoke roiled from both injuries. It gripped at each of them flutily.

"You don't have to resist the fire," Jason called out, his voice a bit hoarse. "Let it purge you of the darkness, deliver you from it. You can choose to yield to the High King of All Realms."

If before the Sombra had looked furious, it was now frothing with hatred that went beyond words. Though Jason was certain blasphemies and curses in multitudes were launched from its lips in the Sombra's foreign tongue, the language of the person it had been before becoming a monster.

In a last bid for vengeance, it reached into its cloak and pulled out a set of shuriken. It slung them at Jason, but the shadowy star-like blade discs never made it to him. Each burned away into ash before getting within two feet of needing to be blocked. The burning injuries glowed brighter, and Jason watched as the light consumed the shadowy assassin and it was no more.

Somehow, its destruction felt as deep a loss to him as any ally's might have been. Though wicked and determined to murder him, beneath the sorceries of shadow lay a person. One who had rejected the Kingdom of Light to the bitter end. It was a heavy thing, and Jason felt certain he was enduring a fractional taste of the sorrow the High King must feel at the loss of this and so many other rebels like it.

All at once, Jason came back to the moment. He looked around.

I have to find Dr. Antoni!

THIRTY-FOURTH INTERLOGUE: UNFORESEEN HEROISM

Dashing through the railyard, Jason leaped in between the stopped train cars, looking up and down in both directions. He moved farther away from the boxcars and into an area where tanker cars were lined up. There, he found Dr. Antoni leaping across the top of another rail car a dozen yards away. A pair of Sombra pursued him, but more like a cat toying with a mouse than assassins after their mark. One would leap and disappear into a swirling mass of obsidian only to reappear in Antoni's path and force him to change course, which would lead him to the other's path. How long they kept it up before finishing the doctor wasn't something Jason cared to wait and find out.

Jason sprinted over and, seemingly in the next instant, was upon them. He caught one of the Sombra unprepared and smacked it across the face with the flat of his spiritsword. The flames crackled as they seared its sallow skin.

Sweeping his spiritsword out in a wide arc, he forced back the other Sombra, who seemed little interested in closing the distance after what had happened to its compatriot. Still, in felid pursuit, it circled at the periphery, sizing up its quarry, which meant Jason had precious few seconds to spare before it would attack.

Getting next to Dr. Antoni, Jason asked, "Are you hurt? Have they injured you anywhere?"

The other man winced and nodded to his left arm. There was a shallow cut. Not too deep, but not the sort of thing one could ignore for long. "We have to get out of here. Boxcar plan was top of the line, but we don't have time to sort it out."

For a moment, Antoni's sweat-drenched face twisted up in a thoughtful expression as if he were piecing together a puzzle for the first time. "You, you defeated one of them, didn't you?"

"What? Oh, yeah." Jason hadn't had a moment to pause and process that, but he had faced and overcome a shadowy adversary. "One of them. By the High King's favor and aid," Jason replied, forcing himself to focus on the situation at hand. "Come on. We'll have to take our chances on the train leaving the station ..."

Jason peered down the line in the near distance and saw a train was already lined up at the platform. If it was the one he was thinking, that was the train they needed to be on, and it could leave any minute. "*Ah!* Right now!"

Antoni didn't speak, but when Jason tugged for him to follow, he didn't hold back anything as they sprinted toward the platform. They didn't have tickets, and with no time to purchase them, their best bet was to jump onto the caboose and climb along the sides to sneak onboard while it was already riding down the rails.

They were about a hundred yards from the platform when Jason felt Dr. Antoni jerk him to stop. Whirling to face Antoni, an acerbic protest ready on his tongue, Jason's eyes widened. He leaped to the left as a tanker car came barreling down the line and hit a switch track too fast, jumping the tracks and rolling on its side past Jason and the doctor.

The horrible screeching of the tanker's hull along the rails was one of the most horrific sounds Jason had ever heard. All the more, because it blocked their path and from the way the Sombra slowly marched forward, they had somehow caused the derailment. It had very nearly killed him and Dr. Antoni outright, but like any clever move in a game such as this, it served a secondary purpose.

"Oh, dear," the doctor coughed, his face dirtied and bearing scratches ruddy and fresh over his exposed forearms and cheek.

Jason smelled it. Petroleum was leaking out of the tanker. Definitely not what they needed right now.

Holding his spiritsword up in a wary guard, Jason tried to think of a way to handle this. There were too many to fight. At least he thought there were. Did the High King always deliver all of the enemies over to his servants?

No, he must not, because Sir Cinaed of Black River fell defeating Count Eidolon and the wyvern. Beyond that, he understood that hard things waited for servants of the Great King, and those moments shaped a Knight into the servant he or she was meant to be. So, in that moment, Jason resolved to follow the High King to death and beyond, if asked.

A pressure on his shoulder startled Jason out of his thoughts. Dr. Antoni squared a concerned look at his face. "One of us must make it to the others to share what we know."

Sparing a glance back at the horde of Sombra closing on them, Jason knew they had only moments. "Quick! Follow me,"

The doctor resisted. "No. I know what we need to do," Antoni spoke up.

Jason almost missed it as he scrambled over the tanker's side and turned to reach back for Dr. Antoni. "Come on. We can still make it."

"Your optimism is inspiring, but, my boy, more so is the adherence you demonstrated to your oaths of fealty to the High King. You haven't shrunken back in fear no matter what we've faced. Thank you for that."

"Dr. Antoni?"

"Promise me that when your time comes to stand bold against unspeakable evil, you will stand firm."

Unable to properly comprehend what he was hearing, Jason watched the doctor reach down into hidden folds of fabric on his outfit and produce his spiritsword. As the flames rushed up the blade, Jason realized what Antoni intended.

"Doctor, no, I can't let you do—" a Sombra, over eager, broke ranks and surged forward, his arm slinging around as a swift stream of blackest intent and from it formed a morning star tethered by a chain. Faster than he could react, the spiked ball crashed squarely into Jason's chest.

The impact was hard enough to knock him off the wrecked tanker, and he landed a few feet away, rolling to a stop. The wind was knocked out of him, and he writhed there for an awful handful of seconds, trying to regain it. His plate armor hidden beneath his shirt had saved him from a fatal injury, but he wasn't without aches.

I should've been on guard!

A scream of pain cut through the evening air just as Jason's breath returned to him in a rush. The scream hadn't been from him. A coil of smoke twisted into the sky, and he guessed the opportunistic Sombra had met his end. Struggling to his feet, Jason staggered toward the tanker again. Another sound echoed through the yard—the train's whistle giving its parting call.

Jason made it a few steps before a tear rolled down his cheek, and he turned and ran full sprint or the closest he could manage now, after the train. Every fiber and sinew of him raged against the choice, but what alternative did he have? Antoni was right. One of them had to press on, and turning back now only dishonored his noble sacrifice.

"Greater love has no man than to lay down his life for a friend."

Those words were etched on both Antoni's and Jason's spiritswords. And today, the spindly timid and confounding Antoni embodied them. The train had made it half a mile away with Jason hanging onto the caboose when he saw a flash of light from the rail yard. Whether it was the tanker igniting or Antoni's fiery loyalty and passion for the High King setting ablaze the night, Jason could only guess. He hoped so desperately for the latter. His knees collapsed from under him, and he dropped to the platform with the railing bars the only thing holding him upright. That and his promise that he would never forget what had just happened or fail to live up to Antoni's heroism when his hour did indeed come.

7

———

DISCOVERY

*"One never knows what can be found in forest depths—for good
or for ill."*

*—Anargen's King's Day Journal
25 Misbyr 1607 Middle Era*

Anargen motioned for Seren to stay back. There was no point in risking both of their lives. He didn't watch long to see how she felt about it. He already knew she would think a risk to one of them was one that needed to be shared. Perhaps she was right, but Anargen had already lost so many he cared about. If anything happened to her or his father, he would be destroyed whether he escaped physical harm or not.

Pressing forward into the clearing, the rain was both a blessing and a curse. It hid the sound of his footfalls and dampened his senses to other things. Creeping up to the cottage, Anargen noticed its construction was quite rough. Whoever built it didn't really know what they were doing,

136

which made its presence out here in this forest all the more peculiar.

Anargen worked his way around to the front of the structure to find the door was just a tanned hide. Pushing it aside, the smell of smoke and damp wood dominated the tight spacing. Judging from the volume of the smoke produced, the modest hearth formed from small stones had been lit and then extinguished by the rains some time ago, which begged a number of questions. When would the occupants be back? What had spooked the pheasants?

"You there, don't move unless you want to be run through," someone called at Anargen's back.

Turning around slowly, Anargen held his hands up. "Easy, I don't mean to trespass. We heard some noises in the woods and stumbled on this cabin."

"Yes, well, you can 'stumble' your way on into the corner and sit there till I decide what to do with you," replied the other, who was a younger teen, as Anargen had expected. What he hadn't expected to find were the other elements of his appearance. The boy had luxurious clothes, but they were soiled and worn, as no genuinely wealthy person would allow them to get. He had hair growing a bit erratically as if it had been well groomed to a particular style and now been left absent of such care. The boy was also slightly chubby, but his cheeks looked a little sallow, as if he'd lost a fair amount of weight quickly. In his hand, he held a formidable-looking sword.

A spiritsword!

Except the blade was not burning. Which meant the wielder wasn't a Knight. "Where did you get that sword?" Anargen asked, keeping his voice calm and even. No sense getting the boy any edgier than he already seemed.

"I'm sure you would delight to know, but I said into the

corner now, or you will have a closer look at this blade than you like."

"That's not going to happen," Seren called from just beyond the entrance to the cabin. The boy blocked most of the view through the cabin's opening, but Anargen could see Seren's head and that she had her spiritsword drawn, flames coursing along its length.

This startled the boy, and he whirled to face his new threat, letting the skin from the doorway drop between them. Before he recognized his mistake and pulled back up the skin, Anargen had his spiritsword drawn and crackling with flames.

"*Argh!*" the boy stumbled backward out into the rain and fell flat on his back.

Anargen slid out of the cabin, carefully moving slowly and keeping at the ready but not projecting tension. "Easy there, no need to get anxious. We aren't here for a fight," he soothed.

"You're—you're both Knights of Light!" the boy exclaimed, sounding astonished. "Well, but you're Libertians, aren't you?"

The rise and fall in his voice over these two details was puzzling. "We are both," Seren replied on their behalf. "I noticed you have a spiritsword as well. How did you come to possess that?"

Grimacing as he extricated himself from the muddy ground and now careful not to lift his weapon up into anything that could be construed as an offensive or defensive posture, the boy answered, "It was given to me by a Knight of Light, Sir Hurstwell, who was Captain of the Guard for Baron Fenwrest.

"Oh, but you don't know the Baron. Ah, well, he was, or perhaps still is, one of the foremost nobles of Ecthelowall. We haven't heard much of how the War of Restoration is going since we had to flee the prime island."

From the way he read their lack of reaction, the boy was intelligent. Which could mean this was an elaborate ruse to buy time. Especially since he slipped and implicitly mentioned there being others. There was an earnestness about him, though, that made Anargen doubt he was making any of it up. "I'm sorry, but we haven't heard much ourselves. Only that the war isn't going well for the Viceroy's side."

He frowned. "I suppose I shouldn't expect a dirty pair of Libertians to be well apprised on the goings on in Libertias, let alone the Lowlands at large."

The way he said it almost made it seem like he hadn't intentionally been so insulting and condescending. "I suppose not," Anargen responded, keeping his tone amiable. "Though it would be helpful to know who you are and who you are here with right now."

Once more, the boy scowled but then shrugged as if battling with himself over what to do and giving up. "I did mention there were others, didn't I? Well, when they return, you can greet them for yourselves. As for me, I'm Gregor."

Apparently, the boy was still somewhat guarded because Anargen knew Ecthels employed surnames, particularly those among the nobility and wealthy merchants. Anargen suspected that this boy was the son of a noble. Likely Baron Fenwrest.

"Very well, Gregor. I'm Anargen of Black River, and this is—"

"Black River, you say?" the boy interrupted, suddenly enthusiastic again. "Does that mean you know Sir Terrillian of Black River?"

Anargen shot Seren a look, and she shrugged, a little smirk playing at her lips. She was finding this encounter amusing, which meant he could likely relax a few more degrees himself.

"I do know Sir Terrillian," Anargen answered. "Though it has been several months since I've seen him. He left our group to assist with the efforts in Ecthelowall."

It was Anargen's turn to descend from pleasure into pain as

the realization struck him that with the war effort going so poorly by accounts, Terrillian may have perished by now.

"That's wonderful!" the boy said and then seemed to notice Anargen's melancholy. "Nothing to worry, Sir Terrillian is well! Or at least he was. You see, he helped get us off the prime island and then off Emeral when they turned against Baron Sornfold. He brought Viceroy Ecthelion to Kirke, so I don't strictly know how he is now, but he's such an exceptional warrior, I'm sure there's nothing to fear for him."

Even exceptional warriors can fall under the right circumstances.

Pushing past the dark thoughts that led to, Anargen replied, "Thank you. We could use a bit of good news ourselves." With that, he made a point of showing that he was sheathing his spiritsword and nodded to Seren to do the same.

They did so, and the boy, Gregor, reciprocated, albeit a bit clumsily. His ineptitude with the blade reinforced for Anargen that Gregor was being earnest in his claims.

As Seren came to stand beside him, she asked of Gregor, "You know, I haven't heard many Ecthels refer to New Ecthelowall as Emeral. You must be pretty observant to note that they prefer their ancestral name for that land."

Gregor looked a bit like a puppy luxuriating in its owner's praise. "Aw, thank you, but that's a bit of information that is hard to overlook, given Lady Sornfold turned against us and is siding with Monarch Ilyron in the war to gain more independence for her people.

"By the way, I'm such a cad. Would you care to come in out of the rain, my lady?"

Was Anargen imagining it, or was this Gregor suddenly taken with Seren? When the boy offered her his arm to lead her in, Seren shot Anargen a look that told him she was a bit surprised by the sudden shift as well. Anargen shrugged to her, hardly able to blame the boy.

"That would be delightful. I'm Seren, formerly of Stormridge," she replied.

"Such a lovely name. But why formerly of Stormridge, if I may ask," Gregor responded very graciously.

"It will take some telling. Perhaps we can mutually exchange our stories."

Remembering the hole in the cabin roof, Anargen let them go on in and instead set about acquiring some materials to fix the thatching. Along the way, he also retrieved the pheasant that had, by appearance, died shortly after Gregor had wounded it.

The time gathering the materials was good for him to bolster his gains on returning from the brink. Enough so that he hardly noticed the rain, though he knew it was likely only his change in outlook that made it seem like the storm had lessened in intensity.

As he approached the glade once more, he saw that the tent flap was being held aside, and multiple other figures were standing inside. He hadn't been gone that long. Had Gregor deceived them both and really did mean them harm? Dropping the items he'd gathered, Anargen dashed over, hand on his spiritsword's hilt.

THIRTY-FIFTH INTERLOGUE: WELCOME

Though he felt like he was roasting in it, Jason pulled tight the long coat he wore. From the moment he arrived in I'jon, he felt he was being watched. Measured. Weighed. Inspected from every angle, and his every move noted. On his last visit to the important Zilnen city with Aria, he had been less aware of the scrutiny he was receiving. Possibly because then he had Aria with him or because, this time, the High King was with him. In either case, he felt like he had to get to the library. Having lost Dr. Antoni before they could confirm a meeting location, the city's library was his only lead if he was to stick to the "familiar paths."

Not that familiar and pleasant were synonymous. At the secret Knight Hall in the library, he'd had a disastrous encounter with Sadiq Kharoum, Defender of the Southwestern Realm. It was Sadiq's devastating skepticism toward the *Palatini Lucis Aeternae* Order and his personal distrust of Jason that had prompted Jason to leave Cinaed and Aria. Now, he just had to hope that things had changed enough that Sadiq wouldn't try to kill him.

Not being killed was the least he hoped for. Desperately, he tried to keep himself from becoming nauseous over pining to be reunited with Aria.

Navigating through the tall sandstone buildings, many embedded in rocky upthrusts or canyon walls, he made it to the I'jon Library. Entering, he quickly realized something amiss there as well. It had only been about a month since he was last here, but even within the library's thick stone enclosure, the residents' temperature and tone had changed. There were far fewer, and those who were there seemed hyperconscious of his presence and gave him a wide berth. He had to spend a good five minutes on the second floor, staring at the ancient statue of Cinaed, Hero of Tislatna, before he could be sure he was no longer eyed by anyone and could slip to the tapestry bearing Zilnen's symbol, the winged lion. Slipping behind its heavy, minty myrtle-hued fabric, he jogged down the corridor it hid.

As the dark of the passage enclosed him, Jason judged he was far enough from the hidden entrance and pulled out his spiritsword. Immediately, flames traced up the length of the blade and illuminated the rough stony walls and floor. The light was enough to navigate the coarse, uneven surfaces without falling. That is until he reached the small drop-off just before the entrance to the secret chamber where he'd met Defender Kharoum.

Sheathing his spiritsword, he climbed over the ledge and lowered himself. It was about as silent a landing as he'd ever made. Ahead in the passage, the door to the room he sought was slightly ajar, with light shining from within. Aromatic scents drifted to Jason, cinnamon and cardamom, he guessed. Someone was indeed here.

Hopefully, they're in the mood for guests. And to do some listening for a change.

Jason eased into the room, prepped with his apologies for

an unannounced arrival and assurances that he meant no harm. They were without purpose. No one protested his presence because no one appeared to be in the room. Very quickly, however, he began to suspect he was missing something. The door to the adjacent library for Knightly tomes was shut. The light he'd observed was from a collection of white candles around the corners of the large wooden table at the room's center. Looking at each, he could see that the candles were new, perhaps unused until now, and had barely begun to pool wax at the top and leak down the sides. Likewise, a single red rose, an incredible rarity in Zilnen, lay on the table by an open book.

Upon closer inspection, he found it to be a book on the history of the Knight Order in Zilnen. It seemed the reader was concerned with how the Order had fared in the past hundred years, particularly the harm done in Zilnen cultural view by the attempts to bring a peaceful resolution to the conflict with Surcalido:

"The Winged-Lion must soar over the Suncrested Sea. Treaties and understandings will never bring the glory due the Winged-Lion—a golden radiance to be envied by the whole of the Lowlands. Chief amongst the perpetrators of the wrongs against the great Winged-Lion are the *Palatini Lucis Aeternae*. Whose so-called light and king only serve to blind those between the majestic Winged-Lion's paws."

Wow. Whoever wrote this doesn't care for the Knights of Light in the slightest. Which begs the question, why is a book like this here?

A whispered warning clear and clarion as a shout came to him. It was not the oddest instructions he'd been given, though he certainly didn't understand their purpose. Acting on it immediately, he vaulted the table and spun around in a pair of smooth movements.

From a nook Jason had not noticed emerged a man garbed in a black hooded robe with a cowl that hid all but his eyes. The dark stranger held something sharp that glinted in the candlelight.

Another whisper told Jason to drop to the floor. A clink sounded over his head, and he rolled to the side and stood. The mystery man had thrown what Jason had taken to be a dagger but was, in fact, a sleek hook capping a rope. Jason's attacker jerked both back to him.

Slipping into a defensive stance, Jason perceived a fiery, forceful command to not stand ready for a battle. It felt like trying to reach across Aridgulch and pull both sides together, reining in his instinct to fight back. Had he ever turned back from a scrap before? As he watched, straining to keep his position held, the other man reached to his side and drew a sword.

Like a dam breaking before a summer rain-swollen river, Jason drew his own at the High King's permitting and threw up a defensive guard just in time to meet and deflect an attack from the man as the other leaped onto the table and then across at Jason.

He was about to counter, but before he could, the pressure not to fight with his dark-clad attacker returned. The hesitation forced him on the defensive, backing away, blocking high, low, and rolling aside to keep the table between them.

Please, my King, I have to—

Jason let the silent plea drop. Given the space, both physical and mental, to assess his foe, Jason realized the other bore a burning blade as well. Tiny inscriptions glowed white-hot on the slightly curved sword. The other combatant was a Knight of Light!

It must be Sadiq.

Holding up his free hand, he called out. "Defender

Kharoum, please. I mean you no ill. I'm here to find Lady Aria and Cin—er—Defender Black."

His plea at least succeeded in halting the attacker long enough that his dark eyes lighted to the spiritsword in Jason's hands. "*Palatini Lucis Aeternae?*" he questioned.

"Servant of the High King of All Realms," Jason confirmed with a cautious nod. Whomever this was did not have Sadiq's voice, which held in it the distant rumble of an approaching storm.

And then he stood there, fiery sword in hand, his posture not tensed.

Around the man's eyes, there was a noticeable tightening in frustration. He sheathed his talwar-like spiritsword. Removing his cowl and hood, he revealed himself to be a young man, roughly Jason's age, with curly black neck-length hair and a clean-shaven face. A long prominent nose and strong jaw with sun-darkened skin made him much like Sadiq in appearance, but without the hard lines of age and worry and bitterness. His brown eyes shifted from frustrated to apologetic. "I should have listened to the High King's guiding. He assured me you were no foe but friend. Forgive me, brother-in-arms."

"Brother-in-arms," Jason murmured to himself, testing it. That was the first time he'd heard other Knights referred to as such. It was foreign but felt familiar. Welcome, even if he didn't know this man at all. Or did he?

What was the name of Tirzah's star-crossed lover? K ... Ka ... Ka ... Bother! Kav?

I man raised his brows, not in impatience but conflict, seeming concern over his appeal being rejected. "Of course. Can you forgive me for intruding as I have ... Sir Kave?"

"Close," the other replied with an amused grin. "Kaveed Amine, Knight of Light at your service."

"And in defense of the secret library," Jason replied, but

without an edge. "I'm Jason Landsby, green, very, very green, Knight of Light."

"Not so green that you resisted the High King's injunction not to fight," Kaveed pointed out. Putting his hand to his chin thoughtfully, Kaveed mused, "I feel I have heard Tirzah speak of a Jason before. A Jason from the far north."

Jason swallowed uncomfortably. "If that same Jason was spoken of unfavorably, then unfortunately, I would say that would be me. I didn't leave anyone with a good impression of me when I was last here."

Kaveed nodded. "She had some rather sharp words for how the Jason she met wounded our sister-in-arms, Aria." Cocking his head to the side, Kaveed squinted. After a moment of scrutiny that left Jason feeling as if he'd been hung from a butcher's hooks for buyers to ogle, the Zilnian added, "Though I have only met you, I can tell you are not the same Jason she spoke poorly of. Not wholly, anyway."

Shrugging, Jason dug his hands into his pants pockets and replied, "I'm hoping none of that Jason remains after the High King's fire did its work."

"Refining gold takes time, and much heat," Kaveed replied and said no more. He held his hand up thereafter to signal for quiet.

Sounds of footsteps echoed down the corridor into the secret chamber. Several pairs of them staggered.

Kaveed shot Jason a concerned look. His eyes darted around the room until, at last, he directed, "Into the study!"

It didn't occur to Jason to think he was being trapped nor being cowardly for fleeing to leave Kaveed to face whoever arrived. At least not until the heavy door was carefully pulled shut, and he was in that familiar little adjunct room. The one filled with rebellious treatises that defied and denied the High King's character, rule, and very existence. This time, he had no desire passing or purposed to read any of them. The room stank of a strange tobacco and rotted fruit. He spotted a hookah sitting near a chair with stacks of books beside it and pits and peels of various fruits on the ground, along with several empty bottles of wine. Before he turned his attention to listening for sounds outside the door that Kaveed needed help, Jason noticed the book title atop the nearest stack—*Civility and Savagery: The History of Rehalcyon from Inception to Present.*

Jason presumed the heavy smoker and reader were both Sadiq. His obsession with Rehalcyon and paranoia about its motives must be consuming him. Frustratingly, for all his trepidation, and if he admitted it, resentment of Sadiq, the Defender of the Southwestern Realm, was right to suspect Rehalcyon of nefarious doings.

The footsteps couldn't be heard outside the room, but a familiar feminine voice made it past the thick door's sound blockade.

"Kaveed! You're here!" Tirzah exclaimed, sounding equal parts shocked and thrilled.

"Of course, my falconress," Kaveed replied with the velvet pleasure of lovers reunited. "I could not stay away. Especially not after what I learned."

Jason's heart picked up. Was Kaveed going to rat him out? Was Sadiq out there?

It seemed unlikely. If Jason understood correctly, Tirzah couldn't be with Kaveed romantically because her father, Sadiq, had already declared her older sister Naomina would marry Kaveed. Given their lack of secrecy in their affections, Sadiq must not be anywhere nearby. Which meant Jason could come out of hiding. Presuming Tirzah's dislike didn't now extend as deeply as her father's.

Maybe it's best if I stay in here.

"Oh, you!" Another voice called out that almost took

Jason's knees out from under him. "A rose and a sweet treat of halva? All of Tirzah's favorite things in one place."

Before he realized what he was doing, Jason slammed into the heavy door, shoving it open so violently the old cedar door gave a wooden squall as it clacked against the stone wall. His heart pounded. "Aria!" he called out.

ALLIANCES

"In the middle of our darkest days, we may find ourselves among others who understand our pain all too well. Those whose pain needs salve even more than our own. That alone is sufficient adjuration to stand firm and hold tight to our oaths during our own trials. At their end, they may be just what is needed to make us fit to tend to the wounds of others."

Anargen's King's Day Journal
25 Misbyr 1607 Middle Era

Anargen skidded to a halt outside the entry to the cabin, as his approach had been too hurried for stealth even in the rainstorm. From the entry to the cabin emerged his father, Glewdyn. "There you are, son. Good to see you're back. Though Seren was under the impression you had plans to repair this cabin?"

"Oh, uh, yes," Anargen replied, his relief and elation

tripping over into embarrassment. "Right, I saw several new arrivals and was concerned. I'll go get the materials I found."

"Excellent," Glewdyn replied. "Why don't you have Sir Fenwrest here aid you in your efforts?" To someone within, he called out, "Thomas, my son, Anargen, has arrived. Could you please assist him in making the repairs? I think all of us will be in far better spirits if we can get out of the rain, even if the quarters will be a bit cramped."

There was a reply from within the cabin that Anargen couldn't quite perceive, and then Glewdyn stepped aside to allow another teen to exit out into the rain. This Sir Thomas Fenwrest was older than Gregor by a few years but a few inches short and a couple of years younger than Anargen. Unlike Gregor, he wore the armor of a Knight of Light, the inscriptions on which glowed brightly and sizzled a bit as the rain pelted its surfaces. It shamed Anargen some that he and Seren had left their armor back at their camp. Though in his ruinous bout with despair, he hadn't been thinking prudently or perhaps at all.

The other teen raised his chestnut-colored brows, and Anargen realized he had failed to offer a greeting or instructions. "Hale evening," he said hastily. "I'm Anargen of Black River."

"I'm Thomas Fenwrest, from the Isle of Fens in Ecthelowall," the other teen replied. "It's good to finally meet you."

Anargen couldn't mask the quizzical expression that descended on his face at the greeting. Was there some element of Ecthel etiquette that included a sense of destiny in every meeting? Quickly recovering, Anargen nodded back toward the west of the glade. "I left the materials for repairing the thatching along with a pheasant there."

Thomas nodded and gestured graciously, "Please, lead the way, sir."

It felt odd to be addressed with the honorific, given that he was the one in common clothes and Thomas bore the gleaming armor of a Knight, but Anargen didn't argue. As they walked along the pond's perimeter to reach the spot where Anargen dropped everything, Thomas spoke up. "I'm sorry if I seemed strange a moment ago. It's just that Sir Terrillian spoke very highly of you."

"Oh," Anargen said with a little laugh, relieved to have the clarification. "Hopefully, he didn't say too much more than that."

"No, no worries. He was extremely complimentary. Though I had to break it to Gregor a moment ago that Lady Seren is spoken for. Congratulations on your engagement, as well."

It felt strange to hear such a thing from a near stranger. To think about his engagement to Seren at all. Given how the recent months had progressed, their future so uncertain, it never had a chance to solidify into a reality. To become the part of the fabric of himself that it deserved to be. His desire to marry Seren and share a life with her hadn't abated and seemed infinitely more plausible, having turned his gaze from the abyss he had been sinking into. Even so, imagining a future where they could breathe freely enough to recite ancient vows of love and commitment in a ceremony seemed like a fantasy. While weddings were comparatively simple in Black River, they were still such a major occasion that they were key events the whole community would attend. Especially given they had both resided there.

Of course, he was forgetting himself altogether. Black River was gone now. The town of his childhood, at least. Destroyed by Count Eidolon in the raid that altered all of their lives and the Lowlands permanently. Count Eidolon, whom they triumphed over, only to have his schemes of conquest using the wyvern crumble and result in the destruction of Stormridge and Sir Cinaed's sacrificial death.

"I'm sorry. Sir Terrillian made it clear to me that your and Seren's love is the stuff of romantic legend. Gregor is heartily sorry as well. And, well, jealous, but he's a good kid and won't do or say anything inappropriate or untoward to Seren or yourself," Thomas said in an intensely apologetic tone.

Anargen realized he had gone very quiet. Thomas must have interpreted it to be Anargen being displeased over Gregor's infatuation. Shaking his head, Anargen made sure to be very ingratiating. "Oh, no need to apologize for him. I can certainly understand Gregor's attraction. Seren is a rarity, beautiful both outwardly and all the more important inwardly."

There was an easing of the tension in Thomas's young face. Though looking at him now as they walked, he didn't seem so young. His hair was a bit wild in the way Gregor's was, but the set of his jaw and the determination in his eyes were those of someone who had seen and overcome much more than a sixteen- or seventeen-year-old youth normally would. Not that Anargen was anywhere on the "normal" path at this point himself.

Something occurred to him, and he chuckled.

"What is it? Did I walk through a spiderweb or something?" Thomas asked good-naturedly.

"Nothing like that. I'm still digesting the 'romantic legend' bit. Terrillian isn't known for his embellishing. He's definitely got a sense of humor, but normally, he's very to the point and a realist about things."

Thomas shrugged as they reached the pile of materials and began picking them up. "Oh, he still is very much that.

Terrillian just made it seem like there wasn't a woman in the Lowlands who could sway your heart from Seren."

"That's true," Anargen replied quietly. His love for her and its steadiness was never in question. That wasn't among the daunting challenges facing them. A seemingly normal problem compared to facing down monsters and political machinations. A twinge of that earlier melancholy that beset him struck again.

Noticing Thomas eyeing him with some trepidation, Anargen asked, "Did my father tell you what has happened to us all since Terrillian departed from our group?"

"He did. I'm sorry for all you've lost. I recently lost my mentor, Sir Hurstwell."

That added new significance to Gregor having Sir Hurstwell's spiritsword. "You have my sympathies as well then. Gregor told us some of what befell you. Did you pass your full tale on to my father?"

"We did," Thomas confirmed. "More or less."

"Then I won't pester you to relive further what you've faced already. Maybe we can focus on the present?"

"I think that would be best," Thomas replied, his expression easing into a smile before the heaviness of what was to come erased his relief. "We've been trapped here for a couple of months now. Originally, we planned to travel to Kirke to support the Viceroy, but through an … um … ally …"

Anargen raised an eyebrow at the uncertainty in Thomas's designation. "Back story to ask my father about?"

"Yes." Thomas sighed. "We learned of the werebeasts obstructing passage to the capital. Monarch Ilyron is looking for us as well, so we have had to keep in hiding. It was at Mia's insisting that we keep close enough to determine if the werebeasts leave their placements and the path to Kirke becomes open for us."

From the grudging way he mentioned Mia's role, Anargen

guessed she was either a thorn in Thomas's side or so dear to him that the idea of harm to her was itself a thorn for him. "Then your goals align perfectly with our own," Anargen replied, hoisting the last of what he'd gathered up and nodding for them to head back. "We're trying to get to Kirke to warn the Viceroy of a plot against him. He's in danger of harm from a band of shadow assassins known as the Sombra. Though, increasingly, I wonder if the source of all our woes from the beginning hasn't been Monarch Ilyron.

"He was behind the Siege of Ordumair and is at least aiding the Sombra in their assassination plot on the Viceroy. And the Grey Scourge obeyed Count Eidolon in Stormridge. It can't be a coincidence the Grey Scourge served them both. Though Eidolon's hubris seemed to leave little room for the Monarch to direct matters."

"Maybe he wasn't," Thomas suggested. "It's impossible to say. He could have been serving the Count's aims and only now is master of events. Or he may always have been serving himself and had aims that simply aligned with Count Eidolon. The Monarch is certainly a master manipulator."

Anargen noted the bitter edge to Thomas's last assessment but left it be. Much as he had any detailed commentary on Count Eidolon's evils. There was also a third possibility that he didn't want to burden Thomas with for the moment. Perhaps neither Eidolon nor Ilyron was behind the events they'd each experienced, and there was a darker force driving both to ruin the Lowlands. A deep rumbling within Anargen made it difficult to see any other possibilities holding true by compare.

Instead of speaking his concern aloud, he asked, "Is there any chance of assistance coming to you from Ecthelowall?"

"I suppose there's always hope for it. It has been months, though, and we were just happy to hear from your father that the Restoration hasn't been completely swept away yet.

"You aren't in a position to receive any help from the Order or allies in Libertias either?"

They reached the cabin, and there were sounds of laughter coming from within. It was a bit jarring with their heavy talk. Anargen thought he heard his father telling an anecdote from his time in Libertias's militia. Those often included comical antics and misfortunes at his expense.

Keeping his voice low to not disturb the fragile conviviality of the others, he said, "Any others we could draw in would take too long to reach and bring with us. In fact, there's no guarantee any other Knights will join us. Without Cinaed's authority as Defender of the Realm, we have little in way of clout or credentials to draw on the other Halls."

With a grunt of effort, Thomas rolled a large section of a log over that he climbed atop to reach the cabin's roof. "I guess that means we're on our own then."

Handing Thomas a bundle of sticks, Anargen almost said, "I guess so," but stopped himself. "We aren't alone. Beyond each other, we have the High King with us in all we aim to do in his name."

As he took the sticks and applied them to the roofing, Thomas stopped and drew in a deep breath. Something was weighing heavily on him. "I know you're right, and that is what both Hurstwell and Terrillian would have told me ... I just ... it's been months that we've been trapped here. I've tried so hard to hold onto hope, but we've all lost so much. I feel myself losing my grip on it day by day. How can we bear up under such evil? How can there be such evil in the Lowlands?"

Anargen nodded. That summed up well how he had felt no more than an hour before now. Thomas needed encouragement as badly as he had. Beginning slowly, Anargen said, "These are difficult days that challenge all of us. Our oaths, our confidence in all that we cling to. In a time of great darkness, we should not be surprised when evil things happen. Loss, injury, terror abound. It in no way diminishes the light that will be at night's end.

"I cannot promise we will prevail. What I can promise is that the King's Day is coming, and with it, the loss, injury, terror—the evil of the Lowlands will be overturned. Till that day comes, how we live, how we fight the evil, is as important in the sight of others as it is in the ends themselves.

"Does that make sense?"

Thomas smiled, this time without an ambiguous edge of sorrow to it. "Terrillian didn't embellish his other stories about you."

THIRTY-SIXTH INTERLOGUE: RETICENT

Right away, Jason knew his failure to control his impulsive surprise entrance was a mistake. All three of those in the room beyond—Kaveed, Tirzah, and Aria—looked at him with shock. For Tirzah, there was the spark of annoyance, perhaps anger, that quickly covered the rest like the tide coming in submerges the shore. Kaveed was anxious, his eyes fixed on Tirzah and his hands resting gently on her arms, both sheltering her and restraining any violence she might feel compelled to unleash. Last and most tragically was Aria, who stood stoic as a statue. She blinked several times, and her eyes were growing glassy.

"I, uh, I," he fumbled for words. Along the way here, he had to have played this very moment out a dozen different ways in his head and considered a thousand different things to say. All of them eluded him now or felt like the hollow echoes of this weighty reality he could scarce bear up under. "Aria, I'm sorry—"

"Yes, you are," Tirzah snapped. She stepped forward,

drawing her spiritsword, which burned with a fire to match her indignation. The curvy young Zilnian woman's green eyes were accentuated with the striking blue shadow and deep black kohl, intensifying the fury Jason could all but feel rolling off her. Every implicit accusation he'd levied against himself could be found in those eyes, hard as jade. She was half a foot shorter or more than him but still seemed to be looking down her hooked nose at him. "But not half as much as you will be once I've finished with you, Wernstrum spy!"

The latter charge sounded nonsensical, but Jason couldn't move. Couldn't speak. All he could do was look on miserably at Aria, whose persistent silence was the loudest condemnation of him any of them could bring.

"Did you really think you could sneak into the library and murder us before your Empire can? Is it not enough that you brought unprovoked war to us, burning our crops and hacking down innocent civilians who dare to stand in your path?" Tirzah all but snarled. "You have to come to personally attack us in our only haven?"

Kaveed stepped into her path as she drifted panther-like toward him. "Tirzah, my beloved, I do not think that is why he has come."

She didn't look at Kaveed but did hesitate a step. "What?"

"Look at him," Kaveed insisted. "He has no weapon drawn."

Tirzah scoured Jason with her eyes and finally grumbled, "Then what is he here for?"

"Reconciliation," called out a third new arrival in the tone of weathered gravel under a stream. "I would imagine."

Some of the tension and building terror crushing the air out of Jason's chest released. "Cinaed! Sir!" He choked out in a strained voice.

Jason had never been particularly excited to have his father or grandfather return after long absences. It had only ever meant harsh words and stern smacks. But this, this warmth spreading through him—seeing Sir Cinaed now was like he'd always imagined a father's homecoming should feel.

"Defender Black, how can we trust him?" Tirzah protested, though her posture and gait became less predatory. "You and Aria both admit he abandoned you and cursed the High King. Ever since I was a little girl, you told me stories of what the darker things of this world can do to a person unguarded against them. If Monarch Ilyron has returned as you say and is orchestrating Rehalcyon's schemes, then he has to be drowned in their influence."

Monarch Ilyron, having returned, should have startled and captivated Jason's thoughts. But all Jason could do was look at Aria, pleading. Her stony stare was unsoftened.

He took stock of her. As the first time he saw her, her hair was done up into a bun with a ribbon holding it in place. She wore a dress right now. Not as nice as that first occasion, but much like Tirzah's, though plain and dark colored to keep with Zilnen custom. It fit her well. A dark shawl was also over her head, and she must have spent quite a bit of time in the sun since they'd last been together because she had a slight tan. I conflicted set of her lips, absent their usual maroon lipstick, was one he'd seen before. Though her gaze was distant and her expression otherwise neutral, she was torn. And that set Jason's heart to aching in wonder over whether she really believed him a monster.

"No apology begins to cover what I put you through," Jason began, addressing Aria. "But to my very core, I'm sorry. It's true. I'm not the person I was when I left. Except it is the reverse of what Tirzah is claiming, I found refuge in the light, not the dark."

He reached into his coat and showed her the satchel he carried. "I've been following familiar roads. Those roads you showed me, hoping to rejoin you. It may be too little too late, but you were right about everything. If I weren't so stubborn and suspicious of everyone, I would've seen the beauty and nobility of what you were trying to show me."

A single tear ran down Aria's cheek, and her dark green eyes drifted to lock onto the floor. A little tremor ran through her slight frame.

Tirzah cleared her throat. She was looking at Aria, perhaps speaking for her. "That all sounds wonderful. But you were a hustler and a scamp for most of your life. Yours is one of the most corrupt and cruel families in the Lowlands. How are we supposed to believe anything you say?"

"I believe I have a test," Cinaed spoke up, having slowly made his way around the table to stand by Jason. His wizened old eyes gleamed under his heavy brows, and there was a slight set of his mouth within its field of silvery white beard that made Jason think he was indeed up to something. Drawing his spiritsword, the burning blade crackled and popped, its flames danced in the space between himself and Jason as he held it pommel up and point down. He nodded to it. "Jason Landsby, take hold of the spiritsword's hilt.

Jason spared a glance at Aria, and finding no answers or empathy there, he looked to Kaveed for insights. He was rubbing Tirzah's arm gently, soothing and comforting her. If this so wounded her, how must Aria feel?

"Jason," Cinaed intoned as stern as a storm. "Take hold of the hilt."

Licking his lips to bring moisture to them, Jason reached out and held tight to the leather-wrapped grip, first with his right and then both hands as Cinaed made room. The old man only held on now by the top, his old knuckles ruddy and hairy over the bulge of the pommel.

"Now, by the authority granted me as Defender of the Northern Realm, I charge you to speak in all truth. Do you yield yourself to the High King of All Realms and pledge yourself to him, in truth, for all the days you live?" Before Jason could answer, Cinaed added, "Know that any guile will be disastrous to you. Now, speak."

Jason drew in a breath. For all the solemnity and gravity of this moment, he found it rather easy to speak at least one thing freely. "Yes, I pledge myself to the High King of All Realms, the Great King of Light who rules atop the Highlands. And who delivered me from bonds both seen and unseen when I was incapable of escape. In life or death, I will always serve him alone."

"So, you have declared," Cinaed acknowledged and then jerked back his hand, stepping back, aged arms spread wide.

Nothing happened for a moment, and then the lettering on the spiritsword glowed brightly shining to fill the space they were in. Heat rushed off the blade and enwrapped Jason, hitting him like the sea against its breakers. The fire from the sword was all around him, and he found he could not breathe, but he wasn't suffocated—the fire carried to him a sweeter air than the room had contained with its cinnamon and cardamom halva and rose scents.

The heat pressed, probed, and ultimately warmed his skin like a full sun breaking through the clouds to shine on him in the deep of winter. It was rapturous and magnificent and intrigued him freshly every second it lingered. Then, it seemed all at once, certainly too soon for his liking, the heat and fire and light returned to the blade, and the room was left much as it had been before. If as, after he'd seen the High King and vowed to serve him, anything could be called the same any longer.

Jason offered the spiritsword to Cinaed, who nodded, his lips pursed as in thought and restored it to its sheath. Stepping forward, he looked directly into Jason's eyes and then cracked a wry smile that became a laugh and then exploded into a tight embrace. "Well met, Sir Jason Landsby of Brackenburgh. You are indeed a true and right member of the Order."

Cinaed released him and stepped back. Kaveed stepped forward. "Well met, Sir Jason Landsby of Brackenburgh, brother-in-arms."

Tirzah, somewhat reluctant, torn between her hand holding to Kaveed's and her eyes on Aria, did step forward. Facing him, she said with a bittersweet sincerity, "Well met, Sir Jason Landsby of Brackenburgh. Brother-in-arms."

Jason nodded to her and mouthed, "Thank you."

She tilted her head in acknowledgment. Her gaze, as everyone else's in the room, however, quickly fell on Aria. Her hand was on her mouth, and she looked like she was holding back more tears. Slowly, her hand dropped, and she said with a tremulous voice, "Well met, Sir Jason Landsby of Brackenburgh, true and right member of the Order." With that, she whirled about and dashed out of the room into the secret passage.

Tirzah was right after her, calling, "Aria, wait!"

Kaveed started to follow after as well, and Cinaed called to him. "*Hmm*, Sir Amine, if you would, take the girls back here by way of the market and the long route. We'll need additional figs, almonds, and chickpeas for our brother-in-arms."

Kaveed nodded but then hesitated. "Actually, Defender, might it be safer for me to bring us back by the south-central route? The market on that path is friendlier to our Order."

A wan smile turned up the corner of Cinaed's mouth. "That it is, Sir Amine. May the High King's favor rest upon you."

"And upon you, Defender," he replied and went out.

Though brief and innocuous, there seemed to be a significance to the exchange that eluded Jason. A purpose for it, which he could not see from where he stood and only would if he stepped back to take in the fuller tapestry.

Cinaed must have perceived Jason was thoughtful, whether for the right reasons or not, he said, "Do not fret about Aria. Give her time, lad."

Jason nodded, but every sinew in him ached to go after her. If the firm pressure of Cinaed's hand on his shoulder hadn't been there, he no doubt would have still.

"I see you brought my effects back from Jerome. How was the boy?" Cinaed inquired, no doubt to redirect Jason's focus.

"The boy?" he asked, finding it difficult to assign such a moniker to the old man he'd been aided by.

"*Mm.* When you reach my age, just about everyone seems like a child," Cinaed replied with a chuckle.

"Ah, but I digress," he continued. "I take it you also met Antoni?"

Without intending to, Jason winced. "I did. He mentioned that you told him to expect my coming. How did you know I would choose to join the Order?"

Cinaed looked amused. "I didn't. I hoped and pleaded for it before the Great King, but I had no special insight into your future any more than my own. I did, however, receive word from Jerome and Glinda of your visit.

"I'm glad to hear each encounter was beneficial to both you and them."

Shoving his hands into his pockets, Jason tapped the tip of his shoe on the stone tiles of the floor. He desperately wanted to avoid mentioning this at the moment. Sir Cinaed had received him back with warmth and understanding. He hated the idea that that could and likely would change once he understood the losses incurred as a result of Jason's waywardness. "I don't know how to say this or make it any easier ... I think Dr. Antoni is gone. I'm so sorry, Sir."

There was a darkening of Cinaed's countenance. "I had feared that to be the case, seeing only you are here now. What happened?"

"We were being attacked by Sombra while in Yuldistan, and he told me to get aboard the train that was pulling out of the station. I did, and he stayed behind. As the train rushed away, the last thing I saw was a flash of light. I couldn't tell if it was his spiritsword or an explosion. I waited a full day at the train station in I'jon, looking for him, but never saw him again.

"Please forgive me, sir! I know my running away has caused so much pain, and you've been so kind to me ..."

"Enough. You're not responsible for Antoni's passing. Knowing him, you may have actually spurred him to his greatest act of fealty to the High King. One he had scarcely seemed capable of when we left him to come to I'jon.

"I won't mislead you. As any man, I grieve my lost friend and charge. Just as I sorrowed for my granddaughter, whose heart you broke. There are things I could hold against you, but I do not because the High King has absolved my rebellion against him, and I must accept when he does the same for others. Moreover, I must strive to show the same compassion and benevolence.

"I do not hold against you a guilty verdict for every evil in the Lowlands and misfortune that we face moving forward. By the High King's sign, you aren't the same Jason who Tirzah first met. And the Knight you are becoming is one I would have at my side for what lies ahead without the foible of unending guilt. Am I understood?"

"Yes, sir," Jason replied weakly, and seeing Cinaed scowl, he tried again with more certainty. "Yes, sir!"

"Good. Now," Cinaed said as he clapped Jason on the back. "I need to sit. I'm sure you have much to tell of your journey, and I would be delighted to be the listener instead of the storyteller for a change."

His grin was so genuine and hearty Jason couldn't repress a smile of his own. "Yes, sir."

THIRTY-SEVENTH INTERLOGUE: CONSCRIPTION

Cinaed listened to the tale as Jason told it, stroking his beard along his chin. "So, your brother is head of the Wernstrum syndicate and assisting Monarch Ilyron in his accession plans. How does all that fit with them also using your family's business dealings to smuggle materials and rare fruits into Zilnen?"

"I'm not sure, sir," Jason freely admitted. "Dr. Antoni said he'd discovered treachery from Surcalido. But that treachery was to turn Surcalido against Zilnen in favor of Rehalcyon. I don't understand why they would be smuggling goods into Zilnen at all if they have Surcalido as an ally now."

Cinaed nodded, still pensive. "That doesn't make sense. Neither Surcalido nor Rehalcyon has a navy to stand up to an Ecthel blockade, either. It wouldn't be a very fruitful alliance. Not like the one they struck with Knorland."

Jason shook his head. "How did that benefit the Empire? Haven't they prowled along the border of the Vogteremark, practically salivating over it, waiting for the Knors to slip or give up on it?"

"You do know your affairs, lad," Cinaed replied. "At least in the West. In the East, the Knors can help another of Rehalcyon's allies, destabilize the governing league the Ecthels put in place. If they can do that, then the last resistance in the Western Lowlands falls. But it would require an enormous campaign coordinated on fronts across the Lowlands to achieve. A war unlike any the Lowlands has seen before."

"That sounds like Dr. Antoni's assessment," Jason confirmed. "Where does that leave us?"

Cinaed slapped his knees as if to wake his legs from a slumber and rose out of his seat. "Behind where we should be and in a bind. I want to call a Council of Knight Defenders from all Twelve Realms. If we succeed, we will present a united front that helps drive the Lowlands to peace and confront the darker sources of the looming war."

It felt strange just the two of them discussing a war across all of the Lowlands and redirecting the currents of its diverse nations from a secret room in a library. How could they possibly change the course of things at such a scale when they had to be cautious about their own lives here in I'jon?

"You have doubts about the plan?" Cinaed surmised.

"Some reservations," Jason admitted. "It is ... ambitious. I'm not sure how we will convince Defender Kharoum to listen to reason, much less all the Lowlands' peoples."

"Leave Sadiq to me," Cinaed advised. "His position is a precarious one."

Scowling, Jason tried to not let a pithy remark slip out. It was difficult for him to find empathy for the coarse man who had presumed Jason to be evil and rejected him without coming to know him at all.

Isn't that what I'm doing to him in kind?

The thought was jarring and hit him hard. Perhaps part of his attempt to emulate the High King's benevolence and compassion would also have to extend to the odious Sadiq. Crossing his arms over his chest, he forced himself to ask with as little skepticism and irony as possible, "Precarious? How so?"

The old storyteller leveled one of his piercing gazes at Jason. Cutting through, it seemed, all the carefully layered defenses and artifices Jason had learned to construct for himself. At length, Cinaed did answer. "It is perhaps too much to tell in a sitting, but chiefly, Sadiq is the head of one of the ruling families of Zilnen. In his youth, he married Mesnara, heiress to another ruling family. Before it was discovered that he is a Knight of Light, it was anticipated that he would one day rule all of Zilnen as its Beyk."

"But it was discovered?"

Nodding, Cinaed's voice became grave. "Indeed. Mesnara petitioned for a divorce from him, which is unheard of for women in Zilnen. Because of her family's standing and the circumstances of his Knighthood, the other family heads agreed to sanction the split. Most of their combined wealth and prestige followed Mesnara, along with their eldest daughter, Naomina. Sadiq took Tirzah, who was a toddler, and her younger sister. He still commands respect and influence, but it leaves him on odd footing to court those who hate his Knighthood. To help 'buy' back some of that intangible capital, he agreed to Mesnara's plans to marry Naomina, whom she raised, to Kaveed Amine."

"Let me guess, Kaveed is also from a leading family, and Mesnara is hoping to capture the glory they lost. All while having no idea history will repeat itself?"

"Nor any inclination to care that Kaveed and her younger daughter Tirzah are very much in love … and already wedded."

Jason ran his hand through his hair and let out a whistle. "No kidding about being in a precarious position. I'm surprised he let Tirzah marry Kaveed. When I was last here, it sounded like that couldn't happen." As he was speaking, Jason picked up on the growing somberness in Cinaed's countenance. Then it clicked.

"Oh, no. Sadiq doesn't know, does he?"

"No," Cinaed confirmed.

Pondering for a minute, as if it was his rift to repair, Jason asked, "Is it legal for Kaveed to be married to both sisters?"

Shaking his head, Cinaed gestured with a sweep of his hand. "No more so than anywhere else in the Lowlands. The penalties for what they have done in defying their parents are harsh. Never mind those they could suffer for being Knights of Light.

"And even if it were legal, Sadiq could not afford to dilute the gains Mesnara believes she will achieve through this politically. He is counting on it to mount his campaign to save Zilnen."

Jason leaned against the room's expansive table. "So, how are we going to convince Sadiq to join an extraordinarily unlikely alliance to achieve something unheard of in the Lowland's history while preventing a moral and ethical transgression he can't know has already happened between star-crossed lovers who would sooner die than be apart?"

He could almost hear Aria's sarcastic assessment, "Using your great wisdom, of course." And narrowly resisted a reflexive urge to glance at the doorway she'd disappeared down.

Her grandfather just splayed his hands wide. "With the guidance and by the favor of the High King."

Before Jason could respond, the echoes of footsteps in the hall reached them. From the frenetic pause, they either belonged to someone furious for their blood or someone fearful of losing their own. His concerns were confirmed when Cinaed stood and rested a hand on his spiritsword.

Moments later, Tirzah skidded into the room, followed

shortly by Aria. Both girls looked winded from their sprint, and it was difficult not to notice the redness of one of Tirzah's cheeks. "Defender!" she pleaded, her voice a breathy scream for help. "They knew about us and took Kaveed!"

Faster than seemed possible, Cinaed was around the table and took Tirzah in his arms, his voice a consoling hum. "Dear child, I'm so sorry. Where has your husband been taken? By whom?"

"Father. He sent some soldiers to wait for us in the market. They knew Kaveed was here and forced him to go with them," Tirzah managed to get out as sobs choked her words.

When it became clear she could not finish, Aria spoke for her. "Defender Kharoum is forcing Kaveed to join him south of Lago Amurgo, where he's amassed an army to attack the caravans bringing supplies to the Rehalcyon seaport. He said the only way to absolve this dishonor was to die in battle for Zilnen. Tirzah tried to stop them, but they hit her and threatened to turn all of the Knights in I'jon over to the authorities if we 'meddled' any further."

Jason had seen Cinaed faced with dire circumstances before, but he'd never seen him so thrown as now. His old face was a mixture of horror, pity, and revulsion. It lasted only a moment, but when he spoke, Jason wondered if the words were Cinaed's own rather than thoroughly laced by the divine authority of the High King: "Take Jason and gather the supplies, prepare the horses, and meet us outside the city's south entry pass. Go, now. We can afford no more time lost."

THIRTY-EIGHTH INTERLOGUE: PREPARATIONS

Jason's tongue felt like it had turned to ash in his mouth, and it had nothing to do with the hot desert sun beating down on his head as they waited several dozen yards from the cooler canyon opening that served as I'jon's southern entrance point. Fidgeting with applying saddle and bags for his horse, he glanced up at Aria, seated on her horse. She seemed to be seething, whether over him or the situation with Kaveed was difficult to say. He hadn't mustered the courage or wisdom to say a single word to her as they'd worked together at a feverish pace to prepare for the journey south. Whether any words would have mattered or his silence had stoked her annoyance, he couldn't be sure. All he knew was it was torture to be so near her and unable to take the pain away that lay just beneath the surface. Worse still, because he knew he caused much of that pain.

What could he say? His weak apology in the library chamber seemed insufficient, but how would his declaration of love ring true, given what he'd done? In a thousand different ways, he'd reimagined their last moments together. Constructing narratives that led to infinitely better places than where they now stood.

Wiping at the sweat of his brow with his sleeve, he realized how ragged and unkempt he was, which did not help his case. Though more than that, it snapped him back to the present. They were waiting outside I'jon to ride to the aid of Kaveed, who was Tirzah's lover—no, husband—and no doubt, therefore, like a brother to Aria. Instead of focusing on his past failures, perhaps it would be best to tend to Aria's present hurts.

"I'm sorry about what's happening to Kaveed. Your grandfather told me about Tirzah's mother and all the strings attached to the situation."

Aria flicked a sidelong glance at him but said nothing. Her mouth was set in a tight line. Her usually soft cheeks looked hard, taut.

Okay ... try a different tactic.

"They do seem genuinely in love. I think Kaveed was going to surprise Tirzah with the rose and whatever that pastry was that smelled like cardamom and cinnamon."

The last word came out a bit strained. Aria had smelled of cinnamon the first time they met when she was working as a hostess at her grandfather's Black River Inn. He had been smitten with her from the first, more than he even realized.

"I know. And it was halva. I showed him how to make it," Aria replied, her own voice strained.

At least that was an answer.

"You have always been an excellent baker. I can still taste the muffins you made when we first met. They—"

"Jason," she said, her voice on the knife's edge between anger and sadness. "Can we please not talk about that right now?"

"Right," he agreed. "Sorry."

Once more, silence poured into the space between them. As it stretched on with neither Cinaed and Tirzah arriving nor Aria choosing anything else to speak about, Jason knew he had to find something to keep the ponderous quiet from burying them.

"I heard Kaveed call Tirzah 'falconress.' What is that about? Is it a Zilnian thing? Like a term of endearment?"

Aria closed her eyes and sighed heavily. "Yes and no. Falconress is the Ecthelish word for it, but the story behind it is Zilnian." She looked at him briefly as if to confirm he had to know more and rolled her eyes.

"Fine. So, the story goes that there was a Beyk of Zilnen who lost his only heir for vexing a desert hag."

"A what?" Jason interrupted and immediately regretted it for the corrosive ire Aria's expression lade on him.

"It's a witch, okay? The desert witch cursed the Beyk. On his lost son's birthday each year, he would hold a tournament in memory of his son. At the tournament, the women of Zilnen could each come and attempt to tame the Beyk's pet falcon. If anyone could, the falconress would be treated to live in the Beyk's palace in N'jafu and receive enough gold to live comfortably the rest of her days.

"There was a poor girl who tended to the orphaned children in her district of N'jafu. She'd lost everyone dear to her when she was young and, once grown, decided to not let the other orphans experience the sorrow she had felt. Having nothing to meet their needs, she took to training birds that lighted on the windows of the hovel she lived in. Their songs with hers delighted the orphaned children and one of the royal guards overheard her during a performance and brought her to the palace to participate in the Beyk's competition."

Aria paused and arched her eyebrows, seeming to have

noticed that Jason was deeply thoughtful. "Do you want me to stop?"

"No, no. I just was wondering about her name. Did the girl have one in the story?"

"Zebaye," Aria replied. "Usually, she is referred to as the *Falconress*."

"I take it Zebaye wins the competition, then?"

"Yes, she does. And if you want to know the rest, please don't interrupt."

He nodded and gestured for her to continue while he rubbed the side of her horse's neck. "Sorry."

Eyeing him with lingering frustration, Aria picked up again but at a faster pace, "Zebaye wins the contest and becomes the Falconress, tending to the Beyk's bird. While caring for the falcon, she visits the orphans again and uses most of the gold she won to care for them.

"After a long time caring for the Beyk's falcon, he flies off from the palace. Without being asked, the Falconress follows the bird all across the Ziljafu Desert and the Ash Dunes until, at last, she catches up with him at the Notiosanemos Sea. When she did, she picked up the bird and kissed him on the beak and …

"Poof, the witch's spell was broken. The falcon she had cared for was the Beyk's son all along. He explains to her he could only be freed by a kiss from one whose heart was truly beautiful and devoted, though some versions emphasize that she was a mother who never bore a child. Then, the Beyk's son asks the Falconress to marry him, and they live out their days in happiness.

"It's one of Tirzah's favorite stories," Aria concluded.

Giving a moment's pause to ensure he wasn't interrupting again, Jason said, "That is a lovely story. Kind, noble, beautiful-hearted. A love that sought across the intractable sands of Ziljafu. I see why Kaveed calls Tirzah his falconress."

"*Mm*," Aria replied absently. Then, scowling added, "The problem with fairy tales is they teach you to expect one thing, and when you find something wholly different, you think it's your fault. Always the tales are 'better to have loved and lost' when it's better never to have ventured to love and felt the sting of loss at all."

Her answer was as effective as any rifle at piercing him through. He could drop from his horse and break his back with continual agony for the rest of his life, and still, the pain of those words would be the one that he would never see past.

"What about real love stories? Like Cinaed and Elena of Tislatna? Ordumair II and Alessia? Or Anargen and Seren?" His voice choked out before he could muster the courage to say, 'Or you and I?'"

"I told you, only one of those stories ended happily," Aria replied, her eyes hard as stone. "That's why real stories are better than fairy tales—they prepare you for the devastation the real Lowlands bring."

"I think all stories can do that," Jason murmured. Perhaps too soft for her to hear because she didn't respond and just looked off into the distance, using her hand to shield her eyes against the beating sun. What hurt him most was that those things she'd said sounded so unlike Aria. It felt as though she was still lost to him. Her body had returned, but not her spirit.

A couple minutes later, Cinaed and Tirzah arrived. The latter wore her shawl wrapped round her face, but he could see through the narrow space for her eyes that the kohl around them had streaked onto her cheeks.

Aria whipped her horse around and brought her alongside Tirzah, who leaned on Aria for support.

At least that much of Aria is still here.

Cinaed spoke up to the whole group. "We have much ground to cover and little time to do it." Then, more directly to Jason, "Kaveed will no doubt have been taken by the Beyk's rail lines to N'jafu. Unfortunately, a new edict was released, and we Knights are not permitted aboard those trains and must find a less direct path. Steel yourself. I have the suspicion that an hour of sorrow may yet lay ahead for us."

9

——————

SHATTERED

*"We are taking a day to collect ourselves, steeling against what is
to come both mentally and emotionally. The latter more of
importance for those of us in the group who are expected to
survive."*

—*Anargen's King's Day Journal*
27 Misbyr 1607 Middle Era

"There." Thomas pointed through the brush and handed over a spying glass that he said had belonged to Arnauld and had been slipped in among their things. Arnauld, the apprentice to Anargen's father who had secretly been an infamous Ecthel privateer in another life—"The Sea Dragon." It was astonishing to think how many lives would have ended if Cinaed and Glewdyn had not taken care of Arnauld at his lowest point. A simple act of charity may have made all the difference for them. It certainly was shaping that way this night.

"I see them," Anargen acknowledged. There were four

178

werebeasts, dashing across a ridgeline over which lay the rolling plain leading straight to Kirke. "They wear those hoods and cloaks to allow them to transform in the day as well?"

Thomas nodded. "We came this far on two different days in the zenith of noon and couldn't find an opportunity to get through. It's been overcast in this region ever since we arrived, or I should say they did. The endless rain is newer, but either way, the diminishment of the daylight and their coverings seem enough to allow them to be in those monstrous forms all the time."

"Something similar took place at Ordumair," Anargen acknowledged.

"How did you counter it?"

"We didn't," he admitted. "An army of Knights from Albaron and the Vogteremark came to our rescue, and with them, the light broke through the gloom.

"I don't think the High King has anything of that sort planned for this hour."

Thomas sighed, "Well, I guess we're left with our current plan."

"Looks like it," Anargen confirmed.

"It's a good plan," Glewdyn consoled as he grunted, getting down low with them. He reached for the spyglass and peered out. "I think the horses we brought will make the difference."

"That's all fine and good of you to say, but neither Seren nor I are particularly fond of this plan," Mia pointed out. "The danger isn't equitably shared amongst us all."

"And that's why there's even the faintest chance of success," Thomas pointed out. "If you, Seren, and Gregor can dash through the opening we create by drawing them off, you can get into Kirke and deliver the warning to the Viceroy. Plus, send us help."

Anargen thought that last bit was a reach. Even if anyone

in Kirke, Knights or otherwise, were willing to help, the likelihood they could reach them in time to be of genuine aid was minuscule. "You'll have Seren with you, and she can protect you in case more werebeasts are lurking past this line. It's the best chance any of us have at getting you into Kirke and rescuing the Viceroy," he reminded her, though his eyes were trained on Seren, who was conspicuously quiet.

Seren's arms were crossed over her breastplate, and her bearing told Anargen she had resigned herself to accepting the plan because they had no other choices. Even so, she wasn't likely to approve of this. Particularly not after Anargen had already spoken with her privately to convey his love and his hope that whatever happened, she would live a long and peace-filled life at the end of this, one of faithful service to the High King.

"If you fall, there won't be much left of me that survives," she had reminded him.

"The Lowlands are better with even a fraction of who you are than none at all," he had told her.

Of course, it did nothing to assuage her concerns, but what could be done? They couldn't sit idly by and let evil run rampant, and other people be cut down wantonly by these beasts.

Among the opinions expressed thus far, Gregor's was the most subdued. He simply stated, "Why should any extra effort be made to keep me safe? I'm not a warrior, poet, or sage."

After that, he had stalked off to don the armor left to him by Sir Hurstwell. At least those parts that fit well enough for him to use. Thomas had tipped Anargen off that Gregor was very much aware that as the only remaining legal claimant to the Monarch's throne through heredity, Gregor was as valuable alive as the Viceroy himself. Both Gregor and Mia represented the terminal points of Ecthelowall's two most powerful noble families, and if the Restoration was to succeed, they needed them.

"It's time to act, lads and lasses," Glewdyn informed them. "They've broken their patrol into small packs. Your time in wait hasn't been in vain. Knowing their behavior this well is a key advantage."

"Precious little good it will do when they all descend upon you," Mia pointed out, her voice bitter and her eyes fixed away from them all. As if to look on Thomas now might shatter her.

"We should reconsider having two ride per horse," Mia insisted. Her hands wrung the edges of the dress she wore. All three of those intended to go before the Viscount had spent time cleaning and patching their garments and making themselves look far less wild. How that would translate after a pulse-pounding flight across the rain-soaked plains on horseback remained to be seen.

"We've been over this," Thomas replied, sounding strained. Little wonder, given each of those not going by horseback had a very real likelihood of perishing before night's end. Which in no way lessened the desire to see the others safe—a painful position that left Thomas, like Anargen and Glewdyn, to be cut both coming and going.

"I don't care if it slows the horses. It's worth trying," Mia retorted. "Seren, please, you're even less enamored with this plan than me. You have to help me make them see reason!"

Her eyes fixed on the forest floor. "I don't like it at all, but we can't keep debating this. We should go get saddled up and ready to ride out."

Mia's expression shifted from hopeful to a grudging resignation. "Very well," she huffed and then stalked off to get ready.

In their absence, Glewdyn announced, "We must get in our own positions. Remember, you both are to head left. I'll go right, and our dear ones will race down the middle. If once they've cleared the ridgeline, and you find an opportunity, make for the moat around the outer wall. There's an outlet there. It isn't much, but it's all we have right now in way of chances to survive this."

Looking at each of them, he nodded. "Good. May the High King be with us and favor us all."

Waiting several minutes, Glewdyn gave them the sign that it was time to make their move. Vanquished or victorious, their fates would be decided in mere minutes.

Thomas shot Anargen a wary glance. As brave as he'd been so far and must have been to reach this point, the teen was still new to Knighthood. Anargen had learned how he lost his family and title to tragedy, how he lived nearly his whole life believing the Knights of Light to be fanciful exaggerations only to discover the truth in his darkest hour.

Pushing back against his own fear and worry, he nodded solemnly to Thomas. A moment later, they broke their cover and marched forward through the rain and gloom. With the fiery gleam of their armor, they must have looked like earthbound stars traversing the darkened landscape.

As they approached the ridgeline, they split their ways. Immediately, Anargen knew they needed to run because the beasts took the bait and began to howl, drawing their kind toward their position.

"Faster, Thomas," he urged as he pumped his arms and legs furiously, driving himself forward, feeling the High King's favor upon him, his *Evaggelion Eirene boots* carrying him faster than he could ever run on his own. They were streaks now, comets shooting across the ebony backdrop of Kirke's Plains— the sign for Seren, Mia, and Gregor to ride out.

Please be with them, Great King.

From behind, too close behind, came the lupine sounds of

the werebeasts, their hot breath almost touching Anargen's back as the monsters gained on the Knights. Thick, wet sounds of massive, clawed palms digging like paws into the mud filled the night, and he pushed himself harder and faster. They had to give the others as wide an opening as possible.

A whisper that should have whipped past at the speed he was going clung to his ear, and he grabbed Thomas's shoulder, using all his momentum to sling them both over the other side of the ridge. As they rolled to the bottom, he caught sight of a werebeast sliding face first into the mud with a whimper. It had tried to cut them off and attack, just missing them. Two of the beasts that had pursued them crashed into the other downed creature and tumbled with yelps down the ridge.

Two more of the pack that had been slower turned with greater ease and bore down on Anargen and Thomas.

Drawing his spiritsword, Anargen called to Thomas, "Back-to-back. Don't let them separate and double team either of us."

"Right." Thomas drew his own burning blade before backing up against Anargen.

Out of the corner of his eye, Anargen caught sight of a lone point of brilliance streaking over the plains and closing on Kirke's gates. Anargen smiled. The plan was working.

Okay, you beasts. She's safe, so let's see whether your bite can match your bark.

The beasts circled them, snarling, their enormous fangs laid bare. These weren't so imposing as the ones Anargen faced in Ordumair and certainly nothing next to the Grey Scourge. For a moment, he considered it might be possible for them to fight through the horde and reach Kirke outright, so long as they only came at them in these small groups.

One of the beasts lunged forward, and Anargen brought his shield up, bashing it against the creature's thick skull. It whined and shook its head. He almost stepped forward to deliver a finishing blow, but Thomas grabbed his shoulder, holding him back. The other beast sailed past, just missing snatching and rending him with its terrible jaws. The first lupine monster growled and went back to circling.

They set a trap. A fine reminder to never underestimate their scheming.

Another attack came an instant later, and this time, Anargen blocked but was ready and swung so swiftly that the sword whistled as it cut through the air and caught the beast across its shoulder.

Having never felt spiritsword fire apparently, the creature squealed, wheeling around in a panic as its fur crackled and smoldered around the wound.

Thomas nudged Anargen, and, picking up his meaning, swung around, separating just for a moment for Anargen to take a swipe at the other beast and Thomas to sortie against the injured one. The attack worked for Thomas, who delivered a devastating blow to the injured beast, but the other was too wary to stay within reach.

If the creature was smart, it would use time to its advantage and wait out the arrival of its kind as aid. Allow sheer numbers to overwhelm the teen Knights.

It seemed that bore out when the other three beasts bounded at Anargen and Thomas from where they'd crashed and tumbled earlier. They had to leap out of the way to avoid being trampled, and Anargen caught one with a glancing blow as it sped past. Rolling back to his feet, he found the other creature bearing down on him, crashing into his hasty block hard enough to drop him to a knee. It snarled and snapped and slashed at his guard until a clarion cry reached its pointed ears. A piercing howl that sounded furious and panicked in one.

Rearing back, the werebeast's face was contorted in wolfish

confusion for an instant. Looking from Anargen, its prey, to the call of the others, which had not halted but instead bore down furiously toward Kirke.

Understanding hit Anargen a moment before the beast. There was still a gleaming dot closing in on the city.

Seren! Those beasts spotted her!

Lunging forward, Anargen missed landing a piercing blow on the confounded werebeast, but it obeyed the summons just in time to ameliorate its distraction. Snapping at him, Anargen had to block, giving it the chance to race off.

Anargen turned to tell Thomas they had to pursue them, but Thomas was already running across the plains, trying to intercept them. Taking in a breath, Anargen joined in forcing himself to move faster and faster and never finding it enough.

Oh, no. Please, my Great King, please help!

If those things reached Seren and the others, they would be overwhelmed by them. There had to be at least nine beasts coming at them. But he couldn't run fast enough, not on his own. He needed his King's favor, the divine blessing he'd experienced only a handful of times. Thomas looked to be so endowed. Why wasn't he? Wasn't he the older, more experienced, and more accomplished Knight?

Right away, that thinking rang hollow, prideful. Pushing aside those thoughts, he ran the best he could and was startled to see a beast go down with a yip—a reddish glowing stripe across its left foreleg.

Thomas struck it as he passed!

Anargen came upon the monster and, barely slowing, delivered his own strike. The creature cried out in fury and agony and dropped. Not fatal, but sufficient to debilitate it for a time. Another creature in Thomas's path fell, and suddenly, Anargen saw a purpose to his slower gait. Beating the beasts there wasn't enough. They could overwhelm them and get past, but if Thomas wounded them as he came on them and Anargen finished in following, then they could weed out enough to give themselves a chance.

Leaping, Anargen delivered a hammering blow to the next hobbled werebeast, pushed off, and managed to keep his balance and momentum to keep going. They were so close now that he could make out the three horses ahead and beyond, only a league ahead, the outer gates of Kirke.

Another beast fell. A fourth after, and Thomas had caught up to the others and whirled around, brandishing his blade in a fiery arc, forcing the first of them to halt their pursuit for an instant.

Anargen suddenly found his speed increasing, and he was there by Thomas's side in moments, facing down five of the werebeasts.

Not the best odds, but once more, they were precious close to achieving their goal of giving Seren, Mia, and Gregor their chance to make it.

The werebeasts tried to move past to find a weak spot they could slip through.

A swift sword or stalwart shield burned in their path for every move, forcing them back with righteous fury.

The presumed leader of the pack eyed the Knights, then its own kind's ranks, and barked an order. They had been attempting to advance one or two at a time. Now they advanced five strong. Anargen and Thomas were forced to give ground.

The creatures edged around them, enfolding the Knights, surrounding them. This wasn't good. Once more back-to-back, Anargen knew this wouldn't work so smoothly as before.

Even so, he wasn't sorry. He knew by now Seren and the others had made it safely to Kirke's gates. Dying with that knowledge would be far from bittersweet.

Once more, the lead werebeast barked a command, and his pack tensed to pounce. Anargen steeled himself for his last fight, which he would make sure to thin the enemies' ranks and leave them nursing wounds long after this night.

"Away from them, you fiends!" Glewdyn cried out, coming into view like a sudden downdraft of flame. He careened into one, battering its enormous bulk aside with a ram from his shield, and turned and buried his spiritsword deep in the side of another before any of them could react.

Then, it was a mad brawl. Fur and claws and teeth against burning swords and shields. Each side fighting for its survival on near-equal footing. Every strike swifter than a falcon's descent. Every parry, every sortie, every lunge and slash timed with such precision as Anargen had never known.

As the werebeast between himself and his father fell to their combined blows, Anargen realized all the beasts were down except the leader of the pack.

Looking toward Kirke, the thing was barreling toward its gatehouse, abandoning all pretense and secrecy in its wild determination to destroy the others before they could reach their objective.

"We have to stop him!" Anargen shouted. Though he needn't have. When he ran, Thomas and Glewdyn were on his flanks at the same instant, the three of them favored by the High King to be alive but unable to take a moment's breath until this last foe was slain.

They crossed over the drawbridge and into the gatehouse, its guards and obstructions demolished by the beast's ferocity, and entered Kirke, closing on their enemy.

THIRTY-NINTH INTERLOGUE: WAR CAMP

The landscape's change was subtle at first and then abrupt for Jason. Having never been in the region, its seas of sand dunes with only a scattering of tiny oases and towns felt endless. They had scarcely rested a single night in the week of travel to get from I'jon to the outskirts of where Aridgulch's canyon and river met the lake, Lago Amurgo. Fortunately, Cinaed's point about the Beyk's rail lines didn't apply to all the lines between I'jon and N'jafu. Otherwise, the journey would've taken almost a month to complete. Even with some of it broken by trips in the boxcars that would admit Knights of Light, it wasn't a journey Jason ever wanted to repeat.

At least not in the excruciating seesaw between silence and surliness he experienced with Aria. Any attempt at cordiality, empathy, or tenderness was rebuffed. Part of Jason was happy to be facing a purely external conflict soon, one which his heart could weather far more readily than the stormy seas surrounding Aria.

It's your fault she's drifted into a maelstrom.

His internal adjudication was as swift and decisive as ever. Fortunately, Cinaed called out to them, "See there, children? We've arrived at what the Zilnen call the body and foot of the 'Great Vase,' that is, Lago Amurgo."

Up soared the dramatically striped stones with ruddy brick-like hues. Intermingled were tame saffron, creamy beige, stalwart slate, and even a mellow blue. Amidst it all were little glints that gleamed in the sunlight, which Jason didn't ask but presumed to be deposits of gold. At the end of the towering canyon walls was what looked like a natural stone fortress encircling a glistening sea. If Jason had not been told it was a lake, its sheer enormity at the edges of the desert would have led him to believe he was looking out on the Notiosanemos Sea. Over its pristine blue waters, he could see little dots hovering, which he took to be birds. All around the lake's lip were larger shapes with little tufts of silver or slate streaming from their tops. No doubt steamer ships, sailing to and from the start of "The Great Vase." Camped at the base of the Lago Amurgo was an enormous sprawl of green tents, soldiers of Zilnen.

"Surcalido calls Lago Amurgo the head of the arrow that divides the Realm," Aria noted. "It certainly looks like an implement of war now."

Tirzah spurred her horse ahead. "All the more cause to hurry. I know my father's tactics. He is at the head of those he leads to battle. We will find his tent at the front of the encampment."

"Easy," Cinaed urged. "We are not guests, and this is not a safe garrison. They have deployed at the base of the lake, and if they are so resting at ease, they must have seized control of it again from the Empire. Even if they took out the telegraph lines en route, no doubt word of what has happened would have reached Falkirke by now."

Turning her mount around to face Cinaed, Tirzah countered, "If my father wants to pretend to be Beyk, how can he fault the Falconress for seeking her charge? Surely when he sees what we've risked, what we're willing to risk, he won't turn a blind eye on our love."

"This isn't a fairy tale," Aria urged, her tone bitter at first, then gentler, pleading, "I can't say how your father will react, and because none of us knows that, we must be cautious."

"But if we sneak in under the cover of darkness, and with a Wernstrum no less, I know Father will think us traitors," Tirzah pointed out.

Jason sighed. Once more, the point of a thorn wounding them all. "Then send me alone now. I'll surrender to him. If he hears me out, then he's merciful enough that I'm sure he'll send for you."

"And if not," Cinaed rebuffed, "You could be killed, lad."

Jason nodded. "Yeah, well, it has been my privilege to know and fight on the right side of this Quest with all of you, even if for a short time."

He felt a yank on his coat sleeve and saw Aria had moved up beside him. "What are you doing?" she whispered with a furious scowl.

Jerking his coat free, he replied, "Reminding you that stories can shape us for the better." Then he spurred his horse on, galloped past everyone, and headed straight for the encampment. At his back he heard Cinaed adjuring the others, "No, let him go. Hard as it may be ..."

The rest was lost to the pounding of the horse's hooves on the tighter-packed rocks and dirt as the sands gave way fully to the cliffs. He did not let up until he was close enough that the camp sentries could see him approaching. He slowed to a trot and held his hands up the entire way to them.

One of them, younger than Jason, rushed to meet him. He

held up a blade, a scimitar or talwar, point first at him. He spoke in short nervous sentences using the Zilnian language, of which, unfortunately, Jason knew precious little.

The other sentry, noticeably more seasoned from his gait and the steadiness of his hands on the rifle he aimed at Jason, spoke in Ecthelish, "All right, you. Stop where you are. State your business."

Reining his horse to a halt with one hand while he kept the other raised, he replied, "I bring urgent news for Sadiq Kharoum."

Holding the rifle steady and not wavering for an instant, the sentry shook his bearded head, causing the bronze tassel of his green fez to swish through the air. "No. I think you are mistaken and need to turn back now."

Jason swallowed as he heard the rifle's safety click off. "I mean no harm. Please tell Sir Kharoum that Jason Landsby has arrived with urgent news from the north."

Cocking his head to the side, the sentry squinted at Jason, scrutinizing his face. Then he fired his rifle.

The shot went wide, and it took Jason clenching every muscle he had control of not to jump off his horse or heed the sentry's advising and gallop off. In truth, the horse he rode now must have seen its share of conflicts in the past to be so bold now and not spook itself. "Please. It is urgent," he repeated.

Once more, the sentry fired a shot, this time not so wide from the mark, coming dreadfully close to hitting Jason's arm. From the precision of his movement, it was intentional, and Jason could understand why this man was on the watch. If he realigned again as he had, he would be aiming straight at Jason's heart, and he had no doubt the sentry would not miss.

Taking a steadying breath, Jason stated again, "I'm here with important information for Sir Kharoum that will have implications for the battle ahead. Please, just send him word that Jason Landsby needs to see him."

"Is this message of yours worth dying for? I won't miss again."

He nodded in reply. "Worth my life, yes. Because it isn't only my life at stake."

The sentry seemed to mull this over for several seconds, his dark eyes peering as deeply into Jason's as they could, examining him. It wasn't so potent as Cinaed's stare but was thorough and forceful. At length, he said, "Nemir, bring word to the Kolağası. If he sees fit to inform Müşir Kharoum, then we bring him. Otherwise, return forthwith."

Trembling a bit, the other sentry sheathed his sword and saluted in the Zilnian fashion. "As you command. 'Jason Landsby, urgent news for Müşir Kharoum.'"

"Good. Now, off with you."

The younger sentry took off, leaving a faint dust cloud behind him. By Jason's estimation, it would take him at least five minutes to pass on the message.

To Jason, the remaining sentry addressed, "If you haven't left by the time he returns, your life's blood will be upon your own hands."

"Understood," Jason replied.

Several minutes later, far longer than Jason felt sure meant good things for him, the other sentry ran up again. The young man kept casting anxious glances at Jason. He whispered something in the older sentry's ear.

"So let it be done," the older sentry concluded. Addressing Jason, he said, "Well, Mr. Landsby, it appears I will need you to come with me." Lowering his rifle, he added, "Please, leave your horse here."

"Of course," Jason replied and climbed down from the horse. As soon as he sat foot on the ground, he knew something was wrong. He managed to turn around just enough to catch sight of the rifle butt as it connected with his jaw. He went down hard, pain exploding at the site of the impact as spots drifted in his vision. He knew what came next. A second strike hit him from behind, and the world went dark.

FORTIETH INTERLOGUE: PARLAY

"*Ugh*," Jason groaned as consciousness returned to him. By now, he should have been well acquainted with being knocked out and rudely woken again, but he supposed this wasn't the sort of thing to which the body ever acclimated. As the pains in his jaw and the back of his head throbbed, he also realized he was soaked. It wasn't until his eyes began to focus properly that he made out the person responsible. It was the sentry from before, bucket in hand. The man snarled something in Zilnian and then spat on Jason.

Though it was by far not the smartest response, Jason chortled and burst into a mad laugh. The similarity between this moment and when he'd awoken a prisoner of the Sombra was so pronounced that it was darkly ironic, tickling his pain-fuzzed mind.

A backhanded slap landed on the already contused jaw, freshly awakening its pains and amplifying them. Apparently, the sentry had not seen the humor in his being captured and tortured for the second time while in Zilnen. This was further confirmed as he launched into a fresh round of hot-blooded

Zilnian profanities and threats. At least Jason took them to be so.

Taking stock of the surroundings, he could see he was in a tent, one for meeting or perhaps expressly for interrogating prisoners. There was only the chair he was strapped into with a rope. His coat was folded up on a nearby table and across it was laid his spiritsword, still in its sheath. It occurred to him they had left the light plate mail he wore underneath his outer shirt.

Another hard smack struck him, and he looked up to see the sentry had a furious expression. Was he honestly upset that Jason had ignored him?

Two more strikes seemed to indicate so. Then, the next smack became a punch. And another. And another. Jason was already too foggy to count them all, but he was strangely clinical about the whole thing. He'd seen it enough times when young. An enforcer was sent to "chat" with someone, and things would take a wrong turn. The thug would lose his temper, and once he started raining blows on the interrogee, it invariably ended in someone having to dig a midnight grave. If his lips weren't so damaged and swollen and his jaw so sore, he would've laughed again at the irony of what was happening. Was there anyone in the Lowlands who didn't want him dead?

From the entrance to the tent came a bellow. Jason couldn't really see who was there. One eye was swollen shut, and the other had his overlong bangs obscuring his vision. Whoever did the speaking apparently had to tear the angered sentry off him and throw him out of the tent.

After those sounds faded, there was a long pause. So long that Jason thought he would slip back into unconsciousness. A gentle smack to his forehead cut that off.

"*Ah.* I haven't much time, so don't waste it by passing out on me," the person before him instructed.

Even without being able to see clearly, Jason knew it was

Sadiq. "Defender," he mumbled through the haze of pain and muffling of his swelling. "Good to see you again."

Sadiq grabbed him by the hair and jerked his head up. "Do not call me that here, you fool. Only a handful know I hold that title."

"Is that why the guard beat me?" Jason asked. "Doesn't like Knights?"

"No," Sadiq replied with a sneer and jerked Jason's head down again. "He hates Wernstrum slime."

"If I see any, I'll let you know right away," Jason retorted, spraying little spittle drops of blood out as he did so.

Sadiq rolled his eyes and stepped back, wiping a few drops off his uniform. "Do you honestly expect to deceive me with such protests? I have evidence of your family's schemes they—"

"Have been smuggling materials to a shipyard on the sea between Surcalido and Zilnen for months. They've also been harvesting some kind of fruit that is of significance, but I don't know anything about that."

"Fruit shipments? Omar must have hit you too hard. Your lies are completely incoherent."

"Rehalcyon is preparing for a war that's bigger than just Zilnen," Jason snapped, his patience faltering. "You must know what's happening in the north and the east. Something big is looming just over the horizon. It could be that the King's Day is rushing now upon us all."

"Poetic nonsense is still nonsense," Sadiq replied, hands behind his back. "Is that why you came here? To attempt to frighten us with your threats of a Lowlands-wide war? If we do not fight now, then Zilnen is lost. Do you truly believe we will just lay down and let you walk over our backs to build your Empire?"

"This is ridiculous," Jason seethed. "We came all the way here to warn you. I've fought werebeasts, Sombra, been attacked by a direnoir and doppelgänger, and beaten by your soldier to get to this moment. And now you're acting like I'm the monster!"

Shaking his head, Sadiq looked a little off-put. "Ah, I see you're employing the same tricks Defender Black uses. Telling spooky tales to push people the direction you desire, *hmm?*"

Jason sighed and sank into the chair. "No, the histories are meant to build you up. Prepare you for what you will face, warn you against dangers, and help you remember what matters."

"As I said, poetic nonsense. The facts are against you, though I still am curious how you came to be in our camp alone. Surely your family doesn't hate you that much."

"Never mind my old family. I'm here as your brother-in-arms, trying to tell you that if you don't change course, it will end disastrously for everyone." Doubting this was getting him anywhere, Jason tried some of the old tricks he knew to get out of bindings and found frustratingly enough that whoever tied him to this chair knew what they were doing.

Sadiq grabbed him by the collar of his shirt and got in his face. "You and I will never be on the same side. Your people must be erased. I will not let millennia of Zilnian splendor be spat upon by you filthy, wretched mongrels."

There was a wildness in Sadiq's eyes. Desperation can either push you to the High King or push you into a spiral toward destruction. Jason feared the latter was true for Defender Kharoum. Gentler in tone, buoyed by a swell of empathy, Jason reminded him, "I'm not here to be your enemy. And neither is Defender Black nor Aria."

Sadiq pushed Jason back and turned away from him, fists clenched. "Defender Black was once a good friend, but he forgets his place and should have been replaced long ago." Turning to Jason again, he pointed at him as if in accusation.

"His judgment is so sorely compromised he actually took you into his inner councils. How many innocent people have you threatened, beaten, and maligned for your family? How many businesses ruined? How many lives ended for profit, power, or both?"

No opportunity to respond to the charges was afforded. Sadiq shook his head, a dreadful scowl making him look dark, menacing in the shadows of the tent. "If he refuses to see reality and respect the boundaries of his realm, he, too, will get swept away."

"Surely you don't mean that," Jason replied, stunned. "Maybe you can't see you and I as brothers-in-arms, but he must be for you."

Drifting toward the tent flap, Sadiq replied. "I cannot tell whether you genuinely believe the virtues you're espousing or merely trying to twist them to your own ends. I have seen enough of the latter in my life to know the former aren't binding in the Lowlands."

How far into doubt and despair has he drifted? He sounds worse than I did when I ran away.

Sadiq opened the tent flap to leave, and Jason called out, "Tirzah came with us. Will you sweep her away too? She feels just as strongly that we must warn you against the dangers you face and how they affect the whole Lowlands. If you can't trust me or Defender Black or Aria, can't you trust your own daughter?"

Releasing the flap, Sadiq marched back over and backhanded Jason hard enough to knock him over in the chair. As Jason coughed from kicking up dust on impact, Sadiq snarled, "I thought all this time I'd raised her better than that. Smarter. But she has betrayed me like her mother. If Zilnen can only be saved by trampling over traitors, dubious allies, and rebellious children, then it must happen."

Jason coughed again and forced himself to say through the scratchiness in his throat, "What about the High King? No man or woman totally eschews guile and self-interest, but he did, and he cares for each of us. I've seen him. He came to me, Defender. You're right that I'm loathsome, and so is my family, but seek guidance from the High King before you act rashly. He will guide you to the truth."

"If he would choose ..." Sadiq stopped himself. He looked torn and started speaking several times before grumbling in Zilnian and exiting the tent.

Heaving out a sigh and wincing from the latest rounds of pain to beset him, Jason closed his eyes and whispered, "Please, Great King, deliver him from this hour of danger. Help him to see your hand and to take it."

Then he closed his eyes and tried to push past the fear and pain. He knew the High King would prevail, even if he couldn't see how from where he lay.

10

WITHIN THE WALLS OF KIRKE

*"It is strange now to think how blind I was to the nature of the
Lowlands and the depth of its shadow. Tens of thousands of
people in Kirke have a monstrous beast stalking among them,
and they do not know. Would they want to know? Is it easier to
go through life unaware of the evil?*

*"No! Terrible as the reality may be, I cannot ever go back to not
knowing the truth and the light. And I wish none remained
unawares of the King's Light and all it reveals. "*

—Anargen's King's Day Journal
27 Misbyr 1607 Middle Era

"**I**t went this way," Glewdyn called, waving them down another side street.

The werebeast's incaution at revealing itself must have diminished somewhat once it burst through the last gatehouse of the city and found itself targeted by arrows and bolts from sentries on the walls. The Knights passed those still shaking from witnessing its entry and from the cries of terror loosed by hundreds of citizens milling about a market space, which was only a few blocks from the gatehouse. Though the arrows and bolts were only nuisances to creatures of its kind, the secrecy in which werebeasts existed was far more damaging to lose. This was no Ordumair, where no survivors were expected to live to tell the tale. If people knew such darkness existed, it might galvanize a disturbing number to seek the remedy of the High King's light. And so, the monster moved them far from the central thoroughfares and places of prying eyes to the seedier, less frequented parts of the city—those which few would desire to visit. Even fewer admit to doing so.

"I think it ducked into that old storage yard," Thomas added as they reached another intersection of streets.

Dashing over to the storage yard and scaling its short wall, Anargen had to leap aside and roll as he came over it because that section of brick cracked and gave way. A collection of weathered barrels and crates alongside the wall were smashed by the stone as well. With all the rain, the soaked wood splintered and muted the sound of the collapse.

Looking up, Anargen saw the werebeast looking at them from atop a building down the street. Scrambling back to his feet, Anargen called out, "He's there!"

The trio raced along the street side as the werebeast loped from rooftop to rooftop. The dinginess and decay of abandonment in the impoverished district gave way again to stone and wooden façade-bearing buildings, which rose nearly twice as tall. Imposing, with refined details and architecture, these likewise yielded in time to still taller, more impressive stone structures. Monuments of Libertias and the most impressive of structures surrounded the three Knights, and they soon found themselves wading through a sudden swell of people and animals. The fiendish beast had changed tactics again and led them into the central market.

As quickly as it had entered the area, it exited, but this time with Anargen and the others unable to pursue. Over the din of the crowds and the ten thousand transactions, Anargen heard his father say, "We've done what we can. We should get to the palace. We had scarce to hope that Seren could bring Mia and Gregor before the Viscount, we never gave thought to how difficult it could potentially be to safeguard the Viceroy."

"He's right," Thomas called out. "The sooner we can get to the Viceroy, the sooner we will be able to turn the tide against Ilyron."

"Lead on then," Anargen replied, still somewhat distracted. There was no shaking the feeling that they were missing something.

Traversing the city from the market to the palace gates felt oddly normal. People pushing past, watching for horses and wagons, and the complications of navigating the city's sprawling streets were utterly unremarkable. Had they really just been battling and chasing a mythical beast? It made Anargen feel as if he were caught somewhere between waking and dreaming.

Things didn't quite become real again until he approached the palace steps. A smaller moat with an ornate stone bridge over the waters surrounded the structure. Beyond this lay a plaza stretching before the gates leading into the palace grounds.

The plaza was wide with tiled designs of an eagle and arrows, the symbols of Libertias. With all the rain, the tiles looked particularly sleek and shiny. About halfway across, Thomas tapped Anargen on the shoulder and nodded toward the square's periphery, where a topiary maze spiraled off in what must be an emerald arboreal marvel during a good sunny day.

Standing over near the maze, under the cover of a sprawling oak tree, were Seren, Mia, and Gregor.

Thank you, my Great King! Oh, thank you!

Faster than was seemly, he rushed over to Seren. She must have caught sight of him and forgotten about propriety, too, because she moved quickly toward him. Totally ignoring decorum in public, he wrapped his arms around her, lifting her off the ground.

Fortunately, the High King's armor was lighter and less bulky than other plate mail. It made the experience far less awkward. And it permitted Seren to reach up and brush his lips with a quick kiss once back on the ground.

"Thank the Great King," she said, her voice catching. "We saw how many of those monsters there were out there. They came very near to catching us."

"I know," he replied, leaning his head against hers. "Those were some of the most harrowing moments of my life. But we're here now, together, delivered by the High King. We can safeguard the Viceroy and finally move forward with the Quest."

Seren leaned away and frowned. She gnawed at her lower lip.

"What's wrong?"

"I'm afraid it won't be that simple. The guards have refused to admit us."

"Apparently, I don't look regal enough to be a noblewoman," Mia called out. She was pressed into Thomas's arms. From the way he held her, there was now little question for Anargen as to the nature of Mia and Thomas's relationship.

Mia continued, frustration and disillusionment weighing down her words. "Nor did they find Gregor impressive enough to be heir to a throne. These commoner soldiers do not know any of the nobility of Ecthelowall. There is no heraldry to display, no seal nor signet that we can produce to sway them."

As if having been rebuked, Gregor scowled and kicked at the stones edging the court. At times, he seemed so sharp, and others, like a much younger child. There was something about him as if Anargen had met Gregor before, though it was completely impossible from what he knew about him.

Setting the peculiar familiarity aside for pondering later, Anargen looked across the plaza at the guards. Sure enough, a pair of them in Libertian blue stood at attention, halberds crossed, steely helms sleek with rain, and neither flinching from their post despite the storm.

Also out, despite the unyielding rainfall, were several others, servants by the look of them, working after a task of unloading some supplies. However, something seemed off about them. The sensation that he was missing something hit Anargen again. What was it about them?

Gregor must have noticed Anargen's scrutiny and perked up out of his dejection. "Of course, we don't look like nobility, so let's go mingle with the commoners. We can come alongside those servants, offer our help, and get into the palace with them!"

Immediately, apprehension about the plan seized Anargen, though he couldn't place why. On its face, it wasn't an awful proposition. All the same, he challenged, "But won't the other servants realize we aren't from the palace? And what about those of us dressed in armor? What servant has that?"

"You'd be surprised about the churn of servants at a big castle or estate such as this. There are always lesser nobles seeking favor, sending gifts with servants and an armed escort," Mia rejoined. "Gregor is right. If you all put down your faceplates, and he and I play up our humbler natures a bit, drenched and dirtied as we are, we can pass for servants. We can even bring the horses with the bags."

"Deception isn't the way of a Knight of Light," Glewdyn commented, wariness in his tone. "We can attempt to slip in unnoticed, but no lies. If they stop us, we must be open with them. There is no other way for us."

Mia scowled but, after a moment, nodded. "Very well. I won't say I like our chances any better for it, but I've seen you Knights do marvelous things." There was a note of awe when she said it, and she glanced at Thomas, who flushed red.

Shutting his helmet, Thomas said quickly, "Right, so we all should get moving. Those other servants are heading for the north side of the palace. We'll need to circle wide to catch up and avoid detection."

Moving swiftly, they made a wide circuit through a parallel topiary with low stone walls and rose bushes interspersed with the common hedges. Mia's dress caught on it and tore a bit, adding to her desired aesthetic. Weaving through the rest of the maze, they slipped in between two groups of servants hauling goods along. None of them asked anything of them, though Anargen noticed one of the men kept eyeing them peripherally. His gaze was unnerving, even if he was unassuming. He had a dark hood draped over a rough, worn grey tunic—an average serf amongst others. Just then, he whispered something to one of the other servants. Both men looked back ever so discreetly at Anargen and the others, then turned around.

What was that about?

Coming upon the north entrance, which was far more functional and far less ostentatious with both its decor and design, Anargen gritted his teeth. There was a porter ahead. Examining each group before making notes on a ledger, he kept safe from the rain by standing under a portico. Along with him guarding either side of the wide doors into the palace were two more Libertian soldiers. Each group of servants ahead paused to allow his once-over and then moved on.

Anargen tried not to let his gait stiffen, but this was the very thing his father had warned about. If they confessed their true intentions and nature, they would surely get placed in irons or kicked out of the city. Either outcome effectively ended their bold endeavor and doomed the Viceroy. Even so, his father was unassailably right. It would go against the core of the Order's nature to not speak truthfully. And from experience, it benefitted no one to subvert the truth.

Every step closer raised his heart's pace. He wondered if the porter would hear it thumping wildly. They were just outside the doors, standing before the porter now. A plump man in a moderately dressy waistcoat and breaches. He mumbled something as he jotted some details into his huge leather-bound ledger. Putting his quill into its inkwell, he looked up, his bristly mustache that wrapped around his face twitching with annoyance. "Well, what are you gawking for? Get inside unless you aim to make merpeople of yourselves and everyone behind you. Planning to take up residence in the moat, *hmm*?"

Anargen looked at Glewdyn, dumbfounded. He couldn't see his father's expression for the faceplate, but the older man's sage eyes were wide with puzzlement like Anargen's.

"Ugh, you aren't the keenest spades digging the garden, are you? Get inside. Now!"

With that, the pair of guards strode forward and ushered them inside rather brusquely.

The group wandered after those ahead, traveling up a set of stone stairs and through several winding corridors until they reached what appeared to be a storeroom for the kitchens.

They were now alone with a gang of servants who had

preceded them into the palace. Among them the shifty-eyed pair.

Everyone from the group unloaded goods, mostly exotic spices, herbs, and dried fruits. There weren't any guards here, just a pair of scullery servants busy looking over some things in the other corner of the room.

"You there," the shifty man addressed them. "Help us unload. It's the least you can do, given I got you into the palace."

"Pardon?" Glewdyn said. "You got us into the palace? Why did you do that?"

The man straightened, and as he did, Anargen felt an icy chill of dread. Like the moment while dreaming, he became aware that he was actually in a nightmare. In a huskier, thicker accent of the southwestern Lowlands, maybe Rehalcy, he replied, "Because I told them you were with us, and I needed someone to take the fall."

"Take the fall?" Mia repeated.

The man grinned wickedly and grabbed the servant he'd spoken to earlier, jabbing something into his side and tossing him into Glewdyn. Slipping backward, he yelped in his less obvious accent, "Help! Murder!"

Dropping to a crouch, he pulled up his dark hood and cowl, disappearing into the shadows in seconds just as everyone else in the room converged on the Knights.

To Anargen's horror, a dark dagger was buried in the other servant's side. The servant groaned and went limp as red spread along his rough spun tunic.

FORTY-FIRST INTERLOGUE: IRREVERSIBLE

Jason winced as he woke up and found, for a change, the sorest part of his body was his back. The sounds of an engine running, a truck's in fact, grabbed his attention. As he sat up, he saw all around him boxes of supplies. Over him was a beige canvas covering. A sudden jarring bump sent a fresh jolt of pain through him.

I'm riding in a truck. Well, being transported in one, anyway.

His hands were bound behind his back, but the swelling in his eyes was better, and his lips and jaw, though not the best, had improved. How long had he been unconscious that he was healing? More importantly, where was he now?

The scenery out the back of the covered truck was no help. Much of Zilnen looked similar to him, though his contused nose did pick up hints of something he couldn't quite place.

A shudder ran through the truck, and it slowed to a stop. Sounds of the engine died away, and Jason could hear a steady sound between scrubbing clothes on a washboard and a sigh.

The sea, I'm smelling the saltiness of the sea. Why would they bring me to the coast?

At the opening of the canvas cover, a pair of Zilnian soldiers stalked up. One pointed a bolt action rifle at Jason. The other undid a gate to the bed and began unloading supplies. Two other soldiers ran into view, ferrying the unloaded cargo out of sight. From their hushed conversation, the mystery of his being brought here didn't seem likely to have an imminent resolution.

Once the supplies were unloaded, the guard with the rifle gestured to Jason. He spoke a command in Zilnian, which Jason took to mean he had to get out. Struggling to comply through his aches and limitations from his bonds, he dropped to the ground beside the vehicle and squinted in the bright sunlight. Sure enough, they were along the coast, though where exactly was the question. This was a slightly higher location, and in the distance, Jason thought he could see the outline of several tall buildings. Out at sea, a dark arc of what must have been ships were arrayed. It was too far away to make out the colors or architecture fully, so he didn't bother speculating what he saw.

A jab to Jason's back took his attention off the distant port and back to walking where directed. It appeared he was being led to an impressive tent, sitting atop a beach dune and colored with the light green of Zilnen. It looked much more akin to the royal tents that would've been deployed in Anargen's day than the practical canvas ones he'd seen at Aridgulch.

Directed up to the entry, the sentries on either side-eyed him with suspicion but allowed him to be pushed through the soft fabric that felt like velour as it brushed over him. Inside, his eyes again needed to adjust, but he could tell right away this was Sadiq's war council chamber. A large table with a map of the area was spread out with carved pieces meant to represent the forces for either side. There were a number of people in the tent—generals, by appearance, or müşir, as the Zilnians called them.

Chatter in the room clamored with many strident, boisterous voices standing out came to a complete end. Defender Kharoum stood in the midst of them, bedecked in an ornate and completely ceremonial uniform of Zilnen design. He wore a fez with a golden tassel and a golden, fringed sash over an otherwise standard officer's suit jacket. His pants were extra billowy and tan, and he wore dark black riding boots with gold inlays. There were medals pinned to the side of his outfit opposite the sash for achievements and honorariums Jason could only guess after. A bejeweled black scabbard with ribbing of gold for a scimitar hung from his hip, and one black-gloved hand rested on the pommel.

There was no sign of a single item of *Palatini Lucis Aeternae* armor on him, and he certainly did not bear a *Thyreos Pistis*, the shield called "Faith." So ardent and imbued with the High King's favor, no projectile could pass through its surface. No fire or acid could burn through it. It would be a simple and obvious choice for imminent battle. The absence of the fiery implements of the King of Light left Jason uneasy. Either Sadiq was not going to fight today, or he would be forsaking the very tools that were his surest defenses.

Sadiq's eyes narrowed as if he was aware of Jason's silent critique and found the appraisal bothersome. He called out something in Zilnian to the others, and they, with noticeable reluctance, quieted and left the tent. One of them intentionally knocked Jason aside with his shoulder as he "brushed" past. When the tent was empty, Sadiq strode forward, his hands clasped behind his back. "Welcome to the outskirts of Port Amurgo. You are on the cusp of seeing history made here. Your Rehalcyon interlopers shall be destroyed today, and the glory of Zilnen's remainder shall stand forth unassailable evermore."

For several seconds, Jason wasn't sure what to say. It all seemed like Sadiq was in the grips of megalomania. Why did he care what Jason thought of this? Perhaps he didn't at all, and there was some other facet to him being brought here to observe. "What about Sir Amine?" Jason inquired, thinking that might be the reason.

"What of Kaveed? Did you manage to fool him, too, with your rumors of wars that aren't being fought?"

It took tremendous control not to sigh. "He's out there, just like Tirzah feared. Isn't he?"

Sadiq scowled. "If he and Tirzah hadn't been so selfishly focused on their own wants, then he would be standing here beside me. He's fortunate for his conniving that he wasn't sent to the Ash Dunes to be devoured by sand scourges."

The flush of heat in Sadiq's voice subsided, and he added, almost as though he were reassuring himself, "Besides, he trusts in the High King. If he is favored, he will live."

The memory of the flash and Dr. Antoni's death struck Jason like a slap. "That isn't how it works. You can be favored and still fall in battle ... or be murdered."

The last he said under his breath, and he didn't think Sadiq heard, primarily because the Zilnian hadn't run his scimitar through Jason right at that moment.

It did succeed in raising the other man's hackles. "What do you know of anything related to the Kingdom of Light? You're just a hustler from the northland. I've been Defender of the Southwestern Realm for twenty years."

"And Cinaed has been the Northern Realm's Defender for probably three times that long. Doubt me if you want, but you're playing into my brother's hands!"

That seemed to take Sadiq aback. "You freely admit your family is behind the atrocities that have befallen Zilnen?"

"I never denied the Wernstrums were behind it. But I've

been hurt by them about as much as anybody. I left that family years ago."

Sadiq's eyebrow quirked up. "That isn't what Tirzah told me. She told me you abandoned Defender Black. Your story is always flip-flopping. Reality isn't a fixed thing for you. It's whatever twisted lie you can concoct to suit your desires."

The Zilnian held up a finger and shook it. "But no more. Look at the deployment before you. We have seized the Aridgulch, cutting off communications and reinforcements for the port. Surcalido and its navy are joining Zilnen's to blockade the port and ensure no one escapes while our armies come in two waves to siege and destroy it."

Jason looked at the map and the positions of all the tokens representing the forces. The orange Surcali navy was adjacent to the minty green Zilnian ships. On land, there were three armies for Zilnen positioned as described. Two had the letter S inscribed on them. The other, far larger, had an *M*.

What did the *M* stand for? Jason felt like he should know, but his thoughts were still disjointed from the beating he'd taken. It seemed an important detail, but all he could say was, "That's a very large map for such a small piece of the bigger picture."

Sadiq huffed. "Oh, this is just the start. Zilnen will take the war to Rehalcyon. First, we liberate the rest of Aridgulch and restore Zilnen's traditional lands. Then Anstara. By the time we're through with your Empire, no one will fear your flags and their silly little bird."

If Jason had been able to conjure a retort or any sort of response, it would've been cut off. A pair of the more resplendent officers from earlier entered and spoke quick words in Zilnian, then departed.

Sadiq smiled, walked to the back of his tent, and pinned the flap open. "It has begun. Come. Witness the end of your Empire's terrors."

"Please, take a moment to pause, breathe, and reassess the landscape," Jason implored. "You've been looking at everything as a Zilnian. You must stop and see it all as a Knight of Light. There is more going on than a flare-up in a regional dispute. You must sense that. Don't you hear the High King's warnings for us?"

Half turning to Jason, Sadiq cocked his head to the side and offered a chilling counter. "Perhaps instead of watching the battle, you would prefer transport to the Ash Dunes. The sand scourges may savor the taste of your foul flesh above the Zilnian criminals they're accustomed to." Waiting a few seconds, Sadiq added, "I didn't think so. Now, watch."

FORTY-SECOND INTERLOGUE: ON WINGS OF CHANGE

There was little to see for certain from the vantage point Sadiq offered. He availed himself of a set of binoculars throughout the hours of combat. Couriers brought steady updates to the progress of the campaign.

The only indicators of something happening in the scene beyond were the sporadic bursts of smoke from ships being struck by cannon fire. There were also occasional curls of smoke around the city itself.

At some point, Sadiq began reciting some history of the port. It, like Aridgulch, changed hands numerous times over the centuries. The city had some high walls built during the late Middle Era and an older city within five-foot walls in various states of crumbling resilience from the Ancient Era. Neither were expected to stop the Zilnian bombards being employed. Though, it would mean the city couldn't be rushed as they had with the Aridgulch settlements.

As the day wore on, Sadiq's enthusiasm morphed into begrudging defiance. It was clear he hoped to take the city before his reinforcements arrived, and a period of stalemate was hampering that ambition.

Jason, in turn, though keeping his eyes on the spectacle and his "head down," was wondering what Cinaed, Aria, and Tirzah had done when he hadn't returned and no word for them to come had arrived. At least, he hoped none had. He loathed the thought that they, too, had been captured and tortured and were now being forced to watch this pitched battle, unable to say or do anything to get through to Sadiq and so hated by all the other Zilnians, they could be murdered at any moment.

As the sun arced toward setting, Jason noticed dark shapes flitting up into the air from the midst of the city. They looked like raptors but would have to be by far the largest birds in the world to reach such sizes to be distinguishable from here. They seemed comically lackadaisical as they circled in the sky over the city, almost like carrion fowl. Suddenly, a group broke off and zipped toward the ships in the bay. There was a flutter of them turning direction, and one of the battleships exploded in a burst of flames. Immediately, the ship listed and keeled over.

As if waiting for that as a signal, the other group of darkling vultures swooped over the city and past its walls. Little flashes of fire and smoke and dust exploded from the path they took. Sadiq, who had been seated reading over some kind of report, leaped to his feet and looked through his binoculars. He said something in Zilnian that Jason had guessed by now to be a profanity.

He looked back at Jason, his face gaunt with bewilderment. As his eyes focused on Jason, however, his expression hardened into the cast of anger. "You! Did you know about these flying deathboats?"

"What?" Jason replied, confused. "Flying death boats? What in the Lowlands do you think I had to do—"

Sadiq backhanded him across the cheek, reminding his contused flesh it had far from fully recovered from his injuries. "Tell me now, what is the secret of these flying machines? I have seen gliders that can fly in and join the birds for the briefest time. These, however, are like monstrous wyverns of steel!"

"I promise I'm just as surprised as you are. I've only ever seen dirigibles and balloons for air travel. I had no idea these existed."

For several seconds, Sadiq glowered at him. Seeming to neither disbelieve him nor to be capable of accepting Jason's words as truth. His indecision was broken by a courier arriving, being carried under each arm by guards. The young man was covered in dust and sand and ash. He had a bright red wound on his shoulder and face.

A flurry of words was exchanged between Sadiq and the guards. A handful of weakly warbled ones came from the courier before he slumped in the other's arms.

Sadiq shouted several things and whirled back to look through his binoculars. The horizon glowed rosy and auburn as more and more coils of smoke rose from where Zilnen's troops and ships were positioned.

The other commanders rushed out onto the overlook. Any apparent awareness of Jason's presence gone. To the commanders, Sadiq issued sharp-tongued orders, but the dynamic of earlier seemed fractured. One in particular, an older fellow with silvery white hair, pushed back, shook his head and countered multiple times before Sadiq grabbed him by his vest and gave him a shake, shouting and pointing toward what was looking more and more like a devastating route.

That was when Jason noticed a wedge of dark shapes on the horizon growing steadily larger. Three, perhaps four, aircraft had broken off from the main squadrons and headed straight for them. "Defender, er, Mus ..., um, Kharoum. They're coming!" Jason fumbled to get out. Still, the cadre of Zilnians ignored him.

Fortunately, the guards at the defensive perimeter around the camp were paying attention and opened fire. One of the dark shapes dropped, but the others were on them, and there was a whistling sound that Jason instinctively knew meant danger. Leaping off the backside of the dune, he tumbled down the sandy slope. Behind him, the ground erupted in a spray of sand and rocky debris.

Jason spat out sand and tried to clear it from his face, complicated by his bound hands, but he was able to right himself and watch as the planes whirled by overhead. Another went down, crashing somewhere dozens of yards past the camp. Ringing in his ears made it difficult for him to hear if it was soldiers in the camp shooting it down or if the planes were malfunctioning. There wasn't a good answer, as the other craft neither crashed nor made another pass. Instead, they formed up and headed back toward the port.

Smoke poured from somewhere nearby, and Jason climbed the dune again to check on Sadiq before giving it a second thought. Atop the dune, Sadiq was half crouched next to the older commander. The officer was lying very still on the ground. Another of the commanders held his head as a fourth tried to speak to him. In this chaos and confusion, Jason realized no one was concerned with his whereabouts. The impulse to run seized him and was withered a breath's space later. The firmly whispered injunction against such an escape came to him, leaving Jason standing there divided. That he had no trouble hearing it when other sounds were somewhat muffled forced him from his flight.

Okay, Great King, what should I do?

Revealing himself seemed like a terrible idea. So, stealthily, he crept back, slipping alongside the tent to crouch behind its corner and some singed beach grass. He lost his line of sight but was hidden. As the ringing faded in his ear, he could make out conversations.

The voices were heated and had threads of fear and fury intermingled until they all suddenly went silent. Jason thought another squadron of planes would attack them, but given there were no sounds of gunfire from the camp, he quickly abandoned that hypothesis. Now that he was listening more attentively, he could hear voices from the camp yelling and the sound of trucks pulling up. From the rumbling, he could make out one had arrived, and many more were coming after it.

Gnawing his lip, Jason crouched tighter to the tent and the long swaying blades of the beach grass, hoping he wasn't visible from the other angles available to these new arrivals. There wasn't much to be done in either case. His muscles quivered from the strain, holding himself tensed at the new angle when he heard fresh discussion begin. Though he couldn't see it to confirm, he thought several new arrivals had stepped out onto the dune. This was born out when Jason heard a woman speak up in the tongue of the Empire, "Of course I have arrived. Such perceptiveness has clearly served your efforts on the battlefield in my absence."

The voice was unfamiliar to Jason. It was a bit high but still had a settled quality that made him suspect the woman was firmly in middle age or older. From the haughty way she spoke, Jason guessed she must be a person of some importance. Zilnen wasn't known for suffering women to use sharp tongues.

"I did not know you spoke the language of our enemy now, Mesnara," Sadiq commented. "Its harsh syllables suit your speech. But now is a rather poor time for your caviling."

A chortle rose from Sadiq's ex-wife, whom Jason almost tried to peek around the tent to see. Ultimately, he thought better of it. "Caviling? Hardly," Mesnara countered. "Would you argue that those planes we observed flying overhead weren't a sign of this battle slipping out of your hands?"

"You know about those infernal desert wasps? These planes?"

"Perhaps," she replied.

A chill shook through Jason. The way she had said it was so pointed that even without seeing or knowing Mesnara well, it was clear this conversation was drifting off kilter.

There was a pause before Sadiq spoke again, "Then help destroy them. You have arrived a day earlier than discussed, and though it will rob me of my honors, Zilnen's glory comes first. We will accept your aid now."

"My aid is not being offered," she replied with a scoff.

Something is wrong with this.

Jason dared to lean out just enough from his safe place to glimpse the corner of the campsite beyond. He could see that more than just trucks were arriving. It was the other army from the map, except instead of camping nearby and sending Mesnara and other commanders to coordinate, the new arrivals were surrounding the perimeter.

Oh, boy. Definitely something wrong.

"We do not have time to play old games and salt old wounds, Mesnara," Sadiq grumbled. He slipped in several other statements, this time in Zilnian.

"The past is indeed dead and entombed, Sadiq. Or it soon shall be."

There must have been a silent cue because there were sounds of a struggle and a scuffle.

"Mesnara, what are you doing?" Sadiq cried out. His question was punctuated by a gunshot that almost made Jason spring out of his hiding spot. His heart hammered in his chest. She shot Sadiq?

FORTY-THIRD INTERLOGUE: FAMILIAL DYSFUNCTION

Jason's fear was immediately allayed as Sadiq grunted, as if fighting against restraints, and shouted, "Mesnara, what treason is this? Have you gone mad?"

"Watch your words, Sadiq, or have you forgotten what the law says about your kind?"

"My kind?" It took a second before Sadiq's confused tone transformed to one of understanding. "The Knights of Light have nothing to do with what is between us or the peril you are placing our people in with this petty play for power. Hate me if you must, but will you doom all of Zilnen to strike back at me?"

Some of Mesnara's poise and superior timbre dissolved like a volcanic fissure opening in a flash of heat. "You deceived and brought shame on me. How dare you dismiss that?"

"It was more than a decade ago!" he bellowed back. "You have done well enough since."

"Don't you try to claim my resourcefulness as sufficient recompense. Especially not as you try to repeat that old ruse to the injury of Naomina!"

Jason flinched at the accusation, so he knew Sadiq must

have. How did Mesnara learn so quickly about Kaveed and Tirzah's secret marriage?

"What are you talking about? I treasure her just as Tirzah. Didn't I arrange a marriage with the Beyk's nephew for her? Is her future as wife of the next Beyk something lamentable?"

Unable to resist the urge to look at the scene, Jason had most of his concerns confirmed. Two guards held Sadiq, and the rest of the commanders were kept in place by swords or gunpoint. At the center of the spectacle was a woman dressed in traditional black, whose hair and face were reminiscent of Tirzah's if sharper and marred by a scowl that the lines on her face betrayed was often an expression she wore. He wondered how contentious her basic nature had been and how much was bitterness and hardship from her position as a divorced Zilnian woman. From the robust makeup and abundant gold jewelry she wore, it would be difficult to say life had been too hard for her. Or at least hard in the ways Jason had become acquainted with.

She tilted her head back at that moment and grabbed fistfuls of her wiry silver-streaked hair. She uttered a frustrated groan. "How can you still be so fixedly deceptive? What am I talking about? *Ugh!* You would have our daughter relive my shame by marrying a knight of folly like you!"

Jason caught the flicker of relief on Sadiq's face, probably because he shared it perhaps in a less potent dose. Jason wasn't an expert on Zilnian culture, but he knew enough that Tirzah and Kaveed's rash decision would've been devastating for both of them, whereas now, perhaps only a loss of face and prospects for Kaveed may take place. Ironically, he may even be permitted to wed Tirzah publicly.

At least, that was Jason's initial hope. But if that was Mesnara's grievance, she didn't need to capture other senior Zilnian military leaders.

How could I be so dense? This is a coup!

From the shrewdness in Sadiq's stare at his ex-wife, he, too, must be coming to see this as more than a family dispute. "Well, if you continue to impede my army, you will not have long to worry about Kaveed. He is on the front lines. He is unlikely to survive without your troops' support and my directing."

Mesnara considered this for a moment. "I suppose that would satisfy the terms of my bargain as well as any other. But I cannot chance his escape. The Emperor's envoy was very clear that Kaveed must die."

"What did you say?" Sadiq asked, his face betraying the same bewilderment, setting Jason's heart pounding again.

"He must die to satisfy the terms of the treaty I signed on behalf of Zilnen with the Rehalcyon Empire a fortnight ago."

"You can be cruel in your mockeries and jests, but surely this is too far. We may see little common ground between us, but Rehalcyon is evil. It is an abominable stain on—"

One of the guards socked Sadiq in the stomach, effectively cutting off his recriminating.

"Rehalcyon is the future, Sadiq. If you could take your head out of the past instead of burying it in the sand like an ostrich, perhaps you would see it too. As a client kingdom of Rehalcyon, Anstara has already begun to outpace Zilnen in terms of industrialization, productivity, and development of every sort. The wealth and strength flowing into Anstara outstrips all of Zilnen, even though Anstara has always been the lesser brother between us. Think of what Zilnen could accomplish if it had the same opportunities and advancements —Zilnen would be the jewel of the South once more!"

"At what cost? Rehalcyon will gut our lands, turn us into mindless slaves for their Emperor, erase everything that defines us as we are."

She shook her head. A sneer of disapproval on her maroon lips. "That is the point. We are now a stodgy, derelict floating into its moors to rot away to scrap wood.

"But why am I arguing the points of this with a man who uses three-century-old battle tactics? You didn't even know planes existed. That they could be used so devastatingly on our forces. All of you are the stony statues of a bygone era weighed with moss and weathering, dragging down all to ruin with you. Burying Zilnen for future ages to uncover and pity."

She all but spat the last bit. "Your execution was the easiest term for me to agree to. I did have some pause over Tirzah's, though."

"You desert hag!" Sadiq screamed and lunged at Mesnara, jerking free of his detainers.

Mesnara drew back a step. Another of her soldiers stepped forward and struck Sadiq square on the chin with the stock of his rifle. As Sadiq reeled backward, the original two gripped him even tighter, forcing him to his knees with his arms jerked back at painful angles.

Approaching him like a feral cat, Mesnara glowered down at him. "If it costs the lives of you and your order for Zilnen to thrive, then so be it.

"Perhaps you can at least take comfort knowing that also newly added to the list of terms is turning over your favorite scapegoat for all our woes. The envoy was clear that Jason Wernstrum, your prisoner, is to be turned over immediately."

Sliding back, Jason's heartbeat sped. It became difficult to breathe silently. He felt suffocated, as though no amount of air could suffice to meet his need for it. The Emperor's envoy wanted him dead too? That meant the envoy was likely his brother.

Dorian, no. What have you done?

FORTY-FOURTH INTERLOGUE: DOUBLY INDEBTED

"Of all the horrid terms which you have no doubt cursed Zilnen to bear, that is by far the one I despise least. However, it seems your Emperor is bereft of his prize. Wernstrum was on this dune before the bombs fell. The smoldering, blackened residue in that gaping hole where he stood is your prize."

Jason found his breathing still further stymied. Was Defender Kharoum actually imagining Jason had been blown to ash, or was he just bluffing to see what Mesnara would do in response?

The outcome could not have been Sadiq's intent. She strode forward, slapped him hard enough to spin him toward the ground, and declared, "That is unfortunate for you. Nothing stands between you and the firing squad, then."

To someone Jason could no longer see, she addressed, "Take him and the rest of these disgraces away. Pass the word— no one loyal to the Beyk and old Zilnen lives. Flank the forces remaining outside the port and wipe them out. Understood?"

"Yes, Your Highness," a gruff male voice replied.

The sounds of shuffling and struggling resumed, but only token resistance was put forth. They must have too much pride to look desperate. And Jason did not hear a single word further from Sadiq as the last of them passed into the tent, and the flap fell shut.

Jason waited a handful of seconds and then crept behind the tent. Hoping he'd heard everything rightly and he was alone now.

He stood there for a few precious seconds, unsure what to do. What he had just heard changed everything. Dr. Antoni's insider information had been misleading. Surcalido wasn't betraying Zilnen—Zilnen was betraying itself. And if this battle were any indication, Rehalcyon would not only have its crucial port, but the vast tracts and resources of Zilnen now among its assets. It could completely cut off Ecthelowall and its western allies from eastern trade routes and supply lines, strangling them. He had to get word to someone, anyone who could use the information to stop this before the war for the Lowlands was already lost.

What am I doing? I have to get to Sadiq. Detestable as he's been, he doesn't deserve this.

Jason impulsively slipped inside the tent. Not even bothering to first listen for sounds within. He tripped on an overturned table and went down, just catching himself enough to not make a ruckus or harm himself. Who was he kidding? He wasn't rescuing anyone like this.

Reaching out to push himself up, his fingertips brushed something warm. At first, he jerked back from it, fearing a burn, but in absence of the contact, his fingers ached as if caught in a peculiar longing for the heat. Pushing aside some debris, he found a bolt of purple cloth. Sticking out from one end was something like a metal stopper. Jason recognized it a second later and frantically unrolled the fabric to reveal the gleaming metal of his spiritsword.

Grabbing it, the flames whooshed up the blade, and a moment later, he had his bonds cut. As they smoldered, he gripped the sword in a tight hug. Sadiq must have been keeping it as a souvenir.

I wonder if he has my shield too.

After a short search, Jason found his little buckler, which he affixed to his arm. With both sword and shield, his chances of survival greatly increased.

What about Sadiq's chances?

It didn't look good for the other man. And as Defender of the Southwestern Realm, he was of enormous importance in overcoming the looming dark.

That did not make it any easier to rescue him, of course, but feeling the heat off his spiritsword once more, Jason knew hope was not lost.

Creeping back out of the tent with his Knightly implements and the dark fabric that had hidden the sword draped around him, he thought he could sneak along the camp's perimeter and locate Defender Kharoum.

Hiding among crates of supplies unloaded with him earlier, Jason watched as the soldiers already present were rounded up and marched, hands over their heads, into the desert. About forty or so soldiers were located at the camp to be removed.

Sadiq isn't with them. Where did they take him?

That's when he spotted him. Already shackled with the other commanders, they were being led to the center of the camp. Thinking to get closer, Jason almost slipped out of his cover, but two of Mesnara's soldiers came over to the supply crates just before he could. Ducking down and covering himself in the fabric completely, he heard one of the pair say, "Hurry up and grab all the petrol you can. Her Highness wants us to set the whole camp on fire. It'll be the perfect distraction."

"Just as long as we're a long way off when it all goes up," the other replied. "You gonna carry some too?"

"Yeah, yeah. Keep your fez on. Here ... *hmph*, I'll take this one."

"So considerate," grunted the other.

It took a few seconds for them to struggle out of Jason's line of sight. Rising slowly, he observed the pair of soldiers a few seconds longer, confirming he understood their plan. Indeed, they were dumping gallons of petrol all over the camp, as were several other teams.

Jason shuddered off a chill. Those soldiers had been speaking the Imperial language, and he understood why now. They weren't Zilnians, only dressed like them. Most of those present were clearly from elsewhere in the Lowlands. There was a scattering of Zilnians among them, but the majority were likely Rehalcyon troops masquerading as Zilnians. Combined with the fire, the retreating true Zilnians would be rushing into a massacre if they tried to join their "reinforcements." He had to rescue Sadiq and get to the front lines as soon as possible. At least with Sadiq with him, the soldiers might not try to shoot him on sight.

To do that, he'd have to make his way around the camp and cut Sadiq free. After that point, he had no idea what he'd do next because although he could imagine it being possible to sneak to Sadiq and even free him, how they would get out thereafter was impossible to conceive.

"Nothing is impossible for you, my King. At least I read that once ... I believe it's true. So, I'm going to need your help now. Please."

Spotting another opportunity to move across the compound, Jason dashed over and ducked behind a tent. It had markings on the side and the size to match a medical tent. The explosion still muffed Jason's hearing, but he guessed that they hadn't decommissioned the medical tent even with the roundup. Or rather, he hoped it hadn't been yet. Injured men don't move very fast, and he wanted to believe they weren't so ruthless as to simply kill them.

The sound of footsteps crunching over rocky soil near the tent startled Jason. He stumbled back from the corner he needed to round and just managed to keep his footing. A soldier walked past. His head was turned right, facing away from Jason.

Scrambling over to the guard, Jason grabbed him from behind, covered his mouth, and threw him on the ground behind the tent. Before he could get out more than a gargled gasp of surprise, Jason struck him on the back of the head with his buckler. The soldier went slack.

Well, he's out for a bit. So, that's one down and only about ten thousand to go.

For a moment, Jason dithered over whether to take the man's uniform. It would certainly look less suspicious than a sheet of cloth if he were spotted. But the man he'd just struck was about a head shorter than him and at least forty pounds heavier. No one who gave him a half-second's look would buy how comically ill-fitting his uniform would be, not with how crisp and formal the Zilnians were. And the Rehalcy, for that matter.

Peering around the medical tent again, Jason spotted a group of soldiers approaching the space where they had lined up Sadiq and the others. The line stopped its formal lockstep, and someone blew a horn. Activity around the camp halted. All eyes turned toward the spectacle unfolding.

Oh, no. I'm out of time.

He'd have to rush over, cut Sadiq free, and then fight his

way out of there. Through a large chunk of those ten thousand troops.

Suddenly, the impossibility of the task felt different to him. It was not as though the High King couldn't empower him for the task. He was sure that was within the Sovereign's power. But there was a pressure, like a hand heavy on his shoulder, holding him back, telling him no.

It was such a peculiar sensation to want to throw himself into certain death for the obtuse man facing execution. Particularly given how readily he would've let just about anyone die to save his own life before he'd begun this Quest before encountering the High King and beginning the process of refining by his fire.

But why? Why is Defender Kharoum going to die? Why did Dr. Antoni, but you rescued me? I didn't deserve it.

Whether through his own thoughts or the familiar whisper, he came upon the point afresh—none of them deserved rescue. They were all rebels by nature. But what Sadiq faced now was different from what the other commanders would endure. The High King promised to bear all his servants living and felled to his Kingdom. For Sadiq, it would be a pause and then a journey beyond description. For the others, it would not be so. Perhaps theirs was the end he should mourn most heartily.

Jason backed away. Though it stung worse than all of the Zilnian soldiers' blows, it would be best for him to go now while everyone was distracted. He could easily slip out, get to Kaveed and the other soldiers, and warn them.

Drawing in a deep breath and steeling himself, he turned and dashed back the way he came, heading for the beach again. He'd run along it and then climb up onto the road once far enough from camp.

He made it onto the beach and started down the coast along the sand, dried and packed tight from the tide being out when the first shot's report reached his ears. Jason lost half a step but pressed on, pushing himself as fast as his legs could carry him. Faster, he was certain, for the special boots the High King had provided. Every wind-cutting step fixed on the thought that Sadiq had finished his task. Twice now, Jason had stared down the insight that he may well come to a like or worse end. He hoped he had the courage to face it and bear his King's banner high to the end.

FORTY-FIFTH INTERLOGUE: TEST OF SUBSTANCE

Crossing over onto the road to the port town was a stark call for attentiveness. Craters were interspersed every so many feet. Some still smoldered from the recentness of the attack. Artillery pieces, soldiers, horses, and others lay fallen. A few destroyed vehicles and even one of the attacking planes marred the landscape. Near sounds of gunfire and explosions were distant enough to be echoes of the living amongst the dead, adding to the macabre sensation of passing through the battlefield.

There were no active forces for either side visible to Jason until he got within thirty yards of where the road wound into the city and, by appearances, had a substantial section of the old outer walls destroyed. What looked like a group of ten soldiers acting as a rearguard rushed out to meet him.

No, no. We don't have time for this!

"You there," called one of the soldiers. "Halt. Identify yourself, or we open fire." In earnest on the threat, the soldier, along with four others, raised their rifles and aimed them at Jason.

How do I get past them, my King?

A rush of warmth enveloped Jason, and he replied in haste, "I'm Jason, and carrying an urgent message for your Kolağası." There was more he meant to say, but he had to pause. All the Zilnians were looking at him in surprise, and he could tell why. He had just spoken to them in Zilnian, and now that he considered it, they had spoken to him in their own language as well. But Jason had never learned enough of the language to speak it so fluently.

Familiar and forceful, the whisper from the High King reminded him he shattered chains, even those shackling men's understanding of one another. And that time was short.

"Please, I must warn him that there's been a surprise attack on the primary camp. Müşir Kharoum has fallen, and an army posing as reinforcements is marching this way."

The first soldier to address Jason tugged at his curly black beard, eyes wide and thoughtful. Another from the group, however, scowled and leveled his rifle at Jason. "You may talk like a Zilnian, but you look like those cursed Imperials and wear useless antique armor. The only sort I've ever heard to do that are those doubly despicable Knights of Light. We should shoot you where you stand!"

"Aydin!" the first soldier called out, reproving. "This battle has already been a strange one. We cannot act in haste." To Jason, he addressed, "What proof do you bear? Be careful, stranger. Answer wrongly or in guile, and we will kill you."

Jason gnawed on his lip. How was he supposed to convince them? His story sounded insane, and his pack of smooth-spoken lies was emptied by pressure from the High King heavy on him, even now. "I ... I'm, as you say, a Knight of Light. I was being held by Müşir Kharoum and witnessed the attack on the camp. His ex-wife, Mesnara, betrayed the Müşir. She has sold all of you into the hand of Rehalcyon in exchange for sole rule as the

Beygum. That is, Beygum under the auspices of the Rehalcyon Empire."

"Lies! A warrior of false light guides us over a pit of scorpions while promising great treasures!" cried another soldier standing beside Aydin.

Jason shook his head. His impulse was to complain he wasn't offering treasures, but he felt sure, somehow, this was a proverbial saying in Zilnen. Much as his trust that the words he spoke were the ones he needed and continued to be rightly translated without his effort. He pinned his hopes on the insights from beyond himself as true. "I'm not bearing you false counsel. Any moment, the camp to my back will burst into flames, and a courier from the Beygum's army will arrive, instructing you to retreat and reinforce the Müşir as though on his behalf."

"Then you will not object to us awaiting the envoy's arrival, you purport as false?" Aydin challenged, sounding incurably skeptical.

"I would happily wait to be proven true, except there is no time. If you wait till the courier arrives to begin the escape, even if you do heed my words, the Beygum's army will have time enough to move to intercept you."

Jason realized his tone had turned desperate, and between his tattered remains of clothes, battered face, and shocking news, he must seem insane to them. He had to turn things around and fast. "Listen, bind me. Take me in shackles, blindfold me, drag me through the streets if you have to, but whatever you do, please don't disregard this warning."

"You heard him. Bind this fool and drag him through the streets," Aydin declared, a snicker on his lips.

In the distance, there was a sound of an explosion. Everyone turned to see a flush of flame rise up like a sudden puff of smoke from a man's pipe. The horizon burned against the indigo backdrop of twilight.

"I can't believe it," one of the other soldiers commented.

Aydin shook his head. "This proves nothing. He is doubtless a pawn pretending to advise us to take a safe route of escape that ends in a trap. I say we kill him and send his body back the way it came on a donkey."

"Aydin, stand down," the first soldier instructed. "I will take him bound to the Kolağası with Timur and Cyrus. You stay here with the others on guard. If what he says of the other messenger comes true before I return, bring the other messenger also bound. We will let the Kolağası sort this out."

"You can't be serious, Farzhad. This spawn of a desert hag deserves death."

The age difference between Farzhad and Aydin looked to be in the latter's favor by Jason's estimation. Aydin's defiance dissolved under the sternness in Farzhard's eyes. Aydin into an abashed capitulation of, "Of course. As you wish." Jason guessed Farzhad must far outrank his outspoken and suspicious compatriot.

"Good. Now, bind him," Farzhad demanded. Four of the soldiers not aiming their rifles at Jason bound him with impressive speed and only a touch of unnecessary roughness. Once finished, they handed the lead tied to the bonds to Farzhad.

"Come now, messenger. You have your desire. Begging the lion's attention, however, may get you eaten." With that, he jerked Jason along after him, heading through the shattered wall segment into the town proper.

That saying, Jason guessed, was from the semi-cultic reverence the Zilnians had for their mythic winged-lion, which was difficult symbolically to distance from their nation itself and its Beyk. The quasi-divine nature each of the three held in their society was part of their hatred for knights, who disavowed all of them. Jason took it as a sign he was still a long way from accomplishing his goal, even if this Farzhad was kind enough not to execute him on the spot.

Within the town of Port Amurgo was a mixture of older structures, some the domed rectangular prisms of Zilnian architecture, some the buttressed and colorful cubes of Surcali design. Still others were less interesting to see, less ornate in detail. These Jason took to be the recent construction of the Empire, which favored function over form in this strategic locality.

Most buildings were still intact, but many were smoking and reduced to jagged bits of rubble betraying the stones and material favored in each culture's composition. This was the first time Jason had been on a battlefield. At least one that wasn't a street under contest between rival gangs and only marked by a spray of bullets. There was a strange potency to the silence of the ruins left behind by the blustering of the cannons and rifles farther in the city, even if fewer bodies were strewn behind.

A jerk from the lead turned Jason's attention from the scene around him. Farzhad led them around a corner and nodded to the other two soldiers. They headed back around the corner far enough for Jason to not be able to hear their booted footfalls against the beige stone of the streets any longer.

Farzhad muttered something under his breath and, turning to face Jason, produced a knife, long and curved enough to qualify as a talwar, and pointed it at him. "You swear you are a Knight of Light? If you are not, now is the time to renounce your lies. The penalty of keeping them is steep."

Jason gulped. Apparently, he had misread Farzhad as the compassionate one. His perspicacity was of a more malevolent sort, it seemed. Even so, wasn't this the very kind of moment

Jason had asked for strength to weather to whatever end not fifteen minutes ago? The High King had brought him swiftly to it, so swiftly he would respond. "I'm the servant of the High King of All Realms. In death and life, bound to my oaths. Which I must honor, whatever the penalties incurred."

At this, Farzhad nodded and replied, "Very well." With a flick of his wrist, he struck.

FORTY-SIXTH INTERLOGUE: SUCCESSION

Eyes shut, Jason felt the wind off the swing against his face and tensed for piercing pain of the wound the sharp weapon had inflicted. In its stead, he smelled singed coir fibers. Looking down, startled, he saw his bonds were severed and smoking. In Farzhad's hand, the talwar was now glowing faintly and licked with flames. "You're a Knight? And not killing me?" Jason blurted out, half wild with giddiness and surprise.

"Not so, loud," Farzhad reproved. "We are not among those friendly to the Order, whether Rehalcyon or Zilnian. I apologize for the deception. I had to see for myself if your oaths were genuine, and the Great King granted my test." He reached out to Jason. "Brother-in-arms Landsby."

Jason gripped his arm back and repeated, "Brother-in-arms, Farzhad." With the shock fading, his wits went to work. "You know my name?"

"I do. My cousin Kaveed spoke about you in the past."

"He did?" Jason wasn't sure whether that was a good or bad thing.

Farzhad looked off to the side. "I said some ungenerous things about the Empire we fight and its people. Kaveed reproved me and used his recent encounter with you as evidence that not all of your people are evil."

"The Empire isn't exactly 'my people' anymore," Jason replied, unable to constrain the wistfulness the admission brought. "I'm sort of wanted by it at the highest ranks."

"I know what that feels like," Farzhad replied, somber as a storm. "Perhaps it would do each of us a kindness to consider that we belong now to a people distinct from our lands of birth?"

Jason nodded. "Yes. I think that might be how to best look at it."

Glancing around the corner, Farzhad whistled a tune and waved toward the other two soldiers. They came like well-trained pets. The pair, who looked so like each other they might have been twins and were no doubt Jason's age, each shot equally surprised and pleased looks at Jason's cut bonds. "Brother-in-arms?" the one called Cyrus inquired.

"Yes," Farzhad answered, quicker and louder than Jason could manage in time. "We're going to take him to the Kolağası as planned. I think we all need to heed his warning as genuine."

The disciplined Farzhad turned and moved through the ravaged streets much faster and freer now. So much so that Jason felt sure he was seeing the fleetness he'd witnessed in Sir Cinaed when he'd first joined the quest. Having experienced it himself, it was still a marvel to behold. Especially since Farzhad didn't even look behind him to see that Timur and Cyrus were following, which they did without question. Jason half-wondered if they would've left him to escape at this point because none of them turned to see that he was following.

An urgency gripped his heart, telling him now wasn't the

time for such idle wondering. "Thank you," he whispered and felt the warmth within his armor seizing into his legs and lungs, and he was in flight, careening down the streets, catching up to the others just in time to watch as their route became erratic, ducking into blasted out shops, vaulting over debris, and cutting corners so sharp it would split a string held perpendicular to the corners. All around, the sounds of the firefight grew more intense.

As he reached Farzhad's side, the others slowed, veered to the right, and ducked through a half-collapsed archway. He was walking now on the other side, his hands raised as if in surrender. Jason kept a hand on the hilt of his spiritsword and slowed to a trot and then carefully crept in with Cyrus and Timur directly to his back. All three emerged into a plaza that had a cracked fountain and some makeshift tents that were hastily erected. Ringing the plaza were curved facades of tall buildings that blended Zilnian and Surcali architecture in ways neither people group would accept in any other facet of their culture. More importantly, however, Jason found about twenty others surrounding them.

"We're here to speak to the Kolağası," Farzhad announced.

"Who's the prisoner?" one of the others, a particularly gruff-looking older man, inquired.

"No prisoner," Farzhad clarified. "Tell Kolağası Amine I've brought Jason Landsby to him with urgent information about the battle."

The old man huffed and, using the same whistling call Farzhad had used earlier for Cyrus and Timur, nodded to a younger Zilnian boy with all his hair shaved. He was maybe fifteen. The teen ran off without further instruction.

"Kaveed is the Kolağası?" Jason asked under his breath, genuinely surprised.

"Yes," Farzhad replied matter-of-factly. "It is a hard thing for a Zilnian to listen to his junior. I have memories of Kaveed from before he could walk or talk. But he is a closer relative of the Beyk than I, and now, it seems he will surpass me in ranks of both my peoples."

It took Jason a moment to realize what Farzhad had meant. It seemed the other took for granted that Sadiq was gone and, therefore, Kaveed was his successor. Though, with his erudite calculations and quick thinking earlier, Jason should have expected him to deduce that as logical, given Jason hadn't said Sadiq had sent him explicitly, and he wouldn't have been his guest.

He wasn't sure what to say. Consoling Farzhad didn't feel right, and they didn't have time to discuss what the hierarchy of the Order implied about servant-leaders or the heavy price those in authority in the Order must be ready to pay to safeguard their charges. He thought about Sir Cinaed from Anargen's era, his sacrifice, and all the times the Cinaed, whom Jason knew had put himself in tremendous danger to keep Aria and himself safe. It was probably for the best that Jason, Farzhad's junior in just about every way that matters, didn't attempt to correct him at this moment.

The perceptive Zilnian raised a brow. "You have something you need to say?"

"Oh, well, I suppose—"

Any further discussion was cut off as a finely dressed Zilnian burst onto the plaza. Garbed in a black vest and fez with a green sash, under which was clearly the armor of a Knight, Kaveed dashed over to Jason and gave both him and Farzhad quick embraces. "Brothers-in-arms, it is good to see each of you. I'm told you have news to share?"

"Yes, Kolağası. It appears matters are worse than we feared," Farzhad replied and gestured for Jason to speak.

Stepping forward, he wasted no time switching gears to retelling what had happened. For Kaveed, he left out none of the details that before would've made it unlikely for a stranger to trust him but ultimately characterized everything properly, including him arriving at Aridgulch with Kaveed's secret bride, Tirzah, and being taken captive and beaten by Sadiq.

At the end, which took far less time to relate than Jason expected, Kaveed looked crestfallen. "I can't believe he's gone. Are you sure?"

Jason shrugged. "I never saw him escape, and there were thousands of soldiers."

"You escaped," Timur pointed out, then blushed and pursed his lips inward, apparently having broken a social protocol by speaking out.

Before anyone could reprove him, Jason replied, "I did, but Sadiq, er, Defender Kharoum, led them to believe I had been killed, and so they weren't looking for me to slip away. He, however, was perhaps the most targeted man in this conflict. I had not realized how deeply Mesnara hated him."

"Hates all of us," the older man from before pointed out. "It seems she would have us all dead."

Kaveed's hand was to his chin, and he looked deep in thought as though the comments hadn't touched him. Or perhaps touched him more deeply than anyone else. He was at the focal point of all the familial turmoil and political intrigue driving the reversals in alliances.

"Indeed," Farzhad agreed. "We are in shifting sands. How will we relay this news to the rest of the forces in the city? I know we are a mixed company, but I can see Bahnam and Javion aren't among us. How many others from the Order are missing?"

"Are you suggesting we abandon our fellow Zilnians?" the older man asked, a challenge in his tone. "They're our own flesh and blood. Surely, we would rescue even the cruelest of them over this Rehalcyon." He gestured with displeasure to Jason.

At this, Farzhad kept silent, though Jason could see the pain and conflict in the man's dark brown eyes and the bend of his thick black brows. Was he afraid to challenge the other man because he was older or higher in station socially? Or was he still conflicted about their freshly agreed-upon identities as Knights of Light over all else?

"Enough of that," Kaveed spoke up. "Jason has been confirmed to be a brother-in-arms and bore us a message of warning when he was under no such obligation and, by all appearances, had every reason not to do so. I can't help thinking of Defender Black's stories of Anargen and how he fought for the Ords who hated him. Would you speak ill of such compassion, Shamsher?"

"No, Defender," the old man replied without a hint of begrudging in his voice. His eyes were still sharp on Jason, but Shamsher seemed deeply committed to honoring the social order.

"I'm not *Defender*," Kaveed corrected him. "But we will need to get word to the others. Timur, Cyrus, come. I trust you each with my life. You must get word to Nizamulmulk on the frontline. Tell him we are withdrawing—he will never retreat, so be sure to describe it as a withdrawal. We must take the Path of the Lion's Back."

At this, the whole encampment erupted into contentious squabbling. Jason gaped at the change.

How bad is this plan if they could hold their peace through everything I told them, and this sets them off?

"Brothers-in-arms! Settle! Settle!" Kaveed called out. "I'm aware of the dangers, but there is no other route. With Mesnara siding with the Rehalcyon Empire, they have no doubt already retaken Aridgulch, and it would place the Surcali in an awkward position to harbor us as refugees. After this devastating setback, they will no doubt reassess their place in the war fast approaching. Our only chance is to reach Qirthen among the Yusbilsi."

"The Yusbilsi are no one's allies!" Shamser protested.

Perhaps it was the continual drone of cannon fire underscoring their current predicament or the supposition that Aridgulch had already fallen and, therefore, Jason may have lost Aria and Defender Black to that monster Mesnara. Whatever the source, Jason didn't hesitate to point out, "Then they aren't the Empire's ally, and at this point, testing our chances with a group of people who can't be bought sounds far better than waiting to die for certain at the hands of those who would cast all of you off without second thought to scrounge out a place among Rehalcyon's ranks. The longer you dither without heeding Kaveed's orders, the closer you all come to forfeiting the chance to escape graciously provided you by the High King."

Once more, silence fell heavily on those assembled. Kaveed patted Jason on the back and spoke with a gentle firmness over the intense cannon fire. "Jason speaks truthfully. But he does not know the dangers of the Lion's Back. You all do, so any of you who wish to follow may. Those who do not, I release you from your obligations to the Beyk with honors." To Cyrus and Timur, he added, "And be sure to convey that message to Nizamulmulk as well. Anyone who fears this path may choose his own."

Drawing in a deep breath, Kaveed finished, "Now, everyone, pack all the supplies you can, and we will exit from the north gate to the city before we lose hold of it. I suspect these Rehalcy will deduce what is happening shortly, so move as swiftly as eagles. May the High King smile upon you and grant you his favor."

As Kaveed concluded speaking, the sounds of the cannons gradually faded. In their place, sirens pierced the air, shrill and terrible as a banshee. "Oh, no," Kaveed mumbled. Then to everyone shouted, "Find cover! Air raid!"

FORTY-SEVENTH INTERLOGUE: ONTO THE LION'S BACK

No sooner had Kaveed issued the warning than Jason heard a whistling. A building three blocks away exploded in a thunderous shower of stone as a plane whizzed past overhead. Staggering backward, Jason scrambled to find cover. Two more planes came into view as the smoke from the first's bomb cleared.

There were so few places of haven on the plaza, particularly since Jason was, by all appearances, the slowest to seek it. He heard the whistle and saw the back half of the plaza explode from the second bomb's impact. Curling in a ball, tiny bits of stone plinked off his armor, and one bigger one clipped his left arm. It hit just right to deflect off his buckler but sent him sprawling from the force of the impact.

Wasting no time now, he dashed for the nearest archway to a shop and, finding it full, rounded the building and ducked down in the space between the two buildings, holding his buckler overhead and closing his eyes. Try as he might not to, he shook a little. This was the worst sort of danger. One that you could hear coming, see coming, and had no real power to escape.

"Please, my Great King. You've brought me this far. Please see us through this. Don't let the hope of uniting your Knights fail now."

There was a cacophonic shout of stone being mortally wounded, and Jason felt the ground shake under him. He could not bring himself to move. The bomb had struck so close, and being between the two buildings, he would easily be crushed by debris from either. Still, he couldn't bring himself to emerge from where he hunkered low.

"Please, my Great King. You must hear me! It was you who shattered my chains. You've safeguarded my steps to come this far. Please, help us!"

Another whistle sliced through the air, and again, Jason felt the ground shuddering under him as if even more terrified than him. Jason smelled smoke, heavy and thick, billowing to him, mingled with dust from pulverized stone. He coughed and unclenched himself enough to get low to the ground, evading the choking cloud. There were moans from those wounded, those dying. Crackling sounds came from the stone close by, threatening to give way. They couldn't take one more hit like this, or they would all die, and the entire quest would falter.

He started to plea again for deliverance, this time angry and bitter that they would fail. Before the words reached his lips, he recalled something from the stories about Anargen. Those of his time in Ordumair during the siege when everything had seemed lost and after they had just narrowly escaped death in Cattingsford but had no certainty of the morrow.

"Sometimes we are called to make a stand, even if it ends in sorrow. Sometimes, the stand is the most powerful implement for the High King to cast off darkness."

"Oh, my Great King. I'm quick to forget. I asked to be kept

bold to the end. Not for the end to be easy and without a fight. Give me the strength to stand firm."

Seconds pregnant with silence ticked past without the whisper announcing the birth of hope to which Jason was growing accustomed. He waited, his breath bated. Though there was no answer audible, no confirming warmth. Jason resolved to trust, to lean upon the very banner he had determined to hold high. Opening his eyes, though it stung with the smoke and dust, he looked around. Above him, he could tell the building wasn't stable and would collapse soon. Outside, those planes could more easily get him with their terrible whistling torments. But here, he was guaranteed to die. Wasn't that the very dilemma he had posed regarding the Lion's Back? Danger along the way versus certain death of staying behind?

Now, he felt sure he was being directed. He had to move forward and trust that every step he made was that much farther the banner was carried to the High King's honor.

Emerging from the alley, Jason staggered to his feet, coughing and swiping to dispel the smoke around him. He found a pocket of clear air and breathed in deeply, astounded by how sweet even the gritty air of this besieged city tasted to him. How close had he just come to suffocating?

"Jason!" Kaveed called out to him. Or so he thought it was. Some of what he'd attributed to silence was really his ears once more being so battered by the terrible bellows of the bombs that he could scarcely hear anything else.

The next instant, he was grabbed by the arms and could see Kaveed, his face dusty and a few scratches dripping red. "Help get the others out of here. Those planes had left us alone, but they somehow figured out where we are."

"Is it safe to move anyone now? Aren't more coming?" Jason shouted without intending to.

"Yes. There are only four of them left. The Surcali had a couple ships they must have bought from Ecthelowall equipped to shoot down the planes. Most of them went down before they realized they couldn't bully them.

"Come on, I think Shamser is over here."

As Jason staggered after Kaveed, a younger Zilnian dashed in front of them. "Defender," Cyrus addressed Kaveed. "I can get to the frontline and deliver the message."

"It's too dangerous, Cyrus," Kaveed said, pushing forward toward where Shamser lay still amidst some rubble. "They hit the front line, too, and even if they're out of bombs, they'll come back round soon enough to rake us with gunfire. We need to get everyone out of the plaza and then try to wait them out to make a break from the city."

"But sir, the cannons haven't started firing again. If they don't, then those things will overrun our positions anyway. I know it's not my place, but since no reinforcements are coming, we have to sound a retreat now if we're going to. Otherwise, we're just choosing one death over another."

Kaveed's face turned stern for a second, but it faded as quickly as a summer storm. "Very well then. Warn them and then keep to the plan. We'll get everyone we can out. May the High King favor you with the feet fleet as a gazelle's hooves."

Cyrus returned a form of Zilnian salute and was off at a full sprint, a blur dashing across the broken landscape, using the newly created paths through several buildings encircling the plaza rather than around them. Jason couldn't quite frame what the exchange meant to him at that moment. That kind of soldierly discipline of salutes and formality, even when both men's uniforms were tarnished with dust, each had lost his fez, and their sashes were shredded. It was utterly foreign to him.

"Sir Landsby, give me a hand," Kaveed instructed. He was helping a wincing Shamser to a seated position.

Jason rushed over and assisted in lifting the old man upright. Shamser was one of those men who was burly in his youth and had no less thickened in his aging, even if he was no longer as spry and limber as he once was. Kaveed asked of him, "Can you walk?"

A gash on the side of his head made it seem unlikely, but already Kaveed was fashioning a compress from Shamser's tattered sash to help staunch the blood staining the man's silvery hair. "I will follow you to whatever end, Defender. Whether that is this body failing me or a sand scourge devouring me, I'm with you."

Whatever his prejudices against Rehalcy, Jason couldn't wholly dislike the old man. If Jason had grown up in Zilnen learning to despise the Empire and watching for decades as its rise further endangered everyone around him, perhaps he would be just as harsh and unfair in his thinking.

To further add to Jason's conflict over the old warrior, he looked up at Jason, gripping his offered hand of support and said, "Thank you, brother-at-arms."

"Anytime," Jason answered with a grunt as he heaved up in sync with Kaveed and ended up supporting the bulk of the old man's weight.

"I see Farzhad. He's got two of the others," Kaveed told him. "I'm going to help him." Whistling a slower tune but freshly saluting Timur as he came up, Kaveed delivered a new round of instructions. "Help Sir Landsby get Shamser to the north gate, and all of you wait for us there. We should be along shortly, but if you hear the planes coming again or the night arrives, go on without us. Understood?"

"Yes, Defender," the young man replied. Timur was under Shamser's other arm and leading Jason as much as Shamser before Jason could say anything.

They exited the plaza through some rubble of a building

that once blocked northward progress. Glancing over his shoulder, Jason watched as Kaveed and Farzhad tended to another trio of injured members of the group. A few others on the periphery bustled about doing something, But Jason couldn't sort it out before he had to pay attention, ducking just in time to not bang his head on a bit of rubble protruding at near face level.

"No worries, Sir Landsby," Timur assured. "We'll see them all at the gate just as surely as the stars will be out tonight to light our way." He chuckled, "They may even best us in reaching there first."

Jason found it hard to share the other teen's sentiments. He had a much more sober view of the dangers they faced. However, if they had starlight to walk by, that would be a welcome comfort. One thing had him particularly concerned, though. "I heard Sir Cyrus say there were 'things' that would overrun the frontline and encampment if we didn't move out right away?"

"Oh," Timur responded, his mood dimming to match the fading light of day. "When we first entered the city after blowing the hole in the wall, some Rehalcyon soldiers rushed out to attack us. Or at least we thought they were at first, but some looked like Surcali and Zilnians and had blank eyes. Since they were citizens and some from Zilnen itself, we attempted to treat them gently, but more and more of them kept coming. No matter what pain they endured or pleas we made, they kept pressing forward. The longer we battled them without being decisive, the more of them there were. It was like they were also turning our own soldiers into their kind."

Swallowing uncomfortably, Jason said, "I've heard about them before. They're called the carrion. Defender Black told me some stories of centuries ago when they were used by a pair of evil sorcerers and before them by Witches of Carmine Glades and tracing all the way back to Tislatna."

"A lot of bad things seemed to originate from there," Timur confirmed. "I don't suppose you know why everyone is afraid of the Lion's Back, do you?"

"Not really."

"Well, it's a long trek, going across a lot of the Ziljafu desert with only a few oases along the route. But we'll have to cut across the Ash Dunes early in the journey."

"I saw those from a distance the last time I was here," Jason recalled. "How did that sand get so dark anyway?"

"That's not really sand. It's mostly ash and volcanic rocks," Timur replied, the edge of a storyteller with something to spook his audience tinging his voice. Jason should recognize it—he'd employed it more than once—a few times in hopes of distracting a mark in a hustle.

"Centuries ago, there were cities where the dunes now are —thriving, important centers of trade and learning. But some desert hags—you'd call them witches, I suppose—came from the south and demanded tribute, or they would destroy the cities. They were refused, so the hags somehow caused these giant fire-breathing lizards that lived under the sands to emerge and destroy all the cities. Nothing is left except the ash and rubble of the dunes, which those things—we call them sand scourges—still guard. Ensuring no one can ever build there again," Timur finished with ominous flair.

Nodding, Jason grunted as he continued to bear up Shamser. "I don't suppose anyone has actually seen one of these sand scourges in recent years, have they?"

"It depends on who you ask and how much you're willing to accept as real," Timur replied. "Sometimes the stories get completely ridiculous and talk about the scourges summoning armies of undead victims to pursue people or turning all the sand around them to glass from the heat of their breath. That all seems unlikely."

"*Hmph,* there's more to it than any Zilnian wants to admit," Shamser put in. "I've seen things gliding in and out of the sands in the distance while watching the Ash Dunes. Things that make me certain I want no part in them."

Jason started to ask if there were any other alternatives to taking the Lion's Back and recalled Kaveed's certainty. Perhaps it was just the other Knight's charisma, but Jason felt he could trust there were no other viable options. "Well, looks like you'll get a close enough look soon," he commented and instantly regretted it.

Given his lack of leverage, Shamser tore loose of Jason's hold with a surprisingly forceful heave and gave him a shove backward. "You think this is funny, Rehalcy? Are you here to torment us and make us feel hopeless?"

"No, sir. I tend to be idiotic sometimes," he replied rather frankly. "In particular, when I'm wearing down."

"*Hmm,* I suppose I pity you then. Because the journey ahead isn't going to be easy or filled with opportunities for naps. You'll be racing for your life, and if you don't keep pace, you'll see those sand scourges for an instant before you're in their gullet going down."

Jason exchanged a hard stare with Shamser. "Thanks for the pep talk," he replied, sardonic.

"The what?" Shamser replied, looking bewildered.

For a moment, Jason had to reign in his urge to deliver another sarcastic zinger. Recalling it wasn't befitting a Knight of Light to do so, particularly to another of the Order. Not to mention he saw Timur was struggling some with the older man resting completely on him.

Looking ahead, Jason asked, "Is that the North Gate?"

The two Zilnians glanced in the direction Jason pointed and agreed. "Yes, about a hundred yards farther."

"Great." Jason took a step toward Shamser, who glowered at him. Sighing, Jason said, "I'm sorry for being snippy and rude. I've never been much of a socialite before if you catch my meaning. Not really, anyway. Today has been both wonderful and terrible beyond anything I've seen. It's not a good excuse, but please, don't take my snark personally. And please, let me help you make it out of here."

"'Wonderful and terrible,'" Shamser repeated. "In what way was it at all 'wonderful'?"

Running his hand through his hair and finding bits of stone in it, he sighed. "I suppose because before I started following the High King, I would've left you all to die and saved my own skin. But I couldn't live with that option now. And even though we faced a fearsome and brutal near-death, we're alive."

Seeming to consider this for a time, Shamser responded, "A bit reductionist, especially for an apology, but I accept it."

Getting back into position, Jason and Timur managed to get Shamser the last yards needed to the North Gate. Unlike Timur predicted, they were totally alone there before the city's open gate. They sat Shamser down to rest against it and turned to watch as the sun sank low beyond the horizon.

"Something is wrong," Jason commented after a few moments resting. "Do you hear that?"

"I don't really hear anything?" Timur replied.

Even with his eyes shut and head tilted back, Shamser was aware enough to know where Jason was heading with the comment. "The sounds of the cannons never resumed. It's strange because even if our forces are in full retreat, the Rehalcyon cannons don't need to hold."

"So, what do we do?" Timur asked, glancing between Jason and Shamser.

"Same thing we're doing now. Wait and hope," Shamser replied without flinching an inch. "And accept that even if we survive this fight today and the insane trek along the Lion's Back, Zilnen is lost."

Just then, there were sounds of gunfire from a few blocks away. The sounds grew closer, and Jason moved to stand in front of Shamser, drawing his spiritsword, which blazed to brilliance, illuminating the area and revealing just how dark it was getting. Settling into a ready stance, Jason watched each of the three streets that fed out to the North Gate for signs of trouble.

From the far right emerged a group of Zilnian soldiers, firing back toward the interior of the city. They ran, hobbled up to the North Gate, and didn't bother pausing as they passed through it and beyond. Jason didn't recognize any of them and glanced at Shamser and Timur.

Neither seemed to know what to make of it, though Timur offered, "I guess Cyrus reached them with the plan?"

"They could have been spies, more traitors planted among us to try and lure any who will follow into a trap," Shamser countered.

"I don't know ..." Jason replied, peering down where the soldiers emerged from. "Something still feels really off."

As if in response, the sallow face of a soldier in the opposing force's army peered around the corner and entered the space around the gate. Jason could see his eyes were glazed, and as the groaning man drew nearer, Jason could make out purplish lines tracing under his skin. Some looked woven into chain-like patterns across his body. He had a gunshot injury to one shoulder and was dragging his own weapon instead of aiming it.

"Wait, is that a ...?"

"That's a carrion," Jason confirmed, and though he was

feeling as uneasy about it, he jogged over, spiritsword held at the ready, and intercepted the thing. "I know them from the story of Stormridge's destruction in the Middle Era. They're bewitched people, controlled by one who knows dark sorceries. They feel no pain, know nothing but to destroy that which their master bids."

The moment the heat and light from the blade were near enough to the carrion, it halted and turned to face Jason. Its face went from slack to a feral anger like a bear whose den had been disturbed. Charging at Jason, it swiped at him with the rifle dangling from its arm, which forced him to dodge, wheeling around, keeping one step ahead. Because of the way it was wrapped, the thing could set off a chambered shot, and there would be little guessing which way the gun was pointed.

After circling in this awkward way for a bit, Jason held up his buckler, swooped forward, and cut loose the straps from which the gun dangled. As the rifle hit the ground, it did fire and clipped the carrion in the leg. It stumbled but shook off the injury and returned to swiping at Jason.

This isn't so hard. He's a little slow, and as long as I keep out of reach, I don't have to hurt him or risk him hurting anyone else.

Batting aside the carrion's latest attempt at snagging him, Jason noticed he was much closer to where the carrion emerged from and could see down that alley. Standing there as if ordered to wait were scores more of them.

Oh, no. That could be a problem.

Jason dodged under the active carrion's attempt to grab him and shoulder-rolled back toward the gate. Charging that direction, he motioned for them to move. "Go, go!" he mouthed, trying not to speak too loudly in case that could trigger the others to come pouring around the block.

He got over to Shamser and helped him to his feet. "What

are you doing?" the old man protested. "Can't you defeat one unarmed man?"

"It's not him I'm worried about," Jason replied through clenched teeth. "He has friends."

Unwittingly, the carrion had reached them, and Shamser grabbed it by the scruff and, with a snarl of, "Back you!" threw it down several feet away.

The carrion landed hard. It lay still for a moment before slowly bringing itself to its feet. It let out an unearthly shriek. Over and over, it made the sound while having a totally blank look on its face.

"What is it doing?" Timur asked, covering his ears.

"I don't know, but I will silence the thing," Shamser replied and hobbled over, his own spiritsword now drawn and burning.

Thinking for a moment, Jason suddenly realized what was happening. "No, no," he called to Shamser and dashed over, blocking his path. "It's calling for the others. We have to run!"

From two of the three streets poured forth at a slow walk the other carrion Jason had spotted. "By the boiling bile of a sand scourge," Shamser grumbled and tried to hobble back in the other direction with Jason's help.

About that time, Kaveed charged forward from the remaining street, fifteen or so men in tow with two camels pulling a cart filled with supplies. As they arrived at the scene, Jason yelled to them, "Run! They're carrion!"

For a moment, Kaveed looked confused, as if trying to place something but having difficulty. Then his eyes grew wide all at once, and he yelled, "Forward men into the desert. We have to leave now!"

The whole group began to run, which drew the attention of several carrion entering the area. They broke off from the main group, which still passively sauntered forward. Walking at first and then baring their teeth with vicious growls, they charged straight for Kaveed and the others.

Jason realized they were going to intercept them. Most of those on foot could probably get away, but if the carrion overturned the carts and kept the supplies from leaving the town, Jason guessed no one would survive the journey ahead.

Taking in a deep breath, he steeled himself. Carrion were second on his list of least-favorite beasts from the stories he'd heard till this moment. Now, they seemed apt to steal the top spot. But that was a thought for when things were calm, peaceful, with all danger far behind and the thrill of horror and revulsion over them only a memory. If that time ever came.

Getting to a full sprint, Jason leaped into a pair of carrion closest to the carts, crashing into them buckler first and landing on top of them. He tried to roll off, but in spite of going down hard and without warning, they both still flailed wildly, and one caught hold of his ankle. As he tried to shake that one free, he used his buckler to bash another walking toward him.

Getting free and to his feet just in time to watch the carrion he'd struck tumble to the ground, two more reached out for him, each growling menacingly. Jason dispatched the first with the flat of his spiritsword, which instantly singed the monster and sent it into a catatonic state. Narrowly sidestepping, Jason thumped the other to the ground with a blow from his pommel to the back of the creature's head.

Jason pulled free of the carrion, gripping his ankle, and turned just in time to be tackled by another he hadn't seen coming. Landing with a bump to his head, spots danced in front of Jason's eyes, and he struggled to block the furious hail of scratches and punches wildly flung at him by the creatures on top of him.

Seconds later, another set of fists began pummeling him, and another. Fresh kicks came from other angles he couldn't see. His armor and buckler were holding firm, but his head wasn't fully protected, and the fiends were finding every chink in the defense he attempted. Barely healed bruises and cuts were quickly agitated. He realized in the blur of pain and strikes that his sword arm was pinned down, and one of them was working at his hand, stomping on his fingers clenched around the hilt to force him to release his hold on it. Jason wasn't sure how, but he knew if he did, then it was over. Letting go of the blade would make the assault much worse, and any hope of survival, faint as it was now, would disappear.

"Get off him, you thugs!" Kaveed yelled from nearby.

Jason saw a burning blade lift high and smelled burning through the mass of flailing limbs. The attacks continued on him but grew fewer. He blocked more and more of them until he finally marshaled his strength and heaved off the last carrion. Scrambling back to his feet, he pivoted and knocked back a quick succession of fresh attackers, but the heap that had been against him was mostly battered away, screeching and clawing at sizzling wounds, likely caused by the flat of Kaveed's spiritsword rather than the edges. In any case, it had been effective. "Thank you," Jason managed to say, his throat and face too sore to say much else.

From the way Kaveed's brow wavered from steady into something very like pity, Jason guessed he must look pretty rough. "Let us get out of this trap, and then we may each say our thanks for a heroic rescue."

More and more carrion poured into the square. A sudden realization struck Jason. This was why the planes had kept their bombing runs to a minimum, and the cannons on the Rehalcyon side stopped. Someone had invoked the curse of the carrion again and now was using them to overrun all resistance.

Dorian, did you do this?

Not the innocent child Jason knew, who had been afraid of

spiders and disliked loud noises and who insisted they keep at least one light on for bed. That Dorian was no such monster. The darkling creature looked like his brother and spoke with his voice, but his heart was an icy rock from the blackest depths of a sunless cavern. Inwardly, Jason wretched that it was all too likely the thing that had consumed his brother had indeed done this.

"Jason!" Kaveed called, already several steps away.

Coming out of his torpor, Jason leaped back, just avoiding being grabbed again. He spun around and followed Kaveed through the gates and into the desert. All around, the landscape was sinking from indigo and violet into the deep dark of night. There were few silhouettes of survivors to discover. Faces he had just learned from arriving at Kaveed's camp were missing. An army had been reduced to less than a troop. Among those absent were Cyrus and Farzhad. Sadiq's death had bought him time with so few delivered for it.

But there was no stopping to calculate the full costs of this battle. They had precious little time to make it as it was, and those things at their backs certainly would not wait. So, when the others began sprinting away across the darkened dunes, he was alongside them and could not stop the hot tears that ran from his eyes.

FORTY-EIGHTH INTERLOGUE: THE JAWS OF DEATH

"I've never ... been ... so thirsty ... in my life," Jason wheezed to no one in particular. Overhead, the desert sun beat down on them mercilessly, driving them like a taskmaster. Onward. Onward. Going where Jason could scarcely remember any longer. Everything was pains and aches and thirst. Oh, the thirst!

Though they had been running swifter than eagles carried by feet shod with the *Evaggelion Eirene,* they were still only on the tail portion of the journey across the Lion's Back. Or at least he thought they were.

Surveying the landscape around them, it was hard to say where they were, given that all the sand dunes looked roughly the same sandy grey color here as the past day's walk. There on the horizon, though, was something. Blurry and indistinct, another army could be dispatched to find and destroy them. That was unlikely since the carrion chased them for a full day before the sun and heat caught up to them. Its relentless heat wore on them, and they fell to the sands long ago. However, those dark forms showed up intermittently.

Pity the carrion can follow us in all of the Ziljafu Desert, but they can't find water any better than us.

What was he saying? Or thinking? Did he say what he was thinking aloud? His thoughts were like birds flitting around in a meadow of flowers grey as steel but soft and shifting as flour. Who would do such a silly thing as to dust the desert with silver filings? With the dust of all this, they could buy all the armies of the Lowlands to fight his brother and Rehalcyon.

I should scoop up some to carry.

Jason stopped and stooped over to grasp a handful of the treasure-powder. It felt gritty and filtered through his fingers, leaving them stained black. Still, he took what he could and stuffed it into his pants pockets.

A few feet away, one of the group members said something to him. He couldn't understand what they were saying. He had only heard the pounding of his heart in his ears for hours now. Jason reached down, and as his fingers slipped into the strange silver, they latched onto something more substantive.

The other member of the group was there, shaking his shoulder gently, then with increasing violence. With some diffidence, he noted it was Kaveed. Why had he come from the front of the column to the back?

He noticed now that the rest of the group was maybe a half mile ahead and moving quickly away. What was their hurry? There was plenty of this ashy silver for them all.

Giving the hefty chunk he'd located a forceful tug that almost knocked him onto his back, he flailed and was caught by Kaveed for an instant. Kaveed let him go, took a step back, and yelled something to the rest of the group. Waving them on emphatically as if he wanted all the dark dust for himself.

Dark, dark dust. And this silver skull Jason now held. Except ... the longer he stared at it ... the less it seemed like silver. It was an argent hue but didn't catch the light like silver should. Part of it broke off and fell back to the ground, and a little plume of ash was kicked up.

Ash ... ash ... dunes. Oh, no!

He flung the skull away and struggled to get up, kicking up a cloud of ash and uncovering more bones as in his feeble attempt at righting himself. They couldn't be here. Couldn't linger. These were the Ash Dunes, around which even the Sombra took care, around which Sir Cinaed had been cautious to lead them when they rescued him from the ksar called Sayeh outside the Gerisk Ruins. The very same region he had been told in no uncertain terms meant death.

After fighting for several seconds, he felt something restraining him and realized it was Kaveed. He forced a skin into Jason's hands and pulled it up to his lips.

Jason stopped fighting as sweet hot water poured forth and struck the desert of his mouth like a monsoon. He drank greedily for a few seconds, hungrier for this water than the sweetest pastry or most savory steak.

It was Kaveed's steady hands alone that guided him to more responsible, rational consumption. With the water came burning sensations and pain. A headache he hadn't known was building struck him hard like hammer blows on the forge of Anargen's family smithy. How did he ever doubt such a thing was real?

After drinking perhaps half the skin, Kaveed pulled it away and took a quick drink himself before tethering it to his belt. "You weren't taking your water rations."

"I ... didn't want us to run out. Wanted the others to have what they needed. I caused all this ... if I—"

"There is no time for this, brother. If you must destroy yourself with guilt, many do it with strong drink. Reserve any such foolishness till after we escape this dreadful place. Do not deny yourself the water you need.

"Now, can you stand?"

Thinking about it was a struggle. The pain of the headache made concentrating difficult, but after several seconds, he was able to coerce his thoughts into a semblance of order. "Yes. Help me up, though."

Complying with the request, Kaveed hauled Jason to his feet. Dusting him off, he slapped him on the shoulder. "Much better. No more digging in the ash and forget what I said about the strong drink if we survive this. Don't throw away anything dearly bestowed by the High King."

"Aria," he groaned. He had cast her aside.

"*Hmm?*"

"Ah, let's get going. Catch up to the others."

"I'm afraid that will be quite the task. I told them to move double time through this leg of the journey, and I don't know if you're able to hold even a steady jogging pace."

Kaveed was right. With his head pounding, keeping to a steady straight-line walk would be an accomplishment. Let alone a jog or the sprint needed. "I'll do my best."

Pausing he looked down at the skull and bones and ashes all around and asked, "The story of the desert hags, it was true, wasn't it?"

"Perhaps," Kaveed acknowledged.

"And the sand scourges?"

"Whatever their origins, they are very much real and the source of this region's devastation. We must tread carefully. We are deep in the Ash Dunes now, and till we are on the other side, our lives are in the balance."

Jason sighed as they walked and already he felt nauseous. "You sent the others on because if they stayed behind with me, they would all die."

"That was my fear. Yes," he admitted.

"You should've left me. No one owes me any better."

Kaveed just tugged him along faster. "If I left you, dehydration and heat stroke would kill you before the day is out. Whatever you think you deserve, I would not wish such a death on anyone."

He paused and eyed him with thoughtfulness and added, "From what Tirzah told me, Aria would not have that for all the Lowlands, either."

"That's just her good nature. She can't stand me anymore. Not that I blame her." He winced as they picked up their pace. His hearing was improving, and there was a faint grinding noise he couldn't place.

Maybe my ears aren't all that better?

"No," Kaveed insisted, pushing them still faster. "She loves you. Even if she cannot yet say it aloud. I should know. I married her would-be sister, and they are of the same fabric from top to bottom."

Jason stumbled, and Kaveed drug him rather than stop to help.

A kind of throaty whistling joined the grinding sound. And should Jason not have needed to focus on his every step being right while his head pounded like parade drums, he would've spared a glance back or asked after it. They were running now.

Louder and louder, the throaty whistle soon overshadowed both the grinding noise and the thumping of his pulse in his ears. From the frantic look on Kaveed's face, Jason had a dreadful notion of the sound's source.

Underfoot, the ashen ground shuddered and shifted. Jason's balance was already precarious, and he gritted his teeth with concentration but knew he had already slowed too much. Kaveed had, too, though he was a few steps ahead, tugging at Jason's arm, futilely fighting to move him faster.

Kaveed looked back toward Jason, and his eyes grew wide. He stopped suddenly and shoved Jason off the left side of the dune they were on, leaping to the right of it. There was a terrible gurgling sound and an awful scent on a strong gust at his back.

As Jason rolled to a halt, coughing and covered in ash, through the haze of all he'd kicked up along the way, he now saw the source of the sounds and scent. An enormous creature was poised atop the dunes and scrambling around to double back. A bit like a monitor lizard crossed with a frog but with tough scales and a beaked face under a crest that pointed back. Strange, jagged claws rose off its forelimbs, and it looked like there were membranes between its back legs, front limbs, and a roundish abdomen. Jason realized as it glared balefully at him was this was the legendary sand scourge he'd been instructed to fear. And as it opened its beaked mouth to reveal wicked teeth and a black tongue, he believed he was looking into the jaws of his death.

FORTY-NINTH INTERLOGUE: ASH TO ASH

The sand scourge reared back onto its haunches and shuddered. Jason watched in terrified amazement, unsure what it was doing, until a whisper ordered him to jump immediately. Against his personal judgment, he launched himself forward as instructed and rolled across a lower dune. He had a clear view of the steady arc of flames that gushed from the sand scourge's mouth. The flames went over his head and scorched the sand with a sizzle and hiss. Smoke and dust billowed up from the impact site. It quickly became so thick that Jason was forced to dash out of the black toxic cloud, coughing and waving his free hand to ward off the fumes. Once clear of it, he checked the ridge top, readying for the sand scourge's next attack. Except that attack didn't come. The huge lizard was missing.

Where could it have gone?

Under his feet, the ground vibrated again, quaking as if terrified of what was hidden within it. Jason looked all around and could not tell where the beast was coming from. Grains of sand mixed with the ash shifted and shuddered, creating little dust clouds like low-floating mist over the ground. The ominous ambiguity of the pending attack set Jason's teeth on edge.

Help me, my King, I don't have the faintest idea what to do here.

There was just silence as the ground shook more and more violently around him. Jason spun in circles, raising his spiritsword up and keeping his buckler lifted at the ready.

I need a bigger shield.

A sudden warning was whispered to him, and Jason flung himself to the left of where he stood, rolling in the ash and staggering to his feet in time to see the sand scourge sail through the air like a missile, its whole body compacted into a sleek reptilian arrow.

With remarkable dexterity for its size, it corrected midair, stretching out its arms and deploying its membrane flaps so it was again in its frog-like shape. It glided for a bit and landed with a noticeable thump several dozen yards away. The beast stamped its forelegs on the ground, clawing at the ashes as it bellowed at him.

"Guess you're not used to having to work for a meal. Sorry to disappoint you," he called out to the thing.

It cocked its head as if it understood him and compacted itself back to its lithe form and charged, moving across the dunes faster than a horse.

Jason watched, listening to some much-needed guidance and dashed up a higher ash dune, spun halfway up the climb, and leaped back off the dune without bothering to see where the beast was or where he'd land.

The soles of his *Evaggelion Eirene* briefly connected with the back of the creature, and he hammered his spiritsword into the tougher-than-stone carapace of the sand scourge. As the burning blade sank deep into its hide, the creature bucked and sent Jason flying to land on his back in the middle of a lower dune.

Through the haze of ashes kicked up, he could see the sand scourge burrow back into the heart of the desert. However, this time, with his spiritsword embedded below its left shoulder blade. With all the dust and ash in the air, getting a good clean breath was hard. What he could get left an awful taste in his mouth and made him want to wretch. Now wasn't the time to throw up what little food and water he had in him.

Making it slowly back to his feet, Jason wiped the soot from his sweat-streaked face. Scouring the landscape for a sign of the creature, he found nothing. Already, the ground trembled in herald of its return. Droplets of ash-tainted sweat dripped into his eyes, stinging them. He tried once more to wipe them clear with mixed success. Those dark shapes he'd seen on the horizon before were back, close now, distinctly the shape of people on horseback.

Not now—things are hard enough.

Up to this moment, he had been quietly working off the assumption those blurs had been mirages or the sand scourge. If it was an advance party to Mesnara's army catching up to them, then this already nightmarish scenario was about to get much worse.

The ground beside Jason exploded away, and he barely raised his buckler in guard before being knocked away as though struck by a battering ram. The creature's head and neck protruded from the dark dune and seemed to savor his shock and pain from the impact. Then it huffed a hot gust from its nostrils and opened its beaked mouth.

Even from where Jason half lay, half crouched, the glow within its maw was unmistakable. He had only a second's breadth to raise his buckler in defense as the flames shot forward and smashed against the small shield, pushing against it like a team of oxen breaking hard soil with a plow.

My King, help me! My shield won't hold this …

As sudden as the monster's arrival came words familiar, but he had forgotten: "*And these shields. They are the Thyreos Pistis. Faith. No arrow or bolt has passed through its surface. No fire or acid can burn through to injure the Knight who allows it to be his defense.*"

Pushing against the jet of flames with the shield and using his free hand to help hold his shielded arm in place, Jason strained. He could not keep holding it back, not when the flames were sure to curl around the little shield's form and consume him.

As he struggled, he saw etched into the interior of the shield the words, "For truly, I say to you, if you have faith like a grain of mustard seed, you will say to this mountain, 'Move from here to there,' and it will move, and nothing will be impossible for you."

If his confidence in the High King's favor and protection were of any size, the shield would hold. He would hold firm.

Taking in a shaky breath as sweat rolled down his face in speedy trails, Jason's vision blurred. If this didn't stop right away, he would faint. But he couldn't. He had to hold on. Had to keep fighting.

"My … Great King … is an unassailable … tower. A fortress … of … refuge," he reminded himself through gritted teeth. He had been purged by the High King's fire, hadn't he? What was this in comparison with that?

Abruptly, the fiery siege ended. Jason almost fell forward from lack of something to push back against. His foe huffed and surged out of its concealment, bearing down on him in a rush.

Jason readied himself to block, dodge, or do anything else to weather this next attack. Nothing new was advised to him except to stand firm.

The creature skidded to a stop and reared up on its back legs, ready to come down on him with its wicked sharp claws. It couldn't have taken more than a few seconds, but it was long enough for Jason to glimpse the horseback riders descending on the sand scourge.

Jumping backward to buy himself some space, Jason had an excellent vantage to see the monster's face change as first one, then another rider, raked a sword along its sides, deeply scoring its legs such that it dropped back down and trembled as it tried to keep itself upright.

Both riders zipped past Jason. They were riding in almost perfect unison. He would have loved to see their next move, but he had clearly heard what he had to do next.

Rushing forward, he ducked and rolled under a swipe from the monster, which dropped onto its face, unable to hold itself upright with only one forelimb. This was the moment Jason had been instructed to act.

Back on his feet, Jason jumped onto the creature's back, and, gripping his spiritsword again, retrieved it from the beast's hide and immediately plunged it in again and again. When his grip did not fail this time, the fire on his spiritsword persisted, and the flames scoured the beast's hide.

It cried in pain, and Jason had to hold his balance as it collapsed completely. Those riders were back upon the sand scourge's flanks. One doubled back to come alongside the thing's head and drove his own glowing sword deep into the creature's neck.

The sand scourge gave a whistling whimper and fell silent.

Jason pulled his sword free from its last attack and dropped off the thing as the fire from the spiritswords roared to a blaze that, in seconds, consumed the beast. The flames danced in front of him, and without looking, he knew the rider had come alongside him. More than that, he was sure now who it was.

"Thank you, Defender. You arrived at just the right moment to save the day."

Over the crackling of the fire, he heard Sir Cinaed grunt. "The day was saved long before we arrived. Ours was merely the task of yielding to be used as agents of aid." Then, with less reproof, he added, "It is good to see you survived yet another trial. We feared the worst when we saw the battle unfold at the Port."

As if waking from a dream, Jason blurted out, "Kaveed! Where is he?"

Cinaed nodded to the other side of the high dune. "It looks like the creature knocked him out early in the attack. We were too far away to see exactly what happened."

"Tirzah went straightway to him."

Relief flooded the space within his heart that panic had claimed. "Oh, thank the High King." Jason sheathed his spiritsword and looked up at the old man.

Cinaed looked very much like Jason imagined a Defender of the Realm should. Wearing his full armor, which glowed with the brilliant inscriptions of the High King's words, he sat atop his horse like a warrior from heraldic legends. Ancient and formidable. He sheathed his spiritsword as well, lifting his helm's faceplate to smile down at Jason.

Those piercing eyes seemed tender for a change. "You look awful."

Running his hands through his hair, Jason laughed, letting the last of his tensions slip. "I've never been one to turn down a scrap. Sand scourges, Zilnian thugs, carrion ... *eh*, just another week."

The old man's face grew grave. "Carrion? Where did you encounter them?"

"In Port Amurgo," Jason replied, surprised he needed to tell Sir Cinaed anything. "After the bombing runs ended, they emerged from the rubble and overran what was left of Defender Kharoum's army." An edge of somberness crept in, pushing aside the humor that had given him a brief respite. "Not many of us escaped."

Nodding, Cinaed looked up over the dunes. "That we knew. You, Kaveed, and what, a dozen others? We also saw they went on ahead. Hopefully, they haven't gotten far. Sand scourges travel in groups. We'll need to be wary till we get across the Ash Dunes."

Then, as if coming to himself, he reached into a saddle bag and tossed something to Jason—a fresh skin of water.

Jason took a shallow swallow, swished out the poisonous taint of the ash in his mouth, and spat. Then he took a deep draught of it, closed his eyes, and breathed out a fresh sigh of relief. It was as hot as the previous drinks Kaveed gave him but was even more welcome. "Thank you doubly."

When Cinaed didn't answer, Jason opened his eyes and followed the old Knight's gaze to where it lingered on another rider also garbed in gleaming armor. This rider, however, was slighter than Cinaed, and he knew right away that his other rescuer was Aria. She stayed where she was atop the dune, but she was looking down at him. With the angle of the sun and the distance, he could not see her expression.

Another horse and rider joined her. Tirzah came alongside her, and walking with her, holding his head and looking a bit worse for wear, Kaveed.

"Come, lad," Cinaed said as the fire burned low, leaving a darker outline of ash against the landscape to demark the sand scourge's defeat. "We have a long journey ahead, and I fear the hardest parts yet remain."

11

INTRIGUE

"The cruelties of how our plans could be undone in a single moment left a bitter taste in my mouth. If we remained and accepted the charges which would be wrongly laid against us, prison and death for a crime we did not commit was not the greatest tragedy that belonged to our predicament."

—Anargen's King's Day Journal
27 Misbyr 1607 Middle Era

Anargen could scarcely draw a breath, watching in horror as the servant slid to the floor. That other man, the shifty-eyed one, had seemed so foul because he was a Sombra. Not a, but *the* Sombra. The assassin they'd come to stop from murdering Viceroy Ecthelion. Now, he was loose in the palace, and anything they did, whether surrendering or fighting or trying to escape, would play directly into his hands, creating an added distraction and allowing him much greater ease in finding his mark and completing his loathsome contract.

"Anargen, help me with this," Glewdyn instructed.

As if swimming through time, Anargen realized his father was below him. Dropping down, the older Knight jerked free the dagger and tossed it a foot away. He grabbed Anargen's hands and forced them to press hard against the sudden rush of scarlet from the man's side.

"Keep good pressure till I say move, then move, understood?" he barked.

Anargen nodded, his eyes riveted to the dying man's lifeblood held at bay pitiably by his unskilled hands. He didn't dare look up to see the horde of those in the room bearing down on them.

With a rush of heat and a loud crackle, Glewdyn produced his spiritsword and commanded, "Move!"

Anargen did, accidentally pulling aside the man's tunic as he did. It proved helpful as Glewdyn lay the broadside of his blade against the man's side. The flames bloomed brighter, and the heat intensified.

At Anargen's knees, the man cried out again in agony that faded into a sigh of relief.

Then they were on them, jerking Anargen and Glewdyn away from the man. Four men each held down Anargen and Glewdyn. Seren and the others didn't move, didn't speak. What could any of them do? In minutes, the room was filled with soldiers who replaced the servants in restraining Anargen and Glewdyn. Another servant had a machete he must have used to open crates and pointed at Seren and the others.

One of the soldiers bearing an officer's regalia stepped into the middle of the chaos and demanded, "What happened here?"

"They stabbed that poor fellow there, Captain Napo," the machete man spoke up. "And if that weren't enough, that one pulled his sword on him too."

Captain Napo regarded Glewdyn coolly, glancing down

and seeing the spiritsword resting on the ground. He then took in the man on the floor. The man's wound was already markedly improved, no longer open. But the black dagger that caused it had disappeared or disintegrated or worse, was circulating amongst those still in the room.

"So much blood. The fiend stabbed him with the sword, did he?"

"Well, I didn't get a good look, but I think he had a knife or dirk he put into him first," the machete man asserted.

"Did anyone else witness this?"

A bevy of would-be witnesses attempted to recount the event with mixed results.

"*Bah*," Captain Napo snarled. Under his breath, he muttered, "First reports of a giant wolf attacking our gatehouses, and now this. Such a night as I never dared desire."

Working his tongue over his teeth, the captain waved to the soldiers restraining Anargen and the others. "Come. Maybe the dungeon's devices will supply one of them with wits to confess what transpired."

Anargen didn't resist as he was tugged along. He felt as if resistance was utterly beyond him. The turns of their fortunes were like a willow's winding roots.

Gregor made a sound as if to protest, but Anargen caught his father shooting him a stern look, silencing the boy.

In the halls, the soldiers tugging them along halted. Captain Napo motioned to a pair of his men. They linked the irons on everyone's wrists. Napo announced, "Silvanus, Pascal, you continue with me. The rest of you, back to your posts."

The other soldiers saluted and tramped off. Once they were alone, the captain conversed in a low whisper with the one called Silvanus and then did the same with Pascal. At the conclusions of those hushed discussions, he whirled to face Glewdyn. "All right, you," he said. "Explain what happened and make it quick. This is your only chance to avoid the rack."

Drawing in a breath, Glewdyn replied, "We are Knights of Light on a mission to protect the Viceroy of Ecthelowall. Word reached us of a plot against him. We snuck in along with some servants, and one of them stabbed that man. We believe he is the assassin threatening the Viceroy's life."

The captain rolled his eyes. "That's a bit much for a tale. Why did you have your sword drawn?" He gestured to the spiritsword.

"To heal the man," he replied without hesitation. "The dagger used on him was a shadow weapon. The High King's fire burned away the corruption it was sowing in his body and sealed the wound."

Even Mia's face twisted with a twinge of disbelief.

It was rather difficult to swallow if one didn't already understand the properties of the spiritsword.

Napo shot Silvanus a look, and the soldier gave a subtle nod.

Sighing, the captain pinched the bridge of his nose.

"The Viceroy knows us," Mia spoke up and immediately looked abashed.

Cocking his head to the side, Napo regarded her for several seconds before scowling. He glanced once more at his underlings. "Very well. Why don't we just take a little trip to see how much of this story holds up?"

With that, he made a crisp turn and walked again at a quick clip. Instead of leading down toward where Anargen expected the dungeons to be found, they went up several floors. The decor became incredibly luxurious, far more so than Anargen felt comfortable around. It reminded him of the opulence of Ordumair's fortress and city in the nobles' quarters and passages.

Stopping in front of a door with intricate carvings and gold-inlaid filigree, Captain Napo rapped his knuckles on the door. There was a brief pause before the door opened, and from it emerged a tall thin man in fine clothes. Though looking older and wearied, Anargen immediately recognized him as the Viceroy.

"Yes, Captain. How may I be of service to you this evening?"

He gestured to the group. "Perhaps you can speak to whether this group here is trustworthy?"

Ecthelion scanned over the group, his eyes lighting on Mia and then Gregor.

"My sakes," he commented. "Captain, why are they in chains, if I may ask?"

"They were accused of a murder. Except no one is dead, and my men tell me they've seen something like this before."

"Like what, Captain?"

"Impossible things. A man with a serious wound healed in seconds." He glanced at Glewdyn and then cleared his throat. "They claim they're here to prevent an attempt on your life."

"I see," Ecthelion said, rubbing his clean-shaven chin thoughtfully. "You may remand them to my custody if you please. I will take responsibility for them."

Napo raised an eyebrow. "Really?" His gaze shifted to the two soldiers. Silvanus again gave a nod. Huffing out a sigh, he muttered, "What a night."

To his charges, Napo instructed, "Very well. Silvanus, you're posted outside the Viceroy's door. Any trouble comes of this, and you'll be ground to mortar for rebuilding the gatehouses, understood?"

For the first time since he arrived, Silvanus spoke audibly enough to hear him. "Yes, sir," he responded in a decidedly Ecthelish accent.

Captain Napo and Pascal departed, leaving Anargen perhaps the most stunned of all at the latest wend of their fortunes.

"Come in," Ecthelion instructed them. "All of you."

Once inside his expansive quarters, he turned and clapped his hands. "I had almost not dared hope you'd made it, Lady Sornfold, Master Fenwrest. When you had not come within a month's time, I despaired of your well-being."

"Would that we could have come to you, your honor," Mia replied. "We were ... detained."

"Giant wolf beasts blocked us from coming to you!" Gregor amended more bluntly. "We thought they were going to rend us to pieces!"

Ecthelion's brows furrowed. "I'm sorry you endured such harrowing hours. I recall my own encounters with such dreadful monsters." Looking from Glewdyn to Anargen down the line, Ecthelion said, "I might guess that your protectors here are Sir Fenwrest, Sir Hurstwell, and Sir Terrillian, but I know for certain the latter most has come and departed to seek support for the Ords and Albarons. So, who might you all be?"

Thomas spoke first, managing to open his helmet in spite of the chains. "You were right, your honor, I cannot be far from Mia or Gregor. I regret to report Sir Hurstwell fell in our defense. Dying a hero worthy of songs and a record in our histories."

Ecthelion's countenance darkened by degrees. "May the High King have received him warmly into his courts." Clearing his throat, he pivoted and said, "Well then, who might the rest of you be?"

Anargen managed to undo his face plate and said, "Anargen of Black River, at your service, your honor."

Ecthelion clapped and gave Anargen's shoulders a hearty shake. "Wonderful! Does this mean you have Sir Bertinand

and, *um*, Sir Caeserus with you? Is that you, Defender MacCowell?"

From the way he regarded Seren and Glewdyn, he must have realized none could be the case, as neither of their body types matched them.

"No, sir," Anargen answered, trying not to let his voice sound as heavy as his heart felt. "They have ... gone a different path since we last spoke. "This is my father, Glewdyn, whom you may remember.

"Your honor," Glewdyn added.

"Ah, that I might just. Well met again, good sir. Thank you again for your aid and for the services you rendered to Captain Nerebold—er— Arnauld. Without him, the Restoration's Navy would be sorely disserviced."

Glewdyn gave a humble nod.

Speaking up again, Anargen said, "And I'm favored to introduce you to my fiancée, Lady Seren."

Seren undid her helmet and offered a small smile. "It is an honor to be in your presence, Viceroy. Not unlike the hero Cinaed of Tislatna and his beloved Elena meeting the first ruler of Ecthalon outside the Golden Forests of Ecthelowall."

Ecthelion's eyes lit up with surprise, and he chuckled. "My, my, I did not know anyone birthed from beyond Ecthelowall's shores knew that legend, much less would use it for such an apt comparison.

"I must say, all I have heard of Anargen's unwavering affections for you were certainly apropos."

Anargen felt his cheeks redden. He glanced at Seren and saw hers were as well. They each laughed, and Ecthelion joined in, looking for an instant far haler than since they'd first come upon him.

"*Ah*, wonderful. Congratulations on your betrothal. Is it too forward to presume Defender MacCowell has the honor of officiating your ceremony?"

As much as he tried not to, Anargen winced and let out a little moan. The mention of Sir Cinaed in the midst of such ease and contentment dealt a potent blow.

"I'm sorry to say, your honor," Glewdyn picked up for Anargen. "But the Defender, much like Sir Hurstwell, gave his life to save many more.

"I would tell you of his heroism and all that has come of things. No doubt you know something of Stormridge's destruction, but I'm afraid there was no embellishment of our purpose in being here. We believe you are in imminent danger once more from the Sombra."

Being a lifelong participant in the theater of politics, Ecthelion must have been quite adept at masking his emotions. But Anargen couldn't help but see how crestfallen he appeared at the news of Sir Cinaed's death. They had delivered him little good news to balance the bad.

"I suppose my son is behind this?"

"It appears so, your honor," Glewdyn replied. "Would that I could offer comfort now, but there is more to tell."

Ecthelion huffed a sigh and, with an acerbic edge, waved to him. "Speak on, then."

"First," Glewdyn said, "do you permit us to undo these bonds?"

Drifting to a mahogany chair with rich indigo cushions, Ecthelion again waved dismissively. "Of course, of course. I will call for Silvanus."

"There is no need, your honor. Forgive me my paranoia, but more will be clear momentarily."

Reaching into Anargen's scabbard, Glewdyn pulled out his spiritsword and, with the burning blade even at such awkward angles, severed the chains binding each of them. When the last shackle fell, he handed the sword over to Anargen to sheath and stretched his arms. "Again, your honor, I wish I had better counsel to deliver, but a member of the Sombra precipitated the incident that led to our capture."

Ecthelion stiffened. "A Sombra is here? In the palace?"

"Yes, sir. He entered masquerading as a common servant. With the distraction and our detainment, he could be anywhere in the palace by now. We must be careful of trusting anyone and assume nothing."

"What do you propose then, Sir Glewdyn? That we flee the palace, the city, the country?" There was a desperate and derisive edge to Ecthelion's words. "I have been here months and only just managed to get an audience with the Viscount that may offer an alliance with Libertias. We badly need it, especially given all the unfortunate tidings you've brought me."

"If your route and meeting are unsecured, it will be extraordinarily dangerous for you," Glewdyn pointed out. "This Sombra is cunning and effective at his trade."

Banging his fist on the round end table near him, Ecthelion retorted, "Did you not hear me? This meeting is our last hope of securing forces sufficient to keep the Restoration alive. I must meet with the Viscount.

"We have exhausted our supplies. The Isle of Fens, Albaron, and Ordumair are all under siege at this very moment. If they fall, we have no allies or recourse left. The ambassador for the Vogteremark has already informed me his people are formally recognizing my son as rightful ruler of Ecthelowall. The Knors have no interest in entering this battle as they stand nothing to gain. Libertias is our last hope."

"What about Rehalcy to the south," Mia spoke up. "Your wife was from there. Perhaps they would be willing to act on the grounds of that alliance?"

Drumming his fingers on the table beside him, Ecthelion

looked pained by that suggestion. "My late wife's people are far more likely to favor my son. He is half Rehalcy, after all, and even chose to keep his mother's surname.

"No. No other options are remaining. We are in the heart of night, and if we want to survive till dawn, we need Libertias to act, and our moment to make that petition is now."

Looking at the others, Anargen could tell those words decimated their optimism. What could they say, though? Ecthelion's gamble was on everyone's behalf. If he did not make it, then he was right. The north lands would fall, and a man who consorted with the darkest sorceries of the Lowlands would rule one of its most powerful nations unopposed.

Thomas broke the silence first. "Well, then, your honor, let's get you to that meeting."

The Viceroy winced. "Actually, my meeting is to take place in a few hours. It's fortuitous because we may utilize the time to provide you with some hot food and fresh clothes. This night, we will all be ambassadors for the Ecthelowall we long to see."

FIFTIETH INTERLOGUE: AMOROUS INSOMNIA

The candle burned low in the room as Jason stared out the window to the streets below. Yusbilsi was such a change from the places he had been. This was the farthest east he'd ever traveled, having left the Western Lowlands for the Central. Albeit the westernmost portions of that region, but it was still significant in ways he couldn't articulate or explain. More than anything, it was a marvel they had survived the journey at all.

Sir Cinaed had been demure over whether he believed they would complete the trek across the Lion's Back. It had been arduous and long. So very long. It had taken two weeks for them to reach Yusbilsi's borders. Once there, they had ridden a train into Hündürqala, the capital. After such an arduous journey, this was a strange sanctuary. He wasn't sure what he had expected from this place. It was like walking into Rehalcyon's past by a hundred years.

No electricity, limited telegraph, no telephony, and no running water. Over the years, he had "roughed" it his fair share of times, but that was normal life here. Most of the people seemed to be nomadic herdsmen or service the herdsmen in some way. Mountains with great steppes stretched all around and further strained his ability to come to terms with Hündürqala. It did not help that his personal relationships had also taken routes different from what he'd hoped.

"Do you mind extinguishing that?" Cinaed asked from the bed opposite Jason's. "An old man needs every minute of rest he can get."

Jason licked his fingers and put out the candle. Immediately, the fuzzy dark pallor of their simple all-wood room became an amorphous ebony mass. Outside, stars shone brightly enough to see some things, and a few streets had torches burning, but being on the second floor of the tall, narrow building, everything was otherwise bleak. Though he knew he should rest while he could, Jason couldn't quiet his thoughts enough to sleep. Not yet. Probably not for hours.

He didn't begrudge Cinaed's request, even if it deepened his desire to have a room to himself. It made sense, though. The wedded couple, Kaveed and Tirzah, had their own room. Most of the other Zilnian soldiers shared rooms. Aria, being the only other woman, had a room to herself. And if he had been able to speak to Aria since the rescue on the Ash Dunes, even if it were to be a fight, he would've been fine. He could likely rest much easier. But that was the rub of it. She might as well be on the moon as down the hall from him.

Worse, who knew how long they would be here? They had arrived and taken up these rooms at the inn using the funds they carried with them. But once Cinaed had spoken with a local peacekeeper, they had quickly been identified as political refugees and were now semi-confined to these quarters. Not under arrest or mistreated, but Yusbilsi was a nation of few Knights before it embarked on the path of neutrality it now anchored its future to. Doing such had made it difficult for them to allow any open expressions of allegiance to the High King, given how many nations expressly disavowed his rule, his very existence, in fact. They weren't likely to risk their special status and the safety it accorded over a few Knights. Which left Jason and the others cut off from outside contact and him frustratingly incapable of sorting out the rift between himself and Aria. He would go talk to her, but guards posted outside their rooms each night for protection meant he couldn't, even if she would speak with him.

He made a sound somewhere between a sigh and a groan and laid his head on the desk, hoping he would nod off eventually.

"You know, I'm not exactly fond of the idea. But I'd imagine the streets are pretty dark by now. If one were to climb out onto the ridge that runs around the roofing of this floor, I doubt anyone would see that person. So long as he accorded himself as a gentleman, I would understand his reaching out to speak with someone dear to him."

Lifting his head, Jason took a few seconds to understand what Sir Cinaed had just said. Had he imagined the old man telling him to risk sneaking outside to see his granddaughter?

"Unfortunately, she's stubborn like me," he added, sounding drowsy. "I know how hard it can be to not be able to tell the woman you love how you feel, knowing it could make a difference."

Jason smiled. "Thanks."

Even with Cinaed's permission, Jason waited for him to nod off and snore to undo the latch and climb onto the precarious ledge wrapping around this floor of the hotel. Shimmering from a few windows away was the candle-lit room of Aria. She hadn't gone to sleep yet, either.

Coming up to the window, he gripped the side of the vaulted overhang that ensconced the window and tapped on the glass lightly. When there was no sign of response, his tapping became more emphatic. He was nearly wrapping on it with his fist when he heard it slide up, and Aria demanded in a hushed voice, "What are you doing?"

"Trying to get your attention." He leaned around to see her. She was hanging out the window, her hair down and slightly askew. Perhaps he had been wrong about her being awake. She certainly scowled at him as though roused from a deep slumber.

"Well, you've succeeded. Along with getting the attention of half our guards, no doubt."

He grimaced. "I'm sorry. I just need to talk to you."

"And you couldn't wait till a more reasonable time?"

"No, I couldn't," he replied, trying not to sound as annoyed as he felt. "You shut me out whenever possible. So, I had to go to extraordinary lengths."

"Did you ever consider that perhaps I have nothing to say to you?"

Jason gnawed on his lower lip. That stung, especially because he had often feared just that. Though she hadn't said she didn't want to talk to him. He clung as much to that nuance as the overhang. "Then let me do the talking for a bit, please?"

She rolled her eyes and looked out on the street below. Of the few people out, it didn't appear as if anyone had seen them.

"I suppose you won't listen to reason like a sensible person and go if I refuse?"

He shrugged. "When have you ever known me to be the sensible type?"

There was a ghost of an almost smile before she replied with her stone-like rigidity, "Fine. Talk fast."

"I love you," he blurted out and immediately hated himself. He had intended to say so much more leading up to that as a culmination, and here he'd flippantly lobbed it out.

There was a little flushing of Aria's cheeks. Maybe his

earnestness had won some points. There was a sincerity in his direct, almost desperate-sounding declaration of love. He tried not to waste his gains. "I know I've impossibly buried that under the betrayal of abandoning you and your grandfather. I said hurtful things. Things I wish I could unsay.

"I'm not asking you to pretend like none of that happened. But please, don't shut me out. We're on this Quest together."

Arms crossed at her waist, Aria breathed out a heavy sigh and looked past him into the distance. "Right. You think you're on a quest. Is that all? I need to get my rest."

Shaking his head, Jason tried to hold back a sudden surge of anger and frustration. This icy, remote mountain of stone shaped like Aria baffled him. He had seen her temper before and her sorrow. But who and what was this that he was seeing? "So, if you forgive me as you say, what is your problem? Why are you still treating me like I'm a carrion trying to maul you?"

Aria looked stunned for a half second and pursed her lips as if trying to hold in what she was thinking. All at once, she huffed a heated sigh and slammed a fist against the window frame. "I don't know what could be wrong with me. I mean, we just watched an entire nation with thousands of years of history destroyed before our eyes because we got there too late to warn them. And in the process, Tirzah, who is my sister in all but blood, lost her father. The Southwestern Realm lost its Defender on the eve of the first time in centuries that all the Defenders were to gather in one place. Oh, and I'm trapped alone in this bedroom in a foreign land." She stepped forward and poked him square in the chest. "If you hadn't been such a fool, we would've made it before all this happened."

She glared at him for several seconds and then turned away, but he caught one of her hands and held it fast. "I don't buy that. Everyone has forgiven me for that, but you. Even Tirzah and Kaveed don't hold it against me. Just you."

Jerking her hands free, Aria looked at the ground. "What do you want to hear?"

"Honestly," Jason replied, some of his verve withering as he had to step back into vulnerability. "I want to hear you forgive me. I want to hear that despite leaving you like I did, you still care just as much for me as I do for you.

"When I left you and Cinaed, I was a fool, okay? You're right."

Aria looked up at him, her expression full of surprise. Apparently, she hadn't expected such an honest admission.

"Yeah. I was a fool. And it took me losing everything and being shackled away in the darkest dungeon in the Lowlands for me to realize it. But you know what? The High King, whose honor I had spat on and whose every overture I spurned, saw me there. He forgave me and freed me. I'm not that fool who left you. The King's fire has burned away everything that took me from you. And as much as you may hate me for what I did, you're hating someone who isn't here anymore.

"So, if you don't want to admit, or if you truly don't love me now," he said and paused to swallow back the pain of saying such a thing, "then fine. You are free to give your love as you choose, but if you keep acting as though I'm not new and different and every bit as committed to the Quest as you are, then all you're going to do is end up sabotaging us as stupendously as I did."

He stood there staring into Aria's enchanting eyes. They were softened from the emerald stones to something else. Then they fell, and she said very quietly, "You should go. Grandfather will be waiting for you."

Jason sighed. "Right." He wasn't sure what he'd expected. Probably a passionate kiss and declaration of her undying love like in all the love stories he knew. Maybe a slap to add cathartic punctuation to all their collective angst before the kiss and declaration?

Stopping at the doorway, he banged his fist on the frame and, without turning to face her, said over his shoulder, "Whatever happens, please know I am sorry for hurting you. And that you're probably the only person, besides my brother, I've ever sincerely loved."

He thought he heard her start to say something, but as the silence stretched seconds longer, he knew he had to leave. "May the High King's favor be on you," he added, shutting the window for her.

Jason was halfway back across the roof when he heard a loud cracking sound and Yusbilsani voices coming from his and Cinaed's room. "You ... there," someone spoke in a thick accent with pauses where he struggled with the Imperial language. "You come ... now. You no come ... you ... die bad."

Frozen by shock, Jason didn't move a muscle. It was unusual for Yusbilsani to have difficulty speaking Imperial— especially those who had escorted them here.

"You will not harm the others, will you?"

"Harm? I ... give ... harm to you!"

Once more, there were sounds of scrambling and furniture being tossed aside.

Jason shimmied over to the window and peered in just in time to see three bulky Yusbilsani warriors dragging Sir Cinaed out of the room.

He started to leap through when he heard a woman's scream.

Aria!

FIFTY-FIRST INTERLOGUE: BOUND BY LOSS

Throwing caution aside, Jason made little jumps to cross the distance back to her room, wobbling as he did. This time, he didn't wait and listen for her to be taken. He smashed through her window and rolled into the room, getting to his feet so smoothly it almost seemed he'd planned it. Aria was already in a corner, reaching for something as two churlish-looking thugs advanced on her. One had just given what sounded like cat calls in their language right before Jason flung himself through the window.

Not even hesitating as they gaped at him, he launched himself like a missile into the nearest of them, slamming him into Aria's table. They both flopped into the floor and even though he was a little dizzied by it, he was back on his feet in time to catch and deflect a sloppy punch leveled his way. As he slung the other man away, he caught a strong stench of spirits on him.

Jason looked over at Aria and was about to ask if she was okay when her hand grasped what she'd been reaching for, and the room suddenly brightened as the flames raced up the length of her spiritsword.

The other Yusbilsani warrior either couldn't see the High King's fire on the spiritsword or completely disregarded Aria's ability to use the blade because he just sneered. The broad-shouldered and hefty man produced his curved sword and a dagger. Still bearing a grin on his big-bearded face, he playfully flipped the dagger in his hand, catching the pointed tip then its hilt, back and forth. Like a viper strike, he snapped around and flung the knife at Jason.

As in more times than he could count now, a whispered warning came just in time for Jason to flatten. The knife stuck fast into the wall behind him. By the time he was up and on his feet, the Yusbilsani wasn't smirking anymore. He struggled to keep pace with the whirling and flicking strikes from Aria's sword as she used the space and speed to keep the more imposing warrior on the defensive.

With some chagrin, Jason remembered his spiritsword was in the other room. Retrieving the knife from the wall, Jason tried to find some way to help. But in the tight confines of the room, there was little chance until, in desperation, the hefty man flailed with his freehand and caught Aria in a glancing blow that set her just enough off balance that she had to stop and get her footing again. A disastrous setback left her open to a hasty follow-up swipe from the big man, who used his weight and reach to corner her.

"Aria!" Jason yelled as she ducked a slice meant to take off her head. In desperation, he flung the knife and grazed the warrior's forearm.

That earned Jason the warrior's attention, and he was on Jason faster than he expected for the man's size. The air rushed off a swipe of the sword, and Jason heard it as much as felt it.

Jason stumbled, dodging it, and fell into the opposite corner of the room.

The warrior took two strides toward Jason and cried out. He dropped his sword and feebly reached for his back before falling to the floor. A sizzling stripe was scored into his back through his leathery Yusbilsani armor.

Aria stood in the warrior's place, trembling ever so slightly. Their eyes met for a moment, and Jason knew he wasn't imagining the relief, the thankfulness he saw in her gaze. Getting to his feet, he walked over slowly and said, "Thank you for the rescue there. You're as incredible as I remember. More."

She blushed. "It looks like I owe you as well. For a change."

There was a faint smile on her lips before she seemed to remember where they were and cleared her throat. "They have grandfather, don't they?"

Jason nodded. "I'm so sorry. They took him before I could get back. I panicked when I realized they were coming for you next."

Aria scowled at the news, and Jason flinched as he realized he had, by rushing to her aid, allowed her grandfather to be taken. No matter what he chose, he had failed her. "I'm so sorry, Aria. I should've—"

She put her hand on his arm and shook her head. In a gentle voice, she redirected, "No, you've said enough apologies tonight. This isn't your fault."

He swallowed back the words he'd been about to blurt out and nodded. "Okay, then." He glanced past her to the hallway of the hotel. No one seemed to be there. "Let me grab my sword, and we can go after them."

She nodded and followed close on his heels, her attention decidedly distant. It took him a couple minutes to rummage and find the scabbard with the spiritsword and his buckler under some debris from the room, which had been thoroughly tossed. Among the debris was also Jason's satchel with Anargen's journal.

"They took all of your grandfather's things but left mine?"

"It probably wasn't intentional." She rummaged through the chaotic mess. "His spiritsword and shield would've been more noticeable. And his satchels as well. He always keeps them in reach … just in case."

Jason strapped on his scabbard and buckler. "They must've caught him before he could wake." Ready to go now, he saw she was staring at something and instinctively put his hands on her arms in a reassuring embrace. "We're going to get him back."

Coming out of her trance, she seemed to note his closeness but didn't pull away. Instead, she quietly commented, "He dropped this on purpose, I think."

Handing it to him, Jason took the scrap of parchment and read the message in swooping letters of an artist's script,

> *"Find your lamp, trim it quick,*
> *Find your way in forests thick.*
> *Night will yield to dawn's light,*
> *Night cannot overcome his might.*
> *When dawn gives way to the Day,*
> *At his side you'll be, so fear allay."*

"It sounds like poetry," Jason commented.

"It's from a very old song," Aria replied. "One he would sing to me to help me sleep. It's about the Great King watching over us. Keeping us safe when all seems lost.

"The ink is fresh. I think he was hoping to get this to me. He always knew when I needed these words."

"Why would they try to take us all?" Jason asked after a lengthy, wistful pause. "We clearly don't have much money, and we haven't caused any trouble."

"None here," Aria amended. "And who says they were taking all of us? Those guys who came for me weren't interested in taking me anywhere ..."

Jason caught her meaning when she trailed off, and a thrill of murderous anger coursed through him. "Those miserable beasts! I'll—"

"*Shh*," she soothed and reproved in one. "We have to be quieter. I'm guessing they took the others for some purpose, and if we let the owners of the inn below know we weren't handled properly, we won't get out of here to help them."

Jason grimaced. Once again, they were going to be outcasts and fugitives. Anyone who saw them would be inclined to report them. "Great. What's the plan, then?"

Aria looked around the room thoughtfully and set her sights on the window. "We must catch up to the kidnappers and follow at a distance. We'll have to travel at night too."

"Looks like we should get underway then."

She nodded. "Follow me. I think I can get us out of town unseen."

Jason raised his eyebrows at her total confidence. Of course, he trusted her, but even if he seriously doubted her, he would've followed along now that they'd already spoken more in the past twenty minutes than in the past twenty days. "Well then, after you, Lady Black."

Without delay, she headed for the window, climbed out it, and waited for him to join her. Once on the roof, Jason watched with some appreciation as she nimbly made her way around the face of the inn to the other side. It took him a bit longer to make the trek. When he caught up to her, she nodded to a tall evergreen with thick limbs that towered well over the building and most of those on the blocks around it. Its nearest verdant needled boughs all but touched the roof of the inn.

"Our way down," she informed him.

He cocked his head to regard her afresh. "How did you even know this was here? We weren't allowed out of the inn rooms, much less the town around it."

She smirked. "You think you're the only one who climbed out of your room? I'm the granddaughter of the most prominent knight in most of the Western Lowlands. I've gotten used to being prepared for trouble."

With that, she bunched up her creamy linen dress and dashed off the room in an impressive leap that landed her in the concealing enclosure of the tree's branches.

Taking a breath and securing his satchel and scabbard, Jason edged back as far as he dared and ran and leaped off as well, smashing through some smaller limbs Aria had managed to slip past without issue from her slighter build.

They climbed down the tree, which required a drop of about eight feet. They each paused for a breath's space as they were essentially in the open now. With a wordless nod to one another, they ran to the edge of the town with its tall, rustic hunting lodge-like buildings.

Beyond was a mountain pass that gave way to a breathtaking steppe of amber grasses, tall and waving under a swift cool breeze. Beneath the canopy of indigo and violet dotted by tens of thousands of brilliant points of light, Jason could almost forget he was in dangerous territory chasing foes. The beauty and wonder of it pulled at him. Reminded of the brilliance of the High King on his throne. And he wondered if this was how the nights had looked to Anargen, unspoiled by the new electric lights and lamps of huge cities.

In the distance, a column of smoke indicating a large camp established on a lower steppe. Without asking Aria's opinion, he knew they had spotted the kidnappers. Resting well outside of Hündürqala for the night.

They climbed down a sloping place on the steppe and

found an overhang to get under. After a few minutes of searching, Jason gathered some small dried-out saplings from nearby and brought them to burn. It wasn't the best fire, but it helped. They both sat beside it. After a few minutes, Aria yawned.

"I'll take the first watch," he informed her. "You can get some rest. I'll wake you if they leave out or come looking for us."

"Thank you." A drowsy note softened and blunted her words.

As Jason stood and stretched his sore limbs, he noticed Aria staring at him. She was wincing.

"You've been through a lot since you left. A lot just since you came to Zilnen."

He shrugged. Maybe the smoky haze and firelight made him look worse. Or maybe he looked as rough as he felt. "A good part of it could've been avoided if I hadn't run off and left you and Defender Black. It's the collateral damage from that mistake that hurts most.

"But for what I've gone through since becoming a Knight of Light? That's nothing."

She arched an eyebrow, and a shadow of the Aria he had known came out in her snarky reply. "*Hmm*, so you got beat up by trade? Were you into boxing or a professional punching bag?"

He laid on his smuggest grin. "I told you when we first met, I've had my share of scraps. Won most too."

Her expression was so dubious he laughed. He was treated for it to the pleasant sound of light laughter from her.

Though with the laughter, he felt himself growing more serious. Something he wasn't accustomed to or wholly intending. "But that's not why the injuries and pain aren't worth noting. The High King delivered me from dark and from suffering I can't begin to explain. I saw him or as much as I could handle. And no matter how many times I think about it or say it, that doesn't become any less a marvel to me. Anything I bear, knowing whom I serve and what he has in wait for those faithful to their oaths to him ... that makes it all bearable. As much as he deems for as long as he deems."

At first, he thought it was a trick of the firelight, but a few seconds later, he heard Aria sniffling and realized the little glimmer on her cheek was a tear trail. "Aria, what's wrong? Is the smoke bothering you?"

Aria shook her head and swiped away the tears. "No, no. It's not that."

Gnawing on his lip, Jason wasn't sure whether to let it go when she didn't elaborate or press for more. In the end, he decided the only way he could help was if he knew where her pain was coming from. "We're going to get them back. Kaveed, Tirzah, your grandfather—they're all going to be okay."

She just closed her eyes and buried her face in her hands.

Well, it looks like I'm just as terrible at this comforting thing as I was before becoming a Knight. I guess that's not among the gifts I was bestowed. Divine armor, shield, and sword—check. Half a lick of sense—not so much.

All of a sudden, she looked up at him and choked back a sob. "I ... I'm sorry," she managed to get out.

"What do you have to apologize for? Nothing that's happened so far has been your fault."

"Because not all your wounds have been on the outside. And I've been cruel to add to the internal ones. Those are the kind that often never heal. I'm so sorry."

He swallowed with some difficulty. "It's okay. I get it."

Shaking her head, she splayed her hands wide. "That's just it, you don't. What you said earlier about yourself, it's true. I've been so busy getting even with the Jason who left us ... left me ... I haven't been willing to see that you're not him."

Jason sighed and leaned back against the incongruous rocks of the overhang. "Don't worry, he's not totally gone. Give me time, and I'm sure I'll mess something up spectacularly."

"Stop it." Annoyance flashed into her voice. Aria stood, walked over, and dropped to a crouch in front of him, her eyes emeralds ablaze. She placed her hands on either side of his face. The sensation of her touch, soft hands, gentle but resolute, startled him.

He hadn't realized how much he missed even the simplest overtures of affection between them. It was like a limb that had been numbed and was suddenly restored its blood flow, tingling in an almost painful way. Painful because he didn't know what to expect next.

She was forceful, insistent when she spoke. "As Knights, we don't completely change, and there's still a lot of work to shape those parts of us that are rough and tarnished into smooth, polished surfaces that reflect the High King's light to others. You're being too kind to notice, but I have my own coarse patches to address.

"I ... *ugh* ... This is so hard to say." Aria drew in a steadying breath, her eyes still on his. "Jason, I do still love you," she said, the intensity in her eyes paired now with a vulnerability. "It would be a lie to say I'm completely over what you did. But I must try because giving you the cold shoulder only chilled my own heart. So ... *ugh* ... this is so hard—"

He leaned forward and kissed her. It took only a second of that for him to recall the rhythm they'd had before. Not just in how they moved at a moment like this but in how they worked together, spoke, and thought. Pulling back from the kiss after several seconds, Jason caught his breath and found a wild sort of humor besetting him. Whether fatigue or the sheer fantastical nature of hearing what he most desperately wanted to, he laughed and teased, "I like the way we said it together."

Aria laughed until her throat caught, and she let out a little squeak, and then they both lost it. It took several minutes for them to calm down enough to settle back against the cavern. She was close beside him now. Her head rested against his arm. "I almost lost you three times now."

Jason rubbed her arm and replied in earnest, "I'm right here. And by the High King's will, I'll never leave you again." And he hoped with every bit of him that he could keep that promise because if he lost her now, it would probably destroy him.

FIFTY-SECOND INTERLOGUE: THE HUNTED

Jason slid down the last several feet of the slope, sending a cascade of little rocks and pebbles scattering before him. Aria stood at the base of the ridge top. She had gathered some berries and collected them in a tattered bit of cloth from her dress. Almost two weeks of tracking the kidnappers across the beautiful but harsh wilderness had taken its toll on their clothes and worn them thin. Even so, he felt an irrepressible urge to give her a goofy grin when he walked up to her.

"Do you have good news?" she asked, hopeful.

"Well, not bad news." He realized he was misdirecting her with his lack of focus on the matter at hand. "They're making camp across the river that comes down off those mountains." He pointed to a pair of peaks in the distance. "It looks like we should be able to cross at some shallows about a mile or two down from here."

"Things could be worse." Her expression turned suspicious. "What was with the silly smile you were wearing? You looked like my pet terrier, Tuffy, I had when I was little.

She'd run up, tongue hanging out, looking like she'd counted the minutes to see me."

"*Ha!* So I look like a dog. Noted. And it was exactly seventy-five minutes since I left you."

Her eyes widened with surprise until he beamed another grin, letting her know he was teasing. "*Ha, ha.* You are starting to resemble Tuffy. Not quite so tawny and brown, but definitely scruffy."

Rubbing at his chin, he found it was sporting a thick matte of hair. Taking the time to shave hadn't exactly been on his to-do list since escaping his brother. "Well, that's what I was hoping for. To evoke memories of a dog. Are you sure I don't look more rugged, dignified? You know, like your grandfather?"

She reached up and touched his face with the familiar tenderness that never failed to win him over. "I loved Tuffy very much. But you should probably shave as soon as possible."

"So, not dignified and rugged like Cinaed?"

Patting him on the cheek, she laughed. "Right. Because every girl dreams of meeting a guy who looks like her grandfather."

He groaned, filched a few of the berries she picked, and scarfed them down. "Point taken. Speaking of your grandfather, how exactly will we get him back from those slime when they reach their destination?"

Aria chewed on some berries herself, a thoughtful expression on her face. "I had hoped the High King would give me some wisdom regarding that, but so far, nothing. From how long and fast we've traveled, we must be getting close to Kizos' Oasis or the Gulf of Halepi."

Jason grimaced. "If it's the Gulf, we'll have to stow away on their ship, or we could lose them for good." Instantly, he regretted his words as Aria's face fell. She was putting on a good front most of the time, but as this trek dragged on, her decision to track the kidnappers back to who hired them seemed like a more and more ill-conceived gambit. And though he knew she was, on the whole, returning to the ease with him they had before he'd left, he was still the guy who'd broken her heart. He was entrusted with a second chance and handled it like he had on boxing gloves, trying to hold a Zhoulong tea set. "Sorry," he offered lamely.

"No, you're right. We have to act soon. It's too risky waiting. We'll have to sneak into the Yusbilsani's camp tonight and free them."

Eyeing her with some trepidation, Jason just clucked his tongue and consented. "Tonight. If we head for the shallows now, by the time we get across and start trekking back toward their camp, it should be nightfall. If we want to be extra careful, we can wait to cross the shallows till dusk, but we will risk the whole thing if there's too much cloud cover or a storm. I don't think these guys can see the Great King's fire, but I'm trying to not gamble with anything precious to me these days." He brushed aside a few stray strands of her hair that had escaped the ponytail she'd kept it in the past several days.

She took hold of his hand and kissed it. "None of this is easy, and things look worse now than when you left. Thank you for sticking around this time."

"Yeah, the old me would've bailed about a hundred miles ago. All those years, I thought living on the streets was tough." Looking off into the direction he knew the camp was located, he drew in a breath. His humor dried up like a noon sun baking away morning's dew. Though he wouldn't say it to her, this would be a rough night. Odds were that one or both of them wouldn't make it out of this in one piece.

Not wanting to think about that, he let his gaze turn northward to the direction where the mountains swelled to double the height. Those were the foothills of the Highland. This trip had brought him the closest he had ever been to where the High King's city and the focal point of his kingdom were located. Wonder's thrill traced down his spine, setting every hair on end.

"I'd go just about anywhere for you," he noted absently. "What your grandfather is trying to do, though—uniting all the Knights of the Lowlands to face the coming darkness—that's worth dying a hundred deaths to see completed."

Aria followed his gaze and leaned against him. "It is. Not many of us are left who understand that, but it most definitely is worth that and more."

They stood there looking into the distance together for another minute before his stomach growled, and Aria insisted he eat more of their berry stockpile. Trying not to eat as much as he wanted felt like trying to hold back a speeding roadster with one hand. Still, he left enough for Aria to have several handfuls, finishing what they had meant to save. Perhaps it was for the best. Soon, dark would fall, and there may be no need to save anything for a return trip.

Whether unconsciously guided to or by fogginess from hunger and fatigue, they managed to lose about an hour of daylight to sitting huddled together at the base of the mountain. He had almost drifted off to sleep when a sound of rocks clattering startled him back to alertness, and he realized how low the sun was on the horizon. "Aria, we have to get up. We need to get down to the river shallows before it gets too dark, or we won't be able to find the way across the river."

She yawned and stretched and was on her feet a few seconds later. As soon as she was through, she tensed and grabbed his arm as he stood up. "Did you hear that?"

Jason shook his head. He hadn't heard anything out of the ordinary and was about to say as much when more rocks tumbled down the slope nearest them. His eyes traced their path up, and he caught sight of something dark high up enough that it blended in with the contours of the mountain by dusk's light. Even so, something was off about whatever it was. Animals didn't tend to move that way. "We need to get going. Now."

Gathering their meager effects, they took off toward the river crossing. They were about two hundred yards away from the shallows when the muted thump of hooves on the grassy steppe reached Jason's ears. Those thumps grew louder far faster than Jason would've believed possible. Sparing a glance behind them, his heart hammered in his chest. A group of ten or more hooded men bore down on them about half over the distance they needed to cover, all of them on horseback. The sickening thought that these could be more Sombra, who had tracked them to this point, brought new energy to his limbs, and he sprinted as hard and fast as he could, all but dragging Aria along.

Maybe if we ford it, they won't be able to follow. Isn't that how all the fairy tales go? Monsters can't cross running water?

"Jason!" Aria called out in between desperate breaths.

He looked back again. Their pursuers were only about fifty or so yards away. "Don't stop!" he wheezed, though his chest and legs burned, and he felt the effort needed to keep Aria apace with him increasing with every step. They were so close —a dozen yards to the water.

Ten yards.

Eight.

Seven.

Six.

He felt a hard jerk from the hand holding tight to Aria, and suddenly, his hand was empty. A breathless cry of "Help!" turned his head. One of the riders had reached them and pulled her away. The rest were coming on her and circling up. If he kept running, he could make it across the river. Maybe still complete the rescue of the others. He was only about three yards from the water, the sound of the river's song as it wended toward the Gulf of Halepi, a siren serenading his ears.

Jason skidded to stop, one foot by the water's edge. "No." He couldn't leave her. Hazy as his thoughts were from breathlessness and panic and days without enough rest or food or any comforts, that much he knew. It wasn't just his love for her either. Somewhere deep within, he felt sure the High King wouldn't want him to abandon her. To trust that he would see them through this to rescue the others and complete the Quest.

Drawing his spiritsword, the flames caught hot and fast across the blade, and he gave a choked shout, "Away from her, you ..." His words failed in his parched, air-starved throat, and he let his actions speak for him, charging at the first rider he could reach.

One of the riders motioned to the others, and a group of three of them broke off and flanked him. The rest formed up and circled in a tightening ring. One of them was dismounted and holding Aria back. Her struggle was furious but futile.

Around Jason, the riders closed their snare still further. With this many foes and his strength spent, he resolved to go down, slashing as wildly as he could. Maybe it would frighten a couple of them, and Aria could make a getaway in the confusion. Funny that now he was hoping she would try for the very thing he had turned back from. No. He knew she would never. Which meant their journey was about to end here.

I didn't make it very far in the Quest, but I won't back down. I'm yours to the very end, my King.

The ring of riders collapsed once more, and now they were each in range of a lunging attack from him. One of the riders addressed him, speaking a string of terse words in the

Yusbilsani language. When he'd been in Yusbilsi, Jason had picked up precious little of the language, so whatever the rider wanted of him, he would have to come and take it. Steadying his breath, Jason gripped the hilt of his spiritsword tight and readied himself for what he had to do next.

FIFTY-THIRD INTERLOGUE: VILE TRADE

Tensing, Jason decided he would lunge for the rider closest to Aria and work his way around from there for as long as he could. He caught Aria's eyes and gave her one last bittersweet smirk.

"You are a member of the *Palatini Lucis Aeternae*, aren't you?" The man who spoke the unintelligible words before inquired. "Answer or die."

Working moisture to his mouth, Jason hoarsely replied, "I serve the High King of All Realms, yes. I do not fear any minions of the darkness."

The rider's head tilted, and it looked like he wanted to ask the others around him for their opinion, but in the end, he just leaned back on his horse. "Many boast bold words, but few keep their courage in the dark."

Jason wanted to lob back a sarcastic retort, but Aria beat him to speaking. "Those who bear the High King's light find in its fire the freedom from fear."

Half-turning in his seat, the rider held up a fist in a sign to hold steady. "Your friend wields a spiritsword. Am I to understand you both have joined the Quest of Fire? Give thought to your answer. These are dangerous lands for those with such oaths. Few pledge them here."

It took a great deal of concentration not to let his ready stance falter. What was this banter between Aria and the rider about? Was she buying time, trying to deceive him in some way, distract them enough to give Jason an opening for an attack?

"We are not from these lands. My grandfather is Cinaed Black, Defender of the Northern Realm. Our task is to unite the twelve Defenders and their realms against a great evil rising in the West."

Is she crazy? She just made us four times as valuable targets. I don't think she revealed half that much to me when we were first together.

The man scoffed. "So, the West begins to feel pain now? Would you be surprised to know the East has faced evil for many generations?"

"This is different," Aria insisted, her voice cracking. "The Day is truly almost at hand."

At this, the man once more looked around. Several seconds stretched by without any words from either party, and Jason could feel tremors running through his arms. Whatever Aria's aim was, if they didn't act now, he wouldn't be able to at all.

"Where is Defender Black now?" asked the rider, breaking from his place in the circle to trot over to Aria. He gave a nod to the other member of his group to release her.

She sucked in a tremulous breath. "He was taken, kidnapped from the Qizilat Inn in Hündürqala. Along with Kaveed Amine, newly appointed Defender of the Southwestern Realm."

"Hündürqala? You are a long way from there, young one. You are deep in the Sykonos Mountains."

"We were trying to track the kidnappers back to who hired

them before attempting to rescue my grandfather and the others. In all, they have ten of our Order captive. All but grandfather are refugees from Zilnen's recent fall."

Some chatter broke out amongst the group, and Jason could scarcely convince himself not to take this opportunity to strike out. What was happening?

"They're camped just up from here on the other side of the river," Aria added, plaintive notes piercing through her attempts to look calm.

Shaking his head, the first rider dropped from his horse and called out something to the other riders in Yusbilsani. Before Jason could react, three from behind grabbed him, and a sack was cinched over his head. Rough hands forced the spiritsword from his faltering grip and bound his arms behind him.

"What are you doing?" Aria demanded, sounding shocked. "I thought you under—"

Her words were suddenly cut off, muffled by something. They must have placed a sack over her head as well. Worse than the capture itself was knowing there had been a moment to act to prevent this, and he had regrettably not taken it.

Rough hands shoved Jason, and from nearby, somebody instructed in less effortless Imperial, "Get go. You walk ... as we say."

Jason had plenty of retorts for the command but complied for Aria's sake. As best he could anyway. It felt like they had walked at least ten more miles before the one Jason considered the leader of the group called out something that brought them to a halt.

There were sounds of daily routines all around, suddenly interrupted by the spectacle unfolding before them, including the hushed but still very charged voices of women and children.

Jason wondered if they were being led through a town when suddenly his mask was whipped off.

He had been right about women and children watching. They watched and whispered to one another, eyeing him as if a griffin had soared out of the pages of a fable and lighted in their midst. Aria was close beside him, and her eyes scanned over the crowd and the buildings beyond. Jason wondered where exactly they were. A few tall structures were made with stone, but otherwise, everything was formed fully of lumber. They had much of the styling of the Yusbilsani architecture, but not perfectly the same. They were in the center of what Jason would call a modest village, but the longer he stared at the buildings and wall, the more he felt like he'd been transported back in time to a Middle Era castle.

That's not possible, is it?

The lead rider from before dismounted and, after handing off his horse to one of the villagers, motioned for Jason and Aria to follow. He led them up a short flight of stairs into the central building dominating the square. The tallest structure in the enclosure looked very much like an old keep. Before him the large double doors seemed to open on their own, with a wooden whine that added to the sense of age to this place.

"It's like we've traveled back in time or something," he murmured, only half convinced that it had not really happened.

"Or something," Aria affirmed in a whisper.

A small retinue of others joined them in what appeared to be a broad entry chamber. Along the walls on either side, stone staircases led straight up and disappeared into a second floor. At the end of the wide mustering area was a small dais and around it an array of twelve chairs with fine upholstering of purple fringed by scarlet patterns that may have been peculiar to their captors' culture. Though ancientness seemed imbued in every stone and timber of the structure, it did not reek of neglect, abandonment, mold, decay, or age. Instead, Jason breathed in the smell of burning candles mixed with other floral and spiced scents, as if incense burned here.

Jason and Aria had just crossed into the center of a large circular seal comprised of an elaborate mosaic that faded to maroon, ochre, and beige from more vibrant colors when their lead detainer came up to them, knife drawn. With a quick flick of his wrist, he cut their bonds free.

"Did I miss something?" Jason whispered to Aria.

"No need to whisper, brother-of-the-hall," the man informed him. He pulled back his hood, revealing a man in his forties with well-tanned skin and wavy ebony hair kept longer than common. Most interesting were the small tattoos he bore on his face in dark blue ink. His exposed forearms also had them. Whether words or symbols, it was hard to tell from the distance. With a sweep of his hands, he gestured to the town. "Welcome to Sığınacaq Yeri. A refuge for Knights of Light in the West Central Lowlands. I'm Kazim Cuzibaum, Defender of the West Central Realm."

Jason shot Aria a surprised look, and she just shrugged. He mouthed, "Seriously? Is he telling the truth?"

"*Ah,* friends, you are not from this Realm. Whispering and secret-keeping are frowned upon. The Emir of Yusbilsani would have your tongues cut out so that you may never speak again if done in his presence."

"Forgive us," Aria began. "We don't know your customs and have been through many hardships."

"So you have said before," Kazim replied, sounding empathetic. "This is a hard land for the High King's light to dispel the dark."

"And it doesn't hurt that you were deceptive yourselves. Aria told you who we are. Why all the secrecy if you disavow it?" Jason asked pointedly. He received a sharp elbow in the ribs from Aria.

For his part, Kazim chuckled grimly. "Lies and bribes are fine so long as the price is the bondage or blood of Knights and innocents. We, of course, have to be careful with outsiders, but I assure you the secrecy in bringing you here was for your own good. Now, should the Emir's peacekeepers find you, you will not be able to surrender this sanctuary. It will go better for you that it is so."

"Thanks?" Jason replied, rubbing the back of his neck and wondering if he was hallucinating all of this. Perhaps those berries they had weren't edible after all.

It would certainly explain a lot. But into his pondering, Kazim commented, "We understand your skepticism. You are no doubt worried for the Western Defenders and wary of those who would put you through such a harrowing experience."

"That is a fair assessment," Aria admitted, squeezing Jason's hand for comfort or to keep him from speaking up. He couldn't be sure. "Especially with the timing. You weren't out there on random patrols or to find us, were you?"

A smirk quirked up Kazim's mouth, and he twitched his mustache for a second as if weighing what he wanted to say. "Your grandfather has not exaggerated at all—your wit is as sharp as a talwar. We had heard rumors that the Emir's merchants had taken a group of Knights of Light for sale in the slave markets. This is a common occurrence for our brethren, sisters, and political opponents of the Emir. We try to watch for such groups and intercept and stop them when possible."

"So, by encountering us, we actually kept you from helping my grandfather," Aria concluded, crestfallen.

Kazim cocked his head to the side. In an almost fatherly tone, he quipped, "Can you stop the winds rolling off the steppes? Or the frosts that beset the mountain peaks? Or the rush of mighty waters of Charis Falls from the Highland?

"You perhaps shoulder too much blame upon yourself. The group you were following was the Emir's personal guard. Whoever is paying Yusbilsi for our dear ones has a deep purse and much power. Doing this risks the Emirate's neutrality and, with it, many profitable services."

Aria looked down at the old stony floor. "It has to be Rehalcyon. They want all of us dead. They know we escaped them in Zilnen and are trying to finish the job."

"I do not think it is the Rehalcyon. It would be simple enough to smuggle them through Zilnen," Kazim countered. "That they've turned toward the Gulf of Halepi tells me they plan to take them to Varliliman. Which we shall, too, once their course is found for certain."

"How can you know that if you're here?" Jason asked, looking around the tall wooden structure for windows to hint at where they were, but there were none. "It's not like we're right by a port's docks."

For a moment, Kazim's eyes narrowed as if unsure how to take Jason's assertion. At length, he relaxed and accepted it as the gambit that it was. "We have placed our own in key positions. The Knights of this Realm have been doing this work for almost five generations. You in the Western Realms have not known our hardships and sorrows. Yet, looking at you now, I do not wish them on you. Trust that we shall be ready to act when the Defenders are brought to the port."

Aria cleared her throat. "Does that mean you are also accepting my grandfather's urgent request to hold the Council of the Realm Defenders?"

Shrugging, Kazim had an imperious glint in his eyes. "Let us succeed in our rescue, then we may speak on matters of the future."

FIFTY-FOURTH INTERLOGUE: DARK DEALINGS AT THE MARKET

"No. I'm well-fed. My thanks," Jason tried to say in Yusbilsani to the grinning man, offering him a raw eel of some kind. The street vendor's face contorted into confusion and then indifference. Someone else was passing by the Grand Market of Varliliman. It was a relief. The scent of the eel was enough to make Jason gag, which he guessed was a bad move here. Everywhere else in the Market smelled intoxicatingly exotic. A mixture of cassia, aloes, cinnamon, and other aromatics had carried him here. But close to the waterfront, the salty smell of the gulf and fragrances of the rest of the Market were lost to the strong smell of fish and other seafood sold under a hot sun. At least here he didn't stand out so badly.

Before the Market stretched the enormous crystalline waves of the Gulf of Halepi. A bright sun shone above, and all around them bustled thousands of people from just about every corner of the Lowlands. Out in the Gulf, just off the Varliliman port's docks, floated an array of warships, mostly Ecthel, ensuring that the trade route that passed through here was kept safe. With the colonial holding of Keraxlaco sending caravans to the port on the opposite end of the Gulf, it was little wonder that the Ecthels were the arbiters of safe travel across these waters. Though for how much longer, he could not be certain.

Business and barter and boisterous calls to acquire myriads of goods and wares continued without any seeming concern for what had happened at Port Amurgo. But there were whispers. Stolen glances between tradesmen and merchants from across the Lowlands who imparted words of caution and planned for how they would weather the change in the tides. Ecthelowall no longer reigned unopposed over the Notiosanemos Sea. That hegemony had comforted many for more than a century, and now, they were suddenly stripped of their covering.

Jason pulled the hood of his blue robe down farther to better obscure the view of his eyes and hopefully deter other street vendors from hocking their goods to him. They and any of the less savory sorts lurking on the fringes of legitimate dealings. He appreciated the robe Kazim had given him. It helped him blend in among the Yusbilsani. Though here in this kaleidoscope of cultures, no one would likely have found it odd that a Brackenburgher was among them.

It was his own ill-conceived curiosity about this place that would get him in trouble. He'd heard of it growing up, even as far away as it was from his birthplace. Varliliman kept Yusbilsi flush with cash, able to afford to defer any attempts to sway them to any regional or Lowlands-wide conflicts that had simmered over the centuries. No one dared try to claim the wealthy nation or challenge its borders, knowing well that to upset the status quo would be to their own detriment. It created a "safe" place where commerce could flourish, leading to its markets, expansiveness, and incredible diversity. So, Jason had to see it, just once, before what everyone in the Grand Market could sense was coming befell it. The status quo was shattered, irrecoverable, and whatever came next would redefine the landscape of the Lowlands for centuries, millennia, to come.

"There you are," Aria said, startling him as she slipped beside him and looped her hand into his with such ease he could scarcely process it. Had they really been like the opposite shores of a strait a few weeks ago—so close but interminably separated? Yet now, her hand fit into his as if the two were separate halves of a whole. He wondered if she felt the same or if, to her, the gesture was simpler, a means of linking them for transport as she tugged him off away from the Grand Market like a train pulling cars out of the station.

She moved quite swiftly in her billowy taupe pants, which he believed were called kamiz. Though he would argue her the most beautiful woman in Varliliman, she barely stood out with the fuchsia shalwar vest and headscarf. Perhaps that was the wisdom Kazim had employed. Carefully ensuring that they neither looked too like they were trying to blend in nor too like they were bold about being foreigners in the Emirate.

"You were supposed to meet us a half hour ago," Aria reproved under her breath.

It was somewhat hard to hear her with them moving so fast and the sounds still echoing from the Market, though the noise had already died down considerably as they wove into less and less reputable parts of the port town. "I'm sorry. I kept getting pulled aside by the vendors. My Yusbilsani is just good enough to get me laughed at and not beaten. I had to be careful how I extricated myself from them.

"That and I tried to see if I could find a way to scrounge enough funds together to buy a maroon anarkali dress for you. When I saw it, the anarkali reminded me of the dress you wore when we first met, but softer, gentler, silken. Almost like you'd be wearing a delicate flower blossom. I know our lives are in turmoil, but I've never given you much beyond grief, and I ... Sorry, I know I'm being silly."

Aria slowed down and looked back at him. Her eyes shimmering. "That's not silly. It's sweet. What's silly is you don't even understand what you've given me."

For a moment, he wanted to flaunt the social rules of this place entirely and kiss her in the open street, right there. But they were both more thoughtful than that. Such was their romance—regaining its presence, potency, vibrance but always giving way to the needs of the moment.

"Come on, I've kept the others waiting long enough," he concluded, taking the lead. After a short time, though, he let her slip back to the front. He hadn't yet mastered all the streets of this place, but apparently, Aria had been here at least once before. She got them to the run-down and abandoned warehouse in minutes.

At the door, she hesitated and turned to him. She leaned up as if to whisper something in his ear and brushed his cheek with a kiss. He must have blushed or smiled goofily because her eyes crinkled with a flash of delight before she nodded to the door. "Remember, we both knock at the same time and recite the phrase."

He nodded, got in position, and silently mirrored her count of three before knocking and saying in Yusbilsani, "By Highland fire, all is set aright."

Jason had no idea where the particular phrase originated, though he understood the sentiment. It didn't seem quite so esoteric as a passphrase should, in his opinion, but perhaps it was its boldness and being unassailably in line with the Order's views, which so few shared, that made it work. In any case, the door was opened to them by an older gentleman from the Udiqui Confederacy.

The man didn't say anything, merely glanced at them, dim

old eyes flickering with recognition. He shut the door and led the way to the tunnel that ran under the warehouse and crisscrossed this entire area of the city. Jason felt a swell of humility come over him as he ducked under the makeshift timber framing that eventually became ancient stone catacombs.

He had been hoping to find another gold coin in the bag he'd been given to buy his girlfriend a dress of all things when, for centuries, the Knights of this Realm had been giving all they had to buy up enough buildings to keep the hidden passages and burial chambers of their ancestors a secret even as they had to lay new ones to keep pace with the growing and developing city above. All of it to keep their brothers and sisters of the hall, as they called them, from being sold as slaves and trophies to some of the cruelest entities of the Lowlands. No wonder some of them looked at him as if he were the anarkali dress—fragile as a flower bloom and too refined for any functional purpose. More and more, he saw his hard life as pampered by comparison.

"You still with me?" Aria asked, giving his hand in hers a little shake.

"To the end," he affirmed.

There was some hesitation whispered from the lack of expression she wore after the declaration. After a moment, she shook her head. "Your mind is somewhere else. Don't forget the plan."

"Right, the plan." Their task was to be in position at the other end of the tunnels near a private wharf where most of the slave deals were made. Kazim and his group were going to use their tunnels to sneak into the auction house where the slaves were kept and extract everyone they could without getting caught. While that happened, they would secure the boat that would let them all sail into the Gulf and make an innocuous trip through the waters deemed fit for leisure craft and then make port on the opposite end of the city where they'd disembark and get out of town as fast as possible. "The next tunnel should take us out by the docks."

"You did pay attention," she approved. "That's a good quality in a boyfriend."

He almost tripped. Was that the first time she had called him that? Jason wasn't sure why it felt so surprising for her to use the relatively new term in a courtship. Or why he was imagining she'd call him "suitor," "lover," or "paramour" instead. Maybe he had never shaken the conviction that she and her grandfather really were far older and as mysterious as he'd once been convinced.

As usual, his befuddlement amused her. Once they got through this, he'd have to turn the tables on her.

Emerging from the tunnel, Jason tensed. There was no one to greet them by the boat. Nobody was by the docks.

Have we been betrayed?

If they had, the High King had not yet whispered a warning nor impressed the conviction deep into Jason's heart.

He and Aria walked a few paces farther along the dock's planks. Looking at the line of ships moored, Jason mumbled to Aria as low as he could, hoping to guarantee she heard, "Our ship was to be called the Azad, right?"

"I think so, yes." Aria peered toward the nearest buildings. Her brow furrowed as she studied them. "Something doesn't feel right about this."

"Something is definitely not right. The Azad isn't here at all," he replied.

Aria's attention whipped to the boats, and her grip on his hand tightened. "We need to get out of here. Right now."

"Agreed."

Just then, the clomping footfalls of someone dashing down

the planks of the dock reached Jason's ears. Instinctively, he spun and put Aria behind him, hand on the hilt of his spiritsword, much as she had done for him back in Brackenburgh. However, instead of a Sombra sliding out of the shadows, it was their old tunnel guide coming on them. Again, Jason felt no impression of warning other than his own misgivings and anxiety.

The man reached them in a minute but took another full minute to catch his breath. "They ... are ... captured," he wheezed in broken Ecthelish.

Pushing from behind him, Aria put a comforting hand on the man's back as he bent over and fought to catch his breath. He was standing with hands on his knees. A blue taqiyah he had been wearing was crumpled in one of his hands, and he used it to fan himself.

"Who was captured?" Aria gently prompted, speaking slowly in Ecthelish after the man had another minute to collect himself.

"All. All ... captured," he replied, steadier now. "We ... fail. All captured."

Aria looked up at Jason, her jaw slack with horror and shock. He put his hands behind his head, knitting his fingers, and tried not to panic.

"How did this happen?" she persisted.

The guide shook his head. "No know. I ... no know ... I ..." He wrung his hat furiously between both hands.

Aria spoke a flurry of words. Jason didn't know what she'd said exactly, but it sounded Zilnian to him. At least that was his hunch, as Aria's sister-like bond with Tirzah meant she was fluent in Zilnian. Which in turn meant his time for freely understanding and speaking the language he'd never learned must have passed. He watched more than listened to a series of exchanges between the two, with the man's voice becoming less fraught. His wringing stopped, and he spoke Zilnian without the start, stop, cadence of before.

At length, Aria looked up at Jason and said, "He says that a rearguard from the attempted raid managed to get word out that they were overwhelmed and captured almost immediately. They've been forwarding the message through the city for the past twenty minutes, getting it to us. He was the last link in the chain." She glanced at him and said something with a heartfelt nod of her head. He obliged her in turn.

"What do we do now, then? We have to help them," Jason insisted, hand resting on the spiritsword again. He'd messed everything up once more. The delay in the Grand Market must have cost them the element of surprise.

Aria nodded. "He also said that he knows where they will bring them. Efram is originally from historic Quimethra of the Uldiqui Confederacy. He knows of a place where they would take slaves who were too high value, dangerous, or controversial to sell here." Once more, she turned to Efram and asked something in Zilnian. He nodded.

"Efram can take us to where they will be. It's across the Gulf of Halepi and up the Quison River to Uthtar."

Crossing his arms over his chest, Jason looked from Efram to Aria. His suspicions hackled him. "How does he know that?"

Aria's face fell a fraction, and she said rather wistfully as if burdened, "Before he became a Knight of Light, he was one of the slavers who ferried the enslaved to Uthtar from here."

"Oh," Jason replied numbly, feeling like he'd been struck. Try as he might, he couldn't help but feel the weight of the admission. He couldn't imagine anyone owning to that fact, even under pretense. Forcing himself to focus, Jason asked, "Can he get us there?"

Once more, Aria inquired of Efram. From the body language and emphatic tone of his words, Jason knew before

Aria even said, "He pleaded with me to do so. Efram is desperate to make amends for what he once did."

"I can relate," Jason muttered and bit his lip. He shouldn't have let that thought slip out.

He looked out onto the gleaming Gulf of Halepi, not wanting to see Aria's reaction. Whether she judged what he said fair or unfair, either would undo him, especially after his latest goof-up.

Without fail, he felt the soft touch of her hand on his cheek, redirecting his gaze to her. Her face was thoughtful and rueful. Not what he'd expected. "You can't keep tormenting yourself over what's past."

He scoffed. "If I could stop myself from ruining things for even a full week, then maybe. You heard Efram. Twenty minutes went by before we found out our newest ally was taken. I blew thirty. If we'd been in position then—"

"Then we would have been taken too. You noted yourself the Azad is gone. They came for both groups."

Jason scowled, not having considered that, though he should have. It seemed like a rather direct intuitive leap— something he would've normally made. Aria added to his musing, "Sometimes the High King guides us onto winding paths because the direct path is more fraught. If we'd been in place when we should have, no one would be left to mount a rescue. You didn't ruin anything, Jason. The High King kept us both from being taken." She cleared her throat, which seemed to have become tight. "And it seems he allowed your love for me to be the conduit by which he did so."

"The dress," Jason recalled. "I didn't feel anything or hear anything directing me to do so at the time."

She shrugged. "Sometimes his directing is obvious when it needs to be. Other times, he has planned and placed things such that we don't even notice he is clearing a road for us as we walk along. The important thing is to trust his wisdom and faithfulness in safeguarding us."

The old Jason would have argued that the others hadn't been safeguarded, but that felt like a quick slope for him to more contentious, rebellious thoughts. If Aria was right, and he knew her well enough to be sure she was, then perhaps all of it was a winding road to something else. Something less fraught, even if they couldn't see it.

He breathed out a shaky sigh, trying to let go of his resistance and apprehensions with it. Adhering to his oaths as Knight of Light proved not always so easy as when he first pledged them. But he supposed that was intentional. Even if the High King knew exactly how true his oaths were, until tested, Jason did not. "Okay. I guess that means we should get going. Efram needs to show us where we're headed next."

FIFTY-FIFTH INTERLOGUE: INTO THE DARK DEPTHS

"This is it," Aria confirmed, gesturing in the dark to a domed palatial estate looming in the distance. It had two tall towers and a hexagonal wall built around it with turrets on each vertice. At even intervals, jagged points stuck out along that wall, and the towers were so pointed that the effect made the whole thing look like the gaping maw of some stony beast. Wan crescent moonlight behind it and being several miles from the town of Uthtar made this look the sort of ominous place where vile acts and atrocities were committed without remorse.

"They've mastered the creepy aesthetic I see." He gave a shudder.

She rolled her eyes at him. "Didn't you get held in the Gerisk Ruins and were almost taken out by a Sombra in a tomb for the last Tislatnean Primus?"

"Well, yeah," he admitted.

"You said the Primus's mummy was sitting on a throne in the room as you battled a shadow assassin for your life barehanded." Aria's tone had grown a bit incredulous by this point.

"Okay, fine, so that's the creepiest place I've ever seen, and this ranks second. But to be at a place where people are shackled as property, and they're holding three of the twelve Defenders of the Realms? You have to admit, this isn't going to be a pleasant stroll."

At that moment, Efram spoke, quick and low. He gestured several times to the fortified palace and then in another direction. Then he bowed in a formal manner and slunk away.

"What was that about?" Jason asked, bewildered to see their guide disappearing into the night.

Aria looked troubled with the moonlight playing off a frown she wore. "He said there's a cistern straddling the estate grounds that is dried up at this time of the year. A well was sealed and covered with stones outside the wall. If we use it to get inside the cistern, we can travel through it toward the back of the grounds and climb up into them from the well on that side."

"That's all really helpful," Jason concluded with some trepidation, "What's the catch?"

"Efram isn't going to go into the estate with us. He said he has another part to play in the rescue and left."

"*Woah.* He's leaving? Where is he going?"

She shook her head as she pulled her hair back into a tight bun. "Efram didn't say. It seemed like he didn't want to tell me, to be honest."

"So, this whole thing might be a trap?"

"Possibly," Aria admitted.

Lacing his fingers behind his head, Jason sighed and closed his eyes. After a few seconds, he stretched and said, "Well, we might as well spring the trap." He stood and offered his hand to help Aria up from where they'd been crouching.

Aria took his hand with a tentative grip. "We're just going to walk in there and get caught?"

"No, definitely not. But there's no getting around the fact that this is probably our last chance to rescue your grandfather. Plus, three Defenders of the Realms are on the line. Like your grandfather says, if the Council of Defenders is the answer, then not acting right now, even if it's dangerous, would cost far more than the Lowlands can afford to lose."

"May the High King be with us," Aria murmured reverently and pulled herself up by his hand. As soon as she was on her feet, she wrapped her arms around him in a tight embrace. He returned it for as long as she held on, and when she let go, she leaned up and kissed him on the lips.

He raised his eyebrows, and she explained, "Just in case."

Jason nodded and looked down the way. Turning his attention back to Aria, he said, "Normally, I would say ladies first. But in this instance, maybe I should be at the front."

Squeezing his hand, she sighed. "As much as I appreciate the intention, if things go wrong in there, it won't matter who goes first."

The somberness stole away any reply he had planned for her imagined snarky comeback or bravado. Had he ever seen her this rattled before?

"Right. Just so you know, I'm still going first. Because I don't want the last thing I see to be you taken, and I'm going to fight till my last breath to keep that from happening."

Rather than argue any further, Aria let him have it his way. Leading them across the open rocky plain toward the estate, about halfway there, he asked, "Which side is the access to the cistern on?"

"Efram said it is the northern wall. Long ago, the estate was a fortress of Knights of Light, and they dug their cistern on the side facing toward the Highland and the Great King's city."

Keeping chatter to a minimum, Jason made the wide cut around and came out of their hiding near a mossy mass of stones. The rocks looked a bit like the rubble from an old cottage, which he supposed was intentional. Surprisingly, they never encountered any opposition while sneaking into the cistern. Which could be seen as a bad sign or a good one, depending on which imagined scenarios Jason chose to indulge in.

It took several minutes to clear the layers of stone, and he was once more surprised by how strong the slight and petite Aria was, but at the end, there was a rather abused-looking well housing. Drawing his spiritsword, Jason held it into the dark recesses of the well. The light pierced the dark for a good forty feet, but beyond that was a mystery. "Can't see the bottom. Hand me a smallish stone. We'll see how deep it goes." Taking the stone she handed him, he dropped it in, counting the seconds. "About seventy feet," he assessed after the muted thump reached him.

"A long way down," Aria summarized. "I have some rope, but it won't be long enough to reach the bottom from up here. Especially not if I tie it to the nearest tree."

"Yeah. None of the rocks are big enough to trust my weight, either." He gnawed on his lower lip. Sheathing the spiritsword, he adjusted his Yusbilsani robe, glad that he still had his trousers on under, and climbed over the lip of the well. He tried bracing himself on either side of it and found he could hold himself up that way. Testing a shimmying method, he found he could do it, but he shouldn't dawdle. He wasn't sure how long he could keep it up. "This way down," he said with a rueful smile.

"Looks that way," she replied, sounding nonplussed. Jason's limbs were long enough, but it would be a stretch for Aria.

"If you fall, I'll catch you," he promised.

"You better," she retorted.

He tried to chuckle as he concentrated on edging down, but

it came out much more choked and far less confident than he meant. One slip, and it would be a long fall and a very much fatal mistake.

As if to confirm it, his foot hit a moss patch just after placing it farther down and slipped. Grunting, he suddenly had his full weight dangling and scrambled to brace himself again. "Watch for moss. No sense having too much fun doing this," he called up to her.

If she responded, he didn't hear. Right away, he started moving faster. That little slip had cost him more endurance than he wanted to admit. He was only about a third of the way down, and already his arms were starting to burn. If he could get down to about ten feet left, he could try dropping the remaining distance and rolling, though he had no idea what the bottom was like. It could very well be a jagged mass of rocks that would make the payoff to that plan painful.

Halfway down, his left arm started twitching. He had to pause to take several deep breaths and rely totally on his legs to give his arms a quick break. This would've been a lot more reasonable for him to attempt if he hadn't been beaten and half-starved for almost a month straight now. Funny how these challenges never seemed to come while he was at peak readiness.

"There's probably a lesson in that somewhere," he grunted as he resumed his descent. "But ponder later, Jason. Move faster now."

Of course, the farther down, the slicker the stones became, and the less he could move as quickly as he wanted. He probably shouldn't have trusted his estimating skills, but after a couple minutes more of descending, he reached the point where he thought he was in the range for his drop and roll plan. Good thing, too, because his legs were now protesting, and his left arm was twitching again.

A whisper of warning rushed down to him in the well. "Don't drop?" he repeated, the strain in his voice causing it to crack. If he had not known from whence the voice came and was so familiar with it, he would be tempted to write it off as a trick of his paranoid mind or the wind. He did know, however, who had spoken to him just now.

Instructed him not to do what his arms and legs desperately wanted him to try. He knew something bad would happen if he ignored the warning. The High King did not idly offer up his counsel nor suffer to give commands only to be ignored.

Jason moved again, swallowing back his unease and fighting to keep his growing unsteadiness in check. Every inch piled up more and more aches and even more hard-fought than the last. He clenched his teeth and wheezed through them as his left arm began shaking. There was no stopping to give it a break now. He had to get as far as fast as he could.

No longer caring whether or not it was slippery, he scrambled downward, pleading with the High King for aid.

He closed his eyes, since it was too dark to see anyway, and kept putting one foot, then hand in place after the other until his foot missed its next mark and he dropped.

FIFTY-SIXTH INTERLOGUE: DESPICABLE DEPTHS DIVULGED

Landing hard on his bottom, Jason groaned. That had been almost a ten-foot drop, and he was sure he had bruised something.

Drawing his spiritsword, he looked up and was suddenly glad he hadn't dropped when he wanted to. Not only had he underestimated the well's depth at that point, and overall, but apparently, the owners of the palatial estate had not left it to chance that no one would try to sneak into their cistern. All along the ground were various swords and sharp pointed bits of metal and hooks and spikes. Jason managed to drop and land between a short sword and an iron spear or javelin.

"Thank you, my King. Thank you. Thank you," he intoned.

A pebble clattered off the walls of the well and landed near him. His head snapped up, and he could just make out that Aria had started her descent. Staggering to his feet, his legs still far from steady, he tried to call out a warning, but his voice cracked and failed him. Knowing how much concentration the climb took, it was probably best not to shout out to her in panic.

Reining himself in and trying again, he called out. "Aria, sweetheart. How far down are you?"

"Far enough," she replied, her voice strained, "to know I really don't like this."

He grimaced. It sounded like she was already at least fifteen feet in. She must have started after him before he'd even reached the bottom.

Of course, she did. Every second matters.

"Sweetheart, how are you holding up?" he asked, his fist held to his mouth anxiously.

"I've been better. Especially ... before you started ... calling me sweetheart. What's that ... about?"

He ran both hands through his hair. Not good. He didn't want to scare her, especially if she was already struggling. Going down was hard enough, so he doubted she could go up, and he knew he wouldn't be able to go up and support her and get them both back down.

More stones clattered down to him as he dithered. If nothing else, she was making good time downward. She was probably thirty feet in now. That also meant she was being a little reckless in how she climbed.

What do I do? What do I do?

Looking around, Jason examined the death trap surrounding him and snapped into action. Wielding the spiritsword, he slashed at a nearby spear and cleaved it through midway up the shaft. For a moment, he just stared, and then it clicked. He began frantically swinging his fiery sword, hacking down all the dangerous and deadly impediments around, cutting them off as low to the ground as he could or knocking them down when possible. The soil wasn't fully dried and was a kind of reddish clay but firm enough.

Above, he could hear Aria grunting and groaning. The

struggle was painfully clear in her voice, and she was still dangerously far up the shaft.

Assessing his progress, it looked like he'd cleared enough that if she fell as he had and didn't land perfectly placed, she would still be safe. Sweat rolled down his face. He looked around the space, noting that he had missed many deadly points. Could she still tumble onto those?

"Jason!" Aria called out, her voice catching. "Honey?"

Uh-oh. Not good.

"Yeah, sweetheart?"

"You know how you promised to catch me if I fell?"

Oh, no. Definitely not good.

His arms were still rubbery to him, and his legs felt ready to give. There was no delaying his answer. "I do. Why?"

"I ... don't ... think ... I'm going ... to ... make it. Don't try to catch me. Just ... finish ... the ... Quest. And I love you ... always."

A little hitched breath escaped her lips, and he realized she would fall any second and asked him to just let her land where she may. From her height, unless she handled it just right, that would likely kill her, and if not kill her, then break enough bones that she wasn't coming back out of the cistern without a stretcher and lift. Neither of which they expected to have.

Another squeak of failing effort echoed to him, and he could see her up about twenty-five or more feet. All her limbs were stretched as far as they could reach and bounced like rafts on a stormy sea's waves.

Oh, please, my Great King. Please. Don't let me lose her now. Help me!

Getting under her as best he could guess and sheathing his spiritsword, the dark closed in on him. As soon as the light vanished, she shrieked and was falling. He held out his arms and braced himself.

It felt like an instant later, her body hit his arms, and he went straight down onto one knee, every muscle straining itself until they felt like a bowstring ready to snap. He cried out in pain, but his arms held fast, and his legs didn't buckle. And before he even understood what had happened, he felt her arms around his neck.

She's okay! We're okay! Thank you, my King!

Shudders ran through Aria's body as he cradled her there in his arms. "Aria? Are you okay? Did you—"

He felt her hands feeling for his face, and finding it, she gripped his head and neck and kissed him with a furious intensity. She took a break seconds later to breathe and kissed him again, little sobs and choked laughter eventually breaking free her hold on him. "You are terrible at listening," she said between throaty chuckles.

"Listening wasn't the issue this time. The living without you part wasn't working for me," he replied.

For just a moment, she rested her head against his chest. "Someday, when we're not racing to save my grandfather, and it's not life or death for us. I'd like to do this."

"Dropping down abandoned wells? Not exactly what I'd advise ..." he set her down and drew his spiritsword.

Aria shook her head and refixed her hair, which had come undone. "You're incorrigible." Looking past him at the rest of the room, she gasped. "And favored to be alive."

"*Mm-hmm.* Our would-be hosts aren't very inviting. I say we go give them our complaints," Jason said and started walking down the length of the cistern, his spiritsword held aloft to help them better see.

"Thankfully, Efram was right about this being dried out," Aria commented.

"It would've made things extra interesting if it wasn't." Jason suddenly stopped and looked at Aria. "We don't need it to be any more interesting because I don't know how we're going to get out of here."

The grimace Aria wore let him know she had no clue, either. "Efram was adamant we could do this."

Efram was also adamant he had to get away as fast as possible.

Seeing no point in arguing, he continued, Aria's hand linked to his free one as he held aloft his fiery sword for light in the broad, dark passage. As they walked, Jason noticed the ground sloped upward. "This must have been a pretty lousy cistern. The water wouldn't have been able to supply the well at the other end of this nearly as successfully as the end we came down."

"I noticed that too," Aria said, her voice holding a note of ill-ease. "It's possible I translated the Zilnian word wrongly, or Efram did. The Zilnian word for cistern literally means, 'vessel of life-giving liquid.'"

"For a largely desert-bound people, that would make sense," Jason allowed. "What would he have possibly meant otherwise, though?"

There was an audible crunch under Jason's foot that startled him. So far, the ground had been like loose-packed clay. But the most recent stuff gave way a bit more, and he felt some kind of rock or something break underfoot. Holding his spiritsword lower to the ground, the flames burned hotter and flared in brilliance. He had stepped on a long, slender bone. A humerus, probably. "Aria ..."

She clung to his arm. "He might have meant this is a tomb. A vessel for blood ..." she said quietly.

Now that Jason looked closer, he could see bits of broken bones poking through the soil all along the corridor. A sickening thought that the red hues to this place were from the blood of those dumped unceremoniously down here, permanently staining the clay, fixed itself in his mind.

"What is this place?" he asked, vacillating from disgust and terror to outrage.

Aria pulled at his arm to get him walking again, and she kept tightly bound to his side as she spoke in a low, rueful tone. "I don't know, but I heard stories about this region. It went through many brutal conquests. It could be this once was a true cistern but was repurposed to dispose of the bodies of those who resisted the latest regime. Or it could be the bodies of slaves not seen fit to sell, and so were discarded here to die."

His throat felt tight. Jason didn't even want to breathe the air in this place. The weight of all the evil that had befallen these people rested heavily on him as any stone they'd removed from the entry well. It was maddeningly awful trekking over and around the bones he could not unsee. "I guess this is now officially worse than the Gerisk Ruins."

"Let's just get out of here," Aria insisted.

Walking the remaining distance in a somber silence, they reached a leveled place in the cistern that terminated into a wall. Overhead, the roof of the cavern had a large hole. To Jason's surprise, something else was there. "A ladder?" The enormous thing stretched high up to where he could see a closure over what must have been the well within the estate walls. The sloping up had been sufficient to bring them to only twenty or thirty feet below the surface.

Aria walked up to it and gave it a rough shake. "It's pretty sturdy. I suppose it made things convenient for those who came here to ..."

Jason didn't blame her for not finishing that thought. Testing the ladder himself, he looked over at Aria and shrugged. "This way up?"

"I'll go first this time," she replied and drew her spiritsword.

The flames from the thin blade brought an added dose of warmth and light to the place, much needed after its chilling nature had become clear.

Wrung by wooden wrung, he followed her, a childish part of him insisting that he keep an eye on the ground below as they climbed to watch for any of the dead so grievously wronged to return for revenge on the living. Knowing what he knew now as a Knight of Light, it was foolish, but the bogeys of childhood, like any of the monsters in the Lowlands, needed banishing by the light.

To his surprise, when Aria pressed her palm against the seal to the well, it lifted away easily, and she was able to slide it aside and slip out into the night. Jason kept his spiritsword out and clamored over the lip as quickly as possible. The courtyard of the estate was unbearably cultured and urbane. Landscaped shrubs and floral presentations ringed marble fountains spewing water from bronze statuaries. Still lit mainly by lanterns, the place had the faux appearance of pleasantness and civility even in the dark. He ran his hand through his hair and found himself coated in cold sweat. It took all his control not to make any unneeded sounds of reviling.

Three steps ahead of him, Aria waved for him to follow her. As they'd seen from afar, the central palace was within the grounds of the estate, but there were also several shorter buildings. One, long and broad, looked very much like a stable. Together, they crouched down beside the corner of what might have been the gardener's shed as Aria pointed out a few guards walking the walls above.

It seemed the pair of torch-bearing and ornately garbed guards had missed Aria and Jason's arrival. Their eyes focused outward. When the two guards began walking down the wall away from the stable, Jason and Aria made their move, dashing across the curated lawn to the side of the stable. True to its form, it was a wood structure that looked like a place for horses and other farm animals. Jason didn't doubt for one second, however, that what waited within would be far less innocent.

On that side of the stable was a normal door, probably a service entrance, with what Jason had noted earlier to be larger primary doors toward the center of the structure. Jason tasted a bit of bile in his mouth when he considered that they perhaps paraded or herded people out of those extra-large doors.

Aria melted the lock on the service door and opened it, slipping in without a sound. Jason followed, pulling the door closed behind him. It was well Aria had her sword drawn still because the stable was utterly dark except for a centrally located table, at which a pair of guards sat playing some sort of table or card game, lanterns hung on broad support posts nearby.

On either side of the "stable" ran cages, most just big enough for an individual, though a few larger ones were scattered amongst them. Dirty tins where it looked like food and water had been served to the captives lay rusted in the corners of the cells. Small bundles of hay old enough to have started sprouting or molding, some both, were allotted in the backs of the enclosures. The place smelled awful, and as he and Aria slunk down the line of cells, it became painfully apparent some of these people had been kept in bondage for weeks, perhaps a month or more. Their clothes were tattered and filthy, and they shivered on the dirt floors.

"This is despicable," Jason whispered to Aria.

"*Shh,*" she shushed and pointed a few cells ahead.

There, braced on either side of a divided cell, were Tirzah and Kaveed, each holding the other's hand between the bars. Before Jason could acknowledge it, Aria dashed over to them and dropped to her knees in front of the cells.

Feeling they deserved a moment to themselves. Jason

walked on, looking for Cinaed. Along the way, he spotted Kazim, whose curly black hair was matted from a blow to his head that had bled some. He was sleeping fitfully on his sparse straw bedding. Cinaed was nowhere to be found on this end of the stable, which left the other half to check.

Jason drew his spiritsword. Getting past the guards would be tricky—unless he wasn't trying to hide.

FIFTY-SEVENTH INTERLOGUE: RIGHTEOUS FURY

Coming right to the edge of where he could be seen, Jason charged out into the open, calling out loudly, "Hale evening, gents," in Ecthelish. The two guards playing a game that involved little colored stones and round pegs on a wooden board were so startled that one fell out of his chair backward, and the other tripped as he scrambled to produce his weapon.

Jason never gave him the chance. Dashing over, he grabbed the back of the man's neck and slammed him down against the table, then threw him to the ground. Flipping the table over on top of him, he was on the other guard and, with his spiritsword, battered away the pistol the guard had produced.

The other guard cried out in pain as the flames seared his hand. He tried to back away, but Jason grabbed him, hoisted him to his feet, and decked him in the face. As he crumpled to the ground, Jason struck him with the pommel of his spiritsword, rendering the man unconscious.

By now, the other guard tried to crawl out from under the table to reach for the stable doors. He raised up and opened his mouth like he was going to scream for help. Jason was there in one leap and held the burning blade next to the man's face. "I wouldn't if I were you," he instructed through clenched teeth.

Slowly closing his mouth, the guard held up a hand in plaintive surrender. Like the guards on the wall, he wore the ceremonial puce vest and a sash with fringe. He had a taqiyah on his head of a slightly darker shade and well-trimmed facial hair. Stammering, he uttered a string of words in a language Jason had never heard before. He guessed it was either the Uldi or Quimethra dialect, whichever province the man was from in the confederacy. In either instance, it did not matter.

Very purposefully, Jason pointed at the man, then covered his mouth. The other man mimicked this and then nodded, growing very quiet. Next, Jason pointed at the cells and made the motion of unlocking them, then pointed at the man.

At this, the guard shook his head and emphatically protested. So much so that Jason wanted to strike the man just to shut him up, but he resisted very narrowly. A pressure against his heart made it feel as though that would take him a step from righteous indignation into cruelty, and that was not the manner of the High King's servants.

Instead, Jason crouched down and once more signed for the man to be quiet. This time, the man was a bit more reluctant but complied. Once he had stopped, Jason pointed at him and made motions for sleep to the man, wanting him to close his eyes.

Apparently, he misunderstood and started to yelp. Bringing down the pommel of his sword on him, the other guard dropped unconscious as well, his strangled cry ending abruptly. It was hard to hear outside whether the noise of Jason's attack or the guard's cry had alerted anyone to what was going on.

Searching on the guard, he found the keys to at least some of the cells and ran back to where Aria was still kneeling in front of the cage with Tirzah and Kaveed. As he approached, she looked up, her eyes filled with tears, and asked, "Did you kill them?"

"No," he shook his head and began working at the locks. "I wasn't exactly gentle with them, but they'll be fine. How are you holding up?"

Aria didn't answer and neither did Tirzah or Kaveed, who each exchanged a glance. For the moment, Aria seemed focused instead on swiping away tears. After Jason finished with Tirzah and Kaveed's cells, Aria took the keys wordlessly and used them on other cages.

Jason helped Tirzah and Kaveed out of their respective cells. Both stretched and then embraced, kissing one another. Jason tried not to intrude as they held each other, but time was short.

"Not to be rude, but what's wrong with Aria? Why is she crying?"

Kaveed sighed and held Tirzah tight to him. "They took Defender Black some time ago. They have done so multiple times since we got here. Whoever is holding us seems intent on torturing the information on our plans out of him."

"Oh, no." Jason put his hand to his mouth and unconsciously glanced back toward the horrible cistern-tomb they'd come out of. How long would it have been before they threw his body in there to join the others? Were they too late even now?

"Do you know where they took him?"

Tirzah released Kaveed and said, "The Defender mentioned the palace at the center of the courtyard. One of the lower rooms. A dungeon, he called it. These Uldiqui are beasts," she snarled acerbically.

"We got a hint of that in the secret tunnel to this place. I didn't know such cruelty existed in the Lowlands," Jason grumbled.

"It very much does," Kaveed replied. "But that isn't what my dear Tirzah means. These Uldiqui are not mere men. They are werebeasts. Whoever employs them has turned to the dark sorceries."

Dorian.

It couldn't be, but Jason's thoughts immediately turned to his brother again. Trying to focus, Jason asked, "Then the Yusbilsani who took you captive are actually darkling creatures too?"

"No," Tirzah replied. "They are simply unscrupulous. Treacherous lot they are, they took their sums of money and left. Precious little it will do for them when the shadows close around and all their precious gold cannot buy deliverance from the horror they unwittingly further."

Rubbing his face, Jason looked toward Aria. She was almost finished with the cells on this side, having ghosted past them to open cells closer to the center of the room. Even now, she was helping Kazim out of his cage.

"Brother-in-arms," Kaveed spoke up, gripping Jason's arm tightly. "We must get Defender Black out of there and to safety. It's all the more pressing that we assemble the Council immediately. The forces of the Dark Prince move against us, and if we do not hurry, the Tower of Light will fall."

Jason's eyes widened. "Tower of Light? Like the stories from Anargen's day? It exists? Or, I mean, it still exists? He and the others succeeded even after scattering?"

Kaveed's brows furrowed, "There is not time to properly answer that. When we are far from this place and daylight restored to us, then we may speak more on this. For now, we must rescue Defender Black."

"Beloved, we don't have our spiritswords, shields, or armor," Tirzah reminded him. "We are hardly a rescuing army."

About that moment, Aria stalked back up, Kazim at her

side. "We've freed all those known to be Knights of Light. The others are all political prisoners or servants who have fallen out of favor with the Uldiqui's Khan. I'm not sure we can trust them not to rat us out in order to barter their way out of their present situation."

"It matters not," Kazim spoke up, holding his head gingerly on the injured side. "We are *Palatini Lucis Aeternae*. Free all ... we must."

Shaking his head, Kaveed asked, "Can we not clear this place? Burn it to the ground forever that none ever be held here again?"

"My beloved," Tirzah rejoined, "Even if they are few in number, they could all be under the werebeast curse. Such a force would be challenging to face even if we were fully armed."

"Fine!" Aria yelled. "You free the prisoners and get everyone to safety. I'm going to rescue my grandfather."

With that, she marched off, leaving the rest of the group in shocked silence.

"I'll get her," Jason said. He dashed over to Aria and got between her and the door.

"Aria, please, we need to think this through," he implored.

"Out of the way. I'm going to get my grandfather." She tried to slip past him.

Jason tried again, backing up and wheeling around in front of her. "Sweetheart, listen to me, we have to—"

"Stop calling me sweetheart. And stop trying to keep me from him. He's the only family I ever knew growing up, and they're killing him! Slowly and painfully. The only way to make it end quicker is for him to betray everything he's ever loved. So, no, I won't calm down and think about this!"

"Fine!" Jason bellowed. He moved one more step in front

of her and drew his spiritsword. "Then let me go down fighting at your side at least."

That stopped her. Now that he had her attention, Jason's tone morphed from passion to compassion. "Let the others prepare for an escape, but you and I—we'll get your grandfather out together, okay?" He brushed his fingers along her cheek, tucking back some strands of wayward hair that always seemed to escape her braids. It was one of the most strangely endearing attributes of her beauty to him.

Aria pressed his hand to her cheek and closed her eyes. Her small frame shuddered as she fought to control the sobs that threatened to shake her until she crumbled to the dirt beneath. After a few moments, Aria seemed to best them and opened her teary eyes. Wiping them clear, she answered, "We probably won't make it."

"Then we'll at least be an undeniable distraction to allow the others to get away," Jason replied, giving her a cocksure smile. "You know how charming I can be."

A light smile touched her lips, and she huffed a heavy sigh. Turning, she found the others had gathered at their backs. "Are we all in agreement then?"

There was a general round of assent. "Good. Then may the High King be with us all," she concluded.

FIFTY-EIGHTH INTERLOGUE: FAMILIAR AND FOREIGN

Jason motioned for Aria to dash across the lawn where he was standing. He marveled at how graceful her stride was, especially under the circumstances. Knowing now that the guards walking the walls could, in fact, be carefully concealed werebeasts and possess the proportional enhancement to their senses made her soundless tread all the more valuable.

From a distance the palace had looked rectangular, but up close, it had a more interesting pattern of rooms which jutted out from the frontage and employed classical architecture emulated from elsewhere in the Lowlands. It had a white-marbled upper portions and brick for the lower third of the levels—an odd and opulent combination that felt strangely aristocratic for such a place. Stranger still, it looked so familiar that Jason suspected it must have an analog he'd seen somewhere along his travels.

"Here, around back," he proposed. "We'll find a dark window and climb in."

"You're not drawing on experience here, are you?" Aria quipped.

He was, in fact, but when he glanced back at Aria, he could tell she meant it in jest. "What can I say? I have skillsets that come in handy from time to time."

Not wanting to broach a discussion of the times he had used this particular skill set, he spotted a lightless window, did a quick kick off the brick portion of the wall, and caught his fingers on the sill of the window above. Pulling himself up, he used the ornate pilasters framing the window to brace himself and employed something new to his person—his spiritsword. Sliding the burning blade into the space between the pane and the sill, he felt the marvelous sword dispatch the catch on the other side. Sheathing it again, he heaved the hefty pane of glass up and slipped in.

Turning around, he reached out to help Aria and found her attempting the same move he had. She made it but gripped his hand instead of the sill. "Our skillsets might align more than you think," she whispered.

"Our sense of humor certainly does," he replied dryly.

Looking around, they had entered into some kind of study. Books lined the shelves with fat spines and esoteric titles inscribed on their leathery covers. Some were quite old looking, and around the room were scatterings of strange metallic trinkets of unknown purpose. Yet something felt off. Again, the feeling increasingly took on the tone of déjà vu for him. As if echoes of some event were reaching his ears, calling to him. There was a strong sense that he loathed this room, even if it was completely new to him.

"We should keep moving," Aria said brusquely, moving toward the door. She gestured to the texts and items on the shelves. "This place is filled with Tislatnean artifacts and tomes."

Hence the creepiness factor. This place just gets better and better.

"Okay. So, Kaveed and Tirzah said your grandfather is on the lower floors of this place. We could always cut through the floor and drop down on them."

Aria had been peering through a crack in the door and turned back to say, "Yeah, and possibly drop the floor cutaway on my grandfather. Or even better, we drop down into a holding cell or something and make things super convenient for them."

"Right, so what's the plan then?"

"You noticed the window in the room to the left was dark, too, right?"

"Yeah. What about it?"

"We can slip into the hall and try to find the staircase down. If someone starts coming, we can duck into there."

Jason shrugged, "It beats dropping through the floor right now."

Peering out, Aria slipped through the tiniest manageable opening in the door and crept down one side of the hall beyond. Jason likewise cleared the hall and then slid out, pushing the door shut behind him. Suddenly thinking about it, Jason checked the door he'd just exited. It wouldn't open. He tried the next door that Aria had suggested and got the same result. The doors were all locked from the inside or at least needed keys to access them from outside.

This isn't good.

He glanced down the carpeted hall in both directions and didn't see Aria. How had she ghosted out of sight so fast?

Following the hall the direction he thought he saw her take, he found himself coming to the central portion of the palace. He again felt the smack of déjà vu as he looked out onto the open foyer with double marble and mahogany banister staircases wrapping up to the second floor from either side. A crystal chandelier of gold hung over the expansive room's center, filled with plenty of candles to brighten the space.

It was so odd. Even the structure of each wing of the house felt familiar. Like the way they'd come into that hallway with doors on either side. Those rooms were one half of the wing with another layer of rooms staggered along in a set just beyond, with a hall also running down their middle. The pattern was so familiar, he suddenly wondered if he could guess where the staircase leading down was.

Just then, a hand gripped his shoulder. He spun and found Aria there. "Hey, come on. I think I found the way down."

"It's not through a room on the far wing behind a surrealist painting of a moonless night, is it?" he asked.

She shook her head, her nose crinkled in utter bewilderment. "What? That's super specific, and no. Just follow me."

For some reason, his being wrong about that was a relief. Following her in the opposite direction from the one he proposed, she took him into a small room that stood as a tip to the wing of the corridor. He noticed the extra stack of rooms and hall converged into this spot just as he imagined it might.

Something else caught his attention. "You cut through the lock?"

"It wouldn't open, and we're running out of time for subtle," she chided.

Entering, Jason's heart thudded. This room looked familiar too. It had a dark carpet and a telescope on a balcony accessible from stairs within the room. Star charts, maps, and assorted other astronomical wares were scattered throughout the room. The stairs that went up were mirrored by a reverse pair that went down to the basement. Jason was certain this wasn't where her grandfather would be.

"*Um*, Aria, I don't think—"

"We have time to look at the stars, yeah, I know. I'm an aspiring astronomer, remember? I'm still focused."

She dashed down the stairs, and he followed, expecting to find precisely what waited at the end for them—a storage room. It was perhaps more cluttered than he expected. Or was it? The eerie déjà vu potency was like gravity now, tugging at him. Trying to pull him back to somewhere, but he couldn't understand where exactly. He'd never been in Uthtar that he knew of.

"A dead end, but look at this," she called to him from across the room. She'd worked over to the opposite corner of the wide room full of tables and shelves with assorted goods. Some foodstuffs that would keep for years. Others were practical items needed for keeping a house and grounds of this sort running. But what Aria found made him smile. "You found a spiritsword."

"Grandfather's," she affirmed. Using the belt and scabbard, she strapped it over her shoulder. "Too bad we didn't lead the others into here. We could've armed one of them to help us. We could be more direct in our search ... instead of poking around futilely ..."

Tears welled in Aria's eyes, and he realized she was on the verge of breaking down. Though it frightened him some, he had to speak up. "Maybe, if we didn't ... know ... what this house is like," he tried to say, faltering as he tried to get the sentence out. "Actually, you know, follow me this time."

Leading her back up to the floor they came in on, Jason pointed to the room on the opposite end of the hall. "There. That's it. Don't ask how I know, but I just know that's it."

He was so focused on leading her there that he rushed out into the open space of the foyer without clearing it first. As soon as they reached the middle, he heard someone call out in the strange language. Jason started to ignore whomever it was and keep running, but a sudden instruction to turn back gripped him forcefully. So much so he swung about, slinging Aria around to skid to a stop deeper into the middle of the room as he raised a block with his buckler.

A few bullets plinked against the little shield. Deftly stopped by his *Thyreos Pistis*, however compact. Out of the corner of his eye, Aria had already drawn her spiritsword and was charging from the side. Producing his own, Jason joined the attack and came straight at the Uldiqui, expecting to take him down quickly.

To his shock, the man spat and leaped inhumanly back several feet into a corner of the room by the doors leading out front to the entry atrium.

Jason glanced at Aria and saw the concern knitting her brow. A second later, the man cried out in a feral snarl that no natural man or beast of the Lowlands would produce. His body quivered, and fur rippled out from his clothes, which shredded away largely to reveal a partially transformed werebeast. It was not the new moon. However, they were close to one, rendering the effect nearly complete. Even so, his snout and fur seemed shorter than the ones Jason had encountered in Brackenburgh. It almost seemed more bear-like than wolf. The rest of the attributes were very much the same. This would not be simple.

The beast pounded his clawed fists on the ground and then charged. Much faster than Jason had been prepared for. He'd forgotten how quickly they moved. A hasty block managed to stop the first of its slashes at him, and he ducked the second.

All of a sudden, the beast lowered its head and battered into him, sending Jason tumbling backward. Trying to roll back to face it, he saw Aria come from the side and just miss nicking it with her blade, the fire crackling as it singed off some fur.

Back on his feet, Jason approached it cautiously, hoping its focus on Aria would turn and he could give her an opening. It didn't, opting instead to barrel toward her.

"No!" Jason cried out and dashed to intercept it, only to be caught by a warning to duck. His momentum was too great to stop outright, so he dropped and slid as the beast turned and swiped to backhand him. Aria was already safely out of the way. The whole thing had been a trick to draw him into another blow.

"Clever beast," he commented and hopped back as it slammed its fist onto the tiled flooring in a tantrum, cracking the tiles into tiny shards. That display, while menacing, gave Jason some hope that they could finish him with feint and flight tactics to annoy him out of his reasoned offensive.

Aria must have had the same thought because she charged forward, only to reverse and wheel to the side as the beast overcommitted to swiping at her and left himself open to a quick sting from Jason's spiritsword.

The beast roared at Jason and once more advanced on him. Aria went for the same pattern, and when the beast didn't take the bait, she changed strategy and lunged, giving a deep strike into its flank.

That got the monster's attention, and it turned and hammered the ground, swiping wildly at Aria. This time, when Jason charged, he knew it wasn't acting—it really wanted to kill her, so he rounded under and plunged his spiritsword deep into its side. Flames licked off the blade and caught on the beast, which gave forth an earsplitting yowl of pain. Its cries doubled in volume as Aria, no longer dodging for her life, rejoined and struck with her sword as well.

Fire local to each wound sizzled, and the beast stumbled backward, clutching its sides and bellowing more than barking at them. It collapsed to the floor, shattering the glass of the doors to the entry atrium. Jason knew this foe wouldn't be getting up.

Which was fortunate because, over the cacophony of its rage and pain, he could hear the thuds of others of its kind converging on them.

"Come on," he called to Aria and offered his hand. "We have to run!"

FIFTY-NINTH INTERLOGUE: EMBATTLED

Aria grabbed his hand, and they dashed toward the hall they planned to reach. As they crossed under the doorway, Jason looked back and saw three more beasts career into the foyer from outside, smashing through the entry atrium like it was paper instead of glass and iron. Atop the overlook to which the two staircases on each side adjoined, two more of the things came from alternate directions and leaped down into the foyer. A range of colored furs and slight size differences, they were all of the same stocky snub-nosed bear type as the last.

"So much for stealth," Aria commented.

"It's all right. Your grandfather can probably take what, all five, by himself?"

"You mean my elderly grandfather who has been in captivity and tortured for days?"

Jason pulled Aria along again and called, "Right. So, we'll save him four."

Even without looking back, Jason knew from their yowls and the crashing sounds that the creatures were coming after them. His only plan was to barrel to the end of the hall and get to Cinaed.

"Remember Ordumair," Aria yelled as they neared the very door he sought. "Close quarters, we'll handle them that way," she instructed and let go of his hand, peeling off down the other hallway sandwiched between rooms.

"Right," he called and turned and hacked through the lock on the nearest door, kicking it open. Inside was a sitting room with a fancy couch and end chairs near a table. Some small tea tables with matching seats sat on the eves of the room.

Hearing more whispered words of guidance, Jason dashed for the right side of the room, ran, and kicked off the wall just in time for one of the werebeasts to crash through the doorframe, taking most of it with it. The monster skid into the room, just under where Jason was sailing over. He slashed with his sword as he passed over it, leaving a glowing stripe across its back.

The shock caused the creature to crash into the wall, and the vibrations shook the nearby seats enough to tip over. However, there was no chance to relish the minor victory as another whisper told Jason to duck. From the hallway, a second werebeast arrived and sprang at him, swiping with its long, curved claws.

Jason dodged backward and tried to keep from being cornered. Meanwhile, his first opponent was gingerly turning to join the fight again. If one of the things was more monster than this room could handle, two would be absurd.

Tight quarters, Ordumair couldn't have been this close combat.

Throwing up a block, Jason wobbled a bit and forced himself to focus. Humor wasn't going to help him here. Each creature tried to converge on him from opposing angles. He listened for the whispered wisdom, but when he saw the sharp teeth drizzled with saliva from those hungry bestial faces chomping at him, he acted on his own. Dodging to the right, he avoided one monster and braced himself for impact from the other.

His buckler was hammered a moment later as the beast headbutted him as the first had. The force of it sent him flying backward out into the hall. He shook his head, trying to clear it, and just caught sight of something from the corner of his eye.

Jason ducked as another beast swiped at his head and then jumped as it went low to sweep his feet out from under him. The other two nipped at each other, deciding which would exit first and likely help cinch the kill.

Great King, please. I need your help!

There was nothing told to him as the beasts stalked to either side and growled at one another, coordinating the impending attack. He had nothing. They had already forced him to a section of hall with two wall sections still intact. No door to bust down—if he could manage it, no jumping back into the room he left or climbing. This was it. There was nowhere to go.

The tactic from before of prioritizing facing down one attack over the other wouldn't even work. Each beast would have equal opportunity to rend his flesh as he had to face down one or the other. How many times had he placed himself in a tough spot now? Clearly, his street savvy and worldly knowledge only carried him so far, and in the arena of monsters and quests, what he brought to the table was vanishingly small.

He jerked back as one of the beasts made a tentative swipe at him and immediately had to jump back the other way as the other growled and bared its fangs, reminding him he had no room to give. Each beast gave a rumbling ursine chuckle. This was amusing for them.

But from the shift in their posture, they were done toying

with him. They each got into a crouch, tensing for the finishing strike.

This was in precise contrast to Jason's response, which was to let the tension in his body go slack. What could he do now anyway?

A whispered answer came to him like the first cool drops of rain after a long, hot drought. "Wait and see," he murmured, repeating the directive.

One of the beasts twitched its ears and reared back a bit as though it had heard his words and was confused. This, in turn, led the other creature to grumble back as if in derision.

The werebeast on Jason's right raised up on its haunches and bellowed at the monster on the left, which was reciprocated by its comrade. Receiving new guidance, Jason crouched low, sprang up, and pushed off the wall, bracing himself across the top of the hallway just as the two beasts leaped forward and crashed into each other, becoming a tumbling, biting, scratching mess of fur and fury.

As Jason watched the two battle each other, he became aware of the heat spreading in his palm. Pressing against the wall as he was, one palm was directly against the spiritsword's burning blade. It felt tremendously hot but didn't scorch him. The wall, however, was another matter. To Jason's amazement and then concern, it had caught fire. As the lines of flames spread, he watched the blaze trace outward like a river flowing down a mountainside.

Once more, Jason was granted a sudden insight and pushed off the wall, dropping with his sword pointed down to land atop one of the werebeasts and deliver a devastating blow. Jumping off it, he landed with a shoulder roll and raised up and around into a slash that got past the guard of the other monster.

The thing recoiled in pain, and he stepped forward with a smooth stroke to finish it. For just a moment, he marveled at how the High King had worked all of it out in the most unlikely of ways. Perhaps in its unlikeliness was the clear evidence of his intervention.

A low growl issued from behind Jason. He had forgotten about the third werebeast. For the moment, his only imperative was to run.

Jason sprinted to the next room and hacked through the lock, bursting in. He was in some kind of scullery or kitchen prep area. This wasn't such a familiar room, and a second later, the werebeast crashed in after him. With a furious swipe, it took out a solid oak table that had been a food prep station, scattering bits of wood and food across the room.

Leaping back, Jason ducked and dodged attacks. Climbing over a counter, he dropped to the ground as the thing raked its claws across the wall behind where he'd stood.

Back on his feet, he crashed through a swinging door into what looked to be a dining room. The floor was a polished stone so smooth and well-kept he could almost see his reflection in it. Expensive mauve curtains made from costly imported fabrics hung from the windows. At the room's center was an enormous rectangular table composed of two long, polished mahogany tables along the length of the room and parallel with a space in the middle and end capped by a pair of shorter tables. There were perhaps thirty or more chairs positioned around it.

Once more, Jason was gripped by the weird sense of having been here before. It was clear what he was feeling wasn't déjà vu. Nothing about the rooms held a sense of having done the things he was now doing again. Only a recognition of this place in and of itself. But what did it mean?

By now, the werebeast had come into the room, slowly padding toward him, A low menacing snarl echoing in the wide room. The monster wrapped its brutal clawed hand around a chair, and, rearing back, he slung it at Jason. That was easy enough to dodge, but as the beast picked up two more chairs and heaved them at Jason, it forced him to run and jump out of the way. In between tosses, the beast bounded forward and tried to chomp at him while he wasn't yet surefooted.

The first time, Jason had to windmill keep on his feet. Licking its chops, the beast hurled itself at him. He managed to dive out of the way in time, but the fight's momentum wasn't on Jason's side right now.

Keeping space between himself and the monster as best he could, Jason edged away until he felt his back against a longer table. It was firm, not giving at all, effectively putting him to the wall. He gripped a chair tucked under the table and tried slinging it with his free hand. The chair missed the werebeast but succeeded in its true goal of turning its attention away long enough for Jason to roll over and up onto the long dining table. The creature looked up and growled. Tensing, it leaped over him to land with a thunderous crack as the sturdy wood gave under the beast.

At once, the table split, and Jason had to grip the edge he'd backed into to keep from sliding down into the fiend's waiting, snapping jaws.

Jason got a quick word of guidance and jumped, avoiding an attack that further splintered the enormous table. He landed beside the beast, fainted with a jab of his sword, smashed his buckler into its face instead, and delivered the real sword blow in quick succession.

The thing groaned and scrambled back, grousing at Jason as it nursed its injury. Glancing back the way he came, he also noted the pair of double doors demarcating the room's primary entry. In addition, the creature was in front of a door on the opposite end of the room from the scullery entrance, which possibly led to a smoking room. With all the noise and destruction, it was imperative that he get down to Cinaed right away. The monster would try to block him no matter which exit he picked.

Before he figured out his full plan, the werebeast decided for him. Marshaling itself and giving a roar, it loped over at him, slower than before, but desperation can make up sometimes for sloppy technique.

Jason dodged its first swipe and blocked the second and third while nicking its forearm. When the fourth strike came, Jason ducked, rolled forward, and risked it all to sink his spiritsword deep into the monster's abdomen.

Just as swiftly, he had to get back as the monster flailed out of control, smashing the other long table before it went down atop its pile of wooden wreckage and fell still. Eyeing it for a few seconds longer, Jason turned, dashed back into the hall through the shattered rooms, and reached the door to the floor below. Already, the lock had been melted off.

Aria is down there. How long ago did she reach it?

Not that the answer mattered. As Jason slipped in and ran down the winding stairs, all his prior commitment and determination to succeed in this next phase was multiplied, with her well-being unknown.

SIXTIETH INTERLOGUE: FEELING THE STEEL BETWEEN BONE BLADES

As Jason wound his way down the stairs, his heart pounded. He didn't know what was at the bottom of these stairs but knew it would be bad. Whatever tether he had to this place made that inescapably certain.

Voices echoed to him from the passage as he reached the final flight of stairs, and everything transitioned from the refined materials of the upper levels to coarse large cut stones of a much older origin. He padded his steps to give himself some chance of assessing what he was walking into.

He could discern Aria's voice but not what she said. Her tone was defensive, furious.

The responding speaker's words, imbued with condescension, were easier to make out, closer to where Jason would shortly emerge: "I'm afraid neither you nor your grandfather are leaving this place alive. You've saved my associates a great deal of time and effort locating you. It would be such a shame to waste it." Surprising and overtaking the antagonist would be a simple matter of timing and force. But Jason's throat tightened as he recognized the speaker.

Melania—what are you doing here?

Aria replied something, and from a sudden rush of heat that wound its way up to where Jason stood, he knew she had drawn her spiritsword. Creeping a few steps farther down, he found the door ahead was already torn open, laying off its hinges. From within, shone light sufficient to cast shadows of those in the room. There were four others present besides Aria and Cinaed. One shadow revealed the feminine figure of Melania. Another was a tall broad-shouldered man with an arm lifted to block the luminous sheen from the sword—an enforcer for Melania, no doubt. The final two were harder to sort out. Neither were physically imposing and with stances that implied they weren't concerned by the display. Hardened warriors of the dark, basalt from toxic volcanic flows resistant to all but the most intense heat.

To Jason's surprise, the broad-shouldered man spoke up, angling such that his shadow blurred over Melania's. "That was not our arrangement," he appealed in Ecthelish with a heavy dose of Knorish accent. "There is no need to be foolish. You kill them, and a new head will replace it. Keep them here, and it will paralyze their factions. The Glorious Campaign can be allowed to continue."

A jerky motion came from one of the nonchalant pair, and the big man went down with a corresponding groan. Faster than a blink, both smaller men were holding down the speaker. Melania's shadowy arm reached out and patted the kneeling man. "Dear Niklush, the arrangement was simply for you to bring me Defender Black and his chief allies. Your Knorish kinsmen got their part in the bargain, the contested lands by the Glaston River. I must note, however, that you failed to keep the terms for your part."

Niklush's voice was full throated, infamous Knorish heat pulsing in each word, "You are a treacherous witch. I kept my vow and now you turn on me! Do you know what I have risked for my people?"

The shadowy Melania once more patted him on the cheek several times and then slapped him with a smack easily heard where Jason crouched in hiding. "You mean forsaking your loyalty to the king you didn't follow behind closed doors anyway? *Mm*, yes, I suppose you won't be first choice for Defender of the North Central Realm any longer. Certainly, a loss for you ... but maybe not so great as this one."

Quick as a viper's strike, the shadowy outline of Melania drew a dagger and stabbed Niklush in the belly. He struggled against the restraining hold of the two others, crying out in surprise and agony.

"No!" Aria yelled, and suddenly, the light drew closer.

"See to her," Melania instructed. "I'm going to tend to dear Niklush. I'm sure he has at least a few secrets he'll happily part with before he perishes."

Jason sat frozen on the steps for several seconds. Yet another Defender and Realm compromised. Whoever this Niklush was, he seemed to have been important. Someone Aria and Cinaed would have trusted. Another betrayal.

"Betrayers always die twice. Once for their enemies and once for those who had been family." Jason's grandfather had often quoted that maxim. Treacherous as he was, it was a wonder he didn't choke on the words as they left his lips. Melania and Dorian were worse than traitors. Now, they were monsters.

Niklush cried out in Knorish, pulling Jason's attention back to the shadow drama. A keening screech overrode the sound of his horror. Each of his tormentor's shades wavered and swelled in the back as though something was hatching from them.

Jason drifted a few steps farther toward the room and could see one of them through the doorway. When the something was fully formed, it loomed menacingly over its prey. This creature's appearance was like a nightmarish squid or a vicious viper. Its face was certainly serpentine, with a crest behind it that was triangular and stiff looking. Its body looked lean and muscular but with incongruous muscle bands, not like a man's. An array of tendrils, some of which terminated in clawed hands and some pointed hooks, spread wide from its body. There looked to be ten in all and varying lengths and degrees of apparent jointedness or tentacle-like flexibility. Most horrific was the way it anchored itself to the man from whom it hatched, braided around his waist like a belt. The two men in the next room were the direnoir-bearing thugs who had murdered Melania's uncle, Verdun.

Jason ducked back behind the corner to keep out of sight, his heart pounding. Direnoir were the most unnerving creatures from the stories of Anargen's trials.

"Your fear makes for sumptuous fare," one of the creatures hissed.

"Yes, yes, delicious. What then shall the little phosphila taste like?" the other responded with wicked glee.

"We need only hold her grandfather, and she'll collapse into a ball like a toddler."

"Yes, do hurry, Niklush. Tell us where your Realm's defender is and where the others will be so we may enjoy our feast on a true phosphila."

Hearing these horrific creatures talking so flippantly about murdering Aria finally snapped Jason out of his stupor. Casting off all his caution, he drew his spiritsword and leaped into the room. "You will regret your hubris, you overstuffed cuttlefish!" he bellowed.

Both direnoir swung around at once to take him in. They weren't quite so large as their shadows implied. Smaller than the one Anargen had faced centuries before. But there were two of the hideous things, each undulating in unnatural ways as they assessed him.

The room itself was both larger than it had seemed from the outside and smaller than he would've anticipated for a dungeon. Far less ominous and impressive than the one he'd been held in by his brother Dorian in Brackenburgh.

This dungeon had simple but effective devices of torture arrayed around the room's periphery, plus a small row of cells with barbed black bars. At the room's back was Cinaed, lying on the ground, unmoving. Before him stood Aria, whose spiritsword was locked in a contest with some kind of long pole Melania grasped.

Jason had to take in a lot quickly and, most pointedly, the shift in the room's tone and quality with his arrival. Just by crossing the threshold with his spiritsword drawn, he felt as though the whole space had warmed by several degrees and became a good bit brighter. Even so, the surprise only affected a brief unease in the direnoir.

Melania broke off from her clash with Aria. "I knew you couldn't keep away. You always had a touch of the romantic about you. But which damsel are you here to sweep off her feet?"

"*Mm*, your insights are keen as always," one of the direnoirs commented, hissing with glee. "He fears greatly for the phosphila's well-being." With a deft stroke from several of its tentacles, the beast tossed Niklush across the room. "Such strong fear for a phosphila—we gorge this night!"

"Take him alive. Dorian will want to have a visit with him," Melania instructed. A sly smirk turned up the corner of her mouth, and she said something to Aria that Jason couldn't make out, but whatever it was, Aria lashed out and set their battle back into motion.

This meant Jason would face both direnoirs alone and couldn't help Aria if something went askew in her fight.

One of the direnoirs suddenly snapped a tentacled arm out at him, the tiny, clawed hand at the end reaching for his left shoulder.

Jason dodged out of the way. The things moved not quite like the boneless musculature of a mollusk nor the jointed motion of a vertebrate—it was thoroughly unnerving. As was the fact that as he watched both creatures grew some in size. It was as if his discomfort and fears truly fueled them, empowering them to destroy him. Jason had hoped that detail of Anargen's account had been an embellishment or misperception.

Another pair of tentacles from the second swiped at him, and as he ducked, a corresponding pair from the first hooked around his arm, with others smacking him hard. His vision blurred briefly. The first direnoir struck again, slamming a whip-like tentacle into his chest and sending him tumbling back to the room's entrance. Jason groaned as he struggled back to his feet and just missed being hit by an appendage with a wicked hook on the end. The cool air from the speedy swipe tickled the back of Jason's nape, chilling him.

How in the Lowlands was he supposed to defeat two of these things when Anargen scarcely handled one? Especially when every fear swelled their size, and right now, he was terrified. Of them. Of losing Aria. Of failing after the High King absolved him of so many wrongs.

At once, the pair of beasts both reached to grab him.

Jason swung and caught the left creature's appendage, severing it in a single strike. But the second got past his guard and tripped him. As soon as his back hit the floor, he was hoisted up. Each creature had taken one of his legs. Seeing how terribly that could go, he swung with all his might and contorted so that his spiritsword grazed the tentacle of the right direnoir, forcing it to let him go.

Jason dropped haphazardly and had to catch himself on the ground. Neither of these smaller direnoir were strong enough to fully manhandle him alone. That gave him a sudden surge of confidence. Scrambling to his feet, he twisted, bringing his spiritsword down in a hacking slice that chopped through the left direnoir's limb. With two smoldering stumps, that direnoir forced its host to retreat a few steps.

"Now, whose fear is palpable?" Jason taunted.

The direnoir snarled but shriveled some. It looked to its compatriot, but the other direnoir was hesitant to attack again as well.

A look of conflict passed over the direnoir's serpentine face. Then, it turned its head toward Melania and Aria. The two were still locked in furious combat. A sharp hiss that sounded sly issued from its mouth. "Perhaps it is hers that will nourish me when I overwhelm her!"

Though he knew it was likely a bait for him, Jason bellowed, "No!" Surging forward, he leaped at the direnoir, which had just turned its back to him.

It tried to spin and slash him with a blade-like limb, but Jason's buckler intercepted the blow, sending it glancing off. He landed and sprang forward, burying his burning blade deep in the direnoir's chest.

The thing shrieked and flailed, a storm of snapping and swiping appendages, but Jason dodged each and waited till the fire from his sword thoroughly caught before pulling back.

As the monster wailed and moaned, disintegrating into ash, its host collapsed, limp to the floor. Absent that obstruction, Jason could see Aria. Their eyes locked for an instant before Melania caught her in her distraction and struck her cheek with the staff she wielded, sending Aria reeling.

Once more, his heart twisted, and he tried to dash to her aid but only made it a step before something gripped his planted foot and took it out from under him. Landing hard, he barely held onto his spiritsword as he was drug backward and flung across the room like a doll.

Shaking his head as he tried to get his bearings, his mouth lolled open. The other direnoir had doubled in size since he last looked at it, barely finding clearance from the room's ceiling. It laughed viciously. "Excellent. That worthless bungler was stunting me. Drawing nutrients, I can far better use. I must say, though, the fresh swell of terror you aroused in my host as he watched what befell the other host ... that is some of the sweetest, most succulent panic I have yet tasted.

"Though yours over this phosphila woman you long for is very near to it. You, boy, have enough fear in you to make me invincible!"

SIXTY-FIRST INTERLOGUE: FEAR AND FLIGHT

"Come, little phosphila. Come feed me," the direnoir crooned.

It sent out four of its appendages at once, forcing Jason to duck under barbed hooks and over the clawed hands aimed at angles no human could achieve. He deflected the last arm with his buckler and gained a few feet of space to breathe.

This can't be happening.

But it was. A monster as malevolent and massive as any he had heard of in stories and legends would snag him any moment. As skillful as he was at dodging the attacks, he couldn't keep it up forever, and he had no idea when or if the direnoir would tire. He was trying not to panic, but keeping his fear reined in was an increasingly difficult task.

How was he supposed to just stop being afraid? He loved Aria, so much so that even that depth of attachment frightened him, let alone the worry he couldn't defend her.

And he wasn't keeping her safe, as evidenced by all they had been through for weeks now. They were in this mess because of him. If he had just stayed on that train with Aria and Cinaed, just given them time to help get his head right and see the light in the darkness, then none of this would be happening.

He deflected another strike with his buckler. This time, the hit was hard enough to stagger him. Another came, and he swiped with his sword, forcing it away, only to be caught off balance and knocked to the ground by still another appendage that struck like a fist.

Struggling to his feet, he immediately dove over a low-sweeping limb and rolled out of the way as he landed to avoid a successive jab and hammer-like smash of two more. A whip-like slap from a tendril sent him flying backward. He managed to nick an arm reaching for him, but another caught him by the shoulder and hauled him up off the ground. He flailed, trying to bat away the other arms coming at him as he dangled in the painful grip. All the while seeing the hungry glowering eyes watching him as a slick tongue licked its cruel serpentine lips.

A shudder ran through him. It felt so cold in this part of the mansion, and all his limbs were growing heavy. All the abuse, all the unceasing exertion was coming down on him at the worst time possible. He was going to die, and the Quest would falter after millennia. How had he messed things up this badly?

An incoming strike from the creature forced him to make a wild swipe to ward off the hook-like limb, and he accidentally caught himself in the face with his buckler. A hot smarting bruise came right away, and he looked at the little shield. He wasn't even competent enough to use the tiny thing.

Anargen wouldn't be embarrassing himself like this. He'd had a lot of training throughout his life, especially after becoming a Knight. Surely someone like him was who was needed in this moment. A champion. A true Knight of Light.

Unlike me. I've never been a warrior.

He could scuffle and get out of a scrape just fine, but

standing and fighting for a cause had never been a part of his plans. At least not until that first night. The night when he saw the magnificent High King and faced down the werebeasts using the implements the High King provided. Doing so had felt so obvious, and even though he still had a lot to learn, he hadn't given much thought until now to the fact that he had done anything at all right. The spiritsword had pulsed like it belonged in his hand. The shield, though small, was truly his. And ever since then, Jason had been doing things he couldn't have possibly done and in ways he could never achieve. At least not on his own.

In the midst of all his guilt and defeatism, he hadn't stopped to consider that perhaps he was being used by the High King, guided in a way that made even his failure feel as if it could fit within the Quest. No doubt it wasn't the ideal, but why had he never before considered that the High King was great enough to compensate for even his shortcomings and failures? The Quest of Fire had been going on for millennia, and was a nobody like him really going to derail all of it? Anargen's failures certainly hadn't, and he had his own share of shortcomings.

A tingling sensation rang the length of Jason's arms, and warmth coursed up from the spiritsword. When the direnoir struck this time, his shield was ready, and he caught the strike that followed immediately with a parry of his sword that singed the creature.

In the midst of all the focus on rescuing Cinaed and not letting the Council of Defenders be stopped, Jason hadn't considered that all he could do was be consistently devoted to the High King. *His Lord's light and might will be what wins the day in the end. Not Jason's craft or cleverness—the High King had done just fine without those for thousands of years.*

What am I so afraid of right now? Failure?

No. Jason remembered Anargen had said while in Ordumair and after escaping Stormridge that even if he failed, his very stand fulfilling his oaths to the High King was itself a victory.

Why would things be different for me?

There was a growl from across the room. A whisper spoke over it, and Jason had only a hair's breadth to drop to the floor as the latest swipe from the direnoir scored a long groove into the wall behind him.

"Little fool!" the direnoir seethed. "You think you've found a cure for your fears? But you're an onion of them. Peel away one layer, and another tighter and more central awaits!"

Jason noticed that for all its bluster, the direnoir was far less sleek and imposing now. Had it truly become so large and imposing, or merely projected it as an illusion?

"If only you could feed on your own fears. You seem to have far more of them than I do. And you should. You know what the High King's fire did to your friend. You are going to burn too."

"*Argh!*" the thing screeched and leaned forward, swiping with each of its limbs in a furious storm of blows. Curses and obscenities were launched with every strike.

But the whispers guiding Jason were already with him, and he was listening to them, not the monster before him. Dodging left, then right, Jason blocked and jumped, coming down fast to slice the clawed arm, grabbing for him. He felt the heat of the Great King's fire racing through him. Jason ducked under one limb, grabbed it with his free hand, and swung under it to avoid another strike. Spinning up and setting his feet, he hacked off everything past where he held.

Jason brought up his shield for the immediate counterattack. He blocked one, then two, three, four attacks all in a row and, finding an opening, lashed out, severing another pointed tendril in a sizzling blaze of smoke and fury.

He hadn't realized until now, but he'd gradually moved closer to the beast. Half of the direnoir's limbs were now smoldering, twitching stumps, and the look on its hideous, bestial face was one of terror and hatred.

It swiped from both directions at once, trying to scissor him, but he blocked the lower with his buckler and let the edge of his sword catch on the other jagged limb. Sliding along the limb his shield abutted, he battered aside another tendril whipping at him, leaving it a sizzling ruin.

The opening he needed was before him, and he surged forward. With all his might, he slammed his buckler into the direnoir's face. As it reeled, he swung and caught the cords tethering it to its host, and, in the single strike, severed them all.

The direnoir wailed and hit the ground, shriveling considerably. It had to prop itself on two of its remaining four limbs and looked about as menacing as a common snake. Jason backed away, wary of it. Even a common snake could inflict a serious bite if given the chance.

"You ... think you've won," it croaked hoarsely and slapped at him.

Stepping around the fallen host of the direnoir, who, like the other, lay still as stone, Jason parried the attack and removed that limb as well. Sortieing forward, he landed a shallow slice across its abdominal carapace, and the direnoir collapsed.

Looking up at him from amidst the smoke roiling off of it, the thing snorted. "You ... haven't ... bested your worst fear ... Dorian."

Jason didn't give it the chance to draw another ounce of energy from him and firmly planted his spiritsword into its back. As the creature disintegrated, it chided, "You'll … never … escape the … fear … of what he … has become!"

With that, the monster got in the painful bite Jason had thought he was guarded against. His little brother. Try as he might, he still couldn't face it. Not head-on, not in full.

It was truly a feat of the High King's doing that he hadn't fed the direnoir enough and fast enough from that fear alone to undo himself. All the other fears he had relinquished moments ago, but this one was so hard. Even facing the realization he couldn't save Aria felt light by comparison.

Aria!

His attention whipped to the battle between her and Melania. They faced each other down, both panting from exertion. Aria favored one of her arms so that it seemed like she'd taken a serious hit to it. From this distance, he couldn't tell how bad it was, but given the way Melania was sliding into position to push her attack from that angle, any amount of hurt was too easily exploited.

"That's enough, Melania," Jason called out, stalking over with purposeful strides, his sword held in guard. He knew Melania well enough to trust she wouldn't just allow herself to be cornered, whatever the odds.

She spat with a sneer on her lips, or rather, the portion she still had that hadn't been erased from their last encounter. "You were never this chivalrous for me. Does this little scamp truly hold your heart?"

From the icy way she said it, Jason was sure to force her back another two steps before answering. "No. My heart is my King's. And because of that, I'm capable of greater compassion. Even for those who have hurt me. You don't have to be destroyed like your two henchmen."

"*Hmph*, you always did overestimate your chances." Her eyes roved around, taking in the dungeon around them. "A shame your brother isn't here. He would find it apropos to face you in this place, where he first learned about the legends of Tislatna from Monarch Ilyron."

"What?"

Placing a hand on her hip, Melania withdrew another pair of steps, grinning. "You don't remember much before Ms. Phosphila, *hmm*? This isn't your first visit here. Your grandmother was obsessed with the legends of Tislatna, and your brother uncovered this place's deepest secret. Monarch Ilyron has been here these long centuries, waiting. At least until your brother uncovered him. Where do you think he learned all the tricks and trappings of the dark sorceries?"

"That's enough from you," Aria warned, edging closer, her burning rapier pointed at Melania, but her eyes more often finding their way to Jason, filled with concern. He must have looked fragile at that moment, like a teacup on the edge of a tall table.

"Why are you telling me this?" Jason demanded.

Melania shrugged. "For old time's sake.

"And because you need to understand that the powers he brings against you are beyond your comprehending."

With that, she slipped back against the wall of the room and gave a wink. In an instant, she had flattened into a black stain on the wall, then slid along the shadows and out of sight. Jason ran forward, waving his spiritsword around every crevice and crack, but she must have fled completely because he couldn't find a trace of her no matter where he looked.

"I thought she was a doppelgänger, but that was a Sombra trick," he muttered. "What has she become?"

A rumbling answer came to him from the back of the room, "A mistress of evil. So deeply ensconced in the dark things of this world that she dabbles in them all, greedy for the gain they promise."

"Cinaed!" Jason called back and ran over to help him to his feet.

Aria had already gone to him while Jason had been searching for signs of Melania. Hooked under his one arm and Jason under the opposite, they got the old man to his feet and, wincing with every step, brought him over to the stairs to brace against them.

"We need to get out of this wretched place right away," he mumbled through teeth clenched with pain. Jason could trace through his shirt the blows from a lash, and the welts on his lined face confirmed that he had been brutalized to the brink.

"Moving too fast isn't good for you," Aria countered as she worked to get her breath. From the way she was still favoring the injured arm and not using it, Jason guessed a bone had broken in it.

"Aria," he said, finding he couldn't say another word for the ache.

She gave him a weak grin. "You didn't get a good look at her. There's a reason she slithered off."

Cinaed chuckled but quickly faltered into coughing. He waved off any attempts at helping him. "None of us are ready for any feats, but by the High King's favor, we must be on our way. You drove off the consort, but the dark liege is soon coming here. Those direnoir reveled in taunting me with that knowledge."

"What about Niklush?" Aria asked as she once more slipped under her grandfather's arm to help him. "Will Boris still be willing to join the Council after this?"

"Defender Tooadama will do what is right in the end," Cinaed wheezed and motioned for Jason to help again. "We all must, or great evil will befall the Lowlands."

"Maybe you both should conserve your strength," Jason advised as he helped Cinaed up the steps. "It's going to be a long walk back to civilization, never mind figuring out how to escape this cursed place apart from that wretched tunnel."

Cinaed gave a faint nod as they struggled up the first turn in the stairs. "*Mm*, I wish that were the worst of what lies ahead. But wishing is a futile thing. A Knight with confidence beseeches the High King, not casts pennies into fountains longingly."

For a moment, Aria looked like she wanted to say something, but from the way she gritted her teeth, it was clear it wasn't from choosing to do so freely. So, they all just struggled up and up and up, so much farther than Jason remembered descending.

Waiting at the top was a tall, dark man looking down on them. "Defender Black, it is good to see you're still whole."

"Defender Cuzibaum, shouldn't you be with the others and long gone by now?" Jason asked, happy to see him, particularly when he relieved Aria of the task of helping her grandfather.

"*Ha!* You believe we would leave you in such an awful place?" he replied, the mock amusement all the more profound with his stiff Ecthelish and strong accent. "We retook our arms. Those you did not defeat, we did."

Jason looked at Aria, his eyes wide. If he had a single bit of strength to spare, he would've broken down into sobbing. "We're going to get out of here then?"

Grunting, Kazim replied, "As long as we move one foot after another foot."

Aria placed her good hand on Jason's back and rubbed reassuring circles around it. Especially as they passed through the wrecked portions of the mansion. Perhaps she worried the news that he had been to this place before would unsettle him as he saw familiar sights again. If he could've afforded to break down that way, perhaps he might have. But as Kazim advised, one foot and then the other. That was all he focused on, well after they were on the lawn. The others were waiting for them, wagons with horses hitched to them.

Figuratively, he was still just moving forward a step at a time as he and Aria climbed aboard a wagon. Wrapping his arms around her as she lay against his chest, he focused on her breathing and his as they rolled, bumping, away from the ruined remains of the nightmarish mansion.

After they had traveled a mile or more out of sight of the wretched place, Aria asked, "How did we get taken in so badly?" More quietly, she added, "We're servants of the High King of Light. Why didn't we see through the deceptions?"

Cinaed winced from his injuries and leaned back against the rough wooden wall of the wagon. He winced still more from the bumps and jostles. "In an hour of great darkness, sorting friend from foe is especially fraught with mistakes."

"That's not an answer," Jason commented, gingerly rubbing the hand of her injured arm. She looked up at him with eyes eager for comfort and hope but expecting none.

Cinaed cleared his throat and leaned forward. "That is because we are asking the wrong question. Instead of wondering how we were taken in, we should marvel that the aid was already on the way before the deception was sprung on us. Why do you think that was Mr. Landsby?"

Brows furrowed, Jason shook his head. "I don't know, sir. You tell me."

Cinaed pursed his lips and nodded. "Very well." He pointed toward the direction they were driving. Low, over the distant mountains, pale beams of the early morning's light pierced the gloom of the landscape and beyond. Jason could just glimpse a glorious sunrise, setting the clouds afire with the promise of the new day. He felt a pang of longing over the sight of the morning light.

"Because, my children, the dawn has resurged, and with it

shall follow the day. What comes next shall see the night's hold fully shattered."

"How can you be so sure?" Aria asked.

A faint smile quirked up the old man's worn cheek. "That, my dear, is a question worth asking. And one to which I've long held an answer."

SIXTY-SECOND INTERLOGUE: RESURGENCE

The train whistle's long shrill blow was one of the most welcome sounds Jason had ever heard. He settled into the seat and breathed a sigh of relief as the train jerked into motion. Outside the platform, the city of Axala was passing by, and they were back underway. A fresh sunrise peaked over the mountains, ringing it, and set the waters of the lake by the same name ablaze with gold and faint orange, fuchsia, magenta, and a host of shades between, each carried along the ripples of the water's surface and along the winding channels of its tributaries.

Across the cabin from him, Sir Cinaed was looking over the paper he'd bought. From the date on the paper, it was already mid-Misbyr, though it was hard to tell they were only five weeks from spring, given this region seemed seasonless. More importantly, they were weeks past their rescue at the mansion. Jason regularly battled back the specter of fear that hung over any time they lingered in one place long.

He felt a hand gently squeeze his, and he looked beside him. Aria raised an eyebrow. "No worries. It will be a quick trip from here in Keraxlaco to Vov Hilan. Knights of Light are still welcome there, even more so than here, and Defender Miguelso has already sent us word that he'll have an entire delegation of Knights waiting to meet us on the platform in Dor Lessa."

Lifting her hand to his lips, Jason graced it with a kiss. "A delegation, *hmm?* Are you sure a respectable lady such as yourself can be seen with a scoundrel like me?"

Aria kissed his hand back and leaned against his shoulder. "I suppose the contrast will help to make me seem all the more magnanimous. What with taking on the task of taming a ruffian such as yourself."

"I'm beginning to wonder why I was so keen to see you both warmed to each other again," Cinaed commented dryly without taking his eyes off the paper. "You are aware that I'm in the car with you, I hope."

Jason straightened and felt his cheeks flush. Going from the extremes of surviving horrendous attacks to the normalcy of courting an older gentleman's granddaughter was such a peculiar juxtaposition of life events. One he wouldn't turn back from, but certainly an adjustment.

"What's in the news?" Jason asked, hoping to change the subject quickly. Though he shouldn't be surprised, it seemed Cinaed could read fluent Keraxlacoan in addition to Zilnian and who knew how many other languages. The temptation to imagine Cinaed to be centuries old still hung alluringly before him.

"Something good, I hope," Aria added, giving Jason's hand another squeeze. She added a conspiratorial smile meant to disarm his comically typical anxiety at being a suitor in the presence of his love's guardian.

"Unfortunately, there is precious little good to speak of in the Lowlands," Cinaed replied gravely. "Zilnen is officially a client kingdom of the Empire, with Mesnara ruling it. And the Vogteremark has signed a defense treaty with Ecthelowall in anticipation of Knorland invading its lands any day now. Which, if that happens, will start a war that will spread to every Realm. The sides are already digging in and preparing for it. A tinder box just awaiting a single spark to ignite it and consume the Lowlands."

Aria tensed beside him. "The Council of Defenders can help broker peace, though. It would not be the first time the Knights of Light did so."

"In a time of great darkness, we should not be surprised when evil things happen. Loss, injury, terror abound. It in no way diminishes the light that will be at night's end," Cinaed replied, at last putting down the paper and folding his hands in his lap.

Jason thought for a moment and then spoke up, "I remember that from somewhere. It was in Anargen's journal. The latest one you left for me."

Nodding, Cinaed commented, "Very good. I'm glad to see it left an impression. That will serve you well in the times ahead."

For a moment, Jason fell silent, but soon, a question came to him, one he had been meaning to ask for some time now. "So, you have these journals. One for each story you've told me?"

"One for each phase in Anargen's life," Cinaed amended. He sat in the train's seat like a weathered old mountain. It was such a contrast to the youth and fresh beauty of Aria. Though from the way her eyes were blinking and already not so bright and open, she looked to be growing drowsy and in danger of nodding off.

A lump formed in his throat as he brushed his fingers against the exposed skin of her arms and felt her adjust her positioning so that her head rested nearer his heart. Sometimes, it felt so surreal to him that she'd taken him back. The sensation was like stumbling across treasure strewn on the road, wholly undeserved and so astonishing it was scarcely believable no matter how many gold coins were spent.

Jason coughed to clear his throat and looked at the worn satchel he'd managed to keep with him this whole time. The "journey" and "travail" journals Cinaed and Aria had read to him. But there was the last, the one Jerome imparted to him. At this point, Jason was less than halfway through it. He thumbed open the cover and scanned a few lines. He didn't find the specific passage Cinaed had just quoted, but he did find one he wanted to ask after. "'The hours grow short till it arrives. The King's Day. What we have all longed for so dearly we can scarcely whisper it without reverence. Though so many now discount it. I do not. Not even in the turmoil that has consumed my life.'"

"So, the last one here," Jason noted. "What is it called?"

"I call it 'the King's Day Journal.'"

"Things must brighten considerably by the end. What I've read of it doesn't strike me as particularly sunny."

Cinaed huffed. "Have the whole tale before you form opinions of it." His sage eyes under the wizened old brows bore hard into Jason the longer the stare lingered. "Perhaps even then, seeing the good in it will be difficult. It wasn't named so because the events are necessarily light or easy by the measure most apply. They speak of a reverent hope for a time. One which every Knight looks for with inexpressible longing."

"What time is that?" Jason asked, holding the old man's gaze for once.

"The King's Day."

Jason straightened up some. "Dr. Antoni said I should speak with you about it. He made it sound like something as tragic as it was triumphant. What is 'the King's Day' exactly?"

"It is a day when the High King returns to the Lowlands to establish his kingdom anew. When war, poverty, greed, strife, and every evil are slain forever. When his loyal servants, those fallen and found alive yet, may walk anew." Cinaed rubbed absently at his aged knees. "Thousands of years have been spent in waiting. In the heart of a true Knight, that hope is not abated by time's expanse. Only by its realization."

A warm sensation tickled Jason's neck. He shut the tome. "Why the delay? Why hasn't he set up his kingdom already?"

"The Lowlands as they are shall pass. If he had ushered in the new glorious era before now, we would not be having this conversation. The High King's timing is his own. When the full number of loyal servants are gathered, I feel then the Day shall come."

Jason's brows furrowed.

What?

Cinaed must have read the confusion on Jason's face. "There will be no more rebellion from men in that new era. Rule will belong unequivocally to him to whom it has always belonged. Every subject will be willing. But in his wisdom and foresight, he has not revealed to us the full details."

"Why not?"

"Why should he?" Cinaed said with a shrug and a smirk.

"Wouldn't it be better to know?"

"And have a finish line well known to usher in an endless era? I think it better shapes us for such a time to not have all things plain. Besides, the Lowlands is a place of shadow till the King's Day. It is enough to know what we see now, what we know now, is fractional to what will be seen and known and experienced in that era."

Jason started to say something. Stopped. Started again and thought better of it. He sighed.

A chuckle rumbled from deep in Cinaed's chest. "Save

your questions. They are good. Those who seek find. But you ask much of an old man who badly needs his rest."

"Sorry," Jason said. He brushed the side of the journal with his thumb, feeling the pages slip past it each time. "Could I read more of this then while you rest? I don't much feel like sleep right now."

"Can you suspend your judgment till all be told?"

"I can try," Jason replied with a grin.

"*Hmm*. Better to do than to try. Of course, you'll never do without trying first. Read away. I will answer what questions you have when I wake."

"Thank you, Sir Cinaed."

"*Mm-hmm*," the old man murmured, as though sleep already swiftly pulled him into the realm of dreams.

Jason rubbed his hand over the worn leather cover of the journal again. He opened it, hoping to find something to better frame the chaos of the present Lowlands in the pages of the past.

12

A FATEFUL AUDIENCE

—Anargen's King's Day Journal
27 Misbyr 1607 Middle Era

"All this oppressive rain is surprisingly fortuitous in one sense," Ecthelion commented as they turned a corner into the final hall before the Viscount's audience chamber. No matter where they walked, even deep within the palace, the pounding of the thousands of watery hammers outside could be heard. "With days and nights awash, the Viscount has been keeping odd hours. The hour is later than he would normally conduct affairs of state, but through the restlessness this rain induces in him, Viscount Geralian agreed to see me this eve."

"'In good or bad, modest or wondrous things, we are highly favored by the Great King,'" Glewdyn recited a familiar maxim of the Knights of Light.

There was a potent convergence of forces precipitating the directing of this evening—the rain a burden and boon in turn. Viceroy Ecthelion's persistence finally yielded a meeting. Their assassin foe entered the palace minutes before they did, and his plan to frame them being turned on its head as they had been led straight to Ecthelion rather than bound and imprisoned. That they were all alive was in itself a miraculous divergence from what they had imagined earlier this evening.

About fifteen feet from the large oak doors depicting the Libertian eagle on each side, the Viceroy motioned for them to halt. Silvanus, the soldier designated to accompany the Viceroy, held up as well.

"Now, before we enter, I want to make something very clear. I will be handling the negotiations with the Viscount. You from Black River and Thomas must all keep to the room's periphery. Mia and Gregor shall approach with me. We do not wish to worry him with our display, even if I did have need of a cadre of guards and courtiers to seem more solvent.

"Before I exit, after speaking with the Viscount, you may enter the hall to secure it. Keep crisp and officious to emulate the soldiers here. I do not discount your valor, but it is not well known here, and your presentation shall be the measure of your quality in their eyes. Our quality shall be the measure, no doubt, of our worth as allies."

"Probably why he got us the fresh clothes before coming here," Seren commented under her breath to Anargen.

He smirked. "These are a bit more luxurious than I'm accustomed to and um ... frilly." The fine fabrics might have been intended for presentation, but under their armor, did it truly matter whether they wore silk and linen over rougher fabrics? It made sense that Mia was now in a more refined dress and Gregor in vest and trousers befitting a youth of the court.

Seren snickered and whispered, "I don't know, I find you dashing."

Ecthelion wasn't interested in entertaining any complaints if he overheard them. Once more, he strode forward, every movement a graceful, measured step of one accustomed to the regal dance of the well to do. Coming up to the guards, he did not give a courteous bow as Anargen might have—it was beneath his station to do so—and merely announced, "Ecthelion Androsson, Baron of Halifax, Viceroy of the Commonwealth of Ecthelowall, to see, Geralian, Count of Kirke, Viscount of Libertias."

The guards outside the chambers the Viscount received dignitaries to did not flinch or bat an eye or waver an inch as one of them recited what must be the formal response for such situations: "His honor, the Viscount, grants you entry. Speak hale words good to be heard or ware the trouble that shall befall you."

Both doors swung open, and the group strode into the fabulous room of marble floors, columns, and gold-leaf patterned oak walls with a chandelier of gold and precious stones hanging over all. Tapestries and rugs of refined blue and materials too costly for Anargen to have ever seen in person were scattered around the room. Seated at the back of this lordly space was the Viscount, who stood as they entered.

Anargen almost wandered farther in than he was told. Fortunately, his father discreetly held him back. They had to look proper, and he needed to play his part well. Too much depended on it to fail.

Across the room, Ecthelion greeted the Viscount, whom

Anargen had, of course, never seen until now. A man of average height in his mid-forties, Geralian was copper-haired with a bristly beard and mustache. He had stern eyes and wore a deep blue tunic and cape with a silvery chest plate embossed with the eagle of Libertias. Silver bracers on either forearm and his signet ring gleamed from across the room. He spoke with an even voice, neither overly gruff nor mild. It was, however, of a timbre that one would be disinclined to question.

"Hale evening to you, Ecthelion. It has been an unfortunate oversight of my land that you have had to wait so long for us to take counsel together. However, to be blunt, this is not likely to be a meeting from which you emerge contented."

Shooting a glance at his father, Anargen's anxiousness doubled. The older Knight was scowling. Anargen wasn't sure they were even permitted such displays of disapproval. More than that, it was out of the ordinary for Glewdyn to have such an unfavorable expression for anyone.

Geralian continued, "I'm aware of your cause's need and the current state of the war. To aid Ecthelowall at such a time would certainly be a welcome change from the icy relations and hostility of the past—the difficulty being that you do not seek aid. You require someone to fight this war on your behalf. Libertias will not send its sons to die for your place as ruler."

Ecthelion was facing away from them, so they could not read his reaction apart from a momentary slumping of his shoulders. "Viscount, you welcomed me into your palace and tended to my needs. Such kindness should not and will never be forgotten. It is true. I am here to persuade you that my people's plight is dire but not a lost cause. There are no foregone conclusions in war, particularly when the foe one faces is so wretched and twisted.

"Your conclusions are based on the assumption the Monarch will be a reasonable force within the greater

Lowlands, that diplomacy and coexistence with him are not only possible but probable, particularly if you do not take a side in the conflict. These are what is unfortunate, honorable Viscount. I know for certain the Monarch is obsessed with the forbidden sorceries of Tislatna. He is fixated on harnessing dark powers that will ultimately lead his forces into conflict with your nation.

"For now, his armies are weakened, divided. Though our strength may look feeble, it is only for the unrelenting and merciless ferocity of our foe. Choose for yourself which is the wiser path, but be forewarned—the blood of Libertias's people will be shed by the Monarch's forces, whether now or in time to come. If you heed our call for aid, there would be a cord of many strands to restrain the Monarch. If you wait till we are fallen, you will face him alone, and a single cord is far more likely to snap."

Scratching at his bushy beard, Geralian said at last, "I shall take your words under advisement. In the meantime, you may continue to reside in your quarters here, or I can provide an armed escort to the border with the Vogteremark. Perhaps in them, you will find a more eager ally?"

Ecthelion gave a nod. "I shall prepare my things and my retinue to depart on the morrow. May Libertias's days be long and prosperous under your sage guidance."

With that said, the Viceroy turned and walked back toward Anargen and the others. His face and gaze so tightly held in check that a sculptor carving a likeness would be in danger of not knowing which was the stone replica and which the flesh and blood Viceroy.

Once he reached them, Anargen felt there was no point to maintaining the pretentious charade any longer and asked, "Viceroy, do you really believe the Monarch will try to attack Libertias if he wins the war against you?"

They all entered the hall before the Viceroy answered, "I do. My son caught me off guard with his brutality and callousness once. I would be foolish to allow him to do so again. With all I know of him as a boy and as the monster he has become, there can be no other option."

For several minutes, they walked in silence, dejection hanging over them all. If they traveled north as advised, they may not even be permitted to enter the Vogteremark, instead forced to take passage by sea to Albaron, which was currently besieged. They would be nomads, exiles with no port safe to land in.

"A shame your Viscount is a blind, pompous buffoon," Gregor commented sharply. "He didn't even bother to be introduced to Mia or myself. We could have told him what sort of man Monarch Ilyron is and how deep is the evil of his black heart.

"*Hmph.* Maybe then the Viscount would even have posted more guards to keep himself from being targeted for assassination. Certainly, no one in the Lowlands is safe from Monarch Ilyron now."

Thomas's mouth was opened in what was likely to be a rebuke for harsh comments about the Viscount, but he didn't say anything. His eyes widened, and he looked as if someone had said those cruel things about him.

"What's wrong?" Mia asked, placing a hand on his arm. "Thomas? What is it?"

Glewdyn looked at Thomas and muttered, "Oh, no."

Studying his father's expression and Thomas's, Anargen thought for a moment, and then it hit him. "We have to get back to the Viscount. Now!"

Everyone in the group seemed to have reached the same conclusion except Silvanus, who silently followed them to and from the meeting as a dutiful guard. "Wait, you do not have permission to see his honor again! You cannot just barge into his chambers!"

As the group dashed back down the hall, Glewdyn explained, "We have it wrong. The Sombra threatened someone in Kirke, but it needn't be the Viceroy he is after. If Ilyron is willing to go to war with Libertias, what better way to set it off balance than murder the Viscount?"

"And lay the blame at the feet of Ecthelion for refusing to come to his assistance," Seren added.

It all made terrible and tragic sense now. Running as fast as they could, Anargen saw that the Knights had left Mia and Gregor behind, and Thomas had fallen back, staying with them. It seemed a wise move, given they could possibly be wrong again about the Sombra's target, but as they rounded the corner again and came upon the Viscount's chambers, the guards to it were both absent, and the doors were still flung open.

Within each guard lay slain on the floor, and in the room's back, Geralian was diving behind his long table, which was flipped on its side. As he did, a line of dark daggers struck the wood, embedding deep within its surface. Between the Knights and Geralian swirled the dark form of the Sombra.

"Stop, you fiend!" Glewdyn bellowed and charged headlong into the room, only to be knocked aside by the werebeast they had lost track of earlier in the night.

Anargen watched his father tumble along the ground and crash into the wall. An instant later, he was pinned under the massive beast's paws as it snapped at him.

If he did not help the Viscount, the Sombra would finish him off shortly, and all the malevolent schemes of Monarch Ilyron would be initiated. But if he didn't turn aside now, he would lose his father. And whether the Lowlands fell one year or one hundred thousand years after, Anargen did not know how he could live with having chosen his father's death.

Skidding to a halt, he had to decide and fast.

What do I do?

No answer, within or without, came at that moment. Ecthelion rushed past him, but the Viceroy had no weapon, only himself as a distraction, which was noble and brave but only doubled the potential losses of this night. It was happening again. Things were on the edge of disaster all around him.

"Anargen, go," Seren said, giving him an emphatic push in that direction. Her posture was already turned toward the werebeast, and she was bounding toward it the next instant.

Those he loved most were risking their lives in battle with the cunning monster that had already eluded harm from himself, his father, and Thomas. How would the two of them fair?

There was no thinking about it. Seren had given him the best gift she could, herself. She was the part of him that could be there for his father, and he the part of her that could boldly seek rescue for their nation.

My King, your might is beyond compare. Help me!

With that, Anargen charged forward, drew his spiritsword, and leaped at the Sombra, which had out a morning star with a spiked mace attached to the end. It whipped the weapon around and caught Ecthelion in the legs as he tried to dodge. There was a terrible cracking sound as the bones were broken, and the Viceroy went down.

"*Ahh!*" Anargen screamed and swung, catching the Sombra across the back as it realized its danger.

The fiend screeched in pain and dropped to the ground, unable to maintain its more powerful manifestations. Drawing a short, curved sword, it called out, hissing, "Phosphila thinks he can best a Sombra? I delight in extinguishing your sort's fire."

Anargen said nothing and instead pressed his attack, coming at the Sombra with a slash from high to low, forcing him to backpedal. Catching the responding blow on his shield, Anargen stepped forward aggressively, lunging for another quick attack and then wheeling back as the Sombra dodged and nimbly jabbed at him.

"You phosphila, all the same, brave until you understand your powers are insufficient. Then the fear sinks in deep as you understand the depth of your hubris, and the cost of your failure becomes plain," the Sombra taunted.

He lunged and slashed viciously, twisting a bit more into his misty form, keeping low and using it to whip around and attack at angles that forced Anargen to pivot and keep on the defensive continually. They came quickly and seemingly randomly, forcing Anargen onto an increasingly shaky guard.

Why can't he just be silent?

As Anargen just missed taking a slice across his helmet, the answer was obvious. *Words can be weapons too.*

In a battle like this, where neither was guaranteed victory and everything was at stake, the right verbal dart could unsettle him and leave him vulnerable to the Sombra's physical ones. And painfully, he knew which words the Sombra could use to affect the greatest harm to him.

Failure. Insufficient. Fear.

All of them had been besetting him since he first stepped out of Black River on the Quest. First, questioning whether he was worthy or meant to be on the Quest. Then he had failed in Stormridge, so horrendously it cost Sir Cinaed his life. Caeserus leaving. Bertinand leaving. The Quest in shambles. Ecthelion, Geralian, Glewdyn, Seren—all of them in danger of dying—because he wasn't the Knight he should have been. Not the hero that was needed.

"You're just like that false king of yours. Pretending to be something. Pronouncing your judgments. Yet the Lowlands are darker than you understand and harsher than you admit until one such as I show you."

The Sombra's blade caught him across the pauldron, knocking Anargen off his feet. He threw up a block that bought him a few precious seconds as the Sombra's blade bounced off. Rolling to the side, Anargen's blade burned before him as he held it out to ward off an advance.

Though he had seen it hundreds of times over all the days since he first took up the sword imbued with the High King's words, made mighty by the High King's fire, it still caught his eye. Mesmerized him. Surprised him.

Because in much of the time that he used it, he took for granted the flames rolled off the blade because the High King blessed it to do so. Seeing now the glowing letters inscribed on it, he understood the fire was from the words of the High King. They were what gave his weapon its power. They were what made the spiritsword so marvelous. And just as the spiritsword was nothing without them, Anargen wasn't a Knight or warrior or hero of himself. He was an implement of the True Hero, and this was his battle. Or rather the aftermath of a battle he had already won.

The fate of the Lowlands inevitably was sealed and certain. Only his part in the Great Story, the Quest, was left to question. And though that seemingly changed nothing, it changed everything. He was a failure, insufficient and afraid— yet inscribed within and wearing without the High King's words, he could be used to do much more.

Whether the whispers had been trying to reach him before now or had been waiting for this moment, they came to him.

This time, as he gave himself over to their instructions, he saw the results more clearly, not as serving him but as guiding him to serve the High King.

A hasty block with his shield held. The Sombra was sloppy in his confidence that it would land. Anargen stepped forward and punched the Sombra square in the face. The shadow assassin dematerialized, merging with the shadows behind him, and struck, but Anargen was already waiting for him. Again, the assassin tried his trick of whirling and attacking at all angles in a random dance of destruction. Save now, Anargen was ready and waiting each time.

The Sombra hissed in frustration. "Phosphila does not know when to submit!"

Avoiding the subsequent attack by sidestepping, Anargen struck the Sombra with his shield, staggering him. Battering the dark blade out its hand with a blow that grazed the Sombra's arm, he grabbed the Sombra and shoved him down, pointing his spiritsword squarely at his chest. "You're wrong. Every knee will bow to the High King. I have already submitted to him. Yield, and he will spare you."

"Never! You think you've won, but I've heard the inner counsels of the Monarch. When his full might is brought against you, you will wish for so easy a death as I would bring you," the Sombra growled—and then shrieked, his body flattening into an amorphous black mass as he tried to merge into the shadows of the floor in escape. But Anargen had already been told what was next and swept his spiritsword across the stony surface of the floor, catching the Sombra in its total shadow form. There was a flare of brilliance and rush of heat, and then the shadowy pall on the floor was no more.

Anargen ran over to Ecthelion and helped to brace him against the wall the viceroy had been dragging himself to. His legs were a bloody mess, and Anargen wasn't a physician by trade. He needed his father—he would know what to do. Looking across the room, Anargen watched Seren and his father bait and vanquish the werebeast battling them.

His heartbeat thrummed with the thrill of hope. Of joy. The disasters of Stormridge and Cattingsford hadn't been repeated.

Ecthelion groaned, forcing Anargen to focus on the present. "Just a moment, your honor. I'll get you help."

Bounding over to Seren and his father, he gripped each of them in fierce and all too brief embraces. "Father, you have to help the Viceroy. The Sombra wounded him severely."

Glewdyn nodded and rushed over to the Ecthel's side. By this point, Thomas, Mia, and Gregor had arrived. The trio led the shaken Geralian out from his defensive position as Anargen sheathed his sword, and Seren joined him in approaching the Viscount.

"Your honor, we apologize for what has transpired. We—"

"Do not speak, young one," Geralian instructed. "I will see to the Viceroy. Then you may explain to me the origins of the horrific things which have transpired tonight."

The Viscount half stalked, half staggered over to Ecthelion's side, where Glewdyn was already trying his best to help him. It was difficult to watch.

"Your Viceroy has likely won you an ally," Seren commented.

"How do you come by that," Gregor asked gruffly, his eyes still wild from the rush of battle and danger.

"It would be difficult to ignore what he has just been saved from," Thomas explained.

"His bravery will resonate with Geralian, who has led troops in battle," Anargen added.

"I think all of our bravery will be difficult to overlook," Mia offered in amendment. "Which we'll all need much more of in the days to come. Ilyron would not have simply attempted this assassination.

"Having Libertias off balance was a means to an end, not the end itself."

"He'll invade now," Seren surmised, her voice low, weary.

"If he hasn't already begun landing troops," Thomas agreed, taking Mia's hand and squeezing it.

Anargen watched the care for Ecthelion for a few moments longer and then said, "I think you're all right about that. There are very hard things ahead, perhaps the hardest yet. But do you hear something?"

Thomas and Mia looked at each other, and Gregor spoke for them, "Besides my own heart hammering in my ears, nothing."

"The rain has stopped," Anargen said with a wry smile. "And I think if we were to go outside right now, we would see that the night was far deeper than we guessed, and already the sun is returning. Surging through the cloud cover to reveal dawn's arrival and with it much-needed light."

ABOUT THE AUTHOR

Brett Armstrong has been exploring other worlds as a writer since age nine. Years later, he still writes, but now invites others along on his excursions. He's shown readers haunting, deep historical fiction (*Destitutio Quod Remissio*), scary-real dystopian sci-fi (*Tomorrow's Edge*) and dark, sweeping epic fantasy (*Quest of Fire*). Every story is a journey of discovery and an attempt to be a brush in the Master Artist's hand. Through dark, despair, light, joy, and everything in between, the end is always meant to leave his fellow literary explorers with wonder and hope. Always busy with a new story, he also enjoys drawing, gardening, and spending time with his wife and son.

Succession: A Novella

Quest of Fire Series – BookTwo

The heir must prove his worth - or die trying

Son of the Northern Realm's Defender, raised among the dwarves of Ordumair, Meredoch was anticipated to succeed his father. Some whispered he would bring the longed-for peace between Ordumair and their ancient foe, Ecthelowall. All of that changes when Ordumair's Thane is killed and Meredoch and his family are exiled.

From prestige to poverty, the young boy must chart a new course. Battling creatures believed only myths and racing against evil toward the prize, Meredoch must face the truth of his place in the world and claim his right of succession.

Get your copy here: scrivenings.link/succession

Shadows at Nightfall

Quest of Fire - Book Three

The hour has arrived … with all its terrors.

The shadows of Jason's past have caught him. Having stepped into the Quest of Fire, Jason is pursued by a league of assassins formed of pure darkness. To his horror he discovers these creatures were also contracted to eliminate Anargen and his friends as they sought to understand the Tower of Light's oracle. To unravel the mystery of who wants him dead and how he fits into the ages old quest, Jason must travel the lengths of the Lowlands. He'll have to move fast, the darkest creatures in the Lowlands have long waited for this hour. With few concerned for the light and everything falling apart around them, Jason and Anargen will face the shadows of night's falling as their world hangs in the balance.

Get your copy here: https://scrivenings.link/shadowsatnightfall

Desperation: A Novella

Quest of Fire - Book Four

Guarding his nation's last hope, a teen must escape enemy lands.

While Anargen, Caeserus, and Bertinand are held captive in Stormridge, the war to restore Ecthelowall's Commonwealth has been waged for months. Enter Thomas Fenwrest, an orphan and page to the captain of Baron Fenwrest's guard and tasked with escorting the children of Restoration nobility to safety at Castle Yerst. Things quickly spiral out of control when the Monarchists deliver a devastating blow to the Restoration. Ancient sorcery and bitter grudges combine to ensnare them. As desperation sets in for the Restoration and Thomas, to where will they turn for hope?

Get your copy here: https://scrivenings.link/desperation

ALSO BY BRETT ARMSTRONG

Tomorrow's Edge Trilogy:

Day Moon

Tomorrow's Edge Trilogy Book One

AD 2039: Eluding authorities, one teen holds the past and future's key.

AD 2039: Project Alexandria is an initiative to give all humanity safe and equal access to all recorded knowledge. But the prodigious teen Elliott knows something is wrong. There are dark intentions behind Project Alexandria and the key may lie in the last print copy of Shakespeare's complete works that contains a sonnet titled, "Day

Moon." Racing along a path made perilous by federal agents and betrayals from those closest to him, Elliott must uncover the sonnet's secrets. All of history past and to be depends on it.

Get your copy here: https://scrivenings.link/daymoon

Veiled Sun: *Tomorrow's Edge Trilogy Book Two*

2021 Selah Awards Finalist

AD 2040: Every day the world slips further into lies.

AD 2040: Every day the world slips further into lies. Seventeen-year-old Elliott knows that better than most. Project Alexandria is rewriting history, shaping the world according to sinister goals. To stop it, Elliott must assemble the "Veiled Sun", a secret program written by his grandfather.

The only people he can count on are siegers–outlaws who use their coding skills for purposes almost as nefarious as Project Alexandria. Overcoming the schemes and betrayals all around him, he's the world's best hope to save reality, if he doesn't lose hold of it himself.

Get your copy here: https://scrivenings.link/veiledsun

Silent Stars: *Tomorrow's Edge Trilogy Book Three*

AD 2040: Past and future hang in the balance as the stars fall silent.

AD 2040: Barely eighteen, things have become much harder for Elliott. Reeling from the losses during the confrontation that brought Project Alexandria to a halt. Elliott feverishly hunts for the original files needed to finish it off. Finding only dead ends, he instead stumbles upon something dire: messages about the Babel Initiative.

Conceived as a successor that would make Project Alexandria's manipulations seem tame, this new threat once again forces Elliott into alliances with morally grey programmers known as siegers. Beset by continual setbacks and defeats, many siegers abandon the cause and go underground to survive the dangers ahead.

The bleak reality that Elliott and those closest to him are almost certain to die in the fight against Dr. Almundson begins to set in. But Elliott isn't ready to give in. He knows the cost of such a silent surrender will be humanity itself.

Get your copy here: https://scrivenings.link/silentstars

Novella:

The Near Distant—Novella Collection

by Brett Armstrong, Erin R. Howard, and

C. Kevin Thompson

Awards for "By Far and Away" by Brett Armstrong:

2023 Selah Awards Finalist

2023 Realm Awards Finalist

2023 Carol Awards Semi-Finalist

On a day trip into the wilderness around Lake Tahoe, college students Ned, Tyler, and Everly stumble upon a monolith. No one knows its origin or purpose, but structures like this one have popped up all over the world, making national headlines. While not the local legend the group hoped to find, they decide to investigate, only to be engulfed by a blinding, powerful pulse of light. Instantly, the three friends find themselves in separate and drastically different worlds. They must quickly adapt to their new surroundings or perish.

Get your copy here: https://scrivenings.link/theneardistant

Stay up-to-date on your favorite books and authors with our free e-newsletters.

ExpanseBooks.pub (an imprint of Scrivenings Press LLC)